Steven Grimes

Death in Sturgis

Llumina Press

This is a work of fiction. Names, characters, places and incidents either are the product of the author's imagination or are used fictitiously, and any resemblance to any actual persons, living or dead, events or locales is entirely coincidental.

© 2006 Steven Grimes

All rights reserved. No part of this publication may be reproduced or transmitted in any form or by any means electronic or mechanical, including photocopy, recording, or any information storage and retrieval system, without permission in writing from both the copyright owner and the publisher.

Requests for permission to make copies of any part of this work should be mailed to Permissions Department, Llumina Press, PO Box 772246, Coral Springs, FL 33077-2246

ISBN: 1-59526-432-9 PB
      1-59526-433-7 E-Book

Printed in the United States of America by Llumina Press

Library of Congress Control Number: 2006905601

Death in Sturgis

Dedication

To all those long, beautiful stretches of two-lane blacktop I've been lucky enough to ride down over the last fifty years and to all the bikes that have carried me down them. Special thanks to Paula for her selfless help and assistance in the writing of the first book in the Death On Two Wheels series.

The Taste of Bugs

Doc spat into the dusty gravel at his feet and squinted into the hot South Dakota afternoon. Salty, he'd thought. South Dakota bugs tasted salty as hell. Southern bugs were sort of sweet, and the ones from the Northeast were definitely bitter. Being a bug connoisseur came easy when you rode as many miles as he did, year after year, without a windshield or a helmet. Doc had ridden motorcycles since his teens through every part of the country, and like many others, had become somewhat of an expert on the taste of bugs. Bugs from the Midwest tasted more like straw, although the big ones hit at night had a tobacco flavor to them. Experienced riders smiled and offered their opinions about the taste of bugs at seventy-five miles per hour or higher while new riders and wannabes sat in confusion.

He strained his deep blue eyes down the long, straight road towards Rapid City, but it was as empty as the bright, dry land spreading south into the Pine Ridge Indian Reservation from where he stood before the small bar. The hot, arid wind whistled down the road and whipped Doc's graying brown ponytail from side to side. He'd already had five or six beers and more shots of Jack Daniels than was good for him. Hell, too much is never enough, he mused. The hot August sun made him sweat out the alcohol and he felt stone cold sober, an awful feeling for the first day of the annual Sturgis Bike Rally.

The two men he was supposed to meet were already three hours late. Rather than get angry, Doc decided it was wiser to use his time constructively and drink some more. Getting pissed off was not something Doc did regularly, and that was probably a good thing. His slow anger would eventually flow over like burning lava from an erupting volcano and pity the man or woman at whom he directed it. Seldom violent, a fellow rider had once described Doc as "gentle when stroked, fierce when provoked," just like a big dog.

Steven Grimes

    He figured that some people use lateness as an expression of how important they are. Just like riding the biggest, flashiest motorcycles money could buy, some people needed to let others know how vital they were to the entire world, whether the world knew it or not. That summed up the two men for whom he was waiting.
    Rock music, talk, and laughter spilled from inside the dark, air-conditioned bar, and Doc smiled. That was one of the reasons he rode his 1981 Shovelhead Wide Glide across the country to South Dakota every year. He loved meeting people in small, out of the way places along the back roads of America. The little town of Interior, at the extreme bottom of the Badlands, was perfect for this. Here, he could talk to the locals, drink some cold Coors beer, and enjoy being over a thousand miles from the ER where he worked. The bartender was cool and brought Doc another cold draft beer on the low wooden porch that spread across the front of the bar. Together they sat on the wood bench as the lonely wind moved down the street like a tiger searching for prey, almost invisible to the eyes, but obvious to his other senses. You had to sit and be quiet long enough to experience it. Talking or making unnecessary noise spoiled the moment and left you sitting with yourself as the only company. By respecting silence when proper, you could hear an awful lot.
    Around the corner and down the street at the Wagon Wheel Saloon, a guy called Lonny held the reins so people could climb onto his eighteen hundred-pound steer for a picture: "a photo op," the tourists would call it. Tips for some feed or a frosty beer in return was always welcome and tended to make Lonny talkative. He had once furnished a horse for the Kevin Costner movie, *Dances with Wolves*, and showed its picture to everyone that stayed long enough to see it. Doc recalled how Lonny's eyes swelled with tears when he described that horse dying of cancer a few years after the movie. Maybe Lonny had been kicked in the head by his horses or cattle a few times too many, but Doc loved listening to him talk about his life. People, real people, like Lonny, could put you in touch with what was really important. It was like a cool, fresh wind blowing right through you and cleaning out all the crap that accumulated in your soul.
    Doc preferred taking little state roads from his home in northeastern Ohio to the rally every year. He enjoyed stopping at mom-and-pop restaurants where the waitresses plied him with seconds, "Here, have s'more, honey; you look hungry. Don't you get hungry on that old mo-

torcycle?" Sharing beers with farmers, ranchers, and truck drivers in little hole-in-the-wall bars and taverns was a favorite pastime, too. After a few rounds, it didn't matter that Doc's hair hung down past his shoulders, or that his arms were covered with tattoos. Doc would buy a round, and it would be answered by another round from some kindred soul sitting on a scarred bar stool. Doc was at ease with such folks, and he could make them comfortable around him, too. In the greatest confidence, a trucker once swore to him that a half-frog, half-bat creature flew into his cab while driving though Alabama. You sure didn't hear stories like that in the bland, boring, fast food chains along the equally bland, boring, interstate highways.

At night, Doc would stay at little, non-franchise motels, where the owners would promise to watch his bike real close, and often left an old washcloth to wipe off the dew in the morning. Checking in was done in a part of their living room that fronted the rest of the motel. It was as close to Mayberry as you could get.

His musings ended as he heard engines approaching from the west. Two riders were approaching, and the wind began to howl. A pair of powerful motorcycles, highly polished, and glimmering like mirrors in the afternoon sun, came closer. Slowing somewhat uncertainly, they finally pulled into the gravel parking lot. The riders saw Doc and quickly turned towards him. Together, they pulled up next to his dusty Wide Glide. The loud, rumbling engines were silenced, and for a moment, all that could be heard was the tick-tick-tick as hot metal began to cool. Doc ran his tongue over his teeth and spit again. He had no way of knowing that one of the men before him would soon die horribly, or that the other would try to kill him, Doc, before the year's Sturgis rally was over.

2

A Long, Long Time Ago

Five hundred million years ago, South Dakota was covered with a warm, shallow sea, and although you couldn't tell it at the time, Mother Nature was hard at work making the area a biker paradise. What is now the western and central United States was a calm, warm sea, filled with clams, oysters, and innumerable small shell-bearing creatures. Bizarre fish swam in the shallow, brackish waters, leaving behind their skeletons when they died a peaceful death, or disappearing forever in the surging fight for life when they didn't. Huge lumbering amphibians hauled their thick, slimy bodies out of the water and sometimes left their webbed footprints in the warm, soft mud, to be found millions of years later in cold, hard rock.

Inch by inch and foot by foot, the mud and slime was crushed by the muck above, becoming rock over tens of millions of years. Dirty gray shale formed flat, well-defined layers when clay, mud, and sand were forced together over eons. Sandstone resulted when grains of sand were cemented together under tremendous pressures. Billions of tiny creatures lived and died, leaving minute shell fragments in thick layers. Crushed together for millions of years, they created large, flat slabs of light gray limestone, which in turn became caves in the distant future. Along the coast, layers and layers of dead plants were compressed into peat, and under even more weight, formed the sulfur rich coals of South Dakota. Modern schoolboys frequently found fossils of plants and tiny animals in these coals.

Miles and miles of flat rock layers formed the basis for the Great Plains, where half a billion years later, bikers would marvel at the beauty stretching from horizon to horizon. But Mother Nature wasn't done. The immense inland sea that spread from Mexico to western Canada began to change as the Rockies were thrust forcefully upward on its western edge. Millions of streams dumped a million tiny bits of sediment into the sea day in and day out. Ever so slowly, the sea was filled with silt and eventually formed rock layers four hundred feet thick along its western coast and up to two thousand feet to the east.

By seventy million years ago, the sea had been transformed into a lush, warm marsh, home to innumerable dinosaurs. Doc would have called it a not so dry run for the film *Jurassic Park*. The hungry, slavering tyrannosaurus rex hunted cattle-like triceratops and duckbills. Lizard-like mosasaurs crawled in the muck, and plesiosaurs poked their long necks out of the shallow water. A twelve-foot-long turtle skeleton was discovered just two miles south of Rapid City in the western part of the state in 1896. South Dakota would adopt the three-horned triceratops as its state dinosaur. In 1990, a tyrannosaurus rex skeleton was discovered on the Cheyenne River Sioux Indian reservation near the small town of Faith. Named Sue, her skull showed unmistakable signs of fighting with other dinosaurs. Later, the skeleton would be fought over by ranchers, Native Americans, and even the FBI. Her skull was a clue; Doc guessed she was one of those bitches that liked to cause trouble.

Sixty-five million years ago, the earth was just "minding its own business," a phrase Doc frequently heard in the ER. Then, from the depths of space, a huge comet crashed to earth near what is now the Yucatan peninsula. Although little direct impact was felt in South Dakota, animals throughout the world larger than a small cat became extinct in an environmental crisis worse than the worst "nuclear winter." Quickly, the dominant dinosaur species completely disappeared. The only remnants were the small, feathered dinosaurs that went on to become the birds of the world, and those reptiles that survived in a watery habitat. Such a huge loss of life impressed upon Doc's mind how puny and fragile our hold on the planet remained. The small furry creatures that had previously cringed at the approach of the dinosaurs came out of their hidey-holes. They grew and developed and diversified until one day, an ape-like creature could stand, raise a tree limb as a weapon, and beat it against Arthur Clarke's silent black monolith.

Although the bikers who would come to love South Dakota so much were far, far in the future, they would have cheered the next development. Sixty-two million years ago, the forces beneath the Rockies decided to raise another tremendous mass of granite. With the pressure and violence of continents crashing together, a massive part of South Dakota as well as eastern Wyoming and Montana were forced skyward—the Black Hills. Hot molten rock, magma, was forced into cracks and fissures in the ancient granite to form the lighter gray rocks called pegmatite (the white streaks on Lincoln and Washington's faces at Mount Rushmore). This magma cooled far beneath the surface. The huge mass of rock from which Mount Rushmore would be carved, for example, cooled eight to twelve miles down. Over the following eons, layers and layers of the softer sediment laid down in the warm oceans were gradually worn away to reveal the pink and gray granite underneath. Erosion would create the amazing spires and peaks seen along the Needles Highway in the Custer State Park. The new, hot rock also created deposits of gold, silver, tin and tungsten resulting in untold misery in the clash of white and Indian cultures.

Rocks such as Minnekahta limestone and Lakota sandstone resisted erosion to form the long, rugged ridges and plateaus best seen backlit by a South Dakota sunset. The broad valleys and gorges, marveled at by bikers from around the world, formed from softer Spearfish siltstone and Sundance shale. Older rocks were found in the center of the Black Hills, younger rocks scattered around them like a bull's eye. Some of these central rocks were two and a half billion years old. This humbled Doc; he had gone out of his way to find where Bear Mountain, northwest of the town of Custer and Little Elk Creek, west of Tilford, boasted these ancient witnesses to the passage of time. To most people, they were just dark red rocks. For Christ's sake, there weren't even any fossils for the kids back home! A feeling of deep peace and being a part of the flow of time came over Doc whenever he laid his hand on the cool, unfeeling rock that had survived so many years and so much change.

By fifty million years ago, the prairie was flush with countless herds of hoofed animals. For some reason, those with an odd number of toes, such as horses and rhino-like creatures would die out in what would become North America. Hoofed mammals with an even number of toes, known as creodonts, evolved into camels, pronghorn antelope, bison, deer, antelope, sheep, goats, cattle, and pigs. But they were not alone in this beautiful, wild arena. Massive predators such as giant wolves, lions, and saber tooth tigers preyed upon the endless herds. Damn, Doc had thought, this would have been a hunter's heaven!

Still, more changes were yet to come, at least to the eastern part of the state. Over the last ten million years, long cool periods resulted in more winter snowfall than could melt in the summer. After years and years of this, huge mountains of ice, glaciers, crawled out of the north to crush, scrape, and carve the earth on an unbelievable scale. Fortunately, Doc thought, the western half of the state and the Black Hills had been spared. The glaciers reshaped the eastern half of the state and created the beautiful Missouri River drainage system, later to be explored by Lewis and Clark.

These massive frigid monsters carried tons and tons of dirt, rock, and debris with them. The retreat of the glaciers dropped huge boulders weighing over a ton that would later confound bikers as they rolled past them in otherwise flat and simple fields. Long ridges of debris delineated the limit of glacial progress and lay across the valley of the Missouri River where I-29 would one day run. Massive amounts of fine dirt dried out as the streams diminished, resulting in huge dust storms as terrific winds whipped along the glacier's front. This dust dropped miles away to form the beautiful Loess Hills of western Iowa, a beautiful ride for any biker who chose the less traveled state roads.

Today's bikers watched for and dodged deer, pronghorn, mountain goats, and bison throughout the Black Hills. Fifty thousand years ago, Doc would have had to add mammoths, llamas, short-faced bears, and giant American lions to the list. That must have been a sight: a paradise filled with strange and beautiful beasts, free of the overwhelming intrusion of humans. Over time, the glaciers retreated as the climate warmed again, and these large animals died out. Some maintain that Stone Age hunters were responsible; others blamed it on environmental pressures. When he sat back and sipped whiskey, Doc would tell you it didn't matter who was to blame; it happened to make motorcycle riding better in the 21st century. In many ways, he loved old Mother Nature.

3

THE FIRST RIDE

Two men disembarked from the Saab turboprop 340B that had delivered them to Rapid City from Denver. A Boeing 737 had carried them on the first leg of the flight from Akron to Denver. The huge plane provided all the ass-kissing first-class had to offer. The smaller turboprop left a lot to be desired; there was a sense of being cramped, the twin turboprops whined loudly, and the flight from Denver seemed to take forever at only three hundred miles per hour. Plus, the stewardess didn't act very impressed by the "MD" behind the two men's names.

The first man, Dr. Noel Herrod, was in his late 40s. His athletic build resulted from work with an expensive personal trainer because he had never been in good shape naturally. At five-foot-six, he was just short enough to be sensitive about it. Tanned to perfection by his own tanning bed, his dark eyes constantly glanced about him. Straight brown hair thinned in what hospital residents, out of earshot, called "yarmulke pattern baldness." His face featured a long, straight nose, clean-shaven skin, and perfectly capped teeth. His small, confident hands moved nervously whenever he talked. His mother called them the hands of a surgeon, which irritated the hell out of him. He smiled frequently, but the smile seemed condescending to patients, artificial with colleagues, and frightening to residents, interns, and medical staff. His voice was low and well modulated. His words were always well chosen and extremely precise. In fact, he sometimes sounded as though he was reading from a script.

Noel was raised in an exclusive northeastern Ohio neighborhood. His cold and demanding parents looked upon their children as objects to show off and brag about at the country club. He attended private school and learned early to look down on Jews, Catholics, Islamics, and any "dark skinned religion." His uncles were physicians, as was his older brother. Noel always came up just a little short when compared to his brother, something his father regularly did, usually over a very tense and angry dinner table. To his everlasting shame, Noel's older brother always did better than he did and was accepted into a top medical school. Noel had to settle for a school with less prestige, and thus got a slightly less esteemed fellowship. His father was a hard-driving, successful cardiologist. Noel had never detected any apparent love between his parents, who got along as long as his mother played the role of "doctor's wife," held up her end socially, and stayed reasonably sober. His father was rumored to have slept with his more attractive fellows and researchers and to have had affairs with a few of the other doctors' wives.

Outwardly, Noel was very proud of his father, but felt he could never live up to his standards, especially financially. As doctors were paid less and less, he found it increasingly difficult to maintain the lifestyle his father had. Noel felt that not only should he have the very best, he should make it apparent to everyone else that he did. He had the best suits, best wife, and best house. When he decided a motorcycle would enhance his image (and enlarge his dick), he knew he had to have the best, which to him meant the most expensive and visible. Sadly, the beautiful motorcycle spent a great deal more time in his garage and driveway than it ever did being ridden.

Noel became very angry when mistakes or shortcomings were pointed out, and always deflected blame to others. He had never engaged in physical violence, but always managed to find ways to "get even." He once told bigger kids that an enemy of his had bad-mouthed them, he stole and destroyed notes of fellow medical students, and he intentionally failed to pass on a reconciliation message from his roommate to a girlfriend he secretly desired. During his medical training, he had a short affair with another cardiology fellow's wife during a brief separation. The physician, Dr. Todd Lassiter, later became his partner, and although Noel never re-established the affair, he never let her forget it. In fact, she lived in fear that he would reveal it to her husband.

Noel started selling prescriptions while he was a cardiology fellow in order to make money. Enough of the right (wrong?) people entered Noel's circle of contacts that he could engage in larger drug deals. He usually worked through several layers of middlemen; he remained "clean" and regularly moved twenty to thirty kilograms of high-grade cocaine each month in many small deals. Openly, he was very vocal about drugs and drug dealers, and he sternly admonished patients for smoking, drinking, or engaging in insufficient exercise, and saw these as moral weakness. He refused to believe addiction was an illness, especially alcoholism. It may be related to his mother's closet alcoholism, but he subscribed to the old "they could stop if only they wanted to badly enough" theory. Actually, Noel hated those who used his cocaine but saw the men he dealt with as businessmen meeting a societal need. They hadn't created the craving, desperate market for crack cocaine, but they never turned away when it beckoned to them with long, green fingers of cash. He himself had never used cocaine or other drugs, except alcohol. In the past, Noel had paid to have others beaten for bad deals, or stealing drugs from him. One person unintentionally died after a beating, but Noel saw this as "a side effect" of the beating. He felt that in this business, the ends always justified the means. A half-hearted police investigation of the death made him feel secure and infinitely superior to the law. In this way, he reinforced his feelings of invincibility.

Noel felt superior to those without formal education or prestigious social positions and used his position as a doctor to make others feel less important. He always introduced himself as a doctor: "Herrod, Dr. Noel Herrod." He didn't know the medical residents thought he sounded like he was saying "Bond, James Bond" and laughed behind his back. Noel worked many hours per week, but always made sure everyone was aware of how hard he worked. He jealously guarded his own time and screamed at residents or fellows if they dared interrupt him. They heard, "Why are you calling me? Only chief residents are allowed to call me!" He leapt at every opportunity to put someone down.

Next from the plane was Dr. Todd Lassiter. Like Herrod, he was a cardiologist with expensive tastes and desires. Unlike him, however, he was quite overweight, badly balding, and had dark hair with a walrus-like mustache. He talked rapidly and stammered when excited. Lassiter shook his head up and down during conversations, interrupted frequently, and wouldn't allow others to complete sentences. Rheumatic fever as a child had weakened his heart, and he now suffered from an irregular heartbeat and coronary artery disease. He had had more palpitations lately, but he attributed them to the increased stress of the past few weeks. Noel was his cardiologist and had reassured him of the prominence of stress in his symptoms. Exercise was not part of Todd's life and going up a flight of steps was enough to wind him. He knew the importance of diet, weight loss, and exercise, as any cardiologist would, but he preferred to rely on medications and the eventual coronary bypass surgery, rather than change his lifestyle so severely. His secret pleasure was a big plate of spicy chicken wings, although his wife seldom allowed him that luxury.

The two cardiologists had known each other during medical school and had done their residencies and fellowships together. Any residency or cardiology fellowship is competitive enough, but these two had taken it up a notch. Somehow, the other residents and fellows always seemed to lose papers and lab results, or their patients didn't do as well as the team of Herrod and Lassiter. Their teamwork carried on after training to build a very successful practice. Todd had been brought into the drug dealing early and managed the monies, as long as the profits were acceptable, and no one got hurt. He felt that condition made him a very moral person; he turned a blind eye to the nuts and bolts of the deals, leaving them up to Noel.

Their third partner, Jacob "Jake" Epstein, had been as hungry for financial success as they were. Jake had known something unsavory was going on, but felt clean as long as he only contributed money and accepted his share of the profits. It was like playing the stock market. The only difference was that this investment had no yearly statement or prospectus. He knew Noel and Todd and trusted them to make a disgustingly huge profit. Jake had made it clear that he didn't want to know what was going on. He had been as hungry for success as Noel and Todd and had been the first to buy an expensive motorcycle. At first, Noel thought he did this because he spent too much time with that professional embarrassment, Dr. Lovejoy, known to them as "Doc." After seeing Jake's "male menopause toy," Noel felt a $55,000 custom motorcycle made a favorable statement about his youth, vitality, and bank account. It didn't take long for Noel to browbeat Todd into a similar, although less impressive, motorcycle. Both took private riding lessons, but Todd admitted that he didn't feel he'd had enough practice riding his powerhouse of a bike. Sadly, the busy life of a successful cardiologist left little time for riding. Jake had suggested they take this trip, with Doc as guide, but had died unexpectedly about a month before of a massive heart attack.

The small Rapid City airport was simple to navigate, and they quickly headed for the baggage claim. Although neither had ever been in South Dakota before, they were not interested in the posters of beautiful landscapes or majestic animals lining the walls. The paper bison and Mount Rushmore did not seem offended.

The two picked up a few small bags; the remainder of their luggage had been shipped ahead of them. A dark man dressed in leathers identified himself as Tim, the driver of the truck that had transported their motorcycles to Rapid City. In this way, they moved from their life in Ohio to Sturgis Bike Week in a matter of hours, with a minimum of effort or discomfort. While the two bikes were unloaded and made ready, Herrod and Lassiter lounged about, drank Cokes, and did none of the physical work. They walked out to pick up their rides in the hot South Dakota sun, sweating for the first time during their week long 'adventure.'

Herrod's bike was parked at the curb. A beautiful Big Dog Mastiff model, it weighed in at almost seven hundred pounds and sported a 117-cubic inch engine with a $4\frac{1}{8}$" bore and $4\frac{3}{8}$" stroke. A 9.6:1 compression made it hard to start when cold, even with an electronic compression release. An S&S Super E carburetor sucked in air for the hefty mill. The bike was stretched 1", had a 3" backbone, and 35° of rake. The 120/70 front tire was 21 inches in diameter. The dealer had sworn that the hefty 250/40 rear tire would make women go wild. Noel felt the tire was too expensive for a burnout, but he lacked the courage to do one, anyway. The thick triple tree gave the bike a beefy look above the highly polished billet forward controls. A Baker six-speed transmission gave smoothness on the road most riders would envy. Herrod had never ridden the bike for more than fifty miles and found the seat became very uncomfortable. The bike had a deep red House of Kolor base with green flames. Everything that could be chromed had been, before he had ever ridden the bike, and nothing had been added since.

Tim pulled Todd Lassiter's new American Ironhorse Slammer chopper up next to Noel's ride and left it idling, thinking the pair would leave immediately. A thing of beauty, it boasted 2" top stretch and 42° rake (38° frame rake, plus 4° from the raked triple tree). Sporting a huge, wide 280 mm rear tire and a 90 mm front tire, this monster was reigned in by dual disk front brakes with six piston-chromed calipers. A 111-cubic inch S&S Super Sidewinder Plus Evo-style engine that exhaled through a 2-1 dyno-tuned exhaust powered Todd's ride. Keeping the bike in balance, power was delivered via a 6-speed right side drive. Todd's ass sat on a Phantom solo seat with Progressive adjustable air ride. He thought the expensive seat was adequate, but he'd never ridden over fifty miles in one day, either. The deep yellow base paint with silver flames across the stretch tank was Noel's suggestion. Todd agreed although he found a yellow motorcycle nauseating. Custom V-handlebars were a little hard to reach because of his short stature, but he found that if he leaned forward enough, he could hit the gears and reach the bars for short trips. Todd thought his side mounted billet license plate frame a little exciting, almost illegal, although Doc had reassured him that the police didn't really object to it. He found the power of his huge engine threatening, and readily admitted that he hadn't enough experience on any scoot to feel comfortable handling it above fifty-five miles per hour.

For several moments, Tim stood looking expectantly at Noel and Todd. They really gave him the creeps. First, they were the rich wannabe-types that flocked to Sturgis more and more over the last few years. Some guys rode their bikes all the way to South Dakota, some pulled their rides in trailers, and some, like these two, trucked their bikes out and flew to meet them. They were self-important pussies, in Tim's opinion. Second, they had no feeling for the event; they were just here to make themselves feel important. Noel's shifty eyes made him look like a cornered animal, looking for a way out of trouble. Tim would be glad once they rode off.

"These bikes are filthy," Noel said quietly. "I thought they were covered during the trip."

"Of course they were covered! They're fine," Tim responded warily.

"They look all right to me, Noel," Todd offered without conviction.

After a tense pause, Noel replied in a low, threatening voice, practiced on hundreds of residents in training, "They're filthy. If you expect to be paid, they'll be washed and polished. Now." He gave Tim a quick, sharp glance, spun on his heel and returned to the air-conditioned airport terminal. Todd exchanged a silent look with Tim, shrugged, and walked after Noel, mumbling as he scurried along.

"Rich bastards," Tim said to the empty air as he turned to call his two helpers. They would wash and polish the already sparkling choppers. "Rich bastards."

Three hours later, the bikes were deemed acceptable by Noel, and the two prepared to ride. Lassiter felt Noel was just delaying meeting with Doc. The two cardiologists knew Doc from the hospital, of course.

They grudgingly admitted that Doc was an excellent ER doctor and made their job easier: only admitting patients with real heart disease to their service and sending the countless heartburn, anxiety, and chest wall pain patients home to their private doctors. Even the "soft" calls Doc brought into the hospital always seemed to have true heart disease when tested with a stress test, or their coronary arteries were visualized with cardiac catheterization. Todd stated openly that Doc was the best diagnostician around. Noel thought the same, but was too offended by him to admit that someone that looked like Doc (long hair and tattoos), talked like Doc (complete disregard for authority on any level), and acted like Doc (he was friends with the hospital janitors, for Christ's sake!) could really be a "good" doctor. Why, the guy didn't even own a car and parked old, borrowed beaters in the winter next to the BMWs and Porsches in the doctor's parking lot! The rest of the time, he'd park his old Harley Davidson right next to the ER entrance. It didn't make sense that the hospital administrators put out millions for advertising and still kept a disgrace like Doc around.

The two rode, slowly at first, and then with more comfort, the sixty-five miles from the Rapid City Regional Airport to the miniscule town of Interior at the southern end of the Badlands National Park. Doc had chosen this meeting place intentionally. It gave the two cardiologists a little mileage to get used to their bikes, provided a short breaking-in period, in case anything obvious was going to happen to the relatively new bikes, and he would get to see how the two held up on enough of a ride along a state road to get their butts sore. They would then ride slowly up through the Badlands, to give them a chance to do climbs and drops for practice. It would give them some practice riding in a group. Plus, he thought the Badlands one of the most beautiful places in the world.

It was obvious that Todd was developing a bad case of monkey butt as he pulled off the main road and into the gravel parking lot of the saloon, along the main road of beautiful Interior. Monkey butt, a serious condition, resulted when the rider (or passenger) could not get comfortable on the bike's seat, no matter what position they tried. It was a complex problem that was part rider, part seat, part motorcycle, part foot pegs, and part environment. Doc had some "Anti-Monkey Butt Powder" in his saddlebag that he had brought on purpose for these two. He was pretty sure they'd need it, although only Todd would admit it. Doc had promised to help these two on their first Sturgis trip as a favor to Jake Epstein, just before Jake's massive heart attack. Although he knew Jake was diabetic, had high blood pressure, and ate everything bad for him (even non-Kosher, if his wife wasn't around), he was still shocked at losing one of his few doctor friends that rode. He'd made a promise, and he'd keep it.

Doc nodded to the two cardiologists and said, "We need some cold beer." He walked into the saloon, leaving the two to follow him. Todd limped in, scratched his ass, and squinted into the sudden indoor gloom.

Noel walked straight to the bar and cleared his throat to get the bartender's attention.

"Heineken," Noel said in his low voice, without a hello, please, or thank you.

The bartender stared at him for a minute, shook his head ever so slightly, and pulled a green Heineken bottle from the cooler at the end of the bar. He pulled another draft for Doc and asked, "Friends of yer's?" Doc shrugged his shoulders in a meaningful way, and the bartender nodded. He got out another Heineken unasked as Todd approached and sat at the bar between Doc and Noel. They all agreed that the cold liquid tasted great after a hot ride. Todd bitched a bit about his butt being numb after the long journey. Doc merely suggested riding more and farther to build up his tolerance and recommended the Anti-Monkey Butt powder he'd had the foresight to bring.

"Alright, y'all, here's the plan from here, if you think it's okay," he added as he saw the dark look on Noel's face. It was clear that although Noel had never been here before, he resented anyone, especially Doc, telling him what to do. "We'll ride up through the Badlands. The speed limit is thirty-five in most places, and that's a good thing. We'll go up and down some good hills. The ride's beautiful, but don't spend too much time looking at the scenery; watch what you're doing."

"We know what we're doing!" came quickly from Noel. Todd just looked apprehensive.

"Well, there's not many rides like this within two hundred miles of Akron, so unless you've ridden a lot, watch out. Hell, I have to be extra careful along here, and I've been here a number of times. Not only are the roads a challenge but there's plenty of idiots out there who don't know what they're doing. They're the biggest danger you'll find during Bike Week. Here, or anywhere else. Keep an eye open to both sides for deer, and slow way down when a bunch of cars are stopped ahead of you; there may be wild game in the road ahead that you can't see." He paused, and got no response. "At the north side of the Badlands, we'll hit I-90. We can fill up there and then head up to Sturgis and the Chip."

Noel said, "We'll still have some gas."

Doc answered, "Yeah, but it's best to top off when you can. There's nothing worse out here than running out of gas just ten miles from where you're headed. Gas stations are a lot farther apart here, and those choppers don't have the world's biggest tanks."

"Or the softest seats," added Todd, not looking forward to another long, uncomfortable ride.

"Y'all put that powder on your asses before we pull out, and we'll take another break up in Wall before we get on 90. You'll be okay."

Without further discussion, the powder was accordingly applied, and the three started their bikes. Doc explained simple hand signals: left, right, stop, slow down, I need gas, and so on before they pulled out. Initially, Doc rode lead in the short, staggered procession to give them an idea of the speed he had in mind. As they passed into the National Park, he took up a rear position, with Noel in the front and Todd tucked in the middle. Noel tended to approach turns too quickly, and then brake too much. Todd plodded along as though he was afraid the road would suddenly turn or give out, but Doc thought that was better than overreaching your abilities blindly. The monkey butt seemed to be cured for the moment.

4

BADLANDS

It was hard for anyone to keep their eyes off the striking beauty of the Badlands formations. Alternating layers of pale gray and deep purplish-red climbed hundreds of feet to end in intricately carved spikes, pinnacles, and towers. Doc knew that erosion wore these away at almost one inch per year, so the view was ever so slightly different from year to year, but he couldn't tell the exact difference. He did notice that the scenery looked different every year because of the angle at which he saw it, the amount of moisture and water on the rocks, as well as the time of day and amount of sun. He could come here daily for the rest of his life and not get bored of the magnificent, raw, wild beauty.

The trio pulled into one of the many overlooks for a quick break and some snapshots. Doc complimented them on their riding. Noel only smirked, but Todd seemed appreciative and smiled in return. Maybe this trip could really be fun, he thought. It certainly had the scenery, all right. Todd took five or six pictures with his Nikon 35mm camera; Noel used a more advanced digital camera. It was difficult to capture the magnitude of the Badlands, regardless of the camera in use. Doc had given up trying. He was happy just to have beautiful memories and feared that someday Alzheimer's disease (or alcohol abuse) would blur those memories. I'll drink a toast to it, then, he thought wryly.

Doc took a photo of Noel and Todd on the brink of a huge cliff with miles of Badlands and South Dakota behind them. Noel wore his usual non-committal smile, but Todd lifted his walrus-like mustache in a huge grin. He was genuinely happy, maybe for the first time in months. Todd never realized that scenery, other than his beautiful house and carefully manicured yard, could cause such feelings. He turned to Doc. "This is great!"

"Yeah, it is. God really went all out making this part of the world. If you squint real hard, you can make out the edge of the Black Hills on the western horizon over there." Doc pointed into the west, the sun just now starting to make its downward journey. "The Lakota Sioux called this area Mako Sica, or Bad Land, because there's no water to speak of. Long before that, though, there was water, along with rhinos, dog-sized horses, giant pigs, and huge buffalo, although I guess we should call them bison. It was pretty wet back then—ten million years, or so."

Todd listened intently, although Noel seemed bored, as though he'd heard it all before. Doc continued, "They even find fossil beavers, saber-toothed cats, and camels here. Back then, this whole area was a marshy plain. At the bottom of all this is a dark layer of shale called Brulé shale, after the Brulé Sioux. Ash fell from volcanic eruptions far off to the west, probably Yellowstone, and formed the white layers. Water carved it away, over millions of years, to make these deep gorges, spires and buttes. The erosion has slowed as the region became drier and drier. Now, only about sixteen inches of rain fall every year, and that's not much. We get more than twice that back in Ohio."

Noel turned away, but one could tell he, too, paid attention to what Doc said. Todd stood like a schoolboy, soaking up the mini-lecture. Doc had read a great deal about the region and could relay his knowledge to others in easily understood terms. He didn't sound like a professor or teacher, and certainly didn't look like one, either.

"Soil, made of clay or silt, alternated with volcanic ash. Some of these layers contain millions of sea creatures and the bones of creodonts, mammals that evolved into pigs and deer and stuff. It's weird to think of all this being underwater, but the proof is right there in those cliffs. The Sioux were the ones that first told us that all this had once been the bottom of an ocean. Pretty smart for 'savages.' Less than one hundred years later, Adolph Hitler would admire how the United States had identified a racially inferior group and systematically eliminated them through warfare, starvation, disease, and the reservation system."

Doc paused as he stared out into the distance. Coming here to the Badlands made him aware of how, years before him, people with skin the same color as his had desecrated this region and stolen from the people they methodically eradicated. Now, it's called 'genocide'; back then, it was 'Manifest Destiny' and was legal as well as politically correct. Doc still felt guilty for something neither he nor his ancestors had done. Hell, his Irish predecessors at that time were being all but wiped out by the British. Maybe it was part of the great white guilt that made Doc more solemn as he gazed across the miles. Neither of the other riders had a response to Doc's geology information or historical observations.

After a few more minutes of silence, Doc returned to the parking area and started his Wide Glide. The Big Dog and Slammer rumbled into life, and after a brief wait for the car, truck, and motorcycle traffic to clear, Noel roared out and headed northward, toward Wall and I-90. Todd and Doc dutifully followed. Doc felt the others' riding skills were adequate at low speeds, but he reserved judgment until they experienced the higher speeds on the western interstates.

Thirty or so miles from Interior, they stopped for gas in the little town of Wall. Once a speck on the map, Wall was now known around the world for the Wall Drug advertising stickers, if nothing else. Wall Drug became renown after offering free ice water along highway 16A in 1936. They didn't need a Madison Avenue advertising agency, just religious faith, and luck. Travelers to Yellowstone and the newly opened Mount Rushmore stopped, got free water, and bought a little something. The store boomed, in part because of the Wall Drug bumper stickers and signs that simply said "Wall Drug," or indicated the number of miles to Wall. They had been sighted in the London underground, Moscow, and even the South Pole. Today, parents who stopped at Wall Drug as kids themselves made the trip with their own children. Back then, cowboy outfits and six shooters were side by wide side with stuffed jackalopes—jack rabbits with antelope antlers. Now, pizza by the slice, scale dinosaurs, and offerings from the Toy Emporium ruled the roost. You could still get your picture taken by the same carving of George Custer on the same tree trunk as your grandparents. Plus, the coffee was free if you were a veteran or newlywed, a grouping Doc found oddly appropriate. As an odd comment on human nature, the jackalopes remained popular, too.

Out on the interstate, they headed northwest for the eighty miles to Sturgis. Noel had initially complained about the return mileage back to Rapid City, but Doc had reassured him of the importance of bike familiarity and soothed him with the magnificence of the Badlands. At least Todd's monkey butt seemed in remission. The broad Red Valley opened its arms widely as they passed through Rapid City and entered the Black Hills. With Doc anchoring the threesome, they stayed at a stable seventy-five miles per hour most of the way. There was plenty of company, though. Hundreds of motorcycles were with them, as well as trailers and trucks hauling motorcycles. Doc saw plates from South Dakota, Iowa, and Nebraska, of course. The more exotic plates were from Michigan, West Virginia, Rhode Island, Alaska, Florida, and Maine.

Ohio plates looked a great deal like the South Dakota plates—red, white, and blue in horizontal layers. Each year at the Buffalo Chip, Doc even saw plates from such remote places as England, Australia, and Germany!

Traffic increased as the bikes converged on Sturgis, and roadside traffic signs warned about stopping distances, as well as the dangers of riding two-up in the same lane. Doc smiled to himself and slowed as the first Sturgis exit approached. Todd grinned widely and even Noel seemed pleased as they took the exit and pulled into the town itself. Doc took the lead and steered them into the amazing experience that was Sturgis Bike Week.

5

Sturgis

Sturgis wasn't just a place; it was an experience. On paper, it was the county seat of Meade County, named for General George Meade, who defeated Robert E. Lee at Gettysburg. The town was named for Lt. Jack Sturgis, killed at the Battle of the Little Bighorn; it grew from Fort Sturgis (originally Ft. Ruhlen). Nestled in the mouth of a natural gap in the hogback ridge that formed part of the outer rim of the Black Hills, the town was along the path to the holy spot, Bear Butte, and the favorite hunting grounds of the Sioux. Three heavily traveled white settler trails converged at Sturgis—the Bismarck, Fort Pierre, and Sidney trails. For fifty-one weeks a year, Sturgis had a population of 6400. But that fifty-second week was something special.

In 1938, JC "Pappy" Hoel started a motorcycle racing and stunt-riding event with the local motorcycle club, the Jackpine Gypsies. Hoel, who ran the local Indian motorcycle shop, put up $500 in prize money. There were half-mile races, board-wall races, ramp jumps, and even staged, head-on collisions with cars! After World War II, as more and more men turned to motorcycle riding, racing and the Sturgis rally began to grow. Hill climbing was added in 1961 and remains very popular. In 1965, there were 1000 attendees; by 2000, an estimated 630,000 riders from around the world attended.

At one point, attendees were the bemoaned "one percenters," those rare, but badly behaved drunkards and gang members who struck fear in the hearts of mothers and fathers across our fair land. The image of the typical biker was based on Lee Marvin and Marlon Brando in 1953's *The Wild Ones,* in which forty motorcyclists crashed a legitimate race and stole the second prize trophy. In this somewhat dated, but innovative and groundbreaking movie, bikers raced up and down the town streets, drank beer, and clashed with a rival gang. The movie was based on an overblown incident that occurred in 1947 in Hollister,

California, near Monterrey Bay. Photos of this rally, some of which were staged by Life magazine, persisted for years in Joe America's mind. The image offended many riders, who maintained that only one percent of bike riders acted this way. In any event, at one point, Sturgis was somewhat of a dangerous place when Hell's Angels and Outlaws scared people away from the event. Woe to anyone who tried riding a Japanese bike to the rally in those days! Still, in many peoples' minds, anyone who rode a motorcycle was hairy, dumb, smelled bad, drank beer, and would fuck their daughter just before leaving town at the police department's insistence.

For better or worse, over the years, this image had changed. Along Main Street, one was more likely to meet a doctor, lawyer, or policeman than one of those smelly, hairy biker types. To many people, a clear distinction existed. There were bikers and there were riders, two very different groups. Bikers still fit the old image, although they had cleaned up just a bit. Today's bikers held jobs, got married, and paid taxes. Some even shaved and used deodorant! They were more likely to be blue-collar workers, and seldom made lots of money or wrote mystery novels. Still, they lived to ride (a famous Harley slogan), drank lots of beer, and got wild whenever the opportunity arose.

Riders were more often professionals, made excellent salaries, rode very expensive motorcycles, and spent more time polishing and showing off their bikes than riding them. They were disparagingly known as wannabe's (or worse) in the rougher biker community. Riders were changing the motorcycle culture in many ways. Motorcycles were more and more expensive, as were accessories and lodgings at rallies. Some events were even non-alcoholic or non-smoking. In addition, fewer and fewer riders knew much of anything about their machines beyond quoting specifications and price. "Old time" bikers had to be good wrenches to keep their scoots on the road. Many riders couldn't even change their oil or bolt on the simplest add-on accessory. The newest young riders, often on high RPM Japanese sport bikes, were known as "squids." They rode "crotch rockets" or "rice burners" and were known for stunt riding—doing wheelies on busy highways. In the past, there had been a great deal of animosity toward these youngsters at national rallies, but they were becoming more accepted on the road and at motorcycle events. Perhaps one of the most rudimentary differences could be seen as two motorcyclists passed each other on the road. Harley riders and bikers tended to acknowledge each other with a quick wave. The left (non-throttle) hand waved outward and downward, often showing the index finger, or the index and middle fingers as a salute—a show of community and togetherness. Young riders seldom, if ever, used or returned the sign.

Still, there was greater acceptance of different styles and bikes at motorcycle rallies and, overall, Doc thought this was a good thing. He adhered to the saying, "It doesn't matter what you ride, as long as you ride." The commercialization of Sturgis irritated him, however. Vendors began selling rally merchandise in 1974, and by 1988, there were over a hundred licensed vendors within the city limits. This resulted in some fundamental changes. For example, it was more difficult to find swap meet areas where bikers could finally locate that hard-to-find part they'd been seeking for years. Some rallies had lost sight of the biker who still built, fixed, and rode his own scoot. Vendor booths sold everything a biker (or his old lady) could want. Leather clothing was big, along with patches that ranged from veterans group identification to those that said, "I fucked your old lady" in large, bright letters. Anything edible was available—roasted turkey legs, stuffed tacos, succulent Phat Thai fried noodles, and those nutritional nightmares—funnel cakes. One of Doc's favorites was the slab of ribs from Famous Dave's at the Loud American Roadhouse. (Be warned, though, the Devil Spit hot sauce was a killer on lips chapped by hours spent in the wind and sun!) There were literally thousands of T-shirts available with every Sturgis and Black Hills Rally picture imaginable. Some were sanctioned as "official Sturgis merchandise," and some were not. The shirts could be bought hundreds of miles from Sturgis, but somehow that wasn't the same. Designs ranged from simple stenciling of the word Sturgis and the year, to complex, silk-screened designs that cost $50 or more. Key fobs, shot glasses, pins, and knives were a few of the souvenirs found up and down each street of central Sturgis. Tattoo parlors sprang up on Sturgis street corners like mushrooms after a rain, drawing artists from around the country for that one special week, and offering everything from traditional Harley logos, wolves, and eagles for bulging biceps, to pretty little hummingbirds, roses, and Rolling Stone lips for low backs, tummies, and who knew where.

Rallies now catered more to expensive custom bikes and their builders. Some stayed true to "old school," but more and more turned out machines that were more flash and less substance. Doc briefly met Indian Larry at Sturgis a few years back, and although the encounter was short, Doc felt he was someone who built from the heart and had genuine respect for the chopper and its history. The newer companies brought out dozens of look-alike "custom" motorcycles only varying in color and minor features, such as seat leather. All that highly polished chrome caused migraines when Doc spent too much time checking them out. Their short, curvaceous pipes let out a roar and blasted flame when the engine was vigorously revved. The tiny seat left little room for the young, eager hard-bodies the dealer promised would follow these bikes out of the sales area.

It was no longer possible to find reasonably priced lodging close to Sturgis, other than the campgrounds, which were also getting more and more expensive. Until 1983, bikers could camp in the City Park. In fact, camping had always played a major role with Sturgis bikers—a combination of lack of available lodging, as well as a lack of available money. Worst of all, in Doc's opinion, beer was more expensive.

The town of Sturgis was laid out in a basic grid pattern with Main and Lazelle streets forming the center of the rally. Main Street was first blocked off in 1949 for a two-hour award ceremony. Now, car and truck traffic was suspended along these streets during the weeklong rally in order to form four lines of bike parking, with a single lane of travel in each direction. Thousands of motorcycles filled the streets for blocks and blocks around downtown Sturgis. A common fear amongst Sturgis Virgins (first-timers) was that they wouldn't be able to muscle their 800-pound machines into the tight spaces without scratching another bike. A friend once told Doc that he had dreams of hitting the next bike and knocking over a whole line of bikes over, domino fashion. Although it sounded funny and would look good in a movie, it would be impossible, considering how the bulk of the bike leaned against the side stand (jiffy-stand was always a weird Harley-Davison term to Doc).

The Sturgis Police Department and the Meade County Sheriff's Office occupied the first floor of a three-floor building right on Main Street. The jail took up the second floor. Doc had no idea what the third floor contained. He had been on the first floor several times, but not the second floor. This was due more to good luck than good behavior. He had met several of the full-time Sturgis cops and generally had a good opinion of them. Many of the cops on the street during the rally were members of other departments from around the Black Hills, other parts of South Dakota and even outside the state. They were there just for the week of the rally. The police were usually easy to get along with, although drunk and disorderly, DUI, indecent exposure, and reckless driving got a trip to the station just as quickly (if not more so) than any other small town. Doc had always been impressed with the heavy, but subtle, police presence and believed it kept most assholes in line and quiet.

The Sturgis rally boasted numerous beer joints, and Doc had visited most of them (been thrown out of only a few). Doc's favorites included the Knuckle Saloon (where anyone riding a Knucklehead Harley could ride right into the bar), the Firehouse Bar (painted bright red so Doc could find it more easily), the Loud American Roadhouse (the ribs were great), and the Broken Spoke. One of Doc's female friends once got a free Knuckle T-shirt from the radio station located inside the bar by taking off her top on-stage to put on the new shirt. Doc had applauded along with the rest of the mildly stoned audience. The Full Throttle Bar on the eastern side of town was easily one of his favorites because of the ability to ride into the bar area, the bands, and the women. Women, by the way, were allowed to go topless if they were painted and had a tiny little something over their nipples. Doc felt it was a tribute to the beauty of women and wished he had some skill with an airbrush!

There were a thousand reasons for people to come to the Sturgis Rally. Different strokes for different folks, Doc mused. Still, he thought there was an underlying reason. Sometimes subtle and sometimes not, Doc felt that the reason most came here was the ability to be anything they wanted to be. Most visitors did not see anyone they knew except for those that came with them, who had the same desires and wishes. At Sturgis, you could be anyone you wanted to be and do (within limits) anything you wanted to do. Sophisticated lawyers rode like hell through the Black Hills. Staid businessmen wore leather, got tattooed, and listened to loud rock music while they drank whiskey straight. Teachers and shop owners showed cleavage and whistled at men walking down Main Street. Yankees and Confederates alike tried on leather jackets, vests, and chaps, while they pretended they were the mean, bad 1%-ers everyone was afraid of back home. It didn't matter if you were black or white, protestant or Catholic, or if you preferred country music to rock. Here, no one cared, or cared to care. Only prejudice against gay men persisted. Lesbians were accepted—hell, they were cheered. Known as 'dikes on bikes,' he never saw them get any grief; they were often applauded for fondling or kissing each other in public. In the last ten years, women on bikes were the fastest growing segment of the riders going down Main and Lazelle. He loved to sit at the bars fronting the street, put down some beers (and some shots), and watch the cars, the bikes, and the people parading by. Attractive women were celebrated, and they loved the attention, strutting past groups of cheering, half-drunken men. The ruder men shouted, "Show us yer tits," with varying results; some got more than an eyeful with amazing frequency, while others got the finger. While not shouting for boobs, Doc certainly appreciated a good pair when they strolled past.

This was the Sturgis that Doc, Todd, and Noel pulled into that hot, sunny, August afternoon.

6

New Friends

Noel and Todd followed Doc off Exit 32 and into the southern end of Sturgis. The sheer number of people and vendors slowed them considerably as they proceeded north on Junction Avenue. Chain restaurants and motels along the edge of town were host to thousands that afternoon. It seemed every one of the 500,000 predicted riders were in town that very day. As the trio crept towards downtown, more individual, mom-and-pop places took over. The stop and go traffic allowed them to get an eyeful of the young women, old graybeards, and bikes of every style, color, make, and engine. Doc saw mostly Evo's and twin-cam engines, with a scattering of Panheads, Knuckleheads, and Shovelheads. The rare flathead was usually parked carefully, often in a side yard or parking lot. Women were on bikes, too, both as passengers and riding themselves. Some were young hard bodies, but there were more big old fat gals, just as proud as could be, on the rumbling steel. One or two older women, grannies, with gray hair streaming behind them, were in the traffic as well. Most people seemed to be handling the movement of bikes well, but a few couldn't ride slowly or in a straight line. Usually they were on the fancier, more expensive customs. Maybe, they're just newbies, Doc thought kindly.

Many yards were packed with tents and bikes where the owners hosted friends and relatives or rented out space. Some residents got out of town and rented their home for the week. They often came back to houses that were actually cleaner than when they left; you can't say bikers were not appreciative.

People laughed and talked on the streets as they checked out each other's rides. Although most were perfect strangers, they acted as if they'd known each other forever. Backs were slapped, shoulders were punched, and more than a few beards were tweaked. The variation was amazing. There were shaved heads, a few Mohawks, long hair, short hair, and every kind of beard, goatee, and mustache imaginable, plus some that weren't. Do-rags and baseball caps were everywhere, and there was the obligatory buffalo head helmet (complete with full-size horns) seen down the street. Women had on the tiniest tops and shortest shorts possible, and flaunted some of the wildest hairdos. Some were as beautiful as models, some nice to look at, the majority rather plain, and some just downright ugly. The same went for their breasts—some weren't much to look at, some bobbed, and some absolutely knocked the eyes right out of your head. Silicone was not a banned substance in Sturgis, you could bet on that! It was so hard not to stare that most men didn't even try, and most of the women were pretty tolerant. Still, Doc had seen more than one guy get smacked in the head for spending a little too much time in appreciation of the eye candy.

Finally, Doc saw a spot he liked and pulled into a side street with enough room for the three bikes to park side by side. Todd had a little trouble backing his ride in at an angle, but finally managed it with a smile that showed he appreciated each small accomplishment. This guy might have potential, thought Doc.,

"Let's stop here," Doc decided out loud.

"Is this place safe for our motorcycles?" Noel questioned—his first real words to Doc all day.

"Yeah, it's safe enough. You've got an ignition lock don't you?"

"Of course, I do; I just wanted to make sure it's safe," Noel grumbled in return.

Todd ventured, "I don't think the owners look too suspicious," as he gave a little wave to the elderly couple sitting in lawn chairs in the grass yard before them. They nodded back and gave a little wave in return. It was plain that they enjoyed watching the bikes go up and down the street.

Doc said nothing and locked his ignition, but not the fork. He tightened his belt before walking back towards Junction Avenue. Noel and Todd followed him to the intersection, and then crossed into the craziness across the street. They threaded their way down to Main Street, where Doc declared, "I'm thirsty. How about a beer?"

Todd and Noel nodded, and the trio passed into the nearest bar. Probably closed the rest of the year, the walls were covered with motorcycle and NASCAR posters. A plain countertop lined one wall, and about an inch of sawdust covered the floor. With no place to stand at the bar, a number of tables had been crowded into the storefront until it was hard to move around. Doc grabbed three long neck Coors beers and threaded his way to his two acquaintances.

"Here y'all go," he said as he set the bottles down. Todd took his beer and took a long, deep drink. Noel was slower and more deliberate. "Sturgis is pretty easy, but there are a few rules," Doc continued, when no one else spoke. "Don't fuck with people, and they won't fuck with you. If you do fuck with somebody, you'd better be ready to stand up to whatever is coming. Don't touch or sit on somebody's bike unless they invite you to, and the same goes for their women. There're not many unattached women around here, so count yourself lucky if you find one."

"I don't see many women around here I'd be interested in, anyway. They all look like overage, overweight sluts," was Noel's reply. He spoke loudly enough that he was overheard at a few tables. A few hard glares came his way, but no one said anything.

"It all looks fine to me. I've only been here thirty minutes, and I love the place," Todd sounded pleased. "But I've really got to go to the bathroom," was his exit line.

"Listen, Noel," Doc started quietly. "You can be a big asshole back at the hospital, but if you act like one or talk like one here, you're gonna get the crap beat out of you. I'm telling you this as a friend, which I'm not. I don't plan on scrapin' your sorry ass off the floor once one of these guys pounds you into a greasy puddle."

"Fuck you, Doc. I don't care what these lowlifes think—if they do think with their feeble brains. And that goes for their disgusting women, too."

"Hey, asshole, nobody here cares if you're a doctor, lawyer, or Indian chief. Piss off the wrong person, and you'll be just another pile of hurt when they're done. Why don't you chill out, keep your damn mouth shut, and stop trying to win the jackass of the month award?" Doc rose and headed for the john.

Once Doc moved away, a huge, bearded man at the next table, tattooed on almost every visible inch of his body, leaned over and rumbled to Noel, "That's some real good advice, pal. I'd pay close attention if I were you."

Noel said nothing, apparently contemplating what this giant could do to him if he persisted. He saw nothing wrong with his attitude and decided that Doc was trying to rile him and get him in trouble with the unwashed rabble filling the bars and streets. He had only come to Sturgis to meet a drug contact and pick up twenty kilograms of cocaine. He thought it a great idea to ship it back to Ohio in the saddlebags of his motorcycle. If no one found it, that was great. If they did, the dirty, hairy drug addicts who filled every cranny of Sturgis and drove that truck full of expensive motorcycles had obviously planted it on him, a respectable physician. He already had plans for that coward Todd, and he was beginning to form plans for Doc, too. Some very painful plans. Yes, he might find a place for Doc in what was coming, a useful role for Doc, indeed.

    The trio left the bar and stopped at several others. The last one was a favorite of Doc's—a raised wooden platform that extended to the sidewalk and sported a thin wall of chicken wire. (To prevent alcohol from spilling onto the sidewalk? To keep patrons from reaching into women's tops as they walked by? To keep the chickens in?) They got three seats at the narrow counter along the chicken wire, six beers, and three shots. Since Doc was still treating, they got MGDs and Jack Daniels. The hot sun felt great as they sat several feet off the ground and watched the girls and motorcycles parade past. Really nice bikes and attractive women got cheers from the men seated along the counter as they passed. Some came around more than once, enjoying the exuberant appreciation. Todd used up an entire roll of film on the bikes, cars, and women parading past. Doc called to one man, regarding his beautiful companion, "You're a lucky man," to which the guy drunkenly smiled, "I know, man, I know." Everyone had a good time, although Noel said very little and replenished his own drinks with Heineken and Black Velvet Canadian whisky. Noel did not provide rounds for his companions. Doc and Todd did their share of rounds, which began to include those seated near them. In true biker fashion, every time one person bought a round, another person bought the next. People were coming and going, which ensured a large amount of liquor in a very short time. Doc got a good buzz going, and took the time to observe Noel and Todd. Noel drank less than anyone else did, seemed to remain sober, and stayed very quiet. Todd drank a lot of beer and whiskey, but didn't show it. When Doc commented on it, he replied that appearing sober was a skill he had acquired in college, and they both laughed. Doc had not taken that class, and he was getting pretty shit-faced.

    Feeling the need for something solid in his belly, Doc staggered, rather than steered, the trio over to the Loud American Roadhouse. They found a table with five stools and a friendly waitress. Beers and shots arrived just before a fantastic pile of Famous Dave's ribs. Doc poured generous amounts of Devil Spit sauce on his ribs and ate the meat right down to the bone. The others ate with a little more finesse, but did major damage to the huge slab of ribs before them. By the time the ribs were gone and another round was ordered, they were actually starting to laugh.

Death in Sturgis

Suddenly, three people were standing next to the table, a couple in their fifties, and a girl in her mid-to-late twenties. They looked tired and frustrated.

"Hey, would y'all like to share this table?" offered Doc.

"Sure, that would be great," the man replied as he and his companion took the two available stools. Todd moved his stool a few inches to make some room, although Noel stayed motionless. The girl remained standing.

"Have a seat, ma'am," Doc continued, as he stood and pulled his stool into position for the girl. She gave him a funny look for a minute, than sat down. Doc motioned to the waitress and being more than just a little drunk continued, "Chivalry is not dead, darlin'! I'm Doc, this is Noel, and this is Todd."

"Herrod, Dr. Noel Herrod," Noel interjected, with an air of superiority, trying hard to impress the newcomers and establish dominance.

Todd added, "We're here from Ohio. Where are you from?" He had already learned this to be a friendly, non-confrontational opening.

"We towed my Softail out here from Muncie. Muncie, Indiana. I'm Jim Baker, and this is my wife, Tammy. Don't laugh, that's our real names, and we're not TV evangelists!" They all laughed. Apparently, Jim and Tammy had done this introduction more than once. He continued, "Erin, here, is my step daughter. We dragged her to Sturgis, kicking and screaming the whole way."

"Give me a break, Jim," Erin laughed. Doc thought it a nice laugh, a sincere one, from a woman able to laugh at herself. She turned to Doc to explain. "I just broke up with an asshole who somehow forgot to tell me he was married for the whole year we saw each other. Last month, I found out. I said 'Fuck you!' and walked out. When Mom and Jim said I could come out here with them, I thought, 'Why not? Nothing else is keeping me!' and here I am! I feel a little like a third wheel, though. We get along alright during the day, but it's not like I want to hear them bumping uglies at night while I pretend to be asleep, ya know?"

Doc was entranced, Noel bored, and Todd wished he were twenty years younger and single.

"It's not like we're sex maniacs; we're normal people going to Sturgis, and that's kind of a turn on, too. It's a little difficult to put Erin out of the room just because Little Jimmy wants to play," Jim said through their first round of Bud Lights. Erin rolled their eyes at her mom and ordered tequila shots all the way around. The young woman explained to Doc that tequila shots were her weakness. He grinned, feeling that this could get very interesting very quickly. He was no young stud, but he knew he could go a long way towards making this young lady forget her previous man, jerk that he may have been.

"We're staying at the Buffalo Chip," offered Todd enthusiastically, with a slight slurring of his speech. "Doc says that's the wildest place in all of Sturgis, an' he should know; he's been here enough." Todd followed this with vigorous head bob, which made his walrus-like mustache bounce up and down.

"We're camping down at Tilford. That's not too far—about ten miles," rejoined Jim. "Maybe we can get together later this week. Drink some beers. We're going to the Badlands tomorrow, if you want to do it together." Jim was jumping at the chance to have a Sturgis veteran take them under his wing. Plus, if Doc could occupy Erin while he and Tammy had a night or two to themselves, all the better! He trusted him, somehow; after less than an hour, he trusted him. Like many people, he felt instantly at ease with Doc, although he didn't know why. He wasn't certain about Todd. He was pretty sure about Noel, though. After this short encounter, he was pretty sure Noel was an asshole.

"We saw the Badlands today, already. It's worthwhile, especially if you have your own geology professor with you. Tomorrow Dr. Lassiter and I are going through Spearfish Canyon. Wednesday, Doc is going to take us to the Little Bighorn battlefield," Noel supplied their itinerary for the next few days. "I don't know how reconvening would be feasible. I fail to see how it could mesh with our schedule."

After several seconds staring at Noel, Erin asked, "Does he always talk like that? That was scary!" She broke into giggles and downed another tequila shot. Doc smiled and downed another himself.

"Don't mind him; he's jus' not used to this loud music an' all," Todd tried to explain, but after nine or ten beers and six or seven shots, he was quite toasted. Noel had had two to three beers and two shots. Todd wasn't sure what had been poured down Doc's throat, but it couldn't have been less than he'd had so far. He felt very warm and kindly toward Doc and Jim and Tammy and, well—everybody. Everybody except Noel, that is. He could be a real dick sometimes. He resented Noel browbeating him over everything. He was now certain about something else. He was sure he'd finally force his way out of the drug deals, even though the money he was making was sweet. He had enough documentation that he could make Noel let him out. "Maybe we can change our schedule or something."

"Well, I'm going to meet an old friend tomorrow in Belle Fourche. Let's do the Little Bighorn on Tuesday and get together during the day

Wednesday. Kid Rock is playing at the Chip that night. Why don't you go with me?" Doc said, locking eyes with Erin.

"That sounds great!" responded Erin. She was in no great hurry to get romantically involved again, but Doc was interesting in an older, more experienced man sort of way. He was also kind of sexy with his deep blue eyes and tasteful tattoos (the ones she could see). Even the graying sideburns and goatee were sort of a turn on. She had the impression that a night with him would be one to remember for a long, long time. Also, he seemed to play fair with everyone and not be on an ego trip like this other guy—Noel. She had decided she was going to be an equal partner in any future relationship, whether it lasted a day, a week, or a lifetime. Doc made her comfortable. It was a cliché, but she already felt like she'd known him for years. "Super! Let me give you my cell number, and you can call me Wednesday morning. Mom and Jim would be more than glad to get rid of me for a few hours, or a day, anyway. Besides, I love Kid Rock. I'd kill to see him live!" Enthusiasm is a wonderful thing.

They had a few more drinks and left the bar, partly carrying Todd to Jim's pick up, which was, fortunately, not far away. They drove to where the three motorcycles had been parked. Erin and Tammy would follow Doc and Noel east to the Buffalo Chip while Jim rode Todd's Slammer. Everybody seemed happy with the arrangements, especially Jim, as he got on the expensive motorcycle and hit the throttle a few times.

"Ride that machine carefully," Noel warned him. "It probably costs more than you make all year. Just follow Doc out of town to the campground, it's within ten miles." Noel cemented a position in Jim's mind as probably the biggest asshole he would ever meet. He didn't know what to say to him; Noel's intimidation powers were very efficient with blue-collar folks like Jim and Tammy.

As they followed Doc in a little procession, Jim imagined knives in Noel's back. Noel imagined killing Doc with his own hands. Tammy imagined a few nights alone with Jim. Erin imagined what being with Doc would be like. Doc imagined another beer. Todd imagined snoring quietly, which he was. Todd's camera was safely next to him on the front seat of the half-ton pickup.

Their small parade made the short trip out of town and past the VA hospital. The traffic made the drive longer than usual. As they passed the packed Full Throttle Saloon on Route 34, Doc pointed out beautiful Bear Butte to the northeast. At last, among hundreds of other rumbling motorcycles, they slowly pulled into the world famous Buffalo Chip.

Welcome Home, Bikers!

7

THE BUFFALO CHIP

Situated at the very front of the Buffalo Chip was a huge steel gate that reminded Doc of the entrance gates to many western ranches. Over twenty feet high and almost forty feet wide, this one was different, though. Along with the Buffalo Chip's traditional buffalo skull, this gate had the message "Welcome Home, Bikers!" that had brought a tear to the eyes of thousands of motorcyclists over the years.

For over twenty years, Rod "Woody" Woodruff and his crew had made the Chip into what they called "the best party anywhere." Doc, a very good judge of things like this, agreed—one hundred and ten percent. Sometimes he felt that the week at the Chip every year made the other fifty-one weeks survivable.

Woodruff, a Belle Fourche lawyer, hosted tens of thousand of riders and provided them with classic entertainment and a great place to raise hell, as well as meet new and old friends during the Sturgis rally. Hell, there had been times when Doc didn't even leave the campground to go into Sturgis for the day; he had everything he needed and wanted around him.

Not just a campground, the Chip was truly a little city unto itself. Sure, you pitched a tent, hauled a trailer, or even rented a camper once you got there, but the Chip was much, much more. There were dozens of vendors, offering everything from tattoos to hot food and sex toys to motorcycle clothing. There was even a Harley Davidson store although as of yet they didn't sell bikes or service them. There were multiple bars, free morning pancakes from the Sons of Light Ministry, and beers or hot dogs for just a dollar from nine to five—pretty much all Doc needed to live. Showers, laundry facilities, and outhouses rounded out the amenities. Some days he felt like he'd died and gone to heaven!

Woody brought fantastic musical acts to the Chip every year. Doc had seen Steppenwolf, the Allman Brothers, Jethro Tull, Blue Oyster

Cult, ZZ Top, and Alice Cooper. Other classics have included Lynyrd Skynyrd, Styx, Marshall Tucker Band, Grand Funk Railroad, The Guess Who, and Steve Miller. More recent acts, like Tantric, Smash Mouth, and Kid Rock, kept the younger folks happy. There was even a strong flavor of country and western music with Montgomery Gentry, Travis Tritt, and Tim McGraw. Admission to the concerts was part of the fee that covered camping.

The experience of listening to John Kay sing Born to Be Wild while hundreds of Harleys revved their engines was almost a religious experience for Doc during a previous rally. Although the Jack Daniels could have played a role, Doc had thought he felt the earth move from the energy and excitement around him. Somehow, he'd found his way back to his tent that night, although he found one of his boots one hundred feet away the next morning and woke up missing a contact lens. It must have been a very good night.

Doc and Erin stood in line to get the weeklong passes for Doc, Noel, and Todd while Jim and Tammy stayed with Todd, still sleeping in their truck. Jim was very glad that Todd was only drowsy and not vomiting. They had a lot of miles to drive in that truck, and he liked the way it smelled right now, thank you. Noel stayed near his bike as if he expected it to be stolen any minute.

"This is not too bad. Last year, I swear I stood in line for two hours to get my pass. At least it's not raining, huh?" Doc understood the anticipation and excitement Erin felt waiting in line.

"Yeah, it's like being at a concert or something. You can tell these people are here to have fun. They're laughing and smiling even just standing here in line. Anywhere else, they'd be bitching and complaining. This is cool."

"The real fun starts inside. Here at the Chip, you can pretty much do whatever you want and be whoever you want to be. This really is the epitome of libertarianism. You can get drunk, get loud, do burnouts at three in the morning, and generally raise hell—at least as long as you don't bother anybody else. There's over two hundred acres here, some improved for trailers and such for VIPs. For old farts like me, you'll find beautiful little shady spots to pitch your tent. Then you can just sit back and enjoy. Yeah, it's loud and noisy, and there's a lot of nudity, but the people make it fun. I've met people from almost every state and a dozen different countries. It's pretty cool to share a cold one with a rocket scientist from Texas on your left and a down-to-earth blue-collar factory worker from Oregon on your right. The common thread is a love of bikes, mostly Harleys, a healthy respect for individual freedom, and a refusal to grow old. Many of these people are in their forties and fifties. There are a lot of Viet Nam vets, too. They have a traveling wall and have had B-1 bomber fly-over every year for the last few years."

"Traveling wall?" asked Erin.

"Yeah, it's a scale replica of The Viet Nam Wall in Washington, DC. Nearly everyone my age had a friend or relative's name on the Wall. Someone we knew, loved, and still miss. It may have been a lot of years, but that empty spot in your heart just never gets filled."

"Were you in Nam, Doc?" she asked, a bit tentatively.

"No, just missed it. I was signed up to join the Navy at the end of my last year of high school, but then peace broke out. The girl I was going with announced that the baby wasn't really mine, and I figured, 'Hell, let's take a minute here and re-evaluate these plans.' I'm one of those people who say, 'I wasn't there, but I care.' I believe there are still American prisoners over there, unless they've all died. We never got answers on what happened to a lot of people. Answers from the Vietnamese. Answers from our own government. To make things worse, this country turned its back on those guys when they got back, many of them fucked up in their heads. I know one guy, six months older than me, who got to Nam just in time to help evacuate Saigon when everything collapsed. He saw a whole lot of shit in a very short time. The sad thing is, in his head, it's still April 1975, and it always will be. He was a marine, part of what was called Operation Frequent Winds. They were charged with getting the last of the Americans and high-risk Vietnamese out. He saw some pretty awful things. They all did, and as far as I can tell, no one came back unchanged. I knew another guy back in Ohio that weighed around two hundred pounds when he got to Nam, but only eighty-eight when he got out of the POW camp. He went on to be active in Rolling Thunder."

"What's that?" Erin asked. Doc was impressed. Although she hadn't even been born by the end of the war, she was paying close attention to what many people her age considered ancient history. To them, Viet Nam was as real (or unreal) as the War of 1812 or the Spanish American War—a lot of people got killed, but there weren't any great movies or video games made about it. Boring!

"Rolling Thunder is a nationwide group dedicated to teaching people about POW-MIA issues—prisoners of war and missing in action.

Death in Sturgis

They ride bikes and have rallies, especially on Memorial Day in Washington. Ya see, America repeats the same fucking mistakes over and over again. Young people pay the price for our stupid foreign policies, just as they're paying today in hot, sandy places like Iraq and Afghanistan. Our government doesn't listen. I'm not an expert or a politician, and I'm not here to make a speech. I feel the human end of things more, and you really can't ignore or forget that kind of pain. There's a poem I remember, if you'd like to hear it."

"Wow, someone reciting love poetry in the middle of Sturgis!"

"No, at least, not the kind of love you're thinking, darlin'. A Major O'Donnell wrote this before he was killed in action in 1970. It goes like this:

> 'If you are able, save for them a place inside of you and save one backward glance when you are leaving for the places they can no longer go.
>
> Be not ashamed to say you loved them, though you may or may not have always. Take what they have taught you with their dying and keep it with your own.
>
> And in that time when men decide and feel safe to call the war insane, take one moment to embrace those gentle heroes you left behind.'"

It might have been the dust stirred up by the rising evening wind. It might have been squinting into the bright South Dakota sun all day long. It might even have been the exhaust fumes from the surrounding bikes. But it wasn't. It was Doc's soft, low voice reciting these lines that brought tears to those people standing in the sudden silence around him. Without raising his voice or calling for quiet, Doc had captured the attention of the happy people standing nearby, and for just a minute, reminded them of how lucky they were to be there.

"Well, all right, brother," someone boomed out and slapped Doc on the back.

The spell was broken, and the silence shattered. The bustling strangers standing in line were now newfound friends, shaking hands and trading hugs. Erin was amazed that no one seemed surprised by what had just happened. It seemed so strange, but at the same time, it seemed so right. She didn't know if it was the magic of Sturgis, the Buffalo Chip, or this unusual man she had only met a few hours earlier. Her female intuition assured her it was a little of each.

8

First Night

Wristbands in hand, Doc and Erin returned to the pick-up, where they found Jim and Tammy standing together, listening to the music coming from inside the Buffalo Chip and swaying where they stood. Noel waited, glowering; Todd seemed to be waking up a bit. Doc gave Noel and Todd their passes. "Put these on your right wrist and flash them any time you enter the campground over there. Just kind of wave, so the security person at the gate can see it and then just ride on in." He indicated the longhaired man wearing a red Buffalo Chip T-shirt with the word "Staff" stenciled across the back.

"That barely qualifies as security," sniffed Noel.

"Yeah, well, cause some trouble, and you'll see how secure your ass will get, in a matter of minutes. People are here to have fun, and generally take care of their own. As far as I know, the police have never been called to the Chip. There's enough big, bad people here that they can enforce the live-and-let-live policy without breaking a sweat. Anyway, that's what you do whenever you want to go in; you don't even have to stop."

"Very well, let's locate our accommodations. Todd, wake up, I'll not go in alone." Noel's dry, nasal voice almost sounded like an order. Todd opened his eyes, got out of the truck, and walked over to his bike.

"That's a great machine, Todd," smiled Jim. "Anytime you want me to ride it for you, just let me know."

"Thanks for helping out. I just had a few too many, but I'm okay now," Todd answered. He wanted to apologize for Noel's attitude, but figured they would get used to it. He had. Then, with a rare second thought, Todd realized that he should neither apologize for Noel, nor accept his boorish behavior. "Noel and I appreciate your help," he finally said.

"Sure. Let's get together tomorrow or the next day. We'll have a good time." Jim wasn't sure he could ever have any kind of fun with Noel. Todd, however, had potential.

"Good night, guys. See you," Tammy said as she got into the truck and waved.

"Good night, Doc. Call me, okay?" Erin looked into his eyes. They seemed a little deeper and a little bluer than when she first met him back in town.

"Here," Doc handed her a bright pink wristband. "This is for you, darlin'. This way, you can come out here anytime. We can listen to some music, do a few of those tequila shots you like so much, and have some fun."

She happily grabbed his hands as he offered the small strip of plastic. "That's so sweet! I'd love to! Maybe you can recite more poetry for me, huh?"

Tammy raised her eyebrows slightly. Doc's answer was his smile and nod. He leaned over and kissed her softly on the cheek. "I'd like that a lot. Maybe you'd like a poem by an Italian poet from the thirteenth century?"

She grinned, squeezed in beside her mother, and the truck backed out. Doc watched them drive into the dark before turning to his two companions. Todd was fumbling with the compression release and choke knobs on his bike, trying to start it. Doc wasn't sure if he was having trouble because he was drunk or because he didn't understand the features.

"Just use the compression release. You shouldn't need any choke to start it now, it's hot enough from Jim riding it out from Sturgis," Doc suggested to Todd.

"What do those things do, anyway, Doc?"

"Well, you've got a huge fucking engine with a lot of displacement and a lot of compression. That means you burn a lot of fuel under a lot of pressure and get a whole lot of power from your mill."

"Yeah, I'm getting to love this thing."

"However, you've got a much smaller starter motor, saving your leg from having to kick start the engine. To make the starter happier, and to keep from fucking up your rings and pistons, your bike has a compression release button on your cylinders. This causes a leak in your cylinder for the first couple of engine cycles, thus lowering the compression and making it easier for the starter to get the engine turned over. After that, it closes and lets the compression return to its regular, pumped-up level. They really liked them in the old days when we had smaller starters. Stroking the engine often increased its compression so much it couldn't be started. It wasn't perfect, but it saved many a jacked-up leg from trying to kick start a high compression engine."

"Okay. But what am I choking when I pull the choke knob?"

"You need the choke out to decrease the amount of air and increase the amount of gasoline going into the engine. This is important when the engine is cold because gasoline actually condenses on the cold cylinder wall and is not available for burning. Once the engine is warm, you don't need anymore choke. Harley used to call it an enricher, rather than a choke, because it enriches the air-fuel mixture—makes it rich with fuel. A lean mixture has more air, or less gas, depending on how you look at it. Stock bikes usually run lean to meet EPA regulations, but that may result in backfires or coughing when you accelerate. Adding a high flow air cleaner and less restrictive pipes tend to make it even more lean, that is, add more air. Your bike will run on the hot side unless you change the carburetor jets to increase the amount of gas entering the manifold. It's sort of like the three bears—too rich, too lean, or just right. You can get a rough estimate of how well tuned your bike is by reading the spark plugs."

"Huh?"

"In the olden days, when riders did their own maintenance, they would put in new plugs, run the bike for a bit, without actually idling the engine, and then take the spark plug back out to look at it. A light gray discoloration of the spark plug electrode means you're probably not getting enough gas. If the plug is fouled or coated with a dark, wet material, then there is too much gas going into the engine. Things are a lot easier now with electronic fuel injection; the computer uses sensors to determine atmospheric pressure and the amount of oxygen entering the engine. It then adjusts the amount of fuel sprayed into the manifold to mix with air. That pretty much takes care of the problem. We old-timers have to change carburetor jets or move needle valves up and down to optimize engine performance and the ultimate dyno reading sessions. Sometimes it can be a real pain—removing gas tanks and so on."

"Wow! That sounds awfully complicated. I think I'll stick with nice, simple human hearts. Hey, Doc, did you ever hear the one about the mechanic and the heart surgeon? The mechanic said, 'I remove defective parts, replace valves, reroute wiring, and clean out gas lines. We both do pretty much the same thing! How come you get paid so much more?' The surgeon answered, 'Try doing it while the engine is running!'" Todd laughed at his own joke.

Doc replied, "Actually, the human heart is stopped during valve replacement and coronary grafting, you know, just like the motorcycle engine. They both sound pretty hard to me. Come on, let's find your trailer." Doc shot down Todd's joke so painlessly that he didn't seem offended. Noel sneered, however, and took it as an example of how even other doctors didn't appreciate that working with the human heart, the very soul, was the most exacting and demanding branch of medicine. He found Doc vulgar and regretted the man had ever been accepted into a medical school. No doubt a graduate of a foreign school, he thought, not knowing that Doc had graduated with honors from one of the best, if snobbish, schools in the country. Doc was proud of his school for having such a large number of women and minorities as students as well as professors, its commitment to the poor, and its Native American health program, where students became aware of the many biological, psychological, and social aspects of treating people of various ethnic backgrounds.

The trio started their motorcycles and rode through the bike and pedestrian gate. They waved their wristbands at the alert but subdued security guard, turned left, and entered the crowded amphitheater area. There was just enough room to pass the Wolfman Jack stage, where tonight's band was winding up their set. They threaded through the excited crowd and past the Sam Kinison Memorial Stage. The mechanical bull was in full swing, mounted by a young woman wearing only leather chaps and boots. No doubt, her bra had flown off during the ride, and she deeply regretted her frontal nudity. The crowd was sorry about it, too. Yeah, right.

Todd was fascinated by the number of people on the narrow dirt and gravel roads and the fun they seemed to be having. They passed the Emerald Pond, where Doc would pitch his tent after locating their rented camper. The camper idea was pretty new, and Doc thought it was the best idea he'd heard of in years—ride your bike, but enjoy a camper! Theirs was quickly found in the Chip's South 40, an area of improved trailer spots. Each was relatively new and provided all the conveniences of home: stove, air conditioning, heater, microwave, bed, kitchen, and bathroom. Each one could accommodate four adults easily—essential, because Todd's wife was scheduled to arrive in a few days. Noel's wife stayed home, much to Noel's irritation. Prior to their arrival, Noel had arranged for bedding, towels, and kitchen utensils. Todd didn't realize that Noel had also made arrangements with some bikers through one of his many drug contacts. He called them as they arrived at their rented mobile home; five dirty-looking men arrived on motorcycles within fifteen minutes. Two of them spent a whole half-hour conferring with Noel in hushed voices. Todd didn't know who they were but was pretty sure he didn't want an introduction.

With Todd and Noel set for the night, Doc found a suitable site along the Cottle Creek, near the Emerald Pond Camp. Even in the growing gloom, the tent was quickly set up with the insertion of two shock-corded fiberglass poles, providing an adequate two-person tent. He quickly spread his self-inflating air cushion and sleeping bag. Two folding camp chairs completed his furnishings. His housekeeping complete, Doc visited the amphitheater area to buy beer before returning to share good times and newfound friendships with others camping in the area. Life was good for Doc.

Noel and Todd, on the other hand, were in the midst of an intense, if hushed, argument—one that started back in Ohio. After Epstein's death, Todd unhappily found himself reduced to Noel's underling and had decided to pull out of the drug dealing.

"Look, we've made plenty of money. We've gotten everything we wanted. It doesn't make sense to go on. Plus, with Epstein gone, we're having a harder time coming up with the cash for each buy." Todd thought his argument was logical and convincing.

"You fool, we're on the verge of the biggest deal we've ever made and can move up to making five to ten million dollars per deal. That's what we've been aiming at—not the penny-ante crap. Don't think small! And don't think you aren't an essential and culpable component of this venture. This is not the proper juncture to dissolve our partnership. Epstein learned that all too well." Although Noel's voice was low, it was as intense as the hiss of an angered rattlesnake. He regretted mentioning Epstein and hoped Todd had not noticed.

Todd was fully awake and had shrugged off the effects of the alcohol. "What do you mean? What about Epstein?"

"He wanted out of the partnership, and the stress was too much for him. I would most strenuously advise you reconsider. This deal will net us more than we made in the last six months! Do you not see the benefit of continuing? I cannot do this alone," Noel continued.

"What do you mean Epstein wanted out? I know he wanted to talk to you, but I didn't know he wanted out. He was very upset about the cocaine-related death of that youngster in the ER, but— He did go see you! He told you he wanted out and you—it wasn't a heart attack at all, was it? You killed him! You did! I can see it in your eyes!" Todd's voice began to rise.

"Keep your voice down, you fool. Yes. Yes. He insisted on withdrawing from the business. He wouldn't listen to reason, and I couldn't convince him that there were alternatives. He threatened to turn us in, to send you and me to jail. Do you want to go to prison?" Noel saw the hesitancy in Todd's face and knew he had hit home. The fool was so easily manipulated. "He died instantly from an injection. Succinylcholine. Used by the anesthesia department. Painless. Quick."

Todd shuddered. "I'm not stupid. I know what succinylcholine is, and I know it isn't quick or painless. He would have been paralyzed and terrified. You killed him by paralyzing all his muscles, even the ones he needed to breathe. I remember reviewing the ECG you did on him! Was it really his, or did you somehow fake it?"

"Ah, that was indeed the actual cardiac tracing of our poor Jake—after he had stopped breathing for a number of minutes and his heart muscle was dying for lack of oxygen. Unless the coroner looks for a specific poison, they are clueless. Forensic toxicology screens are woefully inadequate and take months for turnaround. We're golden, never fear!"

Todd was shocked, "What do you mean 'we'? I never touched him—that was you! That was you!"

"Ah, but you will never divorce yourself from guilt once drug trafficking is revealed. It would go from a slap on the wrist for the drugs to prison or even the death sentence for what we did to Jake." Noel continued to play Todd, as though he were a small trout on heavy test line, terrified, but unable to pull away.

"Well, I don't want to turn you in or anything," Todd was nervous now, scared for himself, and scared of what Noel could do to him or his career. He decided to use the evidence he had tediously collected over the last ten years. "All I want is to get out. You have to let me, Noel. You don't have any choice."

Noel listened, horrified, as Todd revealed what he had compiled. If true, the documents must be several inches thick. And Todd was just the person to do this to him, the lazy little accountant. He was such a mediocre cardiologist and depended on Noel in a hundred different ways. As fast as the small tongue flicked out by a rattlesnake, Noel changed his approach.

"Alright, Todd. You have me where you want me. You win. Let me complete this last deal, and we will retire. No more deals, no more arguing. The deal will go down here in a few days."

"Here, in South Dakota? Are you crazy? How will you get the dope back home? Oh, man, Noel, this is nuts."

"On the contrary, my friend, it's perfect. Do you want to show me this information, so that I am sure you have me where you want me? I'll look at the papers now, if you wish." Noel was at a loss as to where Todd could be securing the documents. Surely, he didn't have them with him. He had brought only the essentials because his wife was going to join them in a few days. His wife. That's it; she had the incriminating documents. Todd had assured him that his wife didn't know about their illegal business, so she couldn't have made her own copies.

At that moment, Noel decided that he would, after all, have to kill Todd. He had the means of doing him in. It was something so clever that no one else had ever thought of it. In the weeks since Jake had died, some TV forensic science program had used succinylcholine to kill someone. But this new plan was perfect. He had even done an Internet search for any hint of prior use of this means of death, and three search engines, including a forensic medicine search engine and a literature library engine, had come up empty.

Noel's smile should have chilled Todd to the marrow. It was the same look last seen by a small mammal before the motionless snake suddenly leapt into action and sank its fangs into its small, soft body. Todd was a dead man.

9

WHAT HAPPENED TO JAKE

The next morning, Todd left the trailer he shared with Noel and smiled into the South Dakota sun. Although he loved everything that he had accumulated in Ohio—the house, the money, the prestige, and the family—there was something special about Sturgis. He felt like another person, a person he liked better than he did the old Todd Lassiter. The argument with Noel was strong in his memory, but he was glad he'd held his ground. There were other ways to make money, and with his children growing up, he felt worse and worse about the drugs he and Noel had been dealing. It was not as if he actually sold anything in the schoolyard for God's sake, he thought. He was just a middleman, taking his share of the profits. A businessman. Innocent. Blameless. Rationalizing his sins away didn't carry much weight in the bright sunshine. South Dakota made it harder to lie to yourself, he thought. He wondered if Noel felt any of that. After last night, he doubted Noel felt anything at all.

The last of the morning dew was being wiped from the Slammer when Todd heard Noel speak his name from only a few feet behind him. Todd flinched as though he'd been struck and spun around. The two maintained eye contact for fifteen seconds before Noel spoke in his cool, paced voice. "You have made your position very clear. I will make the appropriate adjustments. We'll not need to speak of the matter again."

Relieved, Todd shook his head and waited for Noel to either continue or walk away. The subject was changed as Noel went on. "We will leave for the Spearfish Canyon ride at eleven AM sharp."

With that, Noel walked a few feet to his Big Dog and surveyed the fine coat of dew that had formed when the earth surrendered its heat to the starry sky. As everything cooled, the cold metal condensed the scant South Dakota moisture on its cold surface. Noel flipped open his cell phone and spoke a few sharp words into its trim package. Within five minutes, two bikes pulled up, and several of the men Noel spoke with last night dismounted, took out red garage rags, and began to clean Noel's ride. Noel watched them for a few minutes, and then returned to the air-conditioning of the camper.

Todd just shook his head and walked in the direction of the main stage area, remembering the promise of a free pancake breakfast from the Suns of Light Motorcycle Ministry. He may have been a little drunk last night; he may have been angry last night; he may have even been a little high on being in Sturgis for the first time. But he remembered Doc mentioning a free breakfast. One of his strengths was the ability to recover from nights of drinking with little ill effect. After a few minutes, his nose took over and guided him towards the plain white tents where people milled about, and more importantly, pancakes were being prepared!

In the trailer, Noel was motionless on the camper bed, but his mind moved furiously. Todd had made his position clear, which forced Noel to consolidate his own. He knew he must move quickly, but with surgical precision. His mind went back to the final arrangements he had made with that traitor.

Four years ago, when he had begun doing business with Noel, Epstein never guessed that drugs were involved. He had suspected Noel of shady real estate deals, but never thought his money was bankrolling illegal drugs. Last month, a rash of cocaine overdoses in the ER led Epstein to make a few comments to Todd in the otherwise deserted doctor's lounge at the end of a particularly trying ER shift. Todd's response about 'his business investments at work' had hit Jake like a slap in the face. A quiet, but heated, discussion with Todd gave Epstein all the information he did, or didn't, want. Todd had thought Epstein had been aware of what his 'investment dollars' were purchasing. Todd was floored when he realized Epstein had been ignorant of Noel's business dealings. Both doctors had gone hunting for Noel at once. Todd reached him first, told Noel what had transpired, and underwent one of Noel's verbal lashings. Thus, Noel was prepared when Epstein burst into his luxurious office in the cardiology department later that afternoon.

When Epstein confronted Noel with his suspicions, Noel had laughed in his fat face, and confirmed his fears in the worst possible way. At first, Jake had been like Todd and demanded to be let out of the 'business.' When Noel was unbending, he threatened to go to the police or DEA. Unlike Todd, however, he had no collection of dates, times, or amounts of drugs to use as protection from Noel's wrath. Although he had no hard evidence, the damage to Noel's career and the potential uncovering of the drug dealings were unacceptable risks. It was obvious to Noel that Jake had to be silenced. In the past, Noel had paid others to do such distasteful jobs, but the final meeting with Epstein required such finesse that he only trusted himself to take care of it.

Epstein agreed to come back to Noel's office that night to read a letter that Noel agreed to draft to the State Medical Board, exonerating Epstein of any crime. They would then go to the police. Stupid, trusting Epstein, Noel mused. How could someone smart enough to be a doctor be so very stupid? That evening, Epstein arrived at the silent, deserted cardiology department alone, relieved that no one was there to witness his guilt and shame. He sat in Noel's office and began to sob quietly as Noel went behind him to close the door. Just as he sniffed loudly, he felt a sharp jab in his shoulder and spun around to find Noel standing there with an empty five-cc syringe.

"You bastard, what was that?"

"Just something to relax you. I thought you needed it," replied Noel in his quiet, modulated voice. "Sit down. Sit down."

Epstein couldn't believe Noel would give him something harmful, so he sat back down. He didn't feel any calmer. After a few moments, he tried to speak to Noel, but couldn't. His muscles start to twitch, and he found it hard to breathe. His mind, however, remained alert. His muscled twitched more and more as he became completely paralyzed. Because of the way he was seated, he remained upright in the chair.

Noel came around so Epstein could see him better. "I know you can't move; you will, in a moment, lose the ability to breathe on your own. I once heard your friend Doc mention the use of intramuscular succinylcholine on a violent patient. I must admit it is working nicely. As you recall, succinylcholine prevents the transmission of nerve signals in the peripheral nervous system—a rapid acting paralytic agent. Very rapid, I'm sure you agree. I was afraid you'd thrash about after the injection before the full effects manifested themselves. I needn't have worried. I suspect that by this time you are unable to move or breathe on your own. Shall I use a bag-valve mask to breathe for you for the next five minutes or so until the succinylcholine wears off? No? Very well. It must be horrible to be alert and awake, knowing you're about to die, but unable to move or prevent your fate. I will miss your business company, your money, that is. Are you listening? No? Well, since I'm a cardiologist, let's do a quick ECG. With luck, it will show the massive heart attack you will suffer from lack of oxygen. Should anyone ask, that will be the unfortunate tracing I found after you arrived at my office for the chest pain you'd felt over the past few days. I'll say you came at night to avoid embarrassment if the other staff recognized you. Am I rambling? Let's lay you down and do that ECG. My, aren't we floppy! Let's get you up on the examining table. My dear Epstein, I fear you may be having a fatal heart attack!"

As Noel had predicted, within a few minutes of loss of oxygenation, Epstein's heart tracing showed a large myocardial infarction involving much of the heart muscle. His story convinced everyone that fifty-four year old Jacob Epstein, out of shape, diabetic, with high blood pressure and a family history of heart disease, had indeed died in his examining room. Noel agreed to sign the death certificate, and the coroner released the body for burial. Being a good Jew, Jacob was buried within twenty-four hours, along with any chance of exposing Noel to the authorities. Succinylcholine was rapidly broken down by serum esterases, making it very difficult to detect. Only a suspicious coroner would investigate; finding succinylcholine was rare. Noel's musings ended as Todd returned to the trailer. "It's time to go," he said, full of pancakes and eager to ride.

Yes, Noel thought, time to go. Back in Ohio, Noel had thought of a particularly toxic combination, should he need it for Todd. After last night's argument with Todd, it appeared he would he would need to administer yet another poison.

The two started their motorcycles—Noel's polished to perfection. Todd declined Noel's suggestion of a drink before they left. They rode under the wrought iron gate and left the Buffalo Chip.

Spearfish Canyon

Spearfish Canyon, like many of the gorges and valleys of the Black Hills, was formed between forty and sixty million years ago. Spearfish Creek carved through the softer rocks over millions of years and as the foaming water cut downward, the entire area was lifted from deep in the earth. The result was a deep, narrow canyon. Erosion was complemented by the activity of Ponderosa pine and spruce roots grinding rocks into soil as the trees grew and developed. The cycle of freezing and thawing split rock with the power of a thousand jackhammers.

Both Lakota Sioux and white settlers found the clear waters of the creek perfect for spearing fish and provided a rather mundane name to a beautiful canyon filled with dark green pine and spruce, brilliant yellow aspen, and deep red oak. The canyon opened into Spearfish Valley, where early settlers raised cattle and the hay needed to feed them, as well as potatoes, apples, and sugar beets.

Gold hungry miners first settled the town of Spearfish, eager to wrest gold from ground promised to the Sioux nation by the United States government "for all eternity." So much for government promises and treaties. Doc trusted the current power structure as much as Red Cloud, Sitting Bull, and Crazy Horse trusted the government of the 1870s and 1880s. The town charter was established approximately one month before George Armstrong Custer had his pompous, foolish ass whipped at Little Bighorn.

Compared to its neighbors, Central City, Deadwood, and Lead, Spearfish was practically a nunnery! By 1877, Spearfish was known as a quiet little place to raise kids with real stores and a post office. The whorehouses and bars of local riotous towns fit the miners better than the farmers and ranchers of Spearfish. From 1893 to 1933, a railroad snaked its way though the canyon, first to haul ore for processing, and later to haul the growing numbers of tourists that flocked to the area in the mid to late 1930s after Mount Rushmore was completed.

Three mountain peaks surround Spearfish—Crow Peak, Lookout Mountain, and Spearfish Mountain. Someone felt these massive chunks of rock provided a crown on the head of town, providing the nickname "Queen City" of South Dakota.

Another nice thing about Spearfish Canyon was the wildlife. It was almost like driving through a game preserve—where the animals had no choice but to gather around your vehicle. The canyon offered everything from raccoons and porcupines to mule deer and mountain goats. Overhead, you could pick out ravens, magpies, hawks, and even bald eagles. Fishermen loved the fat cutthroat trout, brilliant rainbows, and brookies that filled the creek.

Todd and Noel had ridden the twenty or so miles from Sturgis along busy I-90. Motorcycles were everywhere and caused them to ride a bit more cautiously and slowly than they would have otherwise. The ride had been uneventful, although Todd was puzzled. Noel had suggested four or five times that they stop for a drink. Todd felt fine after his drinking with Doc and their new friends yesterday, but he didn't really want any alcohol today. He'd had enough, more than enough, yesterday and hoped he hadn't made a fool of himself. He remembered getting in the truck with the two women, Tammy and Erin, but beyond that, he didn't recall much until awakening in the early evening. He vividly remembered the argument with Noel. He was proud of having stood firm and felt better about himself than he had in a long time. Maybe it was being around Doc. Maybe it was Sturgis. Maybe it was standing up to Noel. His wife would be here in a few days. Maybe they'd have sex, something they had not done in six months or more. It was an odd thought, but it felt good to be alive. Maybe he and Doc would go and get a tattoo!

They exited at Exit 14, just east of town. A few miles further on was the exit for Belle Fourche, where Doc was going to meet an old friend. Todd had stopped by Doc's tent that morning. All Doc would say was that he had a very special friend he visited every year. Todd had tried to get Doc to accompany them to Spearfish and had even offered to buy all the liquor Doc could drink. That brought a laugh from Doc and the people who had gathered around his tent. Doc made friends quickly wherever he went. Todd didn't understand. Doc was quiet; he wasn't big or flashy, he just seemed to get along with everybody.

The two bikes went west to US-14A, where they turned south and entered the official Spearfish Canyon Scenic Byway. The deep walls of the canyon were alive with plants and animals. Todd rode carefully, to see what he could, and because he was still a little unsteady on the bike in the tight turns. Sport bikes zoomed past him, and he guessed they were going 100 mph or faster. He was correct. The riders pushed their bikes to the limits, scraping boots and foot pegs as they hugged the asphalt around the turns. As they came out of the turns, they accelerated and sometimes popped wheelies to show their excitement and confidence. The very idea of riding like that scarred the pants off Todd. Noel looked down his nose at them, when he deigned to notice them at all.

Whenever Todd stopped for a rest, or to take some photos, Noel appeared impatient and irritable. Todd ignored him rather than provoke an explosion. He'd seen it before. Noel wanted something, but some obstacle was in the way. He would find a way around it, no doubt. But until he did, he was a pain in ass, and Todd preferred to avoid snarling, sarcastic answers to innocent questions. He packed his old Nikon back into his fanny pack and realized for the first time that Noel had had small, stiff saddlebags installed before they ever left Ohio. That's weird, he thought. Why had he done that? He never packed anything in them and usually relied on a small fanny pack and frequent stops at stores for whatever he needed. The questions faded away as Todd moved again into the beauty of the canyon, only twenty miles long.

At the little town of Cheyenne Crossing, they stopped for lunch. Again, Todd declined alcohol when it was offered. After a quick, but satisfying buffalo burger, they mounted their bikes again and headed up US-85 to the casinos of Deadwood. The scenery was breath taking. Cliffs and gorges provided photo ops for Todd, who frequently pulled over and whipped out his camera. Noel said little and took no pictures.

Deadwood seemed to appear out of nowhere from between the canyon walls. The seat of Lawrence County, it was incorporated in 1876. The town's name arose from the many dead trees found in narrow Deadwood Gulch. Houses, hotels, casinos, and businesses hugged the steep hillsides. More progressive and definitely wilder than Spearfish, Deadwood had the very first telephone exchange in the state in 1878, when transportation was still dependent on the stagecoach. Initially, the city relied on the lumber trade and gold mining. Entertainment revolved around alcohol and gambling. Famous, almost mythical names, such as Wild Bill Hickok and Calamity Jane reflected the wild nature of the town. Today, Deadwood bars and casinos included Aunt Sally's, B.B. Cody's, Bella Union Theater, Best Western, Hickok House, Black Jack, Buffalo Saloon, Bullock Hotel, Carrie Nation Saloon, Casey's, Cousin Jacks, Dakota Territory Saloon, 76 Motel, Deadwood Dick's Saloon, Deadwood Gulch Resort, Deadwood Gulch Saloon, Deadwood Horseshoe, Deadwood Livery, Durty Nellie's, Fairmont Hotel, First Gold Hotel and Gaming, Four Aces, Gold Country Inn, Gold Dust Complex, Goldberg Gaming, Gulches of Fun, Hickok's Saloon, Historic Franklin Casino, Kenny's Restaurant & Gambling, Lady Luck Deadwood, Lucky 8 Casino, Midnight Star, Mineral Palace Hotel & Gaming, Miss Kitty's Casino, Miss PJ's Parlor, Mustang Casino, Old Style Saloon 10, Oyster Bay, Prairie Edge, Saloon 10, Silver Dollar, Silverado Casino, S-Mart Gaming, Tin Lizzie Gambling Hall, Wild Bill Bar and Wild West Winners Casino. Holy shit!

    Todd wanted to try his hand at a little blackjack and pulled into one the convenient casinos. Noel cast a wet blanket over the good time Todd had planned by announcing imperiously that he would wait in the parking lot while Todd wasted his time and money inside. The hell with him, Todd thought. He played blackjack and the slots for over two hours before returning to the hot, dusty parking lot. Noel sat in a shady spot with a dark look on his narrow face. Todd walked briskly to his bike and notified Noel that he was ready to go. Without a word, Noel, too, mounted his bike and brought its huge engine to life. He noted Todd's steady gait and determined correctly that Todd had consumed no alcohol inside. That irritated Noel greatly.

    The pair left Deadwood, turned eastward on 14A, and began the ride back to Sturgis. The scenery along the curving, forested route was beautiful, and Todd enjoyed every moment of the ride; sometimes he leaned into the curves and took them a little more aggressively. He recognized his growing independence from Noel and reveled in it. Noel also sensed the change, but his thoughts were dark and murderous.

    The remainder of the Spearfish trip was uneventful. The pair returned to the Buffalo Chip a study in contrasts. Noel was angry and frustrated, although Todd couldn't tell why. He snapped at Todd at every turn and only brightened when he suggested they go to the amphitheater area, where they could drink some cold beer after their long ride. He glowered and stomped away when Todd declined the offer.

    Todd, on the other hand, was the happiest he had been in months. He had a large buffalo steak dinner with all the trimmings, but avoided alcohol for the evening. He planned on waiting until he got together with Doc; it seemed like a bad idea to get drunk with Noel in such a mood. He even enjoyed listening to the evening band play. He had never heard of them before, but enjoyed the rhythmic rock sound as well as the dancing, swaying young hard bodies. The Miss Buffalo Chip contest held Todd's attention more than he suspected it would. He was sorry to admit he'd had little interest in sex for some time and had spent more time and energy making money, both legally and illegally. On the way back, he visited the burnout pits. That was a new experience, and he watched young men shred their tires in huge clouds of smoke and noise for some time until the smell of burning rubber started to make Todd nauseated. He returned to the empty trailer well after midnight and fell asleep within minutes. His last thought before he drifted off was something he'd heard Doc say the day before—"It's a good day to be alive; it's a good day to die!"

11

Belle Fourche

Doc started his dusty Wide Glide after showering and shaving at the communal facilities near the Chip's main gate. Urinals, sinks, toilets, and shower stalls encircled a cold, concrete floor. Someone had christened them the "Tim McGraw Honorary Shithouses" some time back, and the dubious logo was still painted in bold black lettering on the white outer walls. McGraw, a popular country-rock crossover artist was to have appeared at the Chip, some years past. Rumor had it when he showed up to perform he was so rattled by the thousands of drunken, rowdy bikers that he refused to play, earning the honor of having his name painted on the toilets!

Doc just smiled to himself and pulled his hair into a ponytail. He passed a number of people in line to get their admission wristbands, rode through the wrought iron gate, and exited the Chip. He kept Bear Butte over his right shoulder as he headed west and rode through a sleepy, barely stirring Sturgis. The streets were quiet, as though the small town was girding itself for another day of carousing, vending, and parading thousands of rumbling, ground-pounding motorcycles. He passed through the still town on Lazelle Street and merged onto westbound I-90.

At just a little before seven AM, a final bit of chill air hung on, fighting to the very last to keep a bit of nighttime on the hard, rocky ground. It would surrender as soon as the sun climbed and the warmth intensified. Doc had dressed in layers and enjoyed a bikers' easy ability to meet the day's needs by adding or removing something simple, like a jacket or shirt, rather than needing some bulky, multi-purpose outfit. He had said goodbye to his last pair of underwear sometime in the early 1970s. Boxers? Briefs? What the fuck? However, he often wore long underwear under his jeans, even on hot days. They didn't seem to interfere during the day, as long as he was on the bike and moving. The real killers, however, were those long johns that slipped down your ass when you had to walk any distance. Not only did it look odd whenever you stopped and stuck your hand down your ass to pull the damn things up, it felt weird as they slid down your butt cheeks. Still, that extra layer on the legs helped when you had an unfortunate encounter with asphalt. The give-and-take between the two layers helped keep down road rash more than a single layer of cloth did. A T-shirt, usually sleeveless, was important as a first layer. Most bikers owned a dozen or more black T-shirts for every white, red, or blue one in their closet. Most displayed the Harley-Davidson logo in one form or another. In many cases, the back of the shirt indicated where the shirt had been purchased. No doubt, some sort of anthropological treatise could be written about what these all logos meant and what the wearer intended to state or prove. Often, the wearer had not even been to these places. A popular gift for those back home was a souvenir Harley-Davidson shirt. Wannabes tended to wear shirts listing the exotic resort location where they had spent weeks swimming and lying on the beach. Hell, many real riders who sweat for a living couldn't afford to go to one of the resorts, much less buy the damn souvenir T-shirt! On cold days, Doc usually wore a thick long-sleeve shirt or sweatshirt. The same decorative patterns and rules applied. Many of Doc's shirts had no logo at all or promoted one of the many bars he had visited. Being a generous kind of guy, he once gave a shirt that read, "Get a Fucking Tattoo" to his favorite tattoo artist as a tip. On cool days a neck warmer and good gloves with adequate water protection were essential.

 Leather was not the biker's material of choice without reason. Not only did properly prepared and tailored leather keep out the cold and rain, it also kept in the warmth. Perhaps most importantly, it was the best natural substance to save skin if and when the biker fell. Plenty of people said they had never fallen. Doc said a quick prayer for them because he knew that if you rode long enough you would fall. Leather had saved Doc's ass more than once. Once he was knocked from his bike after riding for hours in a rainstorm. He still attributed his lack of serious injuries (only a broken collarbone and a few broken ribs) to the heavy, shock absorbing abilities of that sodden leather coat! Leather chaps were fantastic for keeping legs warm on cold days that sucked heat from a biker like a greedy ex-wife took money from a softhearted man. Although Doc didn't wear them, he whole-heartedly approved of them on tight-assed young ladies, and he had definitively enjoyed them on No-Panty Day in Hulett, Wyoming!

Doc used I-90 for less than five miles before he got off at Whitewood for State Road 34 and headed northwest through Onge to Belle Fourche. He passed dozens of dry and nearly dry creeks filled with brush and stunted trees. A reddish-brown coyote crept across the two-lane blacktop pavement as it slyly returned from a late night encounter with food, sex, or who knew what. It bore a satisfied look on its face, leading Doc to believe that either the jackrabbit population had been decreased by one or there would be a new litter of coyote pups in about nine weeks. Ahead were the outskirts of Belle Fourche, a small town with very special meaning for him.

It was named after French explorers before the area was acquired in 1803 as part of the Louisiana Purchase. It's amazing what $11,250,000 bought back then—529,911,680 acres! At about three dollars a square mile, the United States added all or parts of Arkansas, Colorado, Iowa, Louisiana, Minnesota, Missouri, Montana, Nebraska, New Mexico, North and South Dakota, and Wyoming. It also acquired over seventy Indian nations that it proceeded to destroy.

The early French fur trappers christened the confluence of what was now known as the Belle Fourche River, Redwater River, and Hay Creek as the "beautiful fork." It was a busy trading area used by Indians and whites alike because of the thousands of beavers (and their beautiful pelts) in the nearby rivers and streams. Beaver fur was extremely popular back east and in Europe for beaver fur hats. Apparently, no self-respecting European nobleman would be seen in public without his favorite beaver fur hat. If not for fashion's fickle turn to silk, North American beavers would have been hunted to extinction by the mid-nineteenth century.

The rough and tough fur traders were replaced by multitudes of farmers, ranchers, and traders as the Black Hills gold rush exploded in 1876. Hey, miners and their beasts of burden had to eat, didn't they? Mr. Seth Bullock arrived to supply these miners on a rather inauspicious day, the day Wild Bill Hickok was killed in a poker game holding what is now known as a Dead Man's Hand—aces and eights. As Seth prospered in his business dealings, he bought land along the Belle Fourche River, which he then sold to the railroad just moving into the area. Being the swell guy he was, he even offered to build the railroad terminal. Of course, this just happened to be near his Belle Fourche Livestock Exchange! He shipped the first livestock back east by railroad in 1890 and within five years, the town had become the nation's largest cattle shipping depot, with up to 2500 train carloads of cattle per month! Even 1895's mysterious fire, which leveled most of the business district, couldn't keep Belle Fourche down; it was largely rebuilt within three months. Some of these newer buildings still stood downtown, over one hundred years later.

Belle Fourche was popular indeed. By 1897, the streets were lined with saloons and whorehouses for thirsty, horny cowboys at the end of hot, dusty cattle drives. The cattle, unfortunately received neither liquor nor a warm companion for the evening. Hardly a fair deal, considering they had just walked hundreds of miles and faced a rather dismal future back east!

In June of 1897, a certain Tom "Peep" O'Day spent the day in one of those Main Street saloons before he led Kid Curry, Flat Nose George, the Sundance Kid, and other members of the Hole-in-the-Wall Gang to the Butte County Bank in downtown Belle Fourche. Unfortunately, the bank window was shattered during the robbery and a large, angry crowd quickly arrived. O'Day was too drunk to remount his horse for the get-away and the total haul was only ninety-seven dollars! Doc liked it when a little of the fierce veneer was removed from those Old West legends, and he got to see them as fallible people, much like himself. He particularly sympathized with poor Peep O'Day who was captured hiding behind the bank outhouse after his horse left him behind.

Over 4500 people now called Belle Fourche home and supported the bentonite mines, as well as the cattle and wool industries. It was still one of the wool capitals of the nation. Bentonite, a form of clay, was formed by volcanic ash settling in shallow water. It had the ability to swell to many times its original volume when wet. This was useful in the drilling industry and had become popular in the last few years as a new age method of purging and cleansing the bowels to remove poisons and other impurities. Doc thought this an expensive alternative to eating extra spicy chicken wings and washing it down with cheap beer—both methods got the same job done using "natural" products and meditation. Actually, when he considered all the time spent in the bathroom reading old issues of Easyriders after such a meal, Doc figured they were pretty much a draw.

Given such a colorful past, there remained a strong thread of hardheaded, practical thinking throughout Belle Fourche's history. Even now, the average resident kept their feet solidly on the earth, their head out of the clouds, and thought in down-to-earth terms that didn't allow for dreamy, art-minded types wearing paisley patterns and sandals. Doc thought country music legend Merle Haggard could have referred to the folks of Belle Fourche in his song "Okie from Muskogee," if only he could have found a way to make it rhyme…

On a still, summer morning, Doc rode his scoot into this dusty collection of cattle, outlaws, and mines to meet with a very special woman named Jeanette.

12

JEANETTE

Doc pulled into the gravel driveway behind the barn-style home and art gallery that sat unobtrusively on the outskirts of Belle Fourche. After he placed the bike on its side stand, he sat very still and very quiet. The hot shovelhead engine began to cool in the morning air. His body remained motionless, but his mind moved rapidly and fluidly. The woman within the house remained motionless, as well. She didn't have to part the curtains to know whose bike had just arrived. It was as if she had somehow felt his approach hours earlier. She knew he would show during the Sturgis Rally, as he usually did, but she never knew the day or time.

Jeanette pulled back her shoulder-length, dark brown, almost black hair as she exhaled. Yes, a bit grayer than last year, and yes, a few more crow's feet, too. She tried hiding neither, they were as much as part of her as her trim, round waist and full breasts, which still seemed to defy gravity's inevitable pull. Her petite, five-four frame maintained the curves with which she was gifted. Now in her mid-fifties, men still looked her up and down whenever she entered a room, and offered to buy drinks on the few occasions she visited a bar. Her dark eyes and olive complexion were due to her Chiricahua Apache blood, somewhere between one-eighth and one-half—the orphanage people had never been sure. Her quiet, knowing, Mona Lisa smile, however, came from deep inside, independent of any specific heritage. Small, well-formed hands showed much use, but her skin remained smooth and soft wherever it was not sun-exposed, such as over the small hummingbird tattoo on her left breast. She moved in the quiet, sure way women have done around campfires for over a million years.

Jeanette grew up near Mescalero, New Mexico. Her first recollections were of cool, silent Sunday mornings just before the call to arise for work, Mass, and more work. Vague, poorly formed memories of a father who visited when she was very, very small and held her high in the air were as ephemeral as the dust devils that danced outside the orphanage on the long summer days that stretched forever into her teens. She had shown artistic talents early in schooling, but the nuns had tried their best to steer her towards more practical training. Their concept of an artistic part-Indian girl always seemed to involve a roadside display selling cheap native artwork of beads, turquoise jewelry, and moccasins. Jeanette, always quiet and subdued, smiled and pursued her changing ideas of what she wanted to express and what media she would choose, while dutifully studying typing and shorthand. The nuns found it distinctly un-ladylike when she banged on scraps of sheet metal and bolted them together in amazingly lifelike caricatures of coyotes, hawks, and even the more recognizable sisters. Her quiet intensity and talent won out over her stenography abilities when she earned a scholarship to attend the Kansas City Art Institute.

Jeanette parted with the nuns, boarded a Greyhound for Kansas City, and changed her life. Part of her focused on pursuing her ceramics and sculpture majors. The rest focused on life in nearby South Moreland, where she met people unlike any she had ever imagined at the orphanage. She met hookers, drunks, and even a few bikers. Still, it was a pretty safe neighborhood. She drove her roommates crazy by leaving doors unlocked and windows wide open. She thrived on the fresh Kansas air, while concentrating indoors on sculpture, welding, and metal preparation. Although her class projects were small and self-contained, she collaborated on a few custom motorcycles her graybeard neighbor put together from used parts and swap meet leftovers. He opened up new vistas of what could be considered art and taught her that the lines of a classic chopper held as much beauty as a Rodin or Michelangelo. Within two years, she had mastered a fifteen-coat paint job with skulls and flames during her nights while studying Modigliani and Rembrandt during the day. Jeanette found tattoo art a valid form of expression relatively unrecognized in this country, but earned a typically close-minded "unscheduled evaluation" with her mentor when she proposed tattooing as a project. She got the same lecture Doc had practically memorized—"You have so much ability. Live up to your potential; don't waste your talent."

Jeanette melded Native American works with Maori facial and body tattoo patterns, TIG welding with turquoise mounting techniques, and contemporary metal finishing with traditional media like bronze, clay, stone, and wood. Some of her professors were offended when she decided to return to Taos to work independently, when she could have joined any of a number of financially successful commercial art groups. Although never rebellious or offensive, she followed her muse to Taos, where she produced art that was critically successful, but commercially dismal.

A few years later, she was preparing to watch the sunset near Mount Wheeler, near Taos. It was an otherwise mundane, but uniquely beautiful afternoon, when she noticed another person sitting in one of her favorite spots. Although not territorial, she was interested in what soul had decided this would be the best spot on this very best day to watch the sunset. She approached, sat quietly within ten feet of him, and said nothing. In silence, the world spun on its axis, giving the impression of the sun moving, and in the process set the sky afire with a thousand colors—black, red, yellow, and blue—all at the same time. As the colors faded, and the first stars began to announce themselves, the man turned and sighed, "I reckon there's nothin' more either of us can add." That was how she met Doc.

They made love that first night. Their lovemaking was tender, gentle, and prolonged. Although her familiarity with men was limited, Jeanette knew she had met someone who genuinely cared that she enjoyed the experience. She had fucked before, but seldom made love, and didn't know it was possible to connect with someone on so many levels. He was there, completely, during the raw grinding, as well as the gentle stroking and cuddling before and after. She'd met few men who thought "afterglow" meant anything other than getting a beer and a sandwich or smoking the furtive cigarette. She had spent more time lying in bed talking with Doc than she had ever spoken to another living person.

Likewise, he truly believed in her art and understood her need to fill the yearning in her heart, rather than her bank account. Doc repeatedly denied any artistic abilities. "That kinda thing skips generations," he'd say, but gave her suggestions or made observations on her art whenever she was stuck or felt she was going in the wrong direction. He never attempted to tell Jeanette how something should be done or where she had erred, instead he made observations about "the color of wet wheat" or a bend "more like a whore's leg than a baby's cheek," things that would drive any normal artist crazy. They stayed together for two years while he worked in the outpatient clinic at the pueblo and local ER. That time seemed golden and endless, and her art had never been so vibrant or fulfilling.

One day, Doc told her he had given his notice at the clinic and was preparing to move on. She didn't ask why, and she didn't cry. She nodded and enjoyed every night they had left, just being close to him in bed after intense lovemaking. Like many others, Jeanette didn't understand Doc, but unlike them, she didn't try to change him. She didn't hate him when he left on his Shovelhead early on a dreary October morning. She'd kept her silent vow not to let him see her cry.

They stayed in touch, and whenever Doc went to Sturgis, he'd come down to Taos for a few days with her. Again, being who she was, and he being who he was, there was no anger or resentment—only acceptance and appreciation of the time and love they could still share. He'd come to her without announcement, and she would somehow know just before he arrived. That small part of each year was when she felt most alive and happy.

The intensity of Jeanette's work increased after Doc moved away and seemed to strike a nerve in the art community. She began to sell expensive pieces and attracted an agent, someone she'd never felt the need for before. He was a friendly, outward kind of guy, and a shrewd wheeler-dealer that made a very large name (and profit) for Jeanette. One day, almost five years to the day that Doc left, her agent, now also her manager, married her and moved her to Chicago, where he arranged for her to have a constant show in her own gallery. None of those who knew Jeanette was prepared for such a move. Marriage and Chicago were the last things they had ever anticipated for her. They congratulated her, smiled, and cried when she walked down the aisle, Doc giving her away. On some level, he understood, but like the morning he left Taos, there were no tears or anger.

For five years, Doc visited Jeanette in Chicago during his trip to or from Sturgis. He saw the changes she was going through and the unhappiness that had wrapped around her like the cold Lake Michigan ice wrapped around the Navy Pier in winter. The lake ice melted each spring, but her sadness did not. He was not surprised when he received the late night phone call indicating she was in trouble and that this was the one and only telephone call allowed by the police.

Not surprisingly, the all-male jury found her guilty of first-degree assault and second-degree attempted murder. The male judge gave her two hundred forty months—twenty years—on each count, to be served concurrently. She would only tell Doc, "All I did was cut his dick off. That seemed so important to him. The affairs. Stealing from the gallery sales. The beatings. It didn't seem wrong, somehow."

For the next seven years, her only visitor was Doc, who came at least once a month, plus visits on her birthday, Christmas, and the anniversary of the amputation. After seven spotless years, she was paroled to Doc, who met her at the prison. He took her to Belle Fourche, where they had stayed on a trip to Sturgis in the late 70s. There, he rented a house and set her up with a small kiln, a forge, and enough metal working equipment to fabricate most things she needed.

Her art did the rest, and now she made a comfortable living selling a wide range of art to an even wider range of clients. Many people came back again and again for her eclectic style. Jeanette had lived on the outskirts of Belle Fourche since, seeing Doc once or twice a year, and enjoying a quiet life. She stopped seeing her parole officer after the prescribed length of time, and she had been accepted by most of her neighbors. She had always dreamed of teaching art, but couldn't get a job at the local school because of her prison record. Although she'd had a few apprentices, she managed on her own with no help from anyone. You could discern a number of influences on her current "style," although she frowned a bit and slowed her breathing to focus inwardly whenever she heard anyone attempt to explain her work. Doc could still see a little Celtic, a little Middle Eastern, and some Native American all blended in a rainbow that made each separate influence brighter. Since her prison time, she had introduced the Earth Mother, sometimes boldly, and sometimes like a mist after a summer rain; you couldn't always see it, but you could never deny its presence. It pleased her to be surrounded by candles, and she had made hundreds, if not thousands, of her own. Almost one-half of her art was now sold over the Internet, something she found a little hard to explain. Jeanette was glad that people liked what they saw on their screens hundreds of miles from the actual piece. But on-line, they could only see it from one angle; they couldn't hold it, smell it, or feel it with their hands. She accepted this remote appreciation and evaluation, but was unable to fully comprehend it.

Jeanette still didn't understand her flight to Illinois and marriage, but no longer needed to. She loved Doc, but would never tell him so and had no other serious relationships. Sometimes, usually on late winter afternoons, when there was no sun to be seen and the sleet came down almost horizontally from the west, she would acknowledge she was growing older alone, but was thankful that she never felt lonely. Alone, but not lonely, was how she phrased it in her head. She was almost monastic or nun-like (shudder) in her celibacy most of the year, and really looked forward to Doc's visits. She knew he saw and slept with other women, and although it didn't anger her, she didn't want to think about it, and the good Lord knew that Doc certainly never mentioned it.

13

Doc

After several minutes, Doc swung his leg off the bike and walked up to the back door. Jeanette was already there to open it, and he walked in. "Hey," he started, as they began a very long embrace.

"Hey, yourself," she replied, but couldn't quite put the same southern twang in it as he had. They both laughed and pulled apart.

"You look awful good, darlin'. I sure have missed you," he told her in simple truth and smiled at her. The smile went straight to her heart and made her own burst forth like sunshine after a long rain. It was a devilish smile that made her feel warm, then hot, between her legs. She knew it had had the same effect on other women, as did his half-closed lids while making love; his wet, probing tongue, his strong, sure hands on her body; or the burning heat of him as he spread her apart and entered deeply. All those things crossed her mind standing in her small, neat kitchen as early Monday morning sunlight began to filter through the curtains.

"Would you like something to eat, Doc?" A pause. "Something from the kitchen, I mean."

They both laughed and stood very close as they stared into each other's eyes. Neither could deny the strong desire between them. As usual, this had to be answered first before they could lie quietly for hours in each other's arms and talk of the year that had passed since last they'd laid together. His smile widened into a grin as he bent and literally swept her off her feet. She laughed and laid her head on his shoulder as he carried her into the bedroom. She lay back as he slowly unbuttoned, untied, unlaced, and slipped off her clothing, covering each newly unveiled inch of skin with a gentle but firm kiss. As he straightened to pull off his own shirt, he felt her eager hands at his belt buckle as she reached into his old, worn jeans. Then he climbed onto the bed and covered her body with his own.

Death in Sturgis

Hours later, as he lay with his head on her belly, she stroked his long hair and listened to him breath quietly as he slept. He, too, showed that another year had passed with just a bit more gray and a few more wrinkles, more pronounced from hours of being in the sun with his true love, his motorcycle.

Doc was banging the door on fifty, if he hadn't gotten there already; she wasn't sure. Jeanette knew as much as anyone else about him, which was really rather little. He was getting just a bit of a spare tire from all the beer and whiskey that had passed his lips over the years. At about six foot, he was fairly well muscled, not "sculpted" the way young men were nowadays from hours in some gym, but from using his body. She could count five of the ten to twelve tattoos he bore. Some Celtic, some Indian, some Harley-Davidson. Some told a story, some did not. The 'No CPR' tattoo over his heart with its red circle and bar with the black CPR letters had scared and amused people in and out of ER's for over fifteen years. Long, naturally curly brown hair shot through with gray was usually tied back in a ponytail. She recalled fondly how his hair hung in hundreds of ringlets after a shower. Gray sideburns to the ear lobes and his graying goatee still showed some red in the proper light. He had full lips and white teeth with a chip or two from old fights. His bright blue eyes could bring a chill to her soul when she saw them harden to a steel-like color before a bar fight, or melt her from within just before he took her face into his hands and kissed her lips so gently that if she closed her eyes, she wasn't even sure his lips were there.

Jeanette knew Doc limped a little, especially in the cold, from old ankle and hip fractures. He walked and rode with his right foot and ankle turned out from an old fracture that was never set. "No money for a doctor back then." His upper body was tanned from working outdoors and riding every chance he got. She loved the freckles across his face, shoulders and back; sometimes they made him look, if only for a moment, like a little boy. She was careful to sit on his right side because he was a little deaf in left ear from playing in rock bands when young and countless loud bikes. She'd never heard of the violent blow he'd received as a child that ruptured his eardrum and caused untold hours of pain, as well as mild deafness. A ragged scar and an old surgical wound wandered across his abdomen, but the exact cause was rather vague. "I'd rather not talk about it," Doc had replied the single time she had asked. Usually, his southern twang came out strongest when he was very angry, very drunk, or very tired.

She listened to him snore softly and reflected on the things she knew about Doc that didn't show on the outside. She knew he'd been born in Tennessee and that his family had been dirt poor, but not "white trash." He'd once told her that he'd learned they were poor when he found his father filling the milk jug back up with water to stretch it out longer. He'd also joked once that he'd learned he was poor when he learned that "miner's strawberries" were just plain white beans. She knew neither parent had graduated from high school and had actually disapproved when he had earned bachelors, masters, and MD degrees with honors. She wasn't sure if he had violated some trust the family held sacred, or if they felt "he was getting uppity" and above his station.

As a child, Doc had a pump in the front yard, a coal-burning, pot-bellied stove in the kitchen, and an outhouse in the backyard. His family lived hand-to-mouth, with little savings. His father loaded trucks while his mother stayed at home and cared for ill relatives. There was a great deal of alcoholism in both parents' families. "The Irish flu," he'd called it. To the best of her knowledge, Doc had two brothers who did manual labor, and both had done short prison terms. Doc had never had a conviction of any type, although he'd had his share of scrapes with the law. Fortunately, he was usually in the right and able to convince the police of his justification, if not his innocence.

Doc's family placed great store on manliness and manual labor but much less on intelligence or independent thought. For reasons of their own, they had never responded to invitations for his graduations or weddings. He saw his family once or twice a year, not because of anger or resentment, but because of a lack of common ground.

As far as she knew, he had few close friends, but many, many acquaintances. Doc began playing with sex, drugs, and alcohol at age twelve with the assistance of an older brother later killed in 'Nam. Doc himself was just one year shy of being old enough to go to 'Nam. He had already signed papers to join the Navy directly from high school, partly, because he thought he'd gotten a girlfriend pregnant. The Navy promised him a college education he didn't think he could afford any other way. Then the war ended, and the girlfriend left for someone else—probably the real father. The Navy didn't look so attractive anymore, and the plan fell completely apart.

Although he had never said much about it, Jeanette could tell that Doc, like so many others in his situation, still felt untried as a man. They had been ready to be tested on Viet Nam's field of battle, but that had been pulled from beneath them. As awkward teenagers, they had yearned to prove their worth, much as a tribal youth kills his first lion. Of course, they had wanted an end to an evil, inhumane war fought for money and profit as much as for honor and glory. But having the anticipated trial snatched from before their eyes had left an ugly, unhealed scar in many men his age that resulted in an emptiness in their souls that culminated in alcoholism, drug addiction, and depression.

She also knew that his nickname had been conferred long before he became a physician. At age fifteen, Doc had a summer job in Kentucky pouring concrete foundations and read paperbacks each day during lunchtime while the other construction workers ate, drank vodka, or tried to out-brag the others about their womanizing abilities. One day, an older black worker announced, "Dat Doc, he always readin' dem books an' dings. He'll go fah, yessuh; he'll go fah!" Although no one perceived him as a bookworm, the nickname stuck through the difficult years of medical school, when he had to work thirty hours a week to support himself.

Jeanette contemplated without jealousy that Doc's greatest love of all was riding. He'd started with Jap bikes and now rode a 1981 Harley-Davidson Shovelhead Wide Glide. Riding was total body stimulation, his arms and legs reaching out to the handlebars and forward controls to embrace whatever life threw his way at seventy-five miles an hour or faster. Riding lasted a whole lot longer than sex or food. The senses were overwhelmed with vibration, smell, taste, vision, sound, and hearing—an ongoing process, rather than a single goal. Doc loved the total immersion in the experience and felt that the best part of a road trip was not reaching the destination, but meeting people along the way. Jeanette knew he used state roads rather than interstates whenever possible. He felt there was more to see this way and more people to meet. They both loved mom and pop places like little motels, restaurants, and gas stations. Doc was riding on the state roads when he stopped to watch the sunset and met Jeanette.

He never felt he was better than anyone he met. In fact, he sometimes felt others were more in tune with the flow of life than he was and almost envied the simplicity of their uncomplicated lives. She had experienced his strongly developed belief in right and wrong, but he was able to see things from multiple points of view. She loved this about him, but Doc said it made him a poor arguer because he could agree with both sides. He felt others were entitled to their beliefs even if he didn't agree with them and never thought he had to change anyone else's mind. "You have the right to your own opinion, no matter how stupid or bigoted it may be!" She'd seen him stand up for the underdog to right an obvious wrong in the medical clinic or ER, as well as in bars. In fact, a good number of his fights and scars were for that very reason. Sometimes he'd help someone he didn't know in a fight or scuffle.

She knew he lived in a small old home in a tiny town surrounded by a National Park between Akron and Cleveland. He somehow survived without what others would consider essentials—a stereo, central air-conditioning, and a dishwasher. Oddly, he didn't even own a car but borrowed one during the colder winter months, usually an old beater. Doc got a perverse pleasure out of parking those dilapidated jalopies in the doctor's parking lot to irritate those with expensive Porsches and BMWs.

Jeanette had seen him function as doctor. He was very forthright, whether the patient wanted it that way or not. He was surprisingly gentle with kids, direct with teens and young adults, and as proper as a southern gentleman with the elderly. He could ask older patients about their sex lives or nuns about dancing on bar counters, and liked to ask broken hip patients if they had been out chasing men/women. He did it with a straight face and in such a way, no one got offended. He was concerned about relieving pain, but also very blunt with drug addicts and drug seekers. Doc acknowledged their pain and drug problem, even if they didn't. In the vernacular, he didn't put up with any shit! She heard he had physically thrown out a patient who threatened one of his ER nurses.

She was proud that he didn't care if a patient had money or not. "I give the same crummy care regardless of race, color, creed, or bank account!" he often joked. She had seen grudging respect from colleagues and administrators when she visited the ER where he worked. She'd been told that other doctors asked, "What would Dr. Lovejoy do in this situation?" Some loved him and some hated him, but his skills and abilities were readily acknowledged. He refused to play political games and this was seen as a hindrance to his career.

One thing she knew for sure about Doc was that he loved beer—ale, stout, cold beer, warm beer, American beer, German beer, dark beer, lite beer—beer beer! Another weakness was Jack Daniels straight, although too much whiskey made him a little nasty and argumentative. From what he had told her, he was deeply into drugs when he was young and would use/abuse whatever drug came within reach. He could see why some addicts would rather be junkies than face their otherwise awful lives. Doc used no drugs at all now, partially because he liked them so much in the past, and partially because he would lose his medical license. He used to smoke cigarettes, but stopped at age twenty. Years later, his mother died of lung cancer because she and every other member of his family smoked like chimneys. He tolerated smoke in bars, but didn't want to kiss a smoker. "Tastes like a damn ashtray."

Really, Jeanette knew very little more about him. He had told her that as a middle child he felt neglected and had never connected with his alcoholic father (now sober) or his depressed mother (now dead). Now he intentionally lived hundreds of miles away from his family. She felt he internalized his anger and rejection as depression. Sadness was much easier to deal with than anger, especially if you were angry with someone you were supposed to love!

She knew he never felt superior to anyone because of being a doctor. In fact, most who knew him used the nickname Doc without knowing that he was, in fact, a doctor. He seldom admitted he was an MD to new acquaintances and would only say he worked in an ER. "It changes how they look at me. I'm not ashamed of being a doctor. I'm just not runnin' up and down the street hollerin' it." At work, he used his first name with co-workers. Other physicians were sometimes appalled when janitors and housekeepers said hello to him using his first name or "Doc." He usually introduced himself to patients as "Dr. Lovejoy—you can call me Doc or Dr. Sean." As far as she knew, he always referred to elderly patients as Mr., Mrs., or Ma'am. He frequently asked elderly men about their war experience and thanked them for what they did in the war, a practice that had been known to bring tears to their eyes, especially Viet Nam vets.

During the time he worked near Taos, Jeanette knew that he hugged patients when he thought they needed it, kissed old ladies on their birthdays, and invited them for motorcycle rides. He'd also been known to smack teens on the side of the head for smoking. He had acknowledged how good a cold beer or a shot would be right at that moment to more than one alcoholic, the difficulty of stopping tobacco, and the challenges of losing weight when the bakeries made such beautiful desserts. Although his demeanor, size, and ponytail may have been intimidating to some, he usually sat down to talk with patients or sat on the floor with kids. The ER had a hard time staying supplied with stickers because Doc gave them out to pediatric patients, siblings, and parents alike because he felt the whole family ached when someone was ill. Jeanette heard that more than one colleague frowned on him as "un-professional in every way," but most patients seem to love him and came back asking for him. Even the hospital staff asked him to take care of them or their families when they were ill. Though he didn't tell her about it, she knew Doc had helped discreetly, lending money, helping a family member, treating an STD quietly, whenever he could. He did it anonymously and sent money to someone who needed it, mailed grocery gift coupons, or paid someone's bills.

Even when he lived with Jeanette, he had almost always worked night shifts. That way there were fewer suits (administrators), sicker patients, more "salt of the earth" patients, no one else to help out (or get in the way). In addition, Doc had readily admitted, "It provided time during the day for 'bikes, beer, and babes.'" He often worked six to eight nights in a row in order to take off a solid week.

Jeanette thought to herself about the simple person whose head was in her lap. He was the most complicated and contradictory person she had ever known. She began to stroke a little further down his body, a little more forcefully. Doc smiled, opened his eyes for a moment, and responded again to her touch.

14

What's a Motorcycle?

Who the fuck was Sylvester Roper? Everybody recognized the names of William Harley and Arthur Davidson. They were featured on millions of T-shirts, jackets, motorcycles accessories, and such around the world. You'd have to live in the jungle and wear a bone through your nose not to have heard of these guys. But Sylvester? Sylvester Roper? What the hell did he do?

Well, in 1869, Mr. Roper, no spring chicken at age forty-six, produced his steam-powered velocipede. Huh? This two-wheeled wonder was exhibited at New England fairs and circuses; it featured a small, vertical, charcoal-fired steam boiler under the seat that drove two small pistons, which in turn drove a crank on the rear wheel via connecting rods. A twist control located on the rigid handlebars controlled the amount of steam delivered to the pistons. Voila, the first motorcycle! Doc smiled. It wasn't recorded if Mr. Roper had any luck with the babes.

People in 1884 England were so afraid of Mr. Edward Butler's steam powered tricycle that they requested legislation to control it! One law reportedly required a man with a red flag to run ahead of the contraption to warn people of its approach (a Victorian version of the biker's claim that loud pipes save lives).

Herr Gottlieb Daimler (as in Daimler-Benz and Daimler-Chrysler) created what may be the first recognizable motorcycle, with two in-line wheels, a wooden frame, iron-banded wagon wheels, a vapor-spray carburetor, and a single cylinder Otto-cycle engine. The frame was commonly referred to as the "Bone Crusher"—the grandfather of the rigid frame. The first model utilized "stabilizing wheels" that made it look much like a child's first bicycle with training wheels.

Back in Pittsburgh, USA, L.S. Clarke's 1897 motorized bicycle had a single cylinder gasoline-powered engine mounted to the frame just ahead of the rear tire and appeared quite modern in old photographs.

No doubt, the good people of Pittsburgh were happy to get rid of the charcoal-burning boiler between their legs.

The predecessor of the Indian Motorcycle Company, the Hendee Manufacturing Company in Massachusetts, produced its first model in 1901, two years ahead of good old William and the Davidson brothers. The Indian V-Twin engine was introduced in 1903. It boasted two and three speed gearboxes. The Hendee Special was produced in 1913 with an electric start. Within just a few years, Indian was producing over 20,000 motorcycles per year, making it the largest motorcycle manufacturer in the world at the time. Indian put out great machines such as the 1919 model 101 Scout, the original 1920 Chief, and the well-received 1935 Sport Scout. Poor management and furious competition with Harley-Davidson during WWII pushed Indian over the edge and into the abyss in 1950. Repeated resurrection attempts have thus far proved futile.

The original ten by fifteen-foot Harley-Davidson shed in Milwaukee is part of Americana. In it was born the first 1903 Harley-Davidson motorcycle with a gas-powered engine boasting a 3⅛-inch stroke and 3½-inch bore. This beauty was intended as a racing machine! It must have been popular; by 1905, the sales bottom line read eleven motorcycles sold. A new twenty-eight by eighty-foot building was in place on Chestnut Street by 1906. The street name was changed to Juneau Avenue and the location expanded. In 1908, Harley-Davison output had increased to 154 motorcycles, built by twenty employees. A 49.5 cubic inch, 45° V-Twin pumped out seven—count them—seven horsepower in 1909. A year later, the famous "Bar and Shield" logo was invented that still graces just about everything Harley-Davidson produces, as well as the torsos of many aficionados.

Confederate General Robert E. Lee once said, "It is well that war is so terrible, else we should grow too fond of it," and this applied to motorcycle sales as well. By the end of WWI, Harley had supplied in excess of 10,000 motorcycles to the US Army. They'd reached the big time. The first American to enter Germany after the signing of the 1918 Armistice was riding a Harley-Davidson, and by the end of the war, Harley-Davidson was the largest motorcycle manufacturer in the world.

In the post-war quiet of 1919, the Sport, a 37-cubic inch, opposed twin cylinder model, rolled off the assembly line to high foreign esteem for performance and quiet operation. There were Harley-Davidson dealerships in sixty-seven countries only a year later, and by 1921, the teardrop gas tank had appeared.

At the end of the roaring twenties (just before the Great Depression began in 1929), Harley-Davidson enthusiasts began giving familiar names to the newest Harley-Davidson engines. A forty-five-cubic inch V-twin engine with flat-vented tops on each cylinder head was unofficially renamed the "Flathead," and was used on Harley-Davidson products until Doc was a high school student in 1972. Valves were located on the side of the cylinder which made the engine less efficient, but much, much easier to service. Power was improved over the F-head, especially at higher RPMs, resulting in slightly less acceleration, but better high-speed performance. By the early 1930s, twin-cam engines and front wheel brakes were available, as was the three-wheel Servi-Car, which would be used by police forces and industry for over forty years.

In 1936, a new era began, with an improved sixty-one-cubic inch overhead cam design, with a recirculating oil system that outperformed the larger flathead. Though fully enclosed, Harley-Davidson engines continued to decorate driveways, living rooms and garages with oil droplets, endearing themselves to bikers (and their old ladies).

Because of the large bolts on the valve covers, the '61 OHV was renamed the "Knucklehead" by enthusiasts because of its resemblance to two large fists with bulky knuckles. The initial E-series had a 6.5:1 compression ratio to produce thirty-seven horsepower, the later ELS-series produced forty horsepower with a higher 7:1 compression ratio. The tear drop tank design added instruments, and a four-speed transmission was introduced.

During World War II, Harley-Davidson suspended production of civilian model motorcycles and focused on supporting the war effort. Over 88,000 military versions of the forty-five cubic inch flathead, the WLA, were produced for service in every theater of the war. Many thousands of the newer Knuckleheads were also produced. More importantly, tens of thousands of young, virile, impressionable men learned to ride and enjoy the freedom of being on a motorcycle.

Harley's new 1948 engine had rounded valve and rocker covers, aluminum heads, hydraulic valve lifters, and oiled the upper assemlbly through rocker arms. The chromed covers looked like upside-down cake pans, hence the name familiar name "Panhead." The next year, modern hydraulic telescopic front forks were added to replace the previous spring-based, leading-link suspension. The new Hydra-Glide cleaned up the front of the bike and almost doubled the travel distance of the front wheel providing a much softer ride over even the roughest roads. Also new in 1952, riders began to enjoy actuating the clutch with their left hand and working the gears with their left foot.

In 1957, Harley-Davidson introduced the Sportster to compete with a flood of European imports from Triumph, BSA, Norton, and others. It was a huge success with a fifty-five-cubic inch engine (the famous 883 cc size) and would terrorize dragstrips until the British bikes were destroyed by a force that almost wiped out Harley-Davidson itself—the Japanese.

In 1966, a new engine was introduced in which the knuckles were smaller, slotted bolts, and the cake pans were replaced by two inverted shovels—the "Shovelhead." Lord, Lord, did Doc love this engine! Deeper breathing cylinder heads and seventy-four inches of displacement (1200 cc) produced sixty-five horsepower!

Due in large part to pressure from Japanese imports, Harley-Davidson merged with manufacturing industry giant AMF in 1969—heck, AMF even made bowling balls! Harley-Davidson increased production to justify received monies from AMF, but all this seemed to do was create horrible quality control problems. In 1971, "Willie G." Davidson, the grandson of one of the founding brothers, produced the FX Super Glide in the styling department. Although not a huge success, it introduced the concept of a "factory custom" motorcycle—a very profitable market segment. The Super Glide featured a stepped seat and a "boat tail" fender. However, to the disgust of many Harley-Davidson riders during these years, their beloved bikes had AMF logos applied alongside the Harley-Davidson name plate! Most buyers removed this badge as soon as possible. By 1981, the company was bought back from AMF, and Harley-Davidson stood on its own once again.

Soon after the employee buyout, the new Evolution engine was introduced. For the first time in years, no cool name arose, although some wanted to call the new engine the "Blockhead." The Evo, as is came to be known, was an aluminum engine with steel cylinder sleeves providing eighty inches of displacement. Harley-Davidson boasted it to be an oil-tight (almost) engine that could run on regular unleaded gasoline, even though it had a higher compression ratio. This was the first computer-aided desgin engine for Harley-Davidson and was cooler and more reliable than previous engines.

Front-end suspension springs returned in 1988 as Harley-Davidson recognized the power of the "retro look." Newer designs were seen as too radical by old-timers, a good-but-bad phenomena Harley-Davidson had to deal with for many years. New riders wanted the newest look, like Japanese crotch rockets, but the mainstream Harley-Davidson rider, older and more conservative, wanted the "old time" look of the V-Twin engine. Supposedly named after the Hiroshima's A-bomb, "Fat Man," and Nagasaki's "Little Boy," Harley-Davidson released their best-seller, Fatboy, in 1990. This was the bike ridden by Arnold Schwarzenegger in the film *The Terminator*.

As a further improvement, the 88-cubic inch twin-cam engine came out in 1999 as a completely redesigned effort, but as with the Evo, no descriptive term evolved. Vibration, long a loved and hated part of any engine, was minimized with internal counter-balancing rods, as well as external rubber engine mountings. Still air-cooled, like all previous engines, the TC-88 kept the cams below the cylinder and the valves over the cylinder, connecting them via push rods, unlike Japanese bikes, where the cams and valve were both over the cylinder. Doc knew this seemed like a trivial difference, but Harley lovers would argue about most everything.

The Revolution engine was introduced in the new 2001 V-Rod with plenty of changes to rile up traditionalists! The newest Harely-Davidson engine was codesigned with Porsche and featured water cooling, four overhead-cams, and a shorter stroke with less displacement, but higher RPM. Plus, the cyclinders were set at 60° to each other rather than the almost religiously maintained 45°.

Doc lay next to Jeanette's small, still body and held her gently. The air from the open window had cooled as the sun began to go down. She was still asleep, a slight smile on her lips. He reflected on the changes in Jeanette, himself, and the Harley engines over the years. What a metaphor for human existence! His favorite, the Shovelhead, was the product of years of change and struggle. Wars and rumors of wars had changed Harley-Davidson, as well as America. Violence and struggle within and without the USA had made the nation, and each individual person, what they were now.

Doc found the wide variety of engines fascinating, whether they were traditional Harley-Davidson products, extensions enabled by technologic advances, or totally new ideas. He didn't revile Japanese bikes, like many others. "Ride what you want; it don't matter to me," he'd muse. He'd cursed a Jap bike only once, when its rider cut him off and clipped his front wheel. The bastard kept going, but Doc stopped quite abruptly when he hit the pavement and ended up with some very uncomfortable rib fractures. Fortunately, and in Doc's mind, most importantly, his bike was okay.

Doc rode a 1981 FXWG Wide Glide, stroked and bored to 80 inches—as they say, there's no replacement for displacement. For the uninitiated, stroking an engine increased the amount of distance the piston moved up and down every time the engine fired. Boring increased the diameter, and thus the area of the cylinder and piston. Both approaches increased the chamber size of the cylinder in which the gasoline/air mixture was burned within the engine. As the mixture burned (smoothly, it was hoped) the expanding pressure pushed the piston down, turned the crankshaft, and delivered power to the transmission and the rear axle. A larger amount of fuel and air (displacement) consumed created more power, thus, the faster your ass went down the highway. Translated to biker-talk—there's no replacement for displacement!

Doc did simple work on his bike—changing the oil and plugs, putting on new pipes and air filters, carburetor jetting, tune-ups and bolt-on add-ons, but he left serious engine work to a trusted wrench, Tony, who he met at a small dealership in Cleveland, Ohio. "Do what you know," was Tony's motto. Doc's scoot had Keith Black pistons, totally rebuilt heads, bored .020 inches over, Crane Hi4 ignition and single fire coil, and an Andrews AB grind cam. It was lowered two inches with solid struts. He put on drag pipes with removable baffles that controlled exhaust volume, and by providing backpressure to the cylinder, exerted maximum power. He understood that the engine must "breathe," that is, get in enough of a fuel/air mix for burning, and have non-restrictive exhaust. The United States Environmental Protection Agency, EPA, wanted everything quiet and pollution-free, and it had decided that motorcycles had to do their part in reducing pollution. Never mind that motorcycles contributed less than 1% of the pollution from motorized vehicles, and never mind that big industry, like those who supported the Republican president so much, created the vast majority of pollution in the country—stock Harley-Davidson motorcycles had to meet the very restrictive EPA noise and pollution limits. Doc could hardly help it if a few changes to his ride violated these rules. Low-resistance pipes helped air move through the engine and just incidentally sounded a million times better than stock pipes. Air entered his scoot through an S&S Super E carburetor. The bike featured Apehanger handlebars, a Fat Bob tank, and a Le Pera basket-weave solo seat with a removable pillion pad. Doc thought the original paint job on his ride sucked, so he had a friend versed in the art of motorcycle painting re-do it. The paint was dark blue with black flames on the tank and fenders.

Although there was a lot more chrome he could put on his bike, Doc believed that understatement was a crucial part of being alive. Doc was in the spotlight early in his various careers, but now preferred to stay out of the spotlight. For a number of reasons, he often promoted others at his own expense and preferred to be one of the shadowy figures that kept things moving smoothly. He almost idolized those discrete workers, dressed in black, silent and out of the spotlight, who labor before, during, and after each scene of the circus, play, or movie to make sure everything happens just right. One of his few pleasant memories of high school was being a stagehand for his senior play. No, there was no desire to be in the spotlight for Doc.

15

Morning Sun

TUESDAY

Doc spent the night with Jeanette and held her closely, but gently. They made love again before dawn. Each time they were together, it was as though it was for the very last time, as well it might be. This made it so sweet and intense that sometimes there was little difference between the laughter and the tears. Before the sun had even risen, she fixed breakfast, wrapped in his shirt, giving him little girl smiles whenever she turned from the stove to see him watching her from the table.

Breakfast gone, they embraced for a long time before he packed and reloaded his small bundle onto the back of the Wide Glide. By 7:30, they had said goodbye, and he pointed his face north, up Highway 85. She pointed her face south, so he wouldn't see the tears in her eyes. Long after the rumble of his pipes faded into the distance, she turned and walked slowly back into her house. He'd see her again during this year's rally, if he could.

Doc pulled into the gas station where Highway 85 intersected with US Highway 212 and waited for the two cardiologists for the ride to the Little Bighorn Battlefield. To the east, US-212 continued through the Cheyenne River Indian Reservation, across South Dakota and Minnesota, to St. Paul. US-85 traveled north through the grasslands of the Dakotas to the Canadian border. Then it continued as Road 35 into the depths of Saskatchewan, where it finally ended at Tobin Lake, as isolated a place as even Doc could wish. Today, their ride would take them west on US-212 as it crossed the Northwest corner of South Dakota, the Northeast corner of Wyoming, and across beautiful, rugged Montana. That beautiful two-lane blacktop would carry them through miles and miles of pine-filled Custer National Forest and the Northern Cheyenne Indian Reservation, until it ended in the Crow Indian Reservation, finally meeting up with I-90 at the town of Crow Agency. A ride to the Custer battlefield could have used only I-90, and this was Noel's suggested route—it was direct, well paved, and had ready access to gas and food. Doc was able to convince him that one could better appreciate the area by getting away from the interstate and enjoying the state roads, seeing the realities of the reservations and, best of all, meet some people along the way. Doc stressed to the pair that the idea was not to get there as fast as possible only to take some pictures or call home and then speed back.

A cell phone could be a slave or a master, Doc thought. Some people carried them and just waited to be summoned by its shrill call. Whether in a bar, a theater, or while driving their cage down the highway, they yielded immediately to its insisting cacophonous chorus. A few others, like Doc, used it to communicate at their desire, not the whim of the phone. He pulled his cheap phone out of a pants pocket and turned it on. It seemed to save the batteries when you only turned it on once or twice a day. Funny, how that worked. After waiting for a signal for a few minutes, he saw that he had two messages—one from Todd and one from Erin, the young girl from the bar.

Todd's message was not surprising; they would be late meeting up with him for the ride to the Little Bighorn. The second message was far more interesting. Erin was hoping he'd be back from today's ride in time to get together for some brews. Her voice lingered just long enough to suggest that after the beers there could be a long, enjoyable evening ahead of them.

What a great life, he thought. Wake up with one woman in the morning and go to sleep that night with another. Doc believed that the male urge to be with as many women as possible was planted deep within the chromosomes. A woman's likelihood of passing on her genes was greatest if she held onto a single partner to help protect, provide for, and raise children. A man, on the other hand, had his greatest chance of passing on his genetic material if he spread his sperm to as many women as possible. Not exactly like spraying it from a fire hose, but he felt that by carefully planting seed in many, many places, the father's genes stood the greatest chance of being carried forward. It was an interesting topic that he had pondered over many a drink with both men and women. Although both sexes seemed to agree on the validity of his argument, only the men ever seemed happy with the idea!

He knew there'd be no cell phone service at Little Bighorn, so he chanced a quick early morning return call to Erin. She obviously had her phone turned on and nearby; she answered on the second ring and seem glad, even excited, to hear from him.

"I met a friend of yours last night," she offered, in a very good mood.

"That could be real, real good, or it could be real, real bad, darlin'. Who was it?"

"Well, we went to eat at Mad Mary's in Black Hawk. What an awesome restaurant! The food was great, and there were about a million bikers there. We had to wait for a table and this really, really big guy almost stepped on me coming out of the bar. He was huge! I mean, my neck almost hurt to look up at him! He must be hairier than any other person I've ever seen in my whole life! Did I say he was huge? He laughed so loud my ears hurt, but he was real friendly. He said his name was—"

"Bear," finished Doc.

"Yeah, that's him! He just about fell over me, and then he apologized like a little kid! I mean, he's so sweet and so, so, so—"

"Huge," Doc was enjoying this conversation.

"Yeah! Anyway, he asked me, Jim, and Tammy if we knew anybody out here, and we said we'd just met you, and you should have seen him laugh! He said you two took turns saving each other's lives at the different motorcycle rallies! I think Jim was a little afraid of him, but Tammy thought he was kinda hot. He's too big and hairy for me, you know. I kinda like my guys—"

"Late forties, ponytail, Wide Glide, big dick—"

"Well, yeah, I mean, I'd like to find out a whole lot more about this guy you're talking about! Anyway, I just wondered when you're getting back tonight. I thought we could get together, just, you know, the two of us. Bear told us a whole lot about you, and I-I just-I just wanted to see you again. I know we only just met, but with Jim and Tammy acting like dogs in heat, I just sorta thought—"

After a brief silence, Doc reassured Erin, "I should be back by 8:30 if everything goes okay, an' these guys don't have any trouble."

"Oh, great. I can't wait!"

"Keep your phone turned on; I'll call you when I get back, and we'll get together. I'll be lookin' forward to it."

"That sounds great, but, why would I turn my phone off? That's weird. You're weird, but I like you anyway, Doc. Call me then, bye!"

Weird, Doc thought. He turned off his cell phone and slipped it deep into a pocket. He smiled into the bright sun that was warming up the August morning around him. He even thought he heard a bird sing, but it might have been some dusty disk brakes on one of the bikes coming and going through the intersection.

By 9:00, Todd and Noel arrived, only an hour behind schedule. "Sorry we're late; we had trouble getting started on time," Todd apologized. He didn't know where Noel had been late last night, but Todd doubted he had been at the concert or the Miss Buffalo Chip contest held at the main stage. Todd enjoyed the show and the young ladies before watching biker after biker perform burnouts at the Buffalo Chip's legendary Burnout Bridge. Finally, the fatigue, the noise, and the smell of burning tires were too much for him. He fell asleep in their rented trailer with a thousand images, smells, and feelings sorting themselves into a lifetime of memories. In his dreams, he and Doc were good friends, roaring down a long straight stretch of road with Noel fussing far behind. He had barely moved when Noel crept in like a dog around three AM.

Noel and Doc merely exchanging long, knowing looks, although Doc felt there was a whole lot about Noel and this Sturgis trip that he didn't know yet. He probably didn't even want to know about it when you got right down to it, but he was beginning to get one of his uneasy hunches that something bad, evil, was going down. At Doc's suggestion, they all refueled and headed on west US-212, away from the life-giving, healthy morning sun.

Just past the Belle Fourche city limits, they passed a huge lot full of old, rusted heavy farm machinery on their right. Doc was always reminded of an elephant's graveyard when he passed the massive junkyard. He imagined that a vicious electrical storm could transform the rusting hulks into stumbling, rambling monsters, lumbering blindly onto the highway. Further on, a huge bentonite mine to the south of the road raised clouds of clinging, pale dust. It had little odor, but cloyed the throat for miles after it had disappeared into the distance.

Soon they came to the Wyoming state line, where they stopped so snapshots could be taken. The cardiologists stood by the large Welcome sign, which was pockmarked by 22-caliber pot shots and the occasional 30-06 hole through the sheet metal. It offered a warm, if unique, welcome to Wyoming. Other bikers and groups were doing the same. Doc suggested they get their pictures taken on the other side of the road showing them entering South Dakota as well.

"Might as well do it now; you may not want to stop on the way back," said Doc.

"Yeah, that's a good idea," said the increasingly enthusiastic Todd. Noel remained silent, as though his thoughts were on the other side of the world, untouched by the magnificent openness of the surrounding country.

The brief trek across the northeast corner of Wyoming took less than a half hour. A few miles further in Alzada, Montana, the trio pulled into the Stoneville Saloon, already doing a brisk business before eleven AM. Doc announced that he wanted a beer already, and that they were welcome to join him. Todd smiled crookedly, and even Noel seemed to take Doc's thirst as a good thing. They entered the saloon, which boasted that it was conveniently located in the middle of nowhere and offered an old west cowboy flavor, complete with sawdust on the floor and hitching posts in front. A long line of iron horses stretched across the front of the building where bikers sat to enjoy a cold beer in the increasingly hot morning. Doc bought beers for the three of them, followed by a round from Todd, and even one from Noel, who said little, but wore his inscrutable smile.

After leaving the Stoneville Saloon, they drove through Hammond and Broadus, through prairie grass and the pines of the Custer National Forest until stopping at Ashland, where the Tongue River crossed the road. Todd and Noel didn't know it but they were following the same path as Custer on that final expedition to his bloody fate along the banks of the Little Bighorn River. Once over the Tongue River, they entered the Northern Cheyenne Reservation, where Doc had attended several of the annual Powwow events held on July 4 in Lame Deer. He always found the history, culture, and power of the nation fascinating, although he felt a lot of guilt over the poverty, depression, and alcoholism. Sometimes the people, the artwork, and the dancing made him a bit lightheaded—even when he was cold sober. He wondered if this was a little of what those proud people felt hundreds of years before the whites appeared and destroyed their lifestyles.

The road passed through even more beautiful country with rugged hillsides and bluffs on either side. They even rode through an area with obvious signs of a recent forest fire. Already, life was taking back the terrain with untold millions of small white flowers atop miniscule green sprigs rooted in thick black ashes. Snakelike trails worn by thousands of small mammal feet crisscrossed the rich earth and coarse gravel, giving it the appearance of woven cloth when seen in the proper light.

The small town of Busby held the dubious honor of being "Custer's Last Camp," where the ill-fated troops spent the night of June 24, 1876, before marching the next day to their deaths and history. Now the town's mini-mart boasted the name proudly in tall white letters on its wooden pole façade, in an effort to bring in a few more tourists and their money. Little else drew attention to the small municipality.

The threesome continued through the Crow reservation, where rolling hills masked the tiny meandering streams that fed scattered trees along their scalloped banks. The road rose up a long final ridge before it opened to the Little Bighorn valley and drifted down to the small town of Crow Agency. Just before reaching the outcropping of buildings, a sign on the left announced their arrival at the Little Bighorn National Battlefield. It had formerly been known as Custer Battlefield, unusual because battlefields were seldom named for one person and certainly not the loser. However, the name Custer had the same negative meaning to Indians as the Confederate flag did to American blacks, and in November 1991, the name was officially changed, although the cemetery retains the Custer name.

Doc, Todd, and Noel pulled into the large parking lot near the cemetery and eased their furiously hot iron steeds alongside each other. The two cardiologists dismounted stiffly after the longest motorcycle ride of their lives. They had finally arrived where George Armstrong Custer made his fame, although it was a fame he did not live to enjoy.

16

At the Little Bighorn

Bullshit! Doc thought calling what happened at the Little Bighorn a "clash of cultures" was putting a favorable spin on what he saw as rampant, no-holds-barred genocide—one group of people trying to wipe another from the face of the earth. Yes, a separate Indian memorial was finally complete. Yes, recognizing individual Lakota Sioux and Cheyenne warriors with markers on the field of battle was a great step forward. Yes, changing the name to the Little Bighorn Battlefield was more appropriate than calling it the Custer Battlefield. Yes, recognizing the validity of eyewitness accounts of survivors (Indian survivors) was an essential part of telling the truth about what really happened that hot June day so long ago. What burned Doc's butt was that this "clash of cultures" continued as a slow, economic stranglehold on the people and culture that Custer and his ilk tried so hard to eliminate over one hundred years ago. Doc knew enough of the past to embarrass him as a US citizen and white person. He had seen plenty of cowboy and Indian movies as a kid, but his eyes weren't opened until he read real history later in his twenties and thirties. More shocking were the chronologies of atrocities committed by the United States government prepared by Ward Churchill, an Etowah Cherokee, who admittedly had an agenda of his own. Fair and equitable America screamed for Churchill to lose his job as a University of Colorado college professor when he dared to suggest that maybe 9/11 was just "chickens coming home to roost" after what America had done to other people and countries over its admittedly brief 200+ year history. Doc strongly believed you needed the past to understand the present and prepare for the future.

The Laramie Treaty was formalized in 1868 after US Army troops invaded traditional Lakota lands in Wyoming by building a line of forts to protect the Bozeman Trail. For two years, the native defenders fought the US Army to a standstill in what was known as "Red Cloud's

War." The government, just three years after Lee's surrender at Appomattox, was exhausted and sued for peace. The treaty guaranteed almost five percent of the continental United States to be the sovereign property of the Indians "for all eternity." Included in that territory was most of what is now western South Dakota (including the Black Hills), and portions of Colorado, Nebraska, North Dakota and Wyoming. The government, in less than ten years, blatantly violated this solemn treaty, sworn to and affirmed by "the people of the United States."

The lands of the Laramie Treaty were as close to paradise as could be envisioned by the native peoples. There were still large herds of roaming buffalo, the winters were mild, and game was plentiful. It was no wonder that Indian warriors would fight and die for their way of life.

Once rumors of the minerals (read gold), resources (gold), and natural treasures (gold) of the Black Hills began to be circulated in the 1870's, the government established a geological team under G.A. Custer to evaluate the area. Custer added fuel to the fire with his inflated reports, and miners poured into the ceded area in unprecedented numbers. The Treaty was thrown out the window, and it became the Army's job to force the Sioux and Cheyenne out of their promised lands and onto bleak reservations.

In 1869, General Phil Sheridan succeeded William Tecumseh Sherman in command of the Missouri Division of the Army. This included the entire plains region, from the Rocky Mountains to the Mississippi River. Sherman was remembered for "making Georgia howl" during the Civil War, the destruction of the beautiful Shenandoah Valley during the Civil War, his ruthless treatment of ex-Confederates after the war, and his sensitive, caring statement that "the only good Indian is a dead Indian." Operating in Texas and Louisiana, he helped topple Maximilian from the Mexican throne and faced charges of 'absolute tyranny.' He was transferred six months later as the perfect person to head the Army and its Indian Wars. Based on his success at destroying his enemies' economic base during the Civil War, Sheridan focused on attacking winter camps and eliminating non-combatants (women, children, the elderly) and the Indian's stock (horses and cattle), as well as adult warriors. In fact, he once remarked, "If a village is attacked and women and children killed, the responsibility is not with the soldiers, but with the people whose crimes necessitated the attack." Doc thought both Sherman and Sheridan were real bastards and would have loved to meet them in a fair fight.

Sheridan used a three-prong attack in 1868 to force Arapaho, Cheyenne, Comanche, and Kiowa tribes onto their reservations in present-day northwestern Oklahoma, a real peach of a place without trees, drinkable water, or any way to feed one's family other than infrequent government handouts. Historians described these "attacks" as massacres on unsuspecting tribes encamped with many non-combatants during winter conditions. One of Sheridan's underlings, a certain George Custer, wiped out Black Kettle's peaceful camp, already located on reservation lands.

Since nothing succeeded like success, Sheridan put forth another three-prong attack in the spring of 1876. General John Gibbon marched east from Fort Ellis near modern Bozeman, Montana. General George Crook moved north into Montana. General Alfred Terry departed from Fort Abraham Lincoln near Bismark, North Dakota, and marched west with Custer in command of his famous Seventh Calvary. Early in June, Crook lost a pitched battle in southern Montana near the Rosebud Creek. A defeated army in the field, he retreated into Wyoming. Lacking the technological advantages of today's armed forces, Terry and Gibbon didn't know this. Although the fancy and useful contraptions of "modern warfare" may have been missing, the courage and fortitude of 1876's soldiers were as admirable as that of today's troops. Nevertheless, one prong of the trap was now missing from Sheridan's plan.

Moving up the Yellowstone River to the Little Bighorn, Custer scouted ahead for Terry. Custer's scouts spotted a large mass of Indians from a viewpoint known as the Crow's Nest on the morning of the twenty-fifth. His scouts told him that their advance had been detected. Although better brains had dissected Custer's reasoning, Doc believed Custer rushed ahead in a foolish attack before the Indians, and his chance at looking good before the American people, could escape.

As the 7th moved into the valley from the east, Custer did what commanders are taught never to do—he divided his forces in the face of a superior enemy. True, Robert E. Lee had done it repeatedly and successfully with his numerically inferior Confederate army during the Civil War, but while Custer may have made a bigger name for himself in the American consciousness than Lee, he was not the superior tactician he thought he was. Custer sent Captain Frederick Benteen with one hundred and twenty men southwest to block escape to the south.

Splitting again, Major Marcus Reno was sent with three companies, one hundred and seventy-five men, to attack the eastern end of the village. Indian accounts described their initial surprise as bullets crashed into the tepees, dropping women and children. The outraged Indian warriors responded with all the anger fathers and brothers could muster and forced Reno's outnumbered soldiers back across the river to the high ground.

Custer took five companies, totaling two hundred and twenty-one troopers and officers, farther west along the ridge and descended at least once to the river. A running battle ensued as Custer realized how big the village was, estimated at anywhere from twenty-five hundred to four thousand warriors, plus their families. He sent bugler John Martin back for help with the much-argued message, "Benteen, Come on. Big village, be quick, bring packs, P.S. Bring pacs (sic)." Lucky John Martin was the last survivor to see Custer alive.

Although the details were sketchy, Custer's men were picked off one by one as they ran for the high ground at what is now known as Custer Hill. The soldiers had woefully meager training with their weapons as Civil War-era cartridges were stingily preserved by Army regulations for killing Indians, not to be wasted for such silly things as practice! In addition, Custer's rifles were much less useful in the close fighting preferred by the Indians, hungry for counting coup, as well as spilling the blood of their enemies. With his men gathered around him, Custer entered eternity along with his brother, a cousin, and over 200 men of the 7th Calvary.

Elated with their success over the "long-knives," Sioux, Cheyenne and Crow warriors turned their attention to Reno's men on the bluff, which had now been joined by Benteen and the pack train, which moved slowly because of all the ammunition they carried. Sharpshooters trapped the soldiers in shallow rifle pits along a bluff above the Little Bighorn River until June 27, when the last of the Indians faded away to the south and west. Terry and Gibbon met and advanced to the deserted village. The pale, skinned buffalo carcasses they noted on the hill were, in fact, Custer's men, stripped, mutilated, and bloated in the stark, revealing sun.

Although the battle was a great victory for the Indians, it was their high water mark. Sheridan flooded the region with thousands of soldiers, and the country's fighting blood was up. It was the beginning of the end for an ancient way of life.

In the twenty-first century, bikers on their iron horses wound their way across the landscape with the never-ending prairie wind in their faces. The military cemetery at Little Bighorn grew rows and rows of identical white gravestones, like watchful ivory teeth. Many were re-interred bodies from other Indian battles from across the western plains. The visitor center did a nice job of presenting a balanced view of a very unbalanced, vicious war. "Clash of cultures, my ass," mused Doc. He guided Noel and Todd up to Custer Hill from the visitor center. Todd took more than a dozen shots of the view from the hill, as well as the haphazardly arranged plain white markers surrounding the single black marker of George A. Custer.

"The markers show where bodies were found, not where they are buried. Most of the enlisted men were buried under the large monument here at the top of the hill, but the officers were returned to their families back east. Custer is buried at West Point, where he graduated last in his class of thirty four."

"Why aren't they lined up? It seems real confused," posed Todd.

"Well, they didn't stand in organized firing lines. It wasn't like Errol Flynn in *They Died with Their Boots On*. These guys were terrified and confused. By this time, Custer's men had realized they were outnumbered and outmaneuvered. They were scared shitless, and they knew they were going to die."

"Knew they were going to die," echoed Todd.

"Plus they knew that their death was not going to be pretty, and that they'd be mutilated after death."

"Mutilated?" queried Todd. Noel merely raised his eyebrows.

"Yeah, they'd be scalped, at least. The women would crush their genitals with rocks, and they'd likely have something, eyelids or fingers, for example, cut off."

"Those bastards," Noel offered for the first time. "Those bloodthirsty savages."

"I guess you mean the Indians," returned Doc. "Actually, both sides mutilated the dead, took scalps, and collected trophies. At the Sand Creek Massacre in Colorado, around 1864, US soldiers scalped most of the dead, gutted living women, tore nursing babies from their mothers' arms and smashed their brains out, paraded amputated women's genitals on sticks, and bragged about making tobacco pouches out of the scrotums of the few warriors that were present. Their commander, Colonel Chivington, justified it all, saying something to the effect that his policy was to 'kill and scalp them all, little and big; that nits make lice.'"

Noel snorted. "That sounds like 1960's revisionism designed to make the white majority feel guilty about how badly the poor Indians were treated by the evil government. Indians merely played the role of the 19th century's welfare niggers. We fed the women and the brats with government rations while the male warriors preyed on innocent white homesteaders. I don't believe your liberal propaganda at all."

"Well, no, that's not the case," Doc replied slowly and evenly. He turned to Noel and moved forward so that they stood less than two feet from each other. "These were eye-witness reports by white interpreters and other soldiers given in testimony to Congress soon after the massacre. The same heartless murdering happened at places like Wounded Knee and My Lai by scared, angry young soldiers. Whether you like it or not, Noel, you can't just deny the past because you're a prejudiced ass who thinks you're better than everyone else, especially if their skin is a different color than yours."

Noel just stared at Doc with a red face and bulging eyes for a full thirty seconds. Doc sniffed before he turned on his heel and headed back down the hill to the Visitor Center. Todd moved indecisively next to the trembling Noel before he was told, "Go on, Todd, and follow your new hero. You nigger lovers can both kiss my white ass!" Noel spit his words out with such venom that Todd was visibly shaken.

"Hey, my ass is white, too," was Todd's only answer before he wandered slowly after Doc and Noel down the hill to the parking lot and their waiting motorcycles. They had been at the battlefield less than two hours, and it was clearly time to head back to Sturgis. Todd was not looking forward to the long ride back. "I've got a bad feeling about all this," he said aloud. There was no one to hear him except the dead.

Screech of Tires

The skies to the southeast threatened rain as Doc filled up on premium gas at the small truck stop in Crow Agency where US-212 and Interstate 90 met. The road back to Sturgis was a long one, no matter which way they went. It was a good eighty miles longer to follow I-90, but as Doc was sure Noel would argue, they could go seventy-five miles an hour or more and it was "easier." The way back down US-212 was straighter, but the small towns and the lower speeds would constrain them with a more tortuous route, speed zones, and stop signs. When Noel merely nodded at Doc's suggestion they use the back roads, Doc was more than a little surprised, and even a little suspicious.

"At least we can stop for a cold beer a lot easier than if we were on the highway," Doc said.

"The more the merrier," Noel responded dryly. Todd and Doc looked at Noel for a quiet moment after the uncharacteristic comment. He seemed to be cooling off very quickly after the argument at the top of Custer Hill, especially for Noel. He was not a man known for a live and let live attitude.

Doc nodded to each and started his Wide Glide. They turned back onto US-212 and began the ride to the southeast. Although they had just come this way, Doc felt the road back always held something new and interesting if you kept your eyes open. He remembered the time he turned around near Hot Springs, South Dakota, for the ride back to Rapid City only to find a buffalo herd walking slowly down the middle of a road he had rumbled through less than one-quarter of an hour earlier. He had come upon them after a sharp turn in the road, and was glad to this day that he took nothing for granted that afternoon.

They passed between showers as they headed back across southeastern Montana. A nice thing about the Big Sky Country, Montana's state nickname, was that you could see a storm from twenty or thirty miles away and by careful throttle management, the storms could often be avoided. Sometimes it only required slowing down three or four miles an hour to let a storm pass before coming to the already drying stretch of highway. If the others noticed the skill it took to stay dry on a long road, they made no comment. Perhaps they thought it was just good luck or the rewards of a good, healthy life and a spotless soul.

As the miles passed beneath him, Doc thought a lot about his two riding companions. He couldn't put his finger on it, but something was going on under the surface. He didn't know if there was a separate agenda for being at Sturgis, but they certainly seemed to have their own individual reasons. He knew Todd's wife was flying in this evening for a few days. They had rented an SUV, and they would fly back at the end of the rally, after they paraded around for a few days on the expensive motorcycles as though they rode them all the time back home. Ah, well, to each his own.

It was close to five o'clock when they pulled into Alzada, where they'd had a few drinks earlier in the day. Again, they topped off their tanks after the one hundred and fifty miles they'd traveled from the Little Bighorn Battlefield. It had been a hot and dusty ride, with the temperature hitting 95 degrees. That dried you out quickly when you're going seventy-five miles an hour without windshields. Doc felt they needed to fill up their own tanks, too. He didn't want to spend too much time doing that, though, because he wanted to get back to the Sturgis area. Erin's voice from this morning was still sweet in his ears. Still, just a few beers would be okay.

"Let's grab a few cold ones, boys," he suggested after the last gas tank had been topped off. He expected some sort of complaint from Noel after their run-in back at the battlefield.

"That sounds absolutely fantastic, Doc," Noel said, almost before Doc could finish his sentence. He had a wide grin on his face that Doc thought looked completely phony, like a fox would smile as it introduced itself to the hen house residents. The argument over whites and Indians seemed a million miles away already. Noel turned to Todd and said, "Wouldn't you like something cold, my friend?"

Todd looked at Noel as though he had two heads. He didn't know exactly what to say, so he stammered a quick "Sure. Sure, Noel. Let's get a drink. After you. After you."

"No, my friends, after you!" Noel said as slickly as a used car salesman offering a complete lemon to unsuspecting customers. He made a sweeping gesture with his arm, indicating that Doc and Todd should precede him into the loud, crowded bar.

Todd stumbled forward, bent slightly at the waist as though he was expecting a knife in his back, or a kick in the pants, and walked onto the low wooden porch. Doc followed warily, stepping around Noel as if he was a poised, venomous viper eyeing him up before the strike. Something's up, he thought. Doc couldn't shake the feeling.

The trio entered the crowded bar and found a table near the back. Loud cowboys and drunken bikers rubbed elbows at the long, bent bar under a number of various wild animal heads. Buffalo, pronghorn, mule deer, and jackelope looked down on them while the scantily clad waitresses hurriedly brought armful after armful of drinks to the bar. A few of the women, no longer spring chickens, probably should have been covered a little bit more, but what the hell.

Noel startled Doc and Todd by ordering shots and beers for them all. Doc felt like he was being set up for something and drank warily. Heavily, but warily. Todd put down a number of shots, to Doc's surprise. He remembered how Todd had gotten plastered the first day in Sturgis and didn't want him getting too drunk to ride. Still, after the tension and hard feelings just below the surface at the Little Bighorn, this was a welcome relief.

Todd ordered some chili-cheese fries to Noel's horror and began wolfing down the heart killers. Doc ordered Rocky Mountain oysters for them all. Noel asked what they were, seeing as how there was damn little water to be seen anywhere in eastern Montana. Without waiting for an explanation, Todd eagerly popped one into his mouth. He chewed, swallowed, and smiled. He swallowed two more before wiping his bushy mustache and calling the waitress over to their table.

"These are great, what the hell did you say they were?"

"Well, honey" she began. "I didn't say, but these here Rocky Mountain oysters are pure 100% Montana bull balls, sliced and deep fried. They'll get yer rooster crowing all night long, if ya know what I mean."

Doc smiled knowingly and pulled another long drink from the frosty mug in front of him. Noel's eyes bulged slightly, but he said nothing. Todd sat very still for a moment with a quizzical look on his face. The waitress and everyone around the table, who had of course been listening in, expected him to vomit or faint. Another fifteen seconds of silence passed before Todd erupted into peals of loud, hilarious

Death in Sturgis

laughter. The whole area joined in with several more rounds of beers and shots. Todd got a number of strong pats on the back for trying the oysters so avidly. It was, Doc thought, rather a good example of biker behavior—rough, but good natured and brotherly.

Another beer later, Doc announced, "Well, fellas, I'd love to stay all night and see those oysters take their aphrodisiac effect, but I've gotta wring out my mop and start heading back into Sturgis. It'll be eight or nine when we get back and there's somebody I want to look up."

Doc walked a little crookedly to the men's room and the others turned their attention away from Todd, Noel, and the empty plate of oysters. Noel quickly pulled his chair close to Todd and spoke in a low voice. "That trash you ate will make you extremely ill, you know. You shouldn't eat food in a hovel like this, much less something as unpalatable as those."

"I don't know, Noel. They were pretty tasty—sort of like Portobello mushrooms, you know. I don't think I'll get sick."

"Well, technically, I am your doctor," Noel added emphatically. "And I'm worried about your heart. You've had a number of palpitations lately, and who knows what is actually in the preparations for this food. For all you know, they even used foxglove!"

"Dig?" Todd asked, a bit slowly and drunkenly. He knew foxglove was the original source of digitoxin, a powerful drug used for irregular heart rhythms. Eating something like that could invoke dangerous, even lethal, arrhythmias and have disastrous results on Todd's weakened heart. It would take a very large dose, but the mere thought of the danger was planted in Todd's slightly drunken mind, and it took instant root.

Noel deftly took a number of large white pills from his pocket and placed them in Todd's hand. He quickly but firmly closed Todd's hand over the pills and hissed, "Take these to protect your heart. Take them now. I'm your doctor!"

Todd stared into Noel's powerful gaze and reached for the pills. He stuffed them into his mouth, spilling a few onto the table. Noel picked them up and pushed them back at Todd with the rest of Todd's beer. Todd gulped them down with a worried look on his face. With a sudden smile, Noel sat back in his chair and exhaled a long, deep breath. He rested that way for only a moment before he laid a fistful of money on the table, helped Todd to his feet, and aimed him at the door.

When Doc returned to the table a few minutes later, he saw that his companions had already left. A single white pill lay on the table amid the plates, glasses and a number of five and ten dollar bills. He picked it up and squinted at it in the dim light shed by the neon lamps and light above the pool table. OP 706 was stamped on it. The identification number meant nothing to Doc.

Before he could do or say anything else, the waitress approached. "Yer all paid up, honey. They've already gone outside," she said. Distracted, Doc looked at her, said good night as he pocketed the pill and followed through the door to the low porch.

Noel and Todd were unlocking the multiple locks on their bikes as Doc approached. He shook his head at their security measures but figured it was reasonable considering their expensive rides. He quickly assessed that Noel was reasonably sober and that Todd, although he'd had more alcohol than was proper for a fine, upstanding cardiologist, could still ride a straight line for a newbie biker as long as the straight line wasn't too crooked. It was beginning to darken, so they quickly fired up their mills and headed southeast on US-212. Noel led the way with Todd in the middle and Doc riding anchor.

After thirty-five minutes of easy riding, Todd began to feel hot and dizzy. He thought fleetingly about the possibility of digitoxin poisoning, but remembered that Noel had given him something to protect him, just in case. What were those pills? Todd didn't recognize them; he had never seen them before. Why had Noel had them in his pocket, ready to administer? Before this line of thinking could be carried to its conclusion, Todd began to feel much, much worse.

Then he began to swerve, just a little, and Doc closed up behind him. Todd felt sweat running down his back, and his legs had become rubbery and numb. A splitting headache throbbed unmercifully and his vision blurred. In his confused state, he didn't realize he should pull over, and like a driver fighting sleep, thought he could just take some deep breaths to feel better. "Maybe it's just the booze," he said to himself. Severe nausea started to creep up on him, but he didn't vomit. His chest began pounding until he thought his insane heart would fling itself from his body, through his shirt and leather vest onto the hot highway passing beneath him. He didn't recognize the moment his heart went from the blistering speed of ventricular tachycardia to ventricular fibrillation's chaos. Had Todd been able to see into his chest, his heart would have looked like a bag of writhing, frantic worms in a red, soggy bag. With no effective blood pumped from his heart, his brain shut down in two to three seconds, and he began to undergo a seizure. His hands were still on the handlebars of the speeding, swerving bike as his body wrenched back in the first gran mal seizure. The motorcycle took an immediate hard turn to the right and careened off the road and into a ravine at nearly seventy miles an hour.

Todd's body and the motorcycle traveled through the air for over sixty feet before hitting the first of several large boulders. The resulting somersault flung the pair high into the air before Doc's unbelieving eyes. Doc began to brake hard, but at the speed he was traveling, it would take over a hundred yards to stop. His eyes were spared the image of Todd's body spinning alongside the huge, still roaring motorcycle before coming to a shuddering, spine-shattering crash against a rock outcropping of ancient granite. Both bike and rider burst apart from the impact, one spewing gasoline and chrome, while the other became a fountain of liquefied brains and pulverized internal organs.

By the time Doc stopped his bike and returned to the site, gasoline from the twisted Slammer chopper had ignited and was beginning to cook Todd's broken body. Doc came as close as possible, but an impact at that speed would have been instantly fatal, even with a helmet. Todd's aorta had surely shorn away from its moorings within his chest, and he would have bled to death in a matter of seconds. The extensive damage to the rest of his body would only have been icing on the forensic cake, so to speak. Doc pulled the barely recognizable body away from the spreading fire, however, if only to keep it more presentable for his wife. Poor bitch!

Doc did the perfunctory assessment of airway (crushed), breathing (none), and circulation (none) with no hope of finding any sign of life. He did a quick sign of the cross and said a silent Hail Mary over the body as Noel pulled up. He did not seem upset or surprised, but sat without moving on his idling motorcycle a blank look on his face. Odd man, very odd, Doc thought. Doc did not know how right he was.

18

Questions

It took the South Dakota Highway Patrol less than a half hour to respond to a barely intelligible cell phone call from a motorist that had come upon the accident site. That woman arrived just in time to see Doc kneeling at Todd's side and Noel still sitting at the roadside as the bike's spilled gasoline slowly burned away. The plant-free, rocky earth supported no spread of the fire although the rocky outcropping was badly scorched. State troopers arrived just minutes before the ambulance team dispatched from Belle Fourche. The paramedics seemed relieved that a real emergency room doctor had pronounced Todd dead at the scene, although they agreed that Doc sure didn't look like any doctor they'd ever seen. Technically, they had to refer back to their hospital doctor because Doc held an out-of-state medical license, but there was no denying that the twisted body before them was as dead as dead could be.

The troopers made their measurements and initially seemed to assess the accident as another out-of-state, inexperienced, half-drunk speeding bike rider that tried to take a corner faster than he could handle. It seemed straight forward enough. After asking Doc a few simple, run-of-the-mill questions, they spoke for some minutes with Noel. Then they began casting odd looks over their shoulders at Doc, and he was taken aside for another round of questions. He had expected questions about their drinking or rate of speed, but instead the troopers started grilling him on his relationship with Todd.

"What were you two arguing about before the accident?" asked a clean-cut young trooper. His close-cropped hair was razor cut around the back of his head where the hat's strap held it motionless. An older trooper stood behind Doc, his gray eyebrows bunched in a permanent scowl. Every time Doc turned around uncomfortably to look at him, he was greeted with a dark frown. Doc didn't know if the older trooper hated longhaired hippy freak, tattooed bikers, or just didn't care for the way Doc smelled.

"I wasn't arguing with him," Doc replied irritably. "I had words this afternoon with Dr. Herrod. Dr. Lassiter and I seemed to get along just fine. Who said we argued?"

"Never mind who said what. Had you two been on bad terms with each other before you came out to the rally?" came the same question, reworded in a poorly disguised attempt to make Doc's headache even worse. It succeeded. Doc felt like his head was going to explode. He had no ibuprofen and figured the cops wouldn't give him any, even if he asked. His rapidly decreasing alcohol level wasn't helping either. At least the troopers hadn't done a Breathalyzer test on him or Noel; he probably would've failed miserably.

The troopers had cut loose the motorists who had come upon the accident. They had talked to Noel for a short time and had obviously responded to his pillar-of-the-community image. Noel's "I'm an important doctor" act had been turned on full force, and they seemed to fall for it. Doc's hair, tattoos, and leathers didn't exactly lend him an aura of respectability. It reminded him of the old Johnny Cash lyric, "It didn't really matter if the truth was there; it was the cut of his clothes and the length of his hair." Noel had left quietly while the troopers had Doc distracted.

Now the older trooper took the younger one's place. "You did work with the deceased, didn't you?" he spat at Doc.

"Yeah."

"And you did have trouble with him in the past, didn't you?"

"Not really, we'd argue about a patient sometimes, but otherwise we got along alright."

"And you did argue earlier today, didn't you?"

"I told you, not with him!" The staccato, repetitious fashion of the questions was getting to Doc, and he realized that getting him angry was probably their intention. He'd spill his guts, the beans, or whatever they wanted him to spill—if they got him angry. He got an idea. "I want a lawyer. I'm tired of answering these idiotic questions. Why do you think we argued, anyway?"

The two troopers exchanged looks and walked to the back of their cruiser for a brief conversation. A few furtive looks were directed his way several times before the two returned to Doc. The younger man asked a final question. "Dr. Lovejoy, at any time did you touch, push, or bump Dr. Lassiter or his motorcycle?"

Doc was shocked. "Hell no! Why do you think that? Who told you that? Did that creep Herrod tell you that? He was over a twenty yards ahead of us and couldn't have seen if I'd hit Todd over the head with a sledgehammer! That stupid bastard and I argued today. I wouldn't put a lot of faith in anything he says; surely you can see that!"

With a final monosyllabic grunt that spoke volumes, the troopers gave Doc his wallet and told him they would be contacting him within the next twenty-four hours. Doc returned to his bike and sat there as that last cruiser pulled away, leaving him in the dark under the Wyoming stars. The meat wagon had taken Todd to a funeral home in Belle Fourche, pending his wife's plan for the body. Jesus! He hoped Noel would tell her, Doc sure as hell didn't want to. He'd had that unpleasant task too many times in the ER; he didn't want to have to tell a colleague's wife the bad news.

By now, it was ten o'clock, and Doc had another hour to go before he'd get to Tilford. He pulled out his cell phone, turned it on, and waited for a signal. He called Erin's number, expecting her to be royally pissed that he hadn't called her yet. It took a good thirty seconds to make the connection and start to ring, but when it did, she answered almost immediately.

"Oh, super! It's you! I thought you weren't going to call."

Doc filled Erin in on the trip, the accident, and his grilling by the police.

"Oh, my God! I'm so glad you're all right! I mean, I'm sorry about your friend and all, but I'm so, so glad you're okay!" She was almost in tears. Doc took the time to reassure her again that he was fine.

"Well, Erin, I still want to see you tonight. It's too late to take in that concert at the Chip tonight, but I could swing by and pick you up. We could get a few beers and something to eat if you're still hungry."

"That would be great. Oh! I almost forgot to tell you! Your friend, Bear, gave me a key to the motel room where he's staying in Black Hawk."

"Oh, he did, did he?" Doc chuckled.

"Well, yeah, it's not like that. He said he'd be gone for two days and that we could stay there if we wanted to. He said you were still a hardhead and stayed at the Buffalo Chip in those cold tents, lying on the ground. Bear said he couldn't do that anymore since that wreck where he said you saved his life. How cool is that? I can't wait to hear more about it. Anyway, here I am with a motel room for the night. Doesn't that sound tempting?"

"It sure as hell does, darlin'. Knowing Bear, though, that room is ass-deep in empty beer cans. But I guess we can make a path through them, don't you?"

"You bet, Doc. At least there's no dirty underwear! He said neither of you guys even own underwear!"

"That was one hell of a conversation you two must have had at Mad Mary's the other night! Did he tell you my eyes are blue?"

"He didn't have to, silly, I noticed that right away. Now how long is it going to take for you to get here?"

It took Doc less than an hour to travel the fifty or so miles to the Tilford Gulch Campground. Not bad time, considering he hit three lights, two stop signs, and had to travel thirty-five miles an hour through Belle Fourche. Where there's a will, there's a way, so they say. He found Erin at the gates to the Tilford Gulch Campground, and they rode down to nearby Black Hawk. There they were lucky enough to find something rare for Sturgis Bike Week—a relatively quiet restaurant where they could eat a late meal and do some drinking while they got better acquainted.

Erin, Doc learned, worked as a dog groomer in a small, north Indiana town. She was the junior employee at Gone to the Dogs, and although she'd only been there a few months, she already felt she could do a better job than the current owner. "I'd have specials and coupons and two-for-one day." When she learned that Doc's dog weighed almost two hundred pounds, she laughed aloud.

"That's an awfully pretty laugh you've got," said Doc.

"Well, thanks," she said. "I haven't laughed that much lately. Since I've been to Sturgis, I've laughed more and smiled more than in the whole last year! That bastard I was seeing took away every happy thought I had until there was nothing left but pissed off and lonely. There were times I couldn't reach him and nights he wouldn't call me back, no matter how many times I called. The bastard's married! You're not married, are you? There's not a Mrs. Doc waiting at home somewhere, is there?"

"Nope. There have been a few wives, but only one at a time, and none now."

"You're sure, aren't you? I'd hit you over the head if I found out you're married now."

"No, I'm not committed to anyone. Or much of anything, for that matter."

After more laughter and drinks, they found their way to the Super 8 Motel in Black Hawk, where they were pleasantly surprised to find that the key really did open a room that was quite clean with no beer cans in sight. Relieved, they quickly found their way to the bed. After some very gentle, exploratory kissing, Doc began to undress Erin slowly. He exclaimed over the freckles across her shoulders and chest. His breath evoked goose bumps up and down her arms whenever he touched her, oh, so gently. After he undid her bra snaps, she removed it and turned to face him, her nipples hard with excitement, and her small, firm breasts heaving with each breath. As Doc stood by the bed, taking off his shirt, Erin leaned forward to undo his belt buckle. She reached inside his jeans, past the thermal long johns, and grabbed his dick firmly.

"Yow!" he said, "those are some cold hands!"

"Well, I'll warm you up pretty quick," she said, breathing heavily through her nostrils. She slipped his hardening cock into her mouth and began to suck on the head. Doc moaned and brought his hands down on the back of her head. She looked up at him through heavily lidded eyes, taking him deeper and deeper into her throat as he got harder and larger.

After a few minutes, Doc lifted her up and took off her pants with one hand while stroking her young breasts with the other. He gently pushed her back onto the bed and began to kiss her breasts and the tender skin, covered with hundreds of tiny brown freckles, between them. As Erin started to move her hips up and down, he began a slow, agonizing trip down her soft front and tongued her belly button. He slipped down her tiny thong, which she finally removed with a kick that sent it across the room. Doc began to swirl his tongue around her swelling clit while running one finger up and down her tender, shaven lips. Erin moaned and tangled her hands into Doc's long hair, pulling his face deeper into her steaming cunt.

Doc brought Erin to climax at least a half dozen times by eating her. He breathed deeply of the hot, fecund pussy as he buried his face in her, licking her juices and sucking noisily on her exquisitely swollen, throbbing clit. Finally, she pulled him up to her, and they exchanged wet kisses with twisting, pushing, hard-probing tongues. He bit her neck gently and sucked her ear lobes while breathing into her ears. Erin came repeatedly as he used his hands and mouth on her. She could feel the tip of his engorged dick just at the opening of her wet pussy.

Doc slowly eased into her, spreading her lips apart as she raised her hips to meet him. He moved slowly, going deeper and deeper with each gentle but forceful thrust. He held his torso up with one arm while he kneaded her breasts with the other hand. Erin writhed under him, uttering little cat-like moans of pleasure as he increased the rate and depth of each thrust. Her pussy wrapped itself around him as though it was a mouth sucking his dick into itself.

Then he rolled Erin over onto her belly, and she raised her butt so he could insert himself in her dripping cunt. He moved faster and faster, holding her hips with his hands to keep her from slipping forward. As she came repeatedly, he put one hand on the back of her head and buried his hand in her short, soft hair, pulling her head back towards him.

After fucking her like this for a good ten minutes, Doc pulled out and lay back as Erin mounted him. She was panting quickly as she guided herself up and down on his thick shaft. Doc spit on his thumb and used it on her clit, rolling it back and forth, as she rode him like a wild animal, uttering louder and louder moans until she came for a full two minutes—shivering and shaking like she had a fever. He massaged her breasts and pulled them close enough that he could lick both nipples at once, making loud sucking noises that drove her crazy with the sound as much as the tactile sensation. She held his head tightly to her chest, as though she wanted to smother him.

Their hips began to roll and thrust in tandem, going faster and faster as Doc forced himself into Erin as she drove her gyrating pelvis down onto him. With a crescendo of movement, sound, and smell, Doc erupted into her spasming pussy as another wild orgasm ripped through her. He let out a low, guttural moan as he pumped into her, each drop of cum sucked into her cunt.

Then she dismounted and sucked the last drops of hot cum from his still pulsing cock. She licked and sucked on his balls and rubbed his dick against her face. He slowed, but still breathed deeply as she alternated kissing the tip of his dick and licking the thick, veined shaft from base to tip and back again. With a final shiver, she crawled up into his arms, which closed warmly around her. They lay tightly in each other's embrace as their breathing slowed, their pounding hearts returned to normal rates, and body sweat dried to a dull sheen.

Ten minutes and Erin looked up at Doc before she giggled impishly. He stretched and gave her a kiss on the forehead. After a moment, with a devilish grin, he asked, "Ready to do it again?"

19

More Questions

She screamed. She cried. She beat her fists against Noel's chest after he told her that her husband was dead. They were sitting in the rented SUV in the parking lot at the Rapid City Regional Airport where Noel had met Tracie an hour after her plane landed.

"If only he'd taken more training classes," muttered Noel.

"He took the one recommended by Dr. Lovejoy; wasn't that enough?" she questioned as though the proper answer would return her husband from the dead. Tracie Lassiter had been against her husband getting that damn motorcycle. The money could have been better spent on buying her a new car. Todd had no business on that thing; she'd told him so over a hundred times. She had been primarily concerned with how the motorcycle, no matter how expensive, would adversely affect his image as a respectable, if uninspired, cardiologist. That would affect his practice, and in turn, their income. She counted on a healthy cash flow to maintain the lovely house and garden she so cherished.

"Well, there are other, more advanced courses that he could have taken but Lovejoy, or Doc, as these biker trash refer to him, never suggested them. He obviously felt that as long as he could pilot his own motorcycle, the hell with everyone else."

"Well, to hell with him, then! You'll see, I'll get the best lawyers around and find a way to make him pay for this. Todd was such a good man. He never hurt anyone. Just last week, he said he never meant to hurt anyone."

Noel held her eyes with his and asked, "What did he mean 'never meant to hurt anyone'? Did he elaborate? Did he, Tracie?"

"Well, no, but he said that things were going to be different in the future, and that he was going to do things differently. And he didn't just mean money."

"I see. Did he elaborate? Did he leave any papers or documents that he said may be important the future? A lock box or safety deposit box, perhaps?"

"No, nothing like that. He never said more than that," she replied, somewhat hesitantly. Noel clearly had something in mind, but she didn't know what.

Tracie shuddered to think of the hold Noel still held over her from their affair of years ago. Back then, Todd had been a workaholic cardiology fellow when she turned to Noel for what she thought was some well-deserved attention and caring. Initially, Noel had been charming and considerate, just long enough for her to fall head over heels for him. Then he showed his true colors, cold and cruel, demanding she perform embarrassing acts that always involved the risk of her being found out by her husband. He debased her, stood her up, and made a mockery of the feelings she had proclaimed for him. Hurt to the core, she had turned back to her husband, who, in typical Todd-fashion, had never even noticed that she had strayed.

Thankfully, Noel had never reinitiated the intimacy of their relationship over the years, but all he had to do was look at her with his cold, fish-like eyes, and she would cringe. That infamous smile of his, which reminded her so much of an evil Mona Lisa, was enough to send chills down her spine. Even the memory of that ruinous affair brought tears to her eyes. When Todd informed her that he and Noel would be partners upon completing their fellowships, she had bitten her lip hard enough to draw blood as she congratulated him. He never saw the look of consternation and fear that crossed her face that day.

Today, however, Noel watched her face closely, but did not press the issue. She felt as though a very good, very subtle, very smart policeman had just interrogated her. She didn't know what Noel was up to, but she had strong suspicions that he and Todd had been involved in something, that if not out-and-out illegal, was very close. Medicare fraud, maybe. Their large home in the very proper neighborhood had been just out of reach of Todd's cardiology income.

Tracie breathed deeply and tried to quiet her mind. What was she to do? Her husband, the main moneymaker, was dead, dead, dead, and Noel had suggested that Lovejoy was somehow to blame. He hadn't quite come out and said it, but he intimated that Lovejoy was involved in something shady that contributed to her poor husband's death. Although she wanted to strike out and call the police, something held her back. It may have been the times she'd met him in the ER when her children were ill. He had treated them very nicely and interacted with the children more directly than he had with her and Todd. When Tracie's mother had her stroke, Doc was present and seemed almost ready to cry himself when he entered the family quiet room to explain how serious her condition was. He'd hugged her, which was a bit startling at the time, but seemed part of the complicated man that included his biker persona.

Noel spoke to her again but she hadn't caught what he'd said as she dredged though her past. "Excuse me?" she stammered. "I'm afraid I didn't hear what you said, Noel."

"I merely suggested that returning to the scene of the accident, even at this time of night, would be beneficial in processing your denial and anger. Those emotions are among the five stages of grieving associated with death and dying—denial, anger, bargaining, depression, and acceptance. I would not have you suffering by yourself. Let us return to the scene of the crime, if you will."

"Yes, yes, Noel. I guess you're right. Shouldn't we be speaking with the police? What are they doing about Lovejoy? Is he in jail?" She still had trouble reconciling the murder of her husband with the gentle, if eccentric, ER doctor. She had heard Todd speak of him before, usually in glowing terms, despite his disapproval of his appearance. Still, there was something else. Something Noel wasn't saying or didn't want to say.

Noel drove the SUV and told Tracie they were taking the most direct route to the accident scene. They drove from the airport westward on US-44 to Rapid City, where Noel turned south on Route 16, Mount Rushmore Road. The SUV moved through the dark night as flashes of heat lightning played in the distance. Tracie stared dry-eyed out the window and at her own reflection when the occasional car passed them. From time to time she sobbed or let out a deep sigh while Noel drove silently south on Route 16, deeper into the night. At no time did Tracie suspect they were actually moving further from the accident scene with each minute. Deer stood transfixed in the headlights as Noel turned south onto US-16A.

After fifty or so curving, treacherous miles through pine-lined roads, they reached the closed, deserted Mount Rushmore National Memorial. Noel pulled into a parking space far into the hushed shadows and turned off the engine. For the first time in over an hour, Tracie turned from her morbid reverie and looked at Noel. Although his face was in shadow, she swore to God that his eyes glowed with a light of their own as they pierced her like scalpels on a cold, unfeeling autopsy room table. For the first time, Tracie felt afraid; but, just like the deer fixed in the headlights, she, too, was unable to pull away, scream, run…

In the early 1920s, South Dakota State Historical Society superintendent, Doane Robinson, visualized a massive monument featuring famous heroes of the old west like Lewis and Clark, Buffalo Bill, George Custer, and even Indians such as Sitting Bull and Crazy Horse. He envisioned something not found anywhere else on the face of the continent that would draw in tourist dollars. Some thought this insane; some thought it a wonderful idea that would truly put South Dakota on the map. Robinson convinced US Senator Peter Norbeck, who wholeheartedly threw his support to the project.

A thousand miles away, famed American sculptor, Gutzon Borglum, son of Danish Mormons, had a falling out with the directors of a project intended to depict a Confederate memorial on Stone Mountain, Georgia. Borglum was excited at the prospect of carving a mountain in the Black Hills and eager to leave the frustrations and infighting in Georgia. From the very start, Borglum decided on enlarging the scope of the work by using national heroes, rather than regional ones. He chose Washington, Jefferson, Lincoln, and Roosevelt, who he felt "have a serenity, a nobility, a power that reflects the gods who inspired them and suggests the gods they have become."

Federal legislation permitting Borglum to sculpt a mountain in Harney National Forest was enacted in 1924, and a similar bill passed in the 1925 South Dakota Legislature. By late summer, Borglum had chosen a mountain sacred to the Sioux—Mount Rushmore—named in 1885 for Charles E. Rushmore, a New York mining lawyer. The mountain was located near Keystone, an isolated mining town. Its southeastern exposure provided direct sunlight most of the day. Relatively solid granite, free from fracture, it was deemed strong enough to support his massive concept.

In 1927, while funds were still being appropriated, President Calvin Coolidge spent his summer vacation in the Black Hills. Coolidge loved mountain life and trout fishing (which was rigged to make him appear a fisherman of epic proportions) so much that his three-week vacation stretched to three months. On August 10 of that year, Coolidge was an instrumental part of the formal dedication of the work at Mount Rushmore, the largest work of art on earth.

Using an ingenious, yet simple, technique of models on the ground and protractors, pivots, and plumb bobs, the heads were roughed out, using carefully controlled blasting. The same measurement system allowed drilling closely placed holes at specified depths, known as honeycombing. A worker then broke away the honeycomb walls manually. Finally, workers called bumpers, using pneumatic drills, smoothed out the rock surface of the sixty-foot tall faces, twenty-foot long noses, and eighteen-foot wide mouths.

The Washington head was formally dedicated in 1930, Jefferson in 1936, Lincoln in 1937, and Roosevelt in 1939. Borglum chose Washington because he represented freedom and a representative form of government, Jefferson because of his vision of a United States that stretched from sea to sea, Lincoln as the Great Emancipator, and Roosevelt due to his vision of America's growing world role.

Doc found Mount Rushmore an insult to Native Americans and had visited it only once. He felt it represented years of broken treaties that had destroyed one Indian nation after another. To Doc, it was American embracement of genocide. Placing the monument in the middle of one of the most sacred Indian places—the Black Hills—was like erecting a monument to Adolph Hitler at the base of the Wailing Wall in Jerusalem. Even the choice of the white male heads was offensive. For example, Teddy Roosevelt is reported to have said "I don't go so far as to think that the only good Indians are dead Indians, but I believe nine out of ten are, and I shouldn't like to inquire too closely into the case of the tenth." Jerk.

Billboards and signs along the approach to Mount Rushmore proclaimed, "See Mount Rushmore! Eighth Wonder of the World!" An Indian interpretation would be closer to "See How a Sacred Indian Mountain Was Named after an Insurance Salesman and Defaced by Vandals." Reagan era politicos were said to have referred to Mount Rushmore as a "Shrine of Democracy." G. W. Bush once held a press conference and arranged the cameras so that his head was in line with the other rock heads in an effort to boost his sagging reputation and his deceit-ridden administration.

Doc thought this was mind-boggling bullshit about an insulting memorial carved from sacred mountains illegally stolen and held by the United States government. Please note that the views expressed by Doc did not represent views held by his duly elected government. It was a damn monument to those who stole, robbed, and murdered a technologically weaker, but spiritually superior, people, a memorial to thousands, if not millions of murders, perpetuated on individuals, as well as groups.

Death in Sturgis

Tracie could barely make out the colossal heads on the mountain through Noel's window. She realized where she was as the starlight lit the monument dimly. She now knew she was nowhere near the accident site, and her blood froze within her veins

"What did Todd tell you about the business?" Noel asked urgently.

"I'm not sure what you mean," Tracie stammered. "Tell me about what?"

Noel spit out, "Don't play stupid with me, you ignorant cow! I know he compiled data that could send me to prison. I know he gave it to you for safekeeping. I know you have it. And I want it, now!"

Noel came across the seat like a striking snake and grabbed Tracie by the shoulders faster than she thought possible. He began to shake her violently, and she cried, "I don't know what you're talking about! Please, Noel, let go!"

"Do you expect me to believe that? Damn you! Damn you both! You can't—you won't—do this to me!"

His hands slipped from her shoulders and wrapped around her thin neck. I could snap this like a twig, he thought. His strong hands, sinews bulging, began to tighten around her soft, fragile neck. In the past, he'd had erections with lifesaving cardiac catheters in his hands, now he began to grow hard as he squeezed and squeezed. His thumbs pressed tightly against her trachea, and he felt the cartilage begin to yield and crack. Her eyes bulged as the blood became trapped in her head and the venous pressure began to build. Small specks of blood were forced through the blood vessels of her conjunctival vessels on the eye surface, forming tiny, but unmistakable, petechiae. He continued to squeeze as he climaxed, and long minutes crawled past.

Slowly, he realized that the woman before him was no longer struggling, no longer breathing. How could she? Her windpipe had been crushed beneath his powerful, muscular hands, just like the twig he had originally envisioned. Her head flopped from side to side because he had also snapped the vertebrae of her neck and the cervical ligaments; bone fragments parted beneath the pressure of his hands.

A small trickle of blood emerged from the corner of Tracie's mouth and ran down her chin. Her eyes glazed over as she focused on eternity. The last thing she had seen was the vaguely illuminated faces high above her on the mountain. The four presidents gazed down on her as impassively as they had ever looked down on a death.

20

Valentine McGillycuddy

Wednesday

Crazy Horse, a son of the Oglala-Brulé Sioux, was without a doubt one of the greatest American warriors of all time. A true hero to all Native American peoples, there was little factual information about him until the last few years of his life. Oral history showed him to be a model of Indian manhood in many ways, but as prone to human weakness as any of us. Books have been written and historians have argued about details of his life that we will never truly know.

He was born around 1842, somewhere on the Great Sioux Reservation, in what is now western South Dakota. How's that for detailed information? His uncle, Spotted Tail, was a leader, and his father, Crazy Horse, was an Ogala medicine man. His childhood name was Curly, and he had killed a buffalo with bow and arrow by the age of twelve. The young man beheld firsthand the wanton destruction incurred on the Sioux by General Harney's punitive expedition. Doc was fascinated by Crazy Horse's visions.

In Crazy Horse's first vision, he saw a horse and rider emerge from a body of water and float in the air. The rider wore a breechcloth with leggings only and in his unbraided hair, he had a single feather. He wore no war paint. Crazy Horse heard a voice speak, "You are to help the people with whatever need they have. You are not to take anything for yourself. If you go to war, bullets and arrows will not harm you, as long as you dress in plain clothes, wear your hair unbraided with only one feather on your head, and carry a small stone behind your ear. Before you mount your horse, throw dust over yourself and your horse." A crowd appeared and grabbed his arms. They tried to hold him back. Crazy Horse rode through them into a thunderstorm full of hail and lightning. When the storm ended, he had hail spots on his body and a zigzag streak of lightning on his cheek. A red tail hawk screamed as it flew overhead, and its scream echoed in the sky. Once again, his people grabbed at Crazy Horse's arms. He pulled away and rode off. His father would interpret the vision to mean that he would never be killed in battle, but would die at the hands of his own people.

Crazy Horse's Great Vision occurred around 1871, after extended fasting and prayer near Bear Butte, northeast of where the Buffalo Chip would lay in the next century. It occurred during a thunderstorm in which hail fell all around him, but never struck him.. His eyes saw things that were far away but saw them as though they were up close to him. There was a huge town of many, many houses filled with white people. They worked constantly, like ants. Coldness radiated from these white people that Crazy Horse could not understand. On the edge of town there were shacks where Indians lived, wore old, castoff, white men's clothes and lay about in the street. The eyes of these poor Indians were sullen and they stank of whiskey. Crazy Horse became very sad because the old spirit had gone from these people. This only happened when one people held down another people. It would be good to die to save his people from this fate. He heard a great voice speak, "This had to be, but it will pass. All the people of Earth must gather like the geese that fly together in the springtime." After this, he saw the peoples' broken hearts and minds. However, the few strong ones who maintained their spirit through the bad times passed this spark to their grandchildren.

The vision changed and Crazy Horse saw many black ribbons moving endlessly across the land. When he looked more closely, he saw that the ribbons were made of rapidly moving bugs of many colors. Within these tiny bugs were people but there were very few horses anywhere. The earth darkened, and the people began screaming. Their pain and grief was obvious to Crazy Horse and he realized their loved ones were being murdered. The people erected more and more buildings and birds flew over them. However, these were not birds but shone with lights. The mountains shook with enormous explosions and fire caused a great pall of smoke. Houses and buildings were destroyed beneath a great cloud of smoke.

The people wore better clothes and lived in better houses after the great wars but the Indians remained separate from most of the whites. A great star with nine points rose in the east and the people's faces disappeared. Some people saw the star's light and reached for it but others did not. In the spirit world, they danced under the sacred tree but the tree was too big for just his people. It was for all men of all colors. They formed a single circle as one people as they danced, different in many ways, but united.

Crazy Horse's great vision sounded to Doc like Crazy Horse saw the future with trains and planes and automobiles. Like a brown skinned Nostradamus, the atomic bomb was forecast in Crazy Horse's dream, and so was worldwide destruction. But he also found hope for the future and a foreshadowing of Martin Luther King's "I have a Dream" speech. Although the destruction of the Indian way depressed him, the promise of peace and brotherhood gave him a good feeling about the possibilities of the future.

Doc had read dozens of books on the Lakota Sioux, Sitting Bull, and Crazy Horse, but he was still a white man inside. To be anything else would not be true to himself. Try as he might, there was still some distance, some gap he had not been able to cross. It was entirely possible that he never would. Maybe it would be a goal he would have to strive for over the rest of his days. He never wanted to be an Indian, but there sure were times he wished he wasn't white!

On many levels, it was easier for him to understand a certain Dr. Valentine McGillycuddy, a little known player in the drama of early South Dakota. Maybe it was because he was a doctor, too, or because Doc had Irish blood. Maybe it was because McGillycuddy strove to understand the Indians and improve their treatment while still being a white man through and through.

Born of Irish parents on Valentine's Day, 1849, McGillycuddy graduated from the Detroit Medical School at the tender age of twenty. By twenty-five, he was already on the faculty of the medical school and had begun a long, close relationship with the whiskey bottle. In spite of this, or perhaps because of it, his medical mentor advised he broaden his horizons a bit and recommended him for a mission to the Great Plains. A year later, he headed for the "Wild West" as a member of the International 49th Parallel Expedition defining the boundary between the United States and Canada. It was on this trip that he first fell in love with the wide-open prairie and met the Sioux Indians that would play such a large role in his life. The expedition completed its work in 1874, and he returned east, smitten with the rugged beauty of the western lands and its native people.

McGillycuddy first came to the Black Hills with the Jenney-Newton expedition in 1875 as the expedition's contract surgeon and mapmaker. Only twenty-six at the time, he accompanied the infamous Calamity Jane and California Joe on the expedition. One year earlier, Custer had surveyed much of the area looking for gold and proclaimed Harney's Peak to be unscalable. Young Doctor McGillycuddy had a tall lodge pole pine felled and trimmed to climb it like a ladder for the final ascent. He became the first white man ever to reach the 7,242-foot summit, the tallest peak between the Rocky Mountains to the west and the Pyrenees far to the east.

During the military campaigns of 1876, McGillycuddy acted as field surgeon for General Crook at Fort Laramie, where he met such western legends as Wild Bill Hickok and Buffalo Bill Cody. Tensions between the white invaders and the Indians increased dramatically, leading to the Battle of the Rosebud, followed closely by the Battle of the Little Bighorn. As Crook pursued Sioux warriors fleeing Custer's defeat, the wary Indians fired the prairie behind them. The soldiers were already on half-rations in order to move more quickly, but were unable to "scrounge" or live off the burnt land. Both horses and men began to starve. Sobbing, the troopers shot and ate their own horses, considered by many to be their best friends, until they crawled into Deadwood, more dead than alive. It was reported that some of the cavalrymen lost their minds in the retreat because of the severe hardship of the march. McGillycuddy accompanied these men and documented it thoroughly. It was infamously referred to as the "horse meat retreat."

McGillycuddy and his wife, Fanny, relocated to Fort Robinson, Nebraska, where he was appointed the post surgeon treating whites and Indians alike. He treated Crazy Horse's wife, Black Shawl, as she lay ill with tuberculosis. The two men, different in so many ways, communicated through an interpreter, and over long, long conversations, Crazy Horse began to trust the white man, reportedly the only white man to ever attain this honor.

As the plains were flooded with US soldiers following Custer's defeat, Crazy Horse was finally convinced to bring in his starving band of renegades. After receiving false promises of safety, a group of reservation Indians and over twenty soldiers came in the night to arrest Crazy Horse. According to McGillycuddy, who was an eyewitness, Crazy Horse burst from the guardhouse, once the true intentions of the soldiers were uncovered, and struggled bravely outside. An Army private plunged a bayonet into him, entering just above the hip. Crazy Horse died that night with McGillycuddy at his side, administering morphine to ease the warrior's pain. The official Army report concluded that the incident was an accident. Crazy Horse obviously fell onto the soldier's drawn bayonet. Following this, the Sioux referred to McGillycuddy as "Tasunka Witko Kola," Crazy Horse's friend.

Soon after, McGillycuddy was appointed to the Indian Agent post at nearby Pine Ridge, at that time the nation's largest reservation. It was not an easy or desirable position. The most influential chief at that time, Red Cloud, felt strongly that the Indian men should not perform demeaning manual labor and were entitled to Washington's promise of food and supplies as part of the terms of the treaty in which the Indians ceded their land to the government. The government felt otherwise and did all it could to encourage the men to farm the dry, dusty ground. McGillycuddy began an Indian police force, started a relatively liberal school for the Indian youth, and insisted that whites and Indians be judged under the same laws. Although strict, and at times patronizing, he truly tried to improve the Indian's life on the reservation. His job as Indian Agent devolved into long, exhausting struggles with "government buncombe and red tape."

When Democratic President Grover Cleveland's cronies replaced the Republican cronies in Washington, McGillycuddy was replaced quickly. It was reported that he was officially and officiously escorted from the reservation with his wife and two pet buffalo. They settled in nearby Rapid City, where McGillycuddy lived as a sort of Renaissance man. He was elected to the state Constitutional Convention in 1890, appointed South Dakota's Surgeon General, served as the Dean of the School of Mines, started the first power company (Dakota Power Company), and was elected mayor of Rapid City. Still, he always labored to improve the relations between whites and the Indians. He was to play a role in trying to keep the peace during the Ghost Dance period and the massacre at Wounded Knee, where he tended to the wounded women and children.

McGillycuddy left Rapid City for California after his beloved Fanny died in 1898. He later remarried, this time to the daughter of a trader he had known at Pine Ridge. In 1918, at age sixty-eight, he aided influenza-stricken patients in Alaska and other western states, often traveling to remote wilderness areas to render aid.

Death finally found McGillycuddy in 1939 San Francisco, and the flag at Pine Ridge was lowered to half-mast. His ashes were returned to the Black Hills and are entombed in a special crypt atop Harney Peak where he stood back in 1875. A small brass plaque reads simply "Valentine T. McGillycuddy – Wasicu Waken 1849 – 1939." Wasicu Waken is translated to mean "Holy White Man" or "Holy Medicine Man"; Wasicu refers to all white men, although it literally means "he who grabs the fat," and Waken means holy or sacred.

By no means perfect, McGillycuddy represented the rare white man who felt the two cultures could and should live in harmony. He realized his own limitations in a corrupt political system where Indian Agents made more money whenever they provided substandard provisions or care to the Indians. The whole system reminded Doc of the modern HMO system—doctors often were paid more for doing less.

In his soul, Doc felt the influence of these diverse western forces, both Indian and non-Indian. The whole concept of ownership of the earth and its treasures seemed foreign to him. He agreed that a person should be judged by what they did and what was in their heart rather than what they drive, their house, or their bank account. He also totally embraced the dream of being completely alive. As Crazy Horse was reported to have shouted when riding into battle, "Hoka hey! It is a good day to fight; it is a good day to die!"

21

Morning Philosophy

Doc woke early, while the sky was still dark. He heard the occasional motorcycles going down I-90 outside the Super 8 Motel. The young girl lay curled beside him, nestled in the curve of his arm. He got up to drain his bladder in the dark bathroom. His aim had always been pretty good, even now that his God-given prostate got a little larger everyday. After what he'd had to drink last night, the last thing he wanted was bright fluorescent light burning his eyes in its evil mission to bring him fully awake.

Returning to bed, he kissed Erin lightly on her freckled shoulder and pulled the covers up over her. She felt the sweet move in her sleep and murmured. He had no idea what she said or who she thought she was mumbling it to, but he smiled in the dark and put his arm protectively over her on the outside of the covers. He fell back to sleep until the sun crawled up the eastern sky and he could hear motorcycles starting up in the parking lot. Erin was sitting cross-legged at the foot of the bed, swinging some trinket around her finger and watching the TV with the volume set very low.

"There was something on the news about your friend. They said he died instantly and that alcohol was a factor. Well, duh! At least he didn't suffer, from what you said." Erin's voice was bright and cheerful despite the sad tidings.

"Yeah, I guess. But there was something strange about that wreck. I don't know—"

"What do you mean, Doc? I thought he just ran off the road."

"Well, yeah, he did. But he kept an awfully straight line for a long while after we left that bar. Miles and miles. Usually when somebody is really shit-faced, they start swerving pretty much right away. He did fine right up until the point where he jerked back and forth a couple of times from one side of the lane to the other, and then just completely lost it. It wasn't as if he passed out or fell asleep, I've seen people wreck when they do that. Todd seemed to get real bad real fast, like he was sick or something—"

Doc felt something tugging at the back of his mind, but he couldn't figure out what it was. He knew that if he left it alone, the thought twisting back and forth in the depths of his consciousness would work its way out on its own until it suddenly stood up to say howdy. If he worried at it like a piece of popcorn stuck between a couple of back molars it would hurt and smart and irritate him, but it would stay stuck as hell. Sometimes he could pry it out, but right here, right now, he was content to let it lay.

"What did they do with his body? Will they do an autopsy?"

"Well, back home, they'd consider him a case for the coroner. The police or paramedics would have taken the body to the county coroner's office, kept it in the cooler overnight, and then examined the body in the morning. They'd do an autopsy and examine the gross organs. Yeah, yeah, I know they're all pretty 'gross.' They'd take microscopic tissue samples and do a tox screen, looking for drugs, alcohol level, and such stuff. Then they decide if the death was natural or unnatural—murder, accident, or suicide—things like that. Maybe the accident was so obvious they won't do any of those things. I know Todd had some kind of heart problem, but it would be hard to tell if he had a heart attack or an irregular heart rhythm of some kind. I don't know any of the details of his heart condition, what medications he took—"

"I never knew anyone who died, although there was someone I wish I'd killed! No, I shouldn't say that. I shouldn't say that at all; it's over, and I'm going to move on. In fact, I liked the way we were moving on just last night!"

Erin began to crawl across the bed to Doc. They heard something fall to the floor, and she stopped. She picked up the small trinket and offered it to Doc.

"Here, I guess this belonged to your friend, it has his name on it. We found in on the seat of the truck after we gave him the ride to the Buffalo Chip when he was so drunk."

"What is it?" He held the small, thin plastic device in his hand and tried to focus on it. The morning lights and the drinks of the night before made it difficult to read beyond the white label stuck to the side with Todd's name written on it in felt tip marker. It was some type of minute electronic device.

"It's a memory stick," she said after a minute. "The kind you store photos on. From a digital camera, you know."

"Oh, yeah, okay. Tell you what, Erin. Put it on the dresser there and then climb back in here with me. There's an old Sturgis tradition that if you make love before you go to sleep, you should do it again once you wake up."

"Is that so? I never heard of that before, but never let it be said that I'd buck a sacred tradition!" she laughed.

"Yeah, well, I did make it up just now!"

She jumped back into the bed and pulled the covers up over their heads.

"Whoa, it's after noon. I mean, I'm having a great time, and I'm glad you like me so much, but aren't you, like, hungry? At least Jim and Tammy stop for air, you know?"

Doc looked up at Erin, mounting him in bed, and smiled his quirky little grin. He brought his hands from her breasts and put them behind his head. "Well, I would kinda like a cold beer. If you like, we could run on up to the Chip for beer and some more entertainment. There's a tattoo artist there I wanted to look up for this year's tattoo. He's pretty good, at least when he's half-drunk. I won't let him touch me if he is sober. It seems to take the artist out of him, and he inks like shit unless he's had a few. I guess it's a good thing he's seldom sober during rally week. I got this one from him a few years ago." He indicated a three-inch tattoo on his left upper chest. A red circle with a diagonal bar across it lined in black; it was the universal symbol for "NO." Inked across it in three-quarter-inch black letters were three letters: "CPR." NO CPR!

She'd wondered about that one. "Does that mean you can't get CPR if your heart stops?"

"No," he replied slowly. "It means I don't *want* CPR if my heart stops. I've seen way too many people that survive to get a pulse and blood pressure back. The vast majority of survivors sort of fall apart and die over the next few days. Their kidneys give out. Their livers give out. Their brains never work again, or they're so gorked that they never wake up and live for years as a vegetable. The brain doesn't do well without oxygen for more than a minute or so. Yeah, kids that drown in cold water sometimes make great recoveries, but adults rarely do. The last thing I would want is to be so brain-fucked that I can't recognize the people I love or think straight, or ride my bike. I wouldn't want to spend my last week or two in some ICU hooked to a dozen tubes and running up huge bills for my relatives. Over the years, I've had time to think this through, and I feel I've made an informed decision. It's the same with my deci-

Death in Sturgis

sion not to wear a helmet when I ride. I'd rather die quickly than live a horrific life, paralyzed. I let others decide what they want, but I don't presume to make their decisions for them. Hoka hey!"

"That's pretty deep thinking. I think I'm too young to want to die, don't you?" Erin furrowed her brow.

"I never said I want to die. I want to live, but I want to live on my terms. The good Lord gave me a brain to decide what I do and don't want for myself. And supposedly, America guarantees me the right to life, liberty and the pursuit of happiness. I really, really want to live. I want to laugh and help other people and love, fuck, and ride down those beautiful two lane blacktops that stretch from one horizon to another. I want to see kids smile when I pull a sticker out of their ear or a hundred-year-old lady giggle when I offer her a ride on my bitch seat. I want to see grandkids some day, and I want to watch the sun set behind a hundred beautiful mountains. I really don't want to die."

"I never thought about it that way, Doc. You're kind of a weird guy, you know, but kind of interesting, too. It's fun talking with you, you don't talk to me like I'm an idiot. Guys try to fuck you in so many ways. Some do it physically. Some do it by making you do whatever they want, by making you wait on them or do things for them, you know, the dishes or their laundry. Some men screw a girl by making her feel stupid or less important than they are. You aren't like that. I think I could like you very, very much, you know? Is that a bad thing?"

"Well, it could be very, very bad, or it could be very, very good. Let's see where it takes us, okay?" Doc planted a gentle kiss on her forehead and looked deeply into her eyes. "Don't forget you're on the rebound from an asshole and are a set up for anyone who's nice to you and shows you some tenderness and care. I know it makes me sound a little cold and analytical, but it's the truth."

"Yeah, I hear you. 'Let's not get in over our heads,' right? 'Last night was good, but—' 'Don't call me, I'll call you.'"

Doc laughed, "I thought I was supposed to say those stupid things. 'Of course I love you, we're in bed, aren't we?' Well, I don't think like that, and I'm glad we're together. I don't know where the fuck Bear is, but let's go. I want you to see the Full Throttle Saloon; you'll love it. Ready?"

"Well, I will be, just as soon as I climb off you and put some clothes on my naked body!"

"Hey, I like that little naked body! Let's go to the Throttle now; hopefully, I'll get to see some more of it later."

22

THE FULL THROTTLE

The Full Throttle Saloon - The World's Largest Biker Bar!. With a claim like that, you just had to try it out. And try it out Doc had, year after year. The best part was that just like your favorite novel or movie, you found something different every year, and you loved it even more. Better than a book or film, new things were added and new friends were made every year. A thousand girls, a thousand thrills, a million ways to spend your time, Hey, Jim?

The Full Throttle Saloon had only been operating out on Route 34 between the town of Sturgis and the Buffalo Chip since the summer of 2000. Like most of the modern Sturgis rally, all bikes and bikers were welcome to join in the party. Chances were you'd see more Hondas, Suzukis, Yamahas, and other metric bikes here than at any other place during the rally. In the past, Doc had started his day at the Full Throttle with their all-you-can-eat breakfast before their eighteen separate bars opened for service. Dozens of vendors offered a wide range of rally souvenirs, as well as merchandise and services such as tattoos, hand-painted elk skins, knives, watches, art work, and leatherwear, guaranteed to make any biker (or their lady) happy. Concerts, contests, and daredevil stunts kept the crowd happy day and night. Tar-gagging burnout pits let anyone who wanted to waste a rear tire do it safely in front of friends, family, and innocent bystanders. The Full Throttle was one of the few bars where you could ride your bike right into the bar. Also offered were dynos to verify your bike's horsepower and torque, a Wall of Death—and who could forget the beautiful ladies who made up the Perfect Angelz?

Like the Buffalo Chip, the Full Throttle offered some fantastic classic rock bands. Past performers included Joan Jett, Nazareth, Molly Hatchet, 38 Special, Georgia Satellites, Pat Travers, Jim Dandy's Black Oak Arkansas, Foghat, and Eddie Money.

One year, Doc met Indian Larry at the Full Throttle's Chop Lot, where custom bike builders displayed their designs and worked on bikes in the midst of the crowds. Born Larry Desmedt, he got his nickname for his early preponderance for using Indian motorcycles. Larry learned much of his trade under Ed "Big Daddy" Roth. In the 1960s Roth turned the hot rod and chopper worlds on their ears with his wild designs, unbelievable customizing, and vitality. The Rat's Hole Chopper group implemented many true-to-form Ed Roth designs, such as Ed's Rat Fink character that Doc loved as a kid. Larry's designs were based on rigid-framed machines using classic Harley-Davidson V-twin engines such as pans, knuckles, and shovelheads ranging from eighty-eight to ninety-six cubic inches. He shied away from the huge, billet aluminum engines boasting up to 145 cubic inches, advanced rear suspension, and computer-aided designs. Many, including Doc, appreciated Larry's bikes for their simple, straightforward designs, and use of 1970-style metal-flake paint. Larry seemed like a good guy, down to earth and as eager to share a frosty beer with Doc, as Doc was to share it. A meeting of like souls, it was not to happen again. Larry died less than a month later doing a bike stunt at the Liquid Steel Classic and Custom Bike Series in Concord, North Carolina. It was, Doc thought, the perfect way for Larry to go—riding. He could only hope for the same some day. Although a major light in the chopper world had been extinguished, Paul Cox and Keino from the Indian Larry Legacy Shop in Brooklyn, New York carried on Larry's old-school approach to choppers.

Other bike designers at the Chop Lot have included Paul Yaffee, Kendal Johnson, Matt Hotch, Hotmatch Custom Cycles, Kim Sutter, K.C. Creations, Aaron Green, Paramount Custom Cycles, Chica Customs, Mondo, and Denver Choppers. It was always a thrill to watch these folks work on bikes, examine their completed machines, and talk to them about their products. Some were obviously business people who wanted to make money off chopper enthusiasm. Others were artists, who frankly didn't give a damn whether you liked their work or not, but felt the need to express themselves. Some artists used oils, some used music, these artists used steel and chrome, and fantastic paints.

Doc and Erin pulled into the Full Throttle parking lot and parked in front because the central area was packed with hundreds of riders and their rides. Loud, pulsating rock tunes poured from within the structure.

They found cold beer within minutes and entered the Chop Lot, where Doc showed Erin the Rat's Hole machines.

"Wow, these certainly are, uh, different, Doc," was all Erin could say at first.

"Yeah, you could say that. They remind me of the stuff that Big Daddy Roth did in the sixties. We all thought his hot rods were cool. I even got the Plastic models at Woolworth's and made them when I was a kid. Hell, you can't even buy the model glue now without parental permission. We got high on the designs, not the fumes, when I was a kid."

"Something tells me you're still a kid inside," she laughed. He was so unpretentious and comfortable with himself, it was just fun to be with him, she thought.

"I guess. Sometimes I act like an adult, usually the second week or so of November, but only if I have to! Here, let's go into—" Doc voice stopped mid-sentence with a sudden expulsion of breath. Erin turned quickly, thinking he was choking or had tripped.

Doc was hovering two feet off the ground with huge, hairy arms wrapped around him from behind. These arms were attached to a giant that fit the size sixteen black engineer's boots anchoring him to the ground. A chain belt held in place with a huge skull belt buckle held up worn jeans. A large belly and even larger chest sprouted hair in such profusion that it took a second look to verify that the creature was, indeed, human. A massive head with a thick black beard and bushy eyebrows above sunglasses was capped with long, tangled black hair and a leather cap.

"Doc, how the hell are ya?" bellowed the giant. "Hey, little girl, I see ya found him. He behavin' hisself?"

"He's great, but I think he's turning a bit purple!" piped Erin, recognizing Doc's friend, Bear.

Bear placed the smaller man down and turned him around. "Wadda ya say?"

"Hey, Bear, fuckin' good to see ya! Where the hell have you been? We appreciate the motel room, but we were starting to worry about you," Doc rejoined.

"Well, if ya'd turn on yer damn cell phone once in a while, ya'd have about a half-dozen messages. I ran down to Bruce's Bar in Severance, Colorado, for a day with some fellas. We missed ya; the balls have never been better! Ya coulda gone with us if you listened to that

Death in Sturgis

damn phone!" Bear's chuckle sounded threatening, even when he was in a good mood as he was now.

"Well, we've been busy. Come on, let's get you a beer," suggested Doc.

"I'm way past beer, son. I'm startin' a second bottle of Jack Daniels up here at the upstairs bar. Come on, you two."

They sat at a small table upstairs with Bear. Hell, any table with Bear at it would appear small. A half-full bottle of Jack Daniels soon disappeared between them, along with some cold beers. "Hey, Doc, I got bad news."

Doc looked up and frowned. "Oh, yeah? What's that?"

"An old friend's gone. Remember Vickie, Vickie Morgan, from Kentucky? She was one hell of a wrench back in the day. Her car was rear-ended on I-65 by a speeding semi driven by some fuck-up and burst into flame. She died instantly, so they say. Happened just a few weeks ago."

"Vickie was a girl I knew from way, way back," Doc sadly explained to Erin. "She was married to one of my best friends. Had a couple of kids with him before they divorced. She worked as a mechanic and did some real fine work. We had a lotta good times together back in the seventies. I remember being out in the woods with her once during a near-tornado of a thunderstorm when we were around twenty years old. She got such a thrill out of the storm and the lightning and the wind. It was almost a religious thing for her."

"Sounds like more of a sexual thing!" suggested Erin with a coy smile.

"Yep, she was my mechanic, an' a good one, too. She did a top end job on my bike once, an' it never rode better. She did first-rate work and stood by it, too. Never charged too much, either," offered Bear with a sniff. "Hell, we'll miss her a lot."

"Here's to Vickie," Doc said solemnly and raised his glass.

The other two joined in and drank a toast to their departed friend. The way the news brought a tear to both Doc and Bear, not exactly what you'd call weak, overly sensitive sissies, made Erin appreciate them even more. They fully appreciated being alive, savoring every minute, she thought. They knew it could just as easily be them toasted tomorrow. All it would take would be a split-second mistake, like Indian Larry, or some asshole crossing left-of-center and plowing into a line of motorcycles, or a speeding trucker running over a stopped car. Life seemed such a fleeting moment, a brief spark in a blazing fire.

The conversation turned to other things, but Erin could tell that the news of his friend's death, so soon after Todd's fatal accident, placed a gloom over him. He may have looked like a hell-raising, hard-drinking, wild man, but he really had a sweet heart. Anyway, she hoped, things would only get better.

After Bear gave Doc some more grief about missing his messages, she suggested Doc listen to Bear's invitations on his cell phone. "You might as well join the 21st century!" she laughed.

"I guess I could, just for a minute or so, before I retreat to ancient history," Doc replied as he lazily fetched his cell phone and turned it on. "Damn, nine messages! You musta been desperate for some company, Bear! Let me listen."

Doc keyed in his security code and played the messages as Bear went on, "Can't all be mine. I only left a couple or three! We just gotta get him up-to-date with technology, Erin, he's sorta old fashioned, ya know."

"Maybe that's one of the things I like about him so much," Erin smiled and nodded. She stopped abruptly when she saw the change on Doc's face. He was staring into space as he hung up the phone. He seemed distracted, almost in shock.

"What's the matter, Doc? What is it?"

They both stared at him.

"The Highway Patrol wants to talk to me again. Soon as possible, if not sooner, the trooper said."

"I thought they already took a statement about Todd. What else do they want?" asked Erin.

"Now they want to question me about killing Todd's wife, too!"

23

Frustrated Noel

"Where in the world could that bumbler have hidden it?" Noel hissed. He had gone through Todd's belongings three times and was no closer to finding what he wanted than when he started. Todd had brought very little with him on the plane; Noel remembered that quite clearly. Todd had even made a comment that all he needed were the clothes on his back and his camera. Damn him! The idiot couldn't even extort Noel properly!

It had taken a bit of finesse, but Noel had been able to go through Todd's pockets after the accident while Lovejoy had been marking the distance of the skid marks back to that miserable Route 212. Although the motorcycle had burned, there had been no documents of any type on Todd's broken body. Slob! His obese body had just lain there without answers. There were no saddlebags on Todd's bike for him to have hidden anything.

Todd had very clearly told him that he had over two hundred documents that revealed everything about their business dealings. Dope deals, he'd called them! Then he'd had the effrontery to be offended at how Noel had dealt with Epstein. Epstein had been another stumbling block to Noel's achieving true financial stability. Well, Noel had managed that predicament, hadn't he? Now he had dealt with Todd, as well. The remaining difficulty was the exact locale of the damnable documents!

That insufferable bitch, Tracie, hadn't been any help either. Todd had told Noel the time of her arrival, and Noel had met her outside the terminal. At such a small airport as Rapid City, there were no transport vans taking customers to their rentals. Tracie walked out the west side of the terminal directly to the small rental lot, where Noel had been waiting for her. He walked up to the SUV and startled her with his sudden appearance.

"I was just trying to call you two; why doesn't Todd answer?" she had asked petulantly. It had been a very long flight, and she was exhausted. Exhausted and angry. She hadn't wanted to come out here in the first place. Nice people didn't live in such boorish places. Why hadn't a limousine met her at the airport like they did back in Cleveland? Now she couldn't reach Todd on his cell phone. Christ, they didn't even have acceptable reception out her! Now Noel was here. He was more than an annoyance; he was a painful memory from her past. She looked back on those naïve days when Todd was just a cardiology fellow. How could she have been such an idiot? Now, whenever he looked at her, she felt dirty. Where the hell was Todd?

"Scoot over," he demanded in his low, nasty voice. She slid over the low console into the passenger seat as he opened the driver's door and climbed in. He turned to her said flatly "Todd is dead. He died a few hours ago. You should know that it's Lovejoy's fault."

After fifteen minutes of disbelief, tears, and shouting, he started the SUV and drove off. He'd driven randomly, he thought, with no definitive plan. No, that wasn't true; he took her to Mount Rushmore because he felt that somehow the stolid presidents represented there would support him, back him up, and help him do what had to be done. He was running a business, after all, and this bitch and her dead husband were trying to ruin him, weren't they?

No matter how he had coerced her, pleaded with her, or threatened her, she had refused to tell him where the documents were. Noel thought he had been reasonable with her and had offered her every opportunity to provide him with the documents. Had she done that, she would have left a happy, healthy person. It was that simple. He had only done what had to be done, and when she wouldn't cooperate, he had taken the next logical step. If she didn't have the information, then she certainly couldn't pass it on to anyone.

But what if Todd had passed it off to someone? Who else could have it? What if Lovejoy was in on it somehow? Noel was glad he had suggested to the Highway Patrol that Lovejoy was involved in the accident! Even if he didn't have the information, he deserved to suffer—that embarrassment to the medical field! When Noel called the police, he told them how very worried he was about Todd's poor widow, and had hinted that there was bad blood between the Lassiters and Lovejoy. Nothing definite, of course, but enough to cast suspicion on him. After Tracie's body had been found, the police had contacted him. He had left the body just off federal land so the FBI wasn't involved. Damn. That would have been perfect! The feds would be pitiless with a reprobate like Lovejoy. Just a few more feet, and the body would have brought all kinds of additional grief down on his damnable, longhaired head!

After cleaning himself up, Noel had searched Tracie's body and her luggage. He found nothing and angrily threw her cold body and belongings to the ground. He started to spit on her, but stopped when he realized that DNA evidence could be obtained easily from such a specimen. Instead, he cursed her soul, climbed back into the rental SUV and drove back to Rapid City as a brief rainstorm washed over her cold body. He parked the SUV back in the same spot, feeling rather smug about how smoothly he had spirited her away and killed her. The police were as stupid here as they were back home, he chuckled. It was a cold sound, like a noise from an open grave. Noel wiped his fingerprints off the steering wheel and exited the SUV. He quickly and quietly crossed the parking lot back to his bike and rode all the way back to the Buffalo Chip. That was late last night and earlier this morning.

Noel had spent the daylight hours taking it easy and talking to the police when they called him on his ever-ready cell phone. In those conversations, he had placed careful bits of suspicion about Lovejoy; nothing blatant, just enough to make the police follow him like hounds after a hare. Then he ate a disgustingly fatty steak dinner. He didn't care that it was lean buffalo meat; it was revolting. And of course, there was no way to raise himself above the chattel around him. He'd stayed at the Chip all day long, forcing himself to stay near the smelly, animal-like bikers. He had searched Todd's few belongings in the trailer one last time, staying up far beyond his usual hours.

At least he had some quiet inside the trailer, even if the noise continued outside. It was three AM, and most of the dirty, uneducated crowd had fallen into what he assumed was a drunken stupor. The moronic bikers he had contacted through his drug contacts were nearby, no doubt taking drugs and fucking their own relatives, creating more of their idiotic offspring. The apple never fell far from the tree, he mused.

Tomorrow he would take a relaxing ride by himself into the Black Hills. It was a beautiful region, he admitted. It had been foresight for those intrepid ranchers and settlers to take this land from the savages. He had seen them along the road and in some of the stores when Todd had stopped for film or they had filled their tanks. On that awful trek to the Little Bighorn, he had seen enough of their poverty, ignorance, and lack of motivation.

Surely, he would have risen above such obstacles and not let himself remain on welfare had he been born in this region. How could people live like this? He often wondered the same thing when he saw images of the ghetto where poor blacks suffered. He certainly gave them enough money in taxes every year. Why did they lie in their own offal? Why didn't they clean up their neighborhoods? Why did the parents let their children follow in their own begrimed footsteps and not try to better themselves? It made him angry sometimes; once he had shouted at the poor, unwashed masses when he had to do an Emergency Room rotation as a resident. He felt no pity for them. They got what they deserved, as far as he was concerned. You reap what you sow, isn't that how the Bible verse went?

Just like those bikers that he'd hired to help him. All brawn and no brain. Well, he'd find something for them to do. He suddenly had a grand idea. They liked to use their bulging muscles, didn't they? Well, he'd find a use for them tomorrow while he was riding far away in the hills. They'd get a good workout doing what they did best. If the police didn't give Doc something to think about, he would. Maybe the application of some muscle was just what he needed, that smug bastard. He'd have them beat him within an inch of his life. Hell, it was Sturgis, after all, let them kill him! He was one of their own, wasn't he? Impudent know-it-all! Let the police sniff up a dead end with a dead Lovejoy. He laughed at his own play on words. He'd give the orders the first thing in the morning when the slovenly bastards rose from their sties.

Now it was time for Noel to sleep. Perchance to dream. Dream of money, drugs, and death.

24

FINALE

After the second finale, the band finally left the stage. The band was exhausted. The crowd was exhausted. Bear, Erin, and Doc were exhausted. Once the lights came back on, they headed for one of the bars toward the front of the Full Throttle. A few more rounds of cold beer added a little to the chill after the sun went down. The thin, dry air and starry sky did little to hold in the heat, and the South Dakota night began in earnest. Erin made it plain that she wanted to spend the night with Doc again, and Doc was happy to have her. Hell! Young, attractive, horny girls weren't so common that you could just throw one away. She was fun to be with, non-judgmental, and so far, non-possessive. Her amorous intentions became clear as she giggled and whispered into Doc's ear. Doc was a little non-plussed as he tried to carry on a conversation with Bear. Erin joined in reluctantly.

"You said Doc saved your life, Bear. What did he do? I mean, what did you do?"

"What did he do? Why he stuck a knife in my chest an' saved my life until the paramedics could get there, that's what. Ya should have seen him, he was shit-faced, an' he still knew just what to do!" Bear lavished praise on the embarrassed Doc. "Tell her; ya know all the technical words an' stuff, Doc."

Doc sat with a slight smile across his lips and said nothing. He thought Bear was doing a fine job without the fancy terms for what had happened.

"Well?" Erin pressed. "What happened? You stuck a knife in him? On purpose? Come on, guys, tell me."

"Well, there we were, Erin. Me an' Doc, crusin' down a little access road along I-95, just north of Daytona. We were at Daytona for Bike Week, you know…well, anyway, there we were, smokin' down the road, mindin' our own business, me an' Doc, when this asshole in a pick-up truck came outta nowhere. An' he came right across the center lane an' chased us both into the ditch. Only this ditch was fulla water and swamp plants an' stuff. Hell, it probably had alligators, an' piranhas, an' all. Anyway, Doc hit the water first, an' made this huge splash, just like he'd jumped off the top of the high dive. I laid my bike down just before it skid into the water, an' I musta hit my chest against the handlebars or somethin'. Anyway, I couldn't get up or breathe. Doc came outta the water like Martin Sheen comin' outta that black water in *Apocalypse Now*. He looked scary as hell. I thought he was dead or somethin' but he came right over to me an' took my pulse an' talked to me real quiet like, an' put his head down on my chest to listen. Cause he could tell I wasn't breathin' too good, ya see. I didn't know what he was doin', but I knew I couldn't breathe worth a shit. My head didn't hurt, but I wasn't thinkin' too clear, an' I knew I was getting' worse. I remember seein' somebody in a cage callin' for the police, but I knew I was about to pass out. Anyway, Doc takes out his knife, pulls my shirt up, an' sticks that fuckin' knife into my chest, just under my collarbone. I was in too bad a shape to object or anything. I heard this big whoosh of air come out of my chest, an' all of a sudden, I could breathe okay again! He held that blade in for ten or twenty seconds, an' then he took it back out. He said it was just relievin' tension, but all I know is that it sure made me a hell of a lot better!"

Erin looked incredulously at Doc. She looked back at Bear who was grinning and shaking Doc's hand like he'd just won some big time award. "What does he mean, you relieved his tension? Is this some kind of joke? I mean, really—"

"Well, darlin', Bear took quite a hit on his chest when he went down. Maybe it was hitting his ape hangers, I don't know for sure. He cracked a few ribs and developed what's called a tension pneumothorax. That's when the lung is leaking, and the air builds up under pressure inside the chest, enough to collapse the lung. If you don't relieve the tension, the blood pressure falls, and the person dies, usually in a matter of minutes. All I did was let the pressure out, and his lung re-inflated. The paramedics took him to the ER, but he didn't need a chest tube or anything. He was pretty lucky, that's all. He owes his survival more to his hard head than to me."

"Bullshit!" Bear bellowed. "I woulda died before they got there; them EMS fellas told me so. If he hadn't put that knife in my chest an' twisted it just a little, I wouldn't be here now. Plus, he did it all with a broken ankle an' a fractured wrist! He didn't tell ya that."

"Doc, that's incredible! You saved Bear's life! I mean, that's so, so amazing!" She gave Doc a big hug and turned to Bear.

"You can hug me, too, kid. I saved his life once, too," Bear grinned widely.

Erin wrapped her arms as far around Bear as she could and gave him a peck on the cheek. "You guys are something else!" She snuggled up against Doc's chest, partly out of affection, and partly from the increasing cold. "Tell me that story. Please. Quick, I'm getting cold!"

"Well, that wasn't so much. He was gettin' the shit beat out of him, an' I jus' sorta convinced those fellas to leave him alone an' go home."

"Erin," Doc started. "I pissed off the wrong people in a bar outside of Laconia. That's in New Hampshire. I still don't know what I did or said, but I must have offended someone. I was sitting at the bar and some guy behind me started to curse. The next thing I remember is getting whacked in the back of the head with a pool cue. Then this guy and his buddies started kicking the crap out of me on the floor. I tried to cover my head, but that's hard to do when they're kicking you in the stomach and balls. They'd only been in the bar for a few minutes, so they didn't know Bear was in the head."

"Yeah, I was there for ten minutes or so. I caught diarrhea from someplace an' was spendin' more time in the shitter than I was on my scoot!"

"Well, he made a timely appearance and proceeded to knock the piss out of those guys. They told the cops we'd started the trouble, but the cops knew them and had had trouble with them before. Anyway, when we rode off into the sunset, my ass was hurtin', I can tell you. I had a black eye, a cut lip, probably a concussion, and some major swelling of my balls, where they'd kicked me. Real brave guys, five on one, and kicking me after hitting me from behind."

"They sure changed their tune when I came out of the bathroom!" Bear laughed. "I think one of them passed out just looking at me bang his buddies' heads together. It was a good time, a real good time."

"It was for you, you orphaned son-of-a-mountain! They beat the hell out of me. When's the last time you were beat up?" returned Doc, smarting at the memory.

"Me? Why, just last... well, no. Maybe it was when I... No, I can't say that anybody has beat me up since I was about four years old!" His roars carried down the long, loud bar so that people turned their heads at the massive man and smiled.

"Well, I'm glad you two had somebody to take care of you! It's a wonder you weren't killed. You're lucky to still be alive with the way you carry on!" Erin scolded half-heartedly. After a few more drinks from her beer bottle, she hugged Doc with both arms and began to move against him. Bear raised his huge, bushy eyebrows, and Doc shrugged his shoulders. It was getting late. Bear didn't want to be a third wheel and began excusing himself for the night.

Doc reminded Erin, "Now, you know I'm in a tent. Like a tent with a sleeping bag on the ground. The cold, hard ground. Right?"

"It sounds like a camp out. I'll love it. Besides, I know you'll keep me warm." She still sounded bubbly after all the beer, whiskey, and tequila she'd consumed during the day. She'd not had anything but beer for the last hour and a half, but she still had a good buzz from before the show. Erin had not slept in a tent since she was ten and spent the weekend with a family friend. They'd come in the house, crying, around two AM, after being convinced they'd heard owls tracking them for a bloody kill. She'd not spent a night in anything more rustic than a futon since.

"Okay, I'll drop you off in Tilford in the morning before I go see the Highway Patrol, if that's alright with you. We can hook up later," Doc suggested. He enjoyed being with the young girl, but he also valued his time alone, and he thought he might stop in on Jeanette after the interview. There was something about Jeanette's quiet smile and few words that did a lot of talking for her. Besides, there were a lot of ideas about this whole Noel/Todd/Tracie thing that he wanted to run past her.

"Why don't you stop by Black Hawk, and we'll ride up to Belle Fourche together," Bear said, as though he could read Doc's mind. "Get some rest tonight, you two. Get some rest," he laughed to himself as he walked out into the parking lot to find his scoot. He found it, kicked it into life, and rumbled off into the night.

"Alright, let's head back to the Chip, darlin'."

"Doc? I'm not crowding you, am I? I mean, you didn't plan to spend all this time with me, and if you don't want me to stay the night, I mean—"

"I hear you," Doc replied softly. "I want you to be with me tonight. Tomorrow morning I'll drop you off at the Tilford Gulch campground before I talk with the police. We each need our own time; I understand that. Besides, we need clean clothes and after a night on the cold ground, you may want to spend some time in a hot shower and a real bed. This sleeping bag and tent routine isn't for everybody. I've been thinking of renting one of those campers at the Chip next year. That way I can ride my bike out, but still take it easy on my old, achin' back. But you're not in the way, darlin', really, you're not."

"Oh, you're so sweet, Doc, you're really sweet. I love being with you."

"Yeah, 'sweet' is my middle name. Come on, you're drunk and we're both horny—" They had reached his ride. Doc waited for Erin to climb onto the back, the bitch seat.

"Well, yeah, I am. But still, you're sweet." She hopped lightly onto his bike and wrapped her arms around him. She managed to get one hand onto his thigh and work it towards his crotch. "Ride on, Doc; I really can't wait to get there!"

25

POLICE INTERVIEW

THURSDAY

Doc walked up the steps of the Highway Patrol building near downtown Sturgis. He felt very sober and wary, like a sheep walking into a wolves' den. He knew the troopers were just trying to do their job—protect the innocent and fight international terrorists. He also knew his appearance would prejudice them against believing anything he said. The trooper, Lieutenant Shelton, had insisted he wasn't a suspect, and that since he wasn't being interrogated, he didn't need a lawyer. If he had brought a lawyer, that may have made him look suspicious. The hard concrete steps lifted him above street level as the main door sought to swallow him up. He had left Bear waiting for him down the street at a local bar, where Doc prayed he would remain inconspicuous and quiet. Lord knows what the cops would have done if Bear had walked through their front door. Doc turned one last time for a quick breath of the hot, dry, but free air. He sighed and entered the building. He couldn't help but recall the old phrase, "Abandon hope, all ye who enter here."

The pretty, young receptionist seemed startled to see him looming over her desk, but recovered quickly and paged Lieutenant Shelton. She showed him to a small, square, nondescript room with scarred, dented tables and chairs plus a mirror on one wall. Come on, Doc thought. This had "Interrogation Room from an old B movie" written all over it! He sat still for a few minutes, waiting for the lieutenant, sure that he was being watched from behind the mirror. All they needed was a bright light for his eyes, a small, hard chair for his butt, and someone to blow smoke in his face. He suppressed the urge to stand close to the mirror, picking his teeth and flexing his muscles. Such humor would be wasted on whoever looked at him through the smoked glass. He sat on the small chair, leaning forward at the waist with his hands folded between his legs.

After ten to fifteen minutes, the frame door opened and a tall, lanky, middle-aged man entered with an easy air of authority. His hair was freshly cut into an old-style crew cut; his teeth were blindingly white, and his skin an uneven brown, with the left arm much darker than the right. Doc figured he did enough driving with the window of his police cruiser down to get a decent farmer's tan. He was wearing the official outfit with highway patrol star, tie, and crisp creases on his shirt and pants. He projected authority, but his manner suggested he was trustworthy. A perfect front to get Doc, or any suspect, to talk and answer questions. He had the "get things done" attitude of the South Dakota Highway Patrol as he shuffled a few papers and began. "Good morning, Dr. Lovejoy. I'm Lieutenant Shelton. We spoke briefly on the phone. Can I get you some coffee? Anything?"

"No, thanks, I'm fine," replied Doc laconically. He knew to limit his responses and only answer the question posed him. Don't offer information. Don't make their work any easier, he'd been told. He hadn't done anything wrong, and had nothing to hide. Still…

"Very good, then," stated Shelton. He sat down opposite Doc, about four and a half feet away, facing him squarely. This was close enough to make Doc comfortable, and yet not threatened. "If you don't object, I'd like to record this interview. Understand that this is only an interview, not an interrogation, and you may have a lawyer present if you wish. We can stop at any time, should you wish to obtain counsel. Is that clear?"

Doc paused for a moment, wondering if he should have found a lawyer. He didn't know one in South Dakota other than the owner of the Buffalo Chip, and Woody was too busy running the greatest party anywhere to do much lawyering today. "What's the difference, Lieutenant? Between an interview and an interrogation?"

The lieutenant paused for a moment and looked Doc squarely in the eye. Doc did not look away. "An interview is non-accusatory; it's used to gain information via questions and answers. I'll try to ask brief, succinct questions, and of course, you'll answer truthfully. An interrogation elicits the truth from a liar, even if the suspect doesn't want to tell the truth. We would do things differently. Understand?"

"Yes, that's okay. Record if you wish." Doc had learned some benign questioning techniques as a doctor. In the ER, it was important to get information from the patient, family members, and bystanders about illnesses and accidents, for example. All too often, patients wanted to tell Doc less than the truth, or spewed out-and-out lies. Parents that abused their child displayed many outward symptoms of lying and discomfort when Doc asked questions about how the injury occurred, or why they delayed bringing the child to medical attention.

"Very good, Doctor." A small, portable micro-recorder was placed between them and started. The lieutenant recited the date, time, Doc's name, and place of interview for the recorder. He watched Doc intently, yet subtly. He paid close attention to Doc's eyes, face, posture, and what he did with his hands. A suspect's hands could move away from the body during questioning, a movement called illustrating, which generally indicated truthfulness. Bringing the hands in contact with the body was referred to as adaptor behavior and was associated with deception. Speeders often brought their hands to their face when they caught sight of a policeman; they scratched their nose, rubbed their forehead, or straightened their hair. Using one's hands to relate a physical activity, was much more likely to infer truth than if the hands remained in their lap the entire time.

The lieutenant paid close attention to Doc's posture, too. This often indicated a person's emotional involvement with the event, their level of interest, and the amount of confidence felt during the questioning. No one posture was as informative as the change of posture during the half-hour interview. The truthful subject often changed posture, while the liar, more often than not, assumed an initial posture and never changed from it. The deceptive subject, it was felt, spent so much effort on what they were saying that they, in effect, became frozen. A motionless posture also indicated a lack of confidence in what the subject was relating.

The fact that Doc was leaning forward indicated that he was nonverbally emphasizing whatever he was saying. This was common early in the interview when the subject was telling the truth, and often changed to a more relaxed position as the interview proceeded. The liar might lean forward the entire time, as a challenge to the interviewer. Alternatively, the liar may maintain a restricted or retracted posture, with their feet and legs pulled up under the chair. This represented a reluctance to provide the truth verbally and nonverbally.

Likewise, crossing the arms presented a barrier or challenge to the interview, while at the same time restricting hand motion. Planting one's feet on the floor initially was normal. The comfortable, truthful subject may cross their legs as they became more comfortable with the interviewing process. It suggested a lie was being told if the subject changed posture in response to a tense question, during their answer, or if they used their hands to assist in the position change.

The interview began with general, obvious questions where the trooper could watch Doc answer truthfully. Later, if he lied, his body language would be useful to uncover the truth. He asked Doc questions about where he lived, his job, and what he was doing in the Black Hills. Doc figured he already knew the answers to these questions, anyway.

After a bit, he changed to more relevant questioning. "I'd like to go over the motorcycle accident involving your friend, Dr. Lassiter. Tell me, in your own words, of course, what transpired that evening." Thus, he invited Doc to provide information beyond simple yes-no answers without giving up any information on his own part.

Doc gave a thumbnail sketch—their ride to the battlefield, the argument with Noel, drinks in Montana, and his view of the accident. He did not express his uneasiness with the sudden change in Todd's riding behavior before the crash. It wasn't much more than a hunch, an uneasy something he couldn't shake. Nothing the trooper would understand. He said nothing about Noel, other than that he was in the lead, at least fifty yards ahead of Doc. He thought it best if the trooper spelled out specific accusations or suspicions.

"At any time did you have any argument, disagreement, quarrel, or dispute with Dr. Lassiter?"

"I did not." Doc kept the answer very short.

"And you maintain that you were at least twenty yards behind him when he lost control of his vehicle?"

"Correct."

"Did you or your motorcycle connect with Dr. Lassiter or his motorcycle just prior to the accident?"

"No."

"Can you think of any reason anyone would want Dr. Lassiter dead?" Shelton peered into Doc's eyes.

Doc hesitated, maybe significantly, he didn't know. But he kept his breathing regular, and he looked right back into the detective's cool, gray eyes. "I do not." But as he said it, enough little thoughts came forward from Doc's subconscious that made him certain Noel had killed Todd. Just as surely as the sun was shining and the grass was green, he knew it was true. He didn't know how, and he didn't know why, but he knew Todd was in his coffin because of Noel. Sometimes things were like that; you couldn't put it all together, but you knew. You knew.

There was a similar long pause from the trooper as he kept his eyes glued to Doc's. Neither said a word until the lieutenant sat back in his chair, as though he believed every word Doc had said.

"How well did you know Dr. Lassiter's wife?"

"I met her when she brought their sick child to the ER. That was the one and only time. No, wait, I took care of her mother when she had a stroke, too."

"Did you ever meet her at any hospital function?"

"No."

"Did you ever meet her outside the hospital?"

"No, I did not."

"Who was going to meet her at the airport?"

"I don't know. I suppose Todd and Noel were going to meet her."

"But Dr. Lassiter couldn't meet her, could he?"

"No." Again, pure truth was revealed to Doc. Noel. Noel had killed Tracie, just as surely as he had killed Todd. Why in the world would he do that?

Again, the lieutenant paused. Maybe he saw something in Doc's eyes. He felt the doctor didn't know what was going on, but was beginning to suspect that something related the two deaths.

"Do you know how Mrs. Lassiter's body got to where it was found?"

"I don't know where it was found, but no, I don't know how it got there." Doc thought, this guy's good; he's not telling me anything.

"Do you know if she was to have a rental vehicle here in South Dakota?"

"Her husband had mentioned an SUV, I believe, when he first arrived. He brought almost nothing with him, explaining that his wife was bringing more stuff with her."

"Stuff? What stuff, doctor?"

"Clothes, stuff like that. He brought only a change of clothes and his toiletries. Dr. Herrod brought more than that in his saddlebags. Lassiter had no saddlebags. Kind of odd, now that I think about it."

"Odd in what way, Doctor?"

"Well, you usually don't see any saddlebags on those big, expensive bikes. I guess Todd's wife was bringing stuff for both of them. I really can't say for sure; I'm only guessing," Doc explained. He didn't want to say too much. He was just starting to put it all together, and he didn't want to appear he was hiding something or knew more than he really did.

The lieutenant felt Doc was being reasonably truthful and ventured a little information.

"I can tell you that Dr. Lassiter's wife was found dead near Mount Rushmore, just outside of Keystone, near federal land." It was a statement more than a question.

"I see."

"Do you have any idea how she got there?"

"No, none at all."

"No? Her body and luggage were discovered there, although the SUV she had rented from the Rapid City airport was still in the airport parking lot. Apparently unmoved. Any thoughts?" His stare bore through Doc as if he was as clear as glass.

"No, none. It's sad."

"Sad? Why do you say that, Doctor?"

Shit. Why did he say that? It was because now Doc realized that Noel had killed Todd and Tracie. The bastard. He'd heard stories about Noel and Tracie, their remote affair. He couldn't imagine why Noel would kill Todd, much less Tracie. What the hell was going on? "I think it's sad for two people to die, that's all. One is bad enough, but why should they both die? I have no idea what's going on! No fucking idea—"

"Yes, you're right, Doctor, very sad, indeed." Long pause. "If you could tell me, please, where you were from the time of the accident until—say noon—on Wednesday, and with whom you spent that time." Pleasant, calm, unruffled. This guy could be both the good and the bad cop at once if he wanted to. He watched Doc like a hawk while appearing to be nonchalant. He picked up every nuance of posture, voice, and inflection.

It was a damn good thing I'm innocent, Doc thought, or I'd be in a world of trouble. Doc gave a nearly hour-by-hour account of his time, as requested. He felt like an idiot when he couldn't remember Erin's last name; he thought for a minute and rolled his eyes upward as he tried to remember. Damn, he fucked the girl and didn't even know her name… "McLaughlin!" he almost shouted after a long pause. "That's it. Boy, I feel like an idiot."

"Is there a way to contact Miss McLaughlin?"

Doc turned on his cell phone and retrieved Erin's number. He gave it as though he expected the lieutenant to call her then and there. He did not. After a few more terse questions, the trooper verified that Doc would be in the area at least until Sunday and requested he stay in touch.

"Keep my cell phone turned on, you mean."

"Something like that. We'll contact you if there are further questions. We are keeping our options open in these two deaths. If you think of anything you would like to tell me, anything at all, please call me." He handed Doc his card. "I think, Doctor, you realize I want to find out what's really going on as much as you do. It's as clear as mud now, but as piece after piece falls into place, we'll know the truth. We only miss the truth when we quit trying. Call me if you think of anything else."

He showed Doc to the front door. Doc felt the troopers' eyes on him as he walked down the steps and across the street to his bike, started it, and rode down Sherman Street to where Bear was waiting. Doc felt that his own eyes should look at Dr. Noel Herrod with just as much interest and intensity.

26

Back in Belle Fourche

The two motorcycles rumbled into Jeanette's gravel drive and came to a stop. Doc's Wide Glide sat next to Bear's dark red, vintage 1947 Knucklehead FL. Bear had done much of the work on the bike himself, using his thick fingers more gently than one would think possible. He kept it near stock, with authentic parts wherever possible, although those were getting harder and harder to find. The engine itself had been rebuilt several times as he had almost 250,000 miles on the machine. Doc imagined him picking the bike up, placing it under his arm and tucking it in bed next to him. Yes, the man loved his scoot.

Doc had found Bear in the Sturgis bar where he'd left him. Doc thought the question and answer session had gone pretty well. The trooper listened to his answers and watched him closely, but he'd seemed fair and reasonable. The two friends had ridden amid hundreds of other bikes along I-90 north from Sturgis after Doc downed a few beers. They'd picked up some food, more beer, and a bottle of wine on the edge of Belle Fourche, which Doc had secured in his saddlebags as they rode to the outskirts of town where Jeanette lived.

Doc's mind had been churning from the time he'd left the small interrogation room. What the hell was going on? That seemed to be the fundamental question, but he was beginning to break the problem down into sub-problems he thought Bear and Jeanette could help him solve. Some food, some booze, and throwing his ideas out for the three of them to chew on seemed to be the best approach.

Jeanette welcomed them both with open arms. She'd not seen Bear for over a year and he was immediately pressed into answering questions while Doc began to fix food in her small kitchen. He'd bought hamburger, tomatoes, onions, refried beans, and taco shells. In short order, he'd whipped up enough Mexican food for six or eight—enough for Jeanette, himself, and Bear. He poured some of the rich, red sangria into deep glasses to go with the frosty beers and set the table at about the time Bear and Jeanette came into the kitchen laughing.

"You've not changed, my friend," Jeanette laughed as she sat down.

Bear replied, "I didn't know you wanted me to, Jeanette. No one else does, do they, Doc?"

"Only the Barbers Association of North America, Bear; they're after both of us!" he laughed in return.

They turned to the fresh food and drink with gusto. After they made a serious dent in the laden table, Doc brought them both up to date with what had happened. Then he asked them for their help.

"I know there's something funny going on here; I just don't know what. I know some things for sure, although I don't have any proof. I need your help. I've major questions that stand out, and I think if we can come up with answers to these, we'll have a better idea of where we stand."

"Go ahead, Doc, we're listenin'," urged Bear.

"Alright. First, why did Noel and Todd come to Sturgis? I think Todd came for fun he'd never had before, a little horizon broadening, if you will. He certainly didn't seem like a big prick like Noel. Noel doesn't seem to be here for the events, the people, or the bikes. He has some underlying plan—I don't know what. He didn't enjoy the trip to Little Bighorn at all. He seems to thrive on being an important person at the hospital, and he sure isn't that here in Sturgis. He looks down on everyone else and loves his money and all the things it can buy."

He paused. Bear drained an entire beer and shook his massive head. Jeanette nodded for Doc to continue.

"Second. Why did Todd crash? I know he'd been drinking some, but I don't think that's it. I believe Noel killed him, but I can't think how he might have done it. He never touched him. He was well ahead of us both when Todd started weaving and went off the road. But if you'd seen the look on his face after the action, you would have known he did it. He wasn't shocked, sad, or even upset, as far as I could tell. At first, he looked satisfied. Moreover, I saw him go through Todd's pockets. He thought I was far enough away, but I've seen it done before in the ER, and there's no mistaking it. He was looking for something, but I don't know what. Todd didn't have saddlebags, so whatever Noel was looking for must have been hidden elsewhere. I could tell he didn't find it just by the way he walked away from the body. So the third question is—why did he kill Todd?

"Fourth, I think Noel also killed Todd's wife, Tracie. But why did he kill her? I think he only killed her after Todd's death didn't resolve whatever problem they had between them. I think he tried to get whatever he was looking for from her after he didn't find it on Todd. Lieutenant Shelton told me the SUV had over fifty additional miles on it, although it hadn't been moved from its parking spot. They check mileage whenever a rental is returned, so it was clear that someone, Tracie, or someone else, drove the SUV that night. Her luggage had been searched before it was thrown out on the road along with her body. Did he kill her because of what she said or knew, or because she didn't know anything?

"Last, why is he still here? I think that's connected to the first question about why he's here in the first place! Noel's up to something, and he's killed at least two people to get it!"

"You think he might have killed more than two people?" asked Jeanette. "Has someone else died?"

"Yeah, another doctor died last month, in Noel's presence. It all looked innocent at the time, but the more I think about it, the more I think Noel killed him, too. I'd like to get this bastard and shake him like a rat until he tells us what's going on," Doc seethed.

"Wouldn't do ya any good. His kind just shuts up even tighter when you scare 'em. We've gotta use strategy here, Doc. Wadda ya think, Jeanette?" Bear growled.

Jeanette sat still for a few minutes with her brows knit together. When she answered, she was quiet, as usual, and correct, as usual. "The key to all this is to find what Noel is searching for before he does. A person only acts this way when they are scared. I agree that he's greedy and money-hungry. That's probably why he's here, there's some monetary opportunity here. I'm not sure what it is, but he's only here for that reason. I don't think he came here to kill anyone, but he's obviously not afraid to do so. When we know what is motivating his actions, we'll have solved this. Dessert, anyone?"

Jeanette rose from the table and brought back fresh apple pie and homemade vanilla ice cream. Somehow, she'd known they would be there that day and had been ready.

"Hah," roared Bear. "If she'd known we was comin', she'd a' baked a cake!"

After they'd finished eating, Doc cleared the table, and Bear offered to do the dishes. "There's not that much, y'all sit down with some coffee, an' we'll hash this out some more. I think we oughta think about the things that bother Doc—those little things irritatin' the back o' his mind, ya know?"

"That's an excellent idea, Bear!" Jeanette agreed. She poured hot cups of rich, black coffee for each of them. She added milk to hers. Bear unexpectedly wanted milk and sugar. Doc drank his coffee black, joking that he'd learned to drink coffee on a Marine base in Georgia, where they emptied the jeeps' oil tanks at the motor pool each night for the morning coffee.

"It's not the training that makes Marines mean, it's the coffee!" he chuckled.

They settled in her living room, lined with various pieces of art she found pleasing. Some were her own, some from contemporaries, and some were hundred of years old. There was some Lakota art and some that Doc felt was Middle Eastern, possibly ancient. They all fit together just as the various influences came together in Jeanette herself.

"You seem unconvinced that alcohol led to Todd's death, Doc," Jeanette began. "Why not? Drunks crash everyday. Do you think his drinks were spiked with something? Something to make him drunker? Do you think Noel slipped him a mickey? Something to make him pass out?"

"No, anything like that would show up on a toxicology screen. They do that as part of any car or motorcycle-related death. They can't test for everything, but those things show up real quick."

"What about somethin' they wouldn't look for? How about the other one? That other doctor back in Ohio—what do ya think killed him?"

"He had a heart attack; I saw the ECG myself, unless Noel faked it. No, I think we're on the right track, though," Doc responded. After a few seconds, he added, "Todd wasn't very healthy, though."

"What do ya mean, Doc?"

"He had heart disease, partly from childhood rheumatic fever, and partly because he lived a very unhealthy lifestyle. He was over weight, ate a lot of fat, and I'll bet he had coronary heart disease. You know, where the heart's plumbing is clogged with cholesterol. When his kid was sick, I asked questions about the family's medical history. Noel was his doctor, and he knew how bad Todd's heart might have been."

"Yeah, we'd never have that problem ourselves, would we?" Bear laughed. "But how would that've helped Noel? Could he make Todd have a heart attack or somethin'? Could he have made Todd take a pill if he didn't wanna take it?"

"Well—" Doc started, and he suddenly stopped. He stood and reached into his pocket. Doc moved apart the coffee cups and placed a single pill on the table. "I think we may have our answer, folks. Jeanette, aren't you online? I need to get on the Internet for a minute."

Jeanette led them into her studio, where she kept a computer for her online sales. While they waited for the little Dell desktop to boot up and go on-line, Doc explained about finding the tablet on the table at the Stoneville Saloon after Noel and Todd had left the table. He'd not known what it was, but had impulsively pocketed the tablet, maybe a habit from his teenage drug abusing days. Meanwhile, Bear poked around, checking out the finished and incomplete works Jeanette had scattered around her neat little work area.

"Hey, will ya look at this?" he laughed aloud. Bear had uncovered a painting she had done of Doc, his back to a beautiful setting sun, surrounded by rugged mountains. "Ain't he a beauty?"

Doc smiled and looked at Jeanette, who suddenly and uncharacteristically looked embarrassed. "It's a memory of the first time we met, near Taos," she mumbled. "I've always liked it and keep it nearby. It's sort of special to me."

"It's beautiful, darlin'. It's really well done," Doc said quietly and kissed her cheek. He'd seldom seen her caught off guard like this.

Saved by the bell, Jeanette turned as the computer made beeping noises as it connected to the World Wide Web. Doc sat on the small, cushioned seat and went to drugs.com to identify the pill he'd found on the table in the Montana bar. He typed in the code imprinted on the small, white tablet: OP 706. In less than a second, the screen changed and displayed an identical tablet. The small text next to the image read "Drug Generic Name(s): DISULFIRAM, Brand Name(s) Antabuse, Strength 250 mg, Imprint OP 706, Manufacturer: Odyssey Pharmaceuticals, Inc." Doc made a sound as if he'd been hit in the stomach and sat back in the chair. The others looked at him in wonder because they had no idea what the information meant.

"Well, what is it? Is it some kinda poison or somethin'?" asked Bear.

"Do you know what it is?" Jeanette followed.

"Yes, I do and no, it's not a poison. That is, normally it isn't, but it sure the hell was for Todd!" Doc continued, "Disulfiram, or Antabuse, as it's more commonly known, is a drug used to treat alcoholics. It's given to try to keep them from drinking any alcohol at all. You see, as long as they stay sober, it doesn't bother them, but if they take a drink or two, the drug keeps the body from metabolizing the alcohol normally. The person begins to build up large amounts of a new chemical called acetaldehyde, in direct proportion to how much alcohol has been consumed. This causes flushing, headache, shortness of breath, vomiting, sweating, and marked thirst. Worse, it can cause chest pain, palpitations, a very fast heartbeat, low blood pressure, and eventually loss of consciousness. The person may feel dizzy, confused, and suffer blurred vision. In severe cases, especially in someone with underlying heart disease, like Todd, there may be cardiovascular collapse, a fatally irregular heart rhythm, heart attack, heart failure, seizures, and death. Plus, the more alcohol you drink, the worse the reaction will be."

"If Noel had given these to Todd after all he'd had to drink at the Stoneville Saloon, within an hour or so, he'd have had a serious reaction and passed out, if not died outright. Riding on the bike, it would've looked like he'd just been drunk and lost control of his bike. They'd never look for Antabuse on a routine tox screen. Never! I've never heard of anyone intentionally using this drug to kill someone. That bastard—"

Bear blurted, "That Noel may be a bastard, but he's an awfully smart bastard!"

27

The Pieces Fall Together

Doc paced around the small computer, hitting his fist into his other open palm repeatedly. His anger was almost palpable in the small work area and seemed to infect his friends.

"My God, Doc. Would he have been in pain?" asked Jeanette. Even though she hadn't been there and had never met Todd, she still felt for him and grimaced as she contemplated his death.

"Maybe. Probably in the last minute or so. He was a little sloshed, so he may not have known what was going on. Like when you're falling asleep at the wheel and don't realize you should pull over to the side of the road until it's too late. I don't know. We'll probably never know what he felt. He wouldn't have suffered once he hit those rocks," answered Doc.

"At least now we know how the poor sucker died," Bear said. "Did ya say we can't prove it? Ain't it in his blood or somethin'? Doctor Quincy could always find stuff in the blood. Man, that used ta be one of my favorites shows!"

"That was about as real as all the new forensic soap operas and crime scene programs on TV now-a-days, Bear. The coroner's office can find this type of stuff, but only if they know they should be looking for it in the first place. Usually the toxicology people just look for cocaine, heroin, and stuff like that. They'd have to use gas chromatography, or some other advanced test to find disulfiram. That kind of test isn't done unless there is a clear reason to do so," Doc informed him.

"Doc, isn't there someone we can tell about this? I don't necessarily mean the police, but somebody?" wondered Jeanette. "Is there someone else we can call or ask for help?"

"Let me think for a minute. You're talking about somebody within the system that can get these tests run for us. We certainly can't do it ourselves. Yeah, I think there is. There's a guy I met once down at the Rapid City Regional Hospital, another ER doctor. He's a pretty good guy; maybe he can help out. Let me see if I can reach him. Where's that damn phone?" Doc fished the small cell phone out of his pocket and started dialing.

Within minutes, he had contacted Dr. Jim Foster in the Emergency Department in Rapid City. Doc had met Jim several times in the past. After the niceties were aside, Doc told Jim about his suspicion of disulfiram in the blood of a recent accident victim. While he thought it very unlikely that someone could ride with both alcohol and disulfiram in their blood simultaneously, Jim promised to contact the pathology department and add the appropriate toxicology tests for disulfiram and acetaldehyde, the alcohol breakdown product Doc suspected. It would take one or two days to get back any results. Doc assured Jim that he would call back and that he now owed him at least a six-pack of his favorite beer. Since Jim was a fellow ER doctor, he'd gained some measure of Doc's trust and readily agreed to both the added tests and the offer of beer.

Bear felt good about their progress so far, but suggested that they needed another round of drinks before they attacked the next problem. They all agreed and retired to Jeanette's dusty back yard swing with the remaining cold beers. Doc and Jeanette settled into the swing while Bear sat on the ground, his head still almost as far off the ground as those seated in the swing. They began brainstorming as the afternoon warmed.

"What brought Noel here? What could he get here that he couldn't get elsewhere that would make money? What's special about this area? Or this week?" Jeanette wondered aloud.

"There's nothing out here, but beautiful scenery an' real good people, as far as I can tell," offered Bear as he swallowed an entire beer in one swallow. He wiped his mouth on his sleeve and leaned back to ponder the problem in the warm sunshine.

"Minerals, mining, gold? Maybe he was going to get gold of some kind?" she continued.

"Too heavy," replied Doc. "How would he get it back? Enough gold to make you rich would also weigh you down. Good idea, though."

"Somethin' radioactive? Somethin' for terrorists?" pondered Bear. He'd seen TV shows where that happened, too.

Death in Sturgis

"Drugs? Heroin? Cocaine? Again, how could he carry enough dope to make it worthwhile? You said he's flying back; it's too risky to take a significant amount of drugs on a commercial airplane," she suggested.

"It only takes ten pounds or so of quality cocaine to make a lot of money. You're right, though; he couldn't take it back on a plane. Maybe he's got another way to get it back to Ohio," continued Doc.

"Maybe he's buying stolen computer software; that wouldn't be too big, would it? I don't know, but I saw a guy on TV get a computer disk worth a coupla million bucks, an' it didn't take up too much space." Bear was on a roll. "But where's he gonna get it, an' who's givin' it to him?"

"Well, I don't know who's giving it to him, but I do know that it's not very big these days. Computer stuff is getting smaller and smaller. You can fit hundreds of millions of bytes onto a CD now." Jeanette was up on modern information technology. "Those memory sticks for digital cameras can hold hundreds of photographs until they're ready to be uploaded to a computer workstation for printing. It's fantastic."

Without saying a word, Doc got up from the swing, motioned them to follow him, and went back into the house. He re-entered the studio and took the small memory device Erin had found from his pocket. "This apparently fell from Todd's pocket when he was in Jim's pickup truck," he said as he sat down to the computer and searched without luck for a spot to plug it in. "It's got his name on it and everything. Plus, I remember he was using a traditional 35 mm model, not a digital camera!"

"Here," Bear said, as he took the stick and deftly inserted it into one of the spare USB slots on the back of the computer. The computer beeped and put up a screen informing them that a new device had been found. Doc and Jeanette turned to him with their mouths hanging open.

"Hey, I'm not as stupid as I look. I don't spend alla my time watchin' old TV shows, ya know!" Bear announced.

After they stopped laughing and slapping Bear on the back, Doc sat down to search the contents of the memory stick. There was a file system on the memory stick, but it was encrypted. Only someone who knew the password would be able to open and examine it.

"Any guesses? We can try as many times as we want, there doesn't appear to be much sophistication to this protection. Any ideas, Bear?" Doc asked.

"Ya mean jus' any word? How about his wife's name, or the names of his kids, or his dog, or somethin'?"

"Good guess, although I'm afraid I don't know his children's names; my memory's not that good. I only saw his daughter once as an ER patient."

Todd's wife's name didn't unlock the files. Nor did Todd's own name, their names backwards, or the next twenty-three guesses.

"Well, damn. I'm startin' to run out o' good ideas," Bear sighed. "Maybe we're beat, guys."

"What do you think was on his mind when he made these files and encrypted them? That might be a clue, you know; understand his mindset," suggested Jeanette. She didn't show her frustration as readily as the two men did. Bear was pacing and cursing while Doc took long drinks from the remaining beer and stared out the window at the waning afternoon.

Doc turned to the keyboard and typed "Fuck Noel." He hesitated and looked into the faces of Bear and Jeanette before he tapped the Enter key. Instantly, the folder names became readable and displayed multiple files within each folder.

"Hell, yeah!" shouted Bear. "Look at the names o' them folders, would ya?"

The three folders were named "finances," "photos," and "timeline." Doc clicked on the photos folder first, hoping against hope to see beautiful western scenery.

There were multiple photo files, but none could be considered candidates for a wish-you-were-here post card. Many of them were of Noel and Todd, as well as some men Doc didn't recognize. One, however, showed Noel, Todd, and Jake Epstein sitting together at a table with a bottle of champagne between them. Doc groaned inside at the thought of Jake being involved in whatever dirty business resulting in his death, too.

Another folder on the stick held Excel files, containing what looked like financial files and accounting information. There were numerous transactions consistent with monies paid out and taken in. None of those gathered around the small screen were particularly savvy about this kind of information. Doc doubted that anyone outside the FBI could confirm that this represented ill-gotten gains for Todd and Noel.

Next, Doc opened up the folder titled "timeline." That single file appeared to hold what they had been looking for—a timeline constructed by Todd describing years of drug deals. The deals started out small, but had increased over the past year until over one hundred thousand dollars was exchanged at a time. The last deal occurred only two months ago. They stared at the screen for ten minutes or more as they read what Todd had documented.

Finally, they all moved back. Silently, they looked at each other for a few long moments before anyone spoke.

"Man, this is crazy," said Bear. "It looks like these dudes were dealin' drugs in a big way, ya know? I think I know why this Noel killed Todd. Todd was threatening to turn him in or somethin'!"

"I think you're right, Bear," said Jeanette. "He must have had all this put together as a threat to Noel or as insurance that Noel would do what he said. This is very incriminating evidence. That, or he was blackmailing Noel for more money; maybe he thought his share was too small. What do you think Doc?"

"I think one of those ideas is probably correct. This memory stick is what Noel was looking for. I bet he thought Tracie had it, too, and that's why he killed her and searched her belongings. I don't know if he knew the stuff was on this stick or not, but this is what he wanted!"

"Well, we got it now. An' now we know that they're dealin' drugs, I bet they were lookin' for a big deal to go down here in South Dakota. We got all kindsa reasons to think that, don't we, Doc?"

"You're right there, brother. What do we do with it? If we take it to the police, all I see happening is that they think either we're involved or they just don't believe it. I don't like either alternative. That trooper, Shelton, seemed okay, but those guys are awfully suspicious of anybody like us."

"I'm afraid you're right, Doc. I doubt they'll find me a very creditable witness to all this—ex-con and all. I wish I could be more help," murmured Jeanette.

"Yer sure right about that, girl; I'm no angel, either. We can't go to the law, Doc, that's fer sure. We need to figure out what to do next an' all, but first we have a worse problem!"

"What's that, Bear? What's wrong?" Doc looked worried.

"Hell, man, we're outta booze!"

28

Battle of Belle Fourche

Doc and Bear took their bikes into town to the Dakotamart for more beer, wine, and food. They made a very incongruous pair, pushing their shopping cart up and down the aisles. It slowly filled with some of the essentials of life—cold Coors beer, salad makings, and thick, South Dakota steaks. More than one head turned as they stood to peruse the choices on the well-stocked shelves. Doc could invoke one of Bear's bellowing roars of laughter by referring to him as "Honey," or calling him his "life partner."

"Sure, baby, get whatever you want! Big Daddy wants to keep Momma happy!" Bear would answer in a sugary-sweet voice that made Doc double over. The fact that they were both more than just a little plastered didn't help matters. The joking seemed to defuse the anger and tension that had mounted like an impending prairie thunderstorm over the course of the afternoon. They still felt justifiable rage towards Noel for the deeds he'd committed, but they were beginning to feel that maybe something could be done.

Doc had begun to see a glimmer of light—some hope that Noel could be brought to bay and his crimes avenged. Maybe it was Doc's desire to pull for the underdog and right unknown wrongs. Maybe it was the sense of righteous rage he felt when some defenseless person was maligned or taken advantage of in some way. Of course, that feeling was also responsible for some of the more memorable beatings of his life. Looking back, Doc could have chosen his fights more carefully, but he would have found it harder to live with himself afterwards than it was to lick his wounds, ice his bruises, and suck down a healthy combination of Jack Daniels and painkillers.

The unusual pair finally reached the checkout counter, where they initially scared the poor checkout girl, and then began to charm her. Bear, as large as he was, could still flirt with the best of them. He'd had

Death in Sturgis

his share of women who wanted to find out if he was as impressively large everywhere they could reach. He seldom disappointed them, and he had the uncanny ability to put people, women at least, at ease when he turned on his size twenty-four personal charm. Doc was always impressed to see him at work and egged him on to ever more impressive efforts.

Today, Bear had the girl, who could barely be out of her teens, giggling, and rolling her eyes at him. This was the only week of the year where she saw more than the endless lines of cowboys and farmers that came through her checkout line. The fact that this gigantic man, who was nothing like anything she'd ever seen before, was talking to her like her longest confidant and beau had her swimming. The pimply-faced bag boy was stumbling and bumbling with their purchases, as Bear struggled with the eternal paper versus plastic debate.

"Gee, we're puttin' those bags on our bikes, ma'am, so you've gotta help me decide. Do you recommend them big, strong, plastic bags, or do ya think I'd do better with good ole' paper? I'm confused!" Bear issued a stage whisper audible from twenty feet away.

The girl continued to giggle and twisted a long, dark curl around her finger as Bear discoursed on the paper versus plastic contest. She pivoted on one foot in her little checkout station before the cash register as she rang up the final total. Doc paid with a credit card, and Bear wished her an intense goodbye laden with promises to return and whisk her away from her otherwise dull and boring life. They made their way back to the blistering asphalt parking lot where the day had begun to sear them and the entire Black Hills. There they creatively crammed some containers into the saddlebags and tied others across their seats, strangely reminiscent of cowboys lashing their meager foodstuffs to their saddles a hundred years ago.

Neither Doc nor Bear could resist the siren call of a sign proclaiming 'Cold Beer' mounted on a small, hole-in-the-wall bar along Route 85—known locally as Fifth Avenue. The cool darkness of the bar beckoned as they parked their bikes near the front door and went in. The food would surely be secure while they enjoyed the hospitality of the aptly named Outlaw Saloon. Doc suggested they limit their libations to "a couple or three" beers, and Bear readily agreed. Once that limit had been exceeded by one or two refreshing brews and a few shots of Jack Daniels, they walked heavily back into the South Dakota sun and re-started their rides. They turned onto National Street and rode ever so carefully back toward Jeanette's.

Doc and Bear were confused when they found a half-dozen bikes parked haphazardly in Jeanette's gravel drive. They didn't recognize any of the near-stock Harleys adorned with moderate amounts of chrome. Jeanette's back door stood open, which was odd, because anyone there to see her artwork would have gone in the front door, into the gallery area. They traded worried glances as they walked quietly into the mudroom and approached the kitchen. They could hear a raised, irate male voice from the studio area.

"Tell me where it is, bitch. I know Lovejoy left it here! Tell me, or I'll beat the living shit out of you!"

This was punctuated by the sharp crack of an open palm hitting solid flesh. Jeanette's cry of pain followed within milliseconds of the blow. Other male voices could be heard in the background, along with loud noises as Jeanette's sculptures crashed to floor one after another. Evil cackles accompanied each crash as the men saw the pain she felt every time one of her lovingly crafted pieces of art found its way onto the floor from its display stand.

The short, swarthy man standing before Jeanette brought his arm back in preparation for another staggering blow. A taller man with dirty blond hair and a dull look on his face held her from behind, trapping her arms painfully high behind her back. His small, pig-like eyes glittered with anticipation as his partner began to bring his arm forward. The blow never landed.

With a shout worthy of any Lakota warrior, Doc screamed, "Hoka hey!" and flew into the room, catching the dark man's forearm from behind. With a wrench that used every iota of energy and every ounce of his weight, Doc pulled back on the man's arm. A satisfying crunch sounded across the room as the man's upper arm, his humerus, fractured in at least three pieces as it was dislocated from the shoulder socket. His scream of pain was the perfect lead-in for the nauseating sound made as Bear grabbed the two men to the right of the door and crushed their skulls together, face-to-face. They immediately fell to the floor, unaware of anything beyond the searing pain they felt in their heads as they passed into blissful unconsciousness. Jeanette was released and the man moved quickly away.

Jeanette's interrogator fell to the floor at Doc's feet, his fractured arm hanging limply at his side. Doc completed his introduction with a savage, well-placed kick to the face that resulted in a sickening, wet sound as facial bones shattered into pulverized jelly. Content with that piece of shit, Doc turned to the two men who had been destroying Jeanette's art. They were already backing away from a Bear that looked like a Norwegian berserker from the Middle Ages. His eyes bulged from his flaming face and his breath whistled through his dilated nostrils. Bear reached out to the first stranger as the other spun on his heel to run. He met Doc's clenched right fist with his solar plexus and fell heavily to the plaster-ridden floor with his breath knocked out. He looked up stupidly at Doc as he lay there fighting for every breath.

Bear wrapped his strong right hand around the other man's neck and lifted him a full two feet off the floor, Darth Vader-like. A small squeeze on Bear's part cut off the passage of air to the man's lungs completely as it ceased blood flow from to and from his brain. With terrified, bug-like eyes, the intruder lost consciousness, and Bear tossed him to the side like a discarded rag doll, unconcerned with whether he was dead or alive.

The fair-haired man who had been holding Jeanette came up behind as Doc looked at the man he had just knocked to the floor. Doc felt something hot sear his right flank and turned to find the last man standing before him with a bloody knife in his hand. The man whirled, and before Doc could reach him, fled for the exit. Bear was a good fifteen feet away, where he had nearly decapitated his dancing partner. Doc staggered a few feet ahead, but Bear stopped the man with a fifteen-pound chunk of broken plaster he had fetched from the debris scattered across the floor. It struck him square in the back, sending the man's limp body sliding a full six feet across the kitchen floor. Each of the strangers was breathing, but none was conscious.

"What the fuck is going on?" breathed Bear heavily as he searched the room with his eyes for another opponent. "Who are these assholes, Doc?"

Silently, Doc knelt at Jeanette's side. She sat holding the left side of her face gingerly. An ugly swelling was rapidly appearing, a dark reddish-purple hue across her high cheekbone. Doc assessed her quickly with his well-honed ER skills. Her airway, breathing, and circulation were intact, and she did not appear to have suffered any intracranial injury. Her eyes were open (four points), her speech was clear, and she was oriented (five points), and she was moving all her extremities with ease and purpose (six points). This gave her a Glasgow Trauma Score of fifteen— normal. Her chest moved symmetrically, and her extremities were warm. She held her abdomen where she had been struck at least once, but it was soft and there was no involuntary guarding of any quadrant. She had contusions, bruises, but was otherwise physically sound.

Doc became more aware of the burning on his right side and reached down to examine his own body. He pulled away a bloody hand. "Shit," he said quietly, to no one in particular. He took a few, tentative, deep breaths and detected nothing that made him think he'd suffered a deep lung injury. His finger carefully probed the ugly gash where the thug's stiletto had cut him. It was about ten inches long, but shallow. He knew this limited exam could be deceptive, but felt further evaluation could wait while they secured these assholes with some small gauge wire he knew Jeanette had on hand. Good. The smaller the better. That would really hurt, and one thing he wanted above all else at this moment was to make these motherfuckers hurt. Hurt real badly.

29

The Dust Clears

Bear began to secure the strange men in Jeanette's workroom with the metal wire he'd found on one of her benches. As the most likely to run off right away, he picked the winded man up from the floor like a paper mache puppet and tied his hands to his feet, placing him heavily along one of the nearby walls. The smaller man made no attempt to struggle or escape once he got a good look at Bear's face; he wisely sat, wide-eyed, without a word. The next three unconscious men were gathered and hog-tied in a similar fashion, except for Doc's patient with the broken and dislocated arm. Bear tied only his good arm to his feet before moving him like the worthless piece of shit he was to the side of the others.

In the meantime, Doc had softly lifted Jeanette from the plaster-littered floor and carried her into the small bedroom. There he gently washed her bruised and battered face. "Stay here," he whispered and went into the kitchen to find some ice for her poor face. "Don't forget this moaning asshole on the kitchen floor, Bear," he called as he re-entered her bedroom. Bear merely grunted and roughly tossed the latest of the collection down along the wall.

Jeanette lay quietly on the bed as the realization of what had just transpired began to sink in. Doc knew that, with time, she'd be okay; she was, after all, a woman. He spoke soothingly to her as he worked for several minutes. She reluctantly winced from the first icy touch of the roughly fashioned cold pack he'd made from ice cubes and a fresh washcloth.

Suddenly, all three heard the simultaneous blaring of a car horn and the screech of tires, followed by the unmistakable crash of bending, clashing metal. Doc was instantly out the back door as Bear emerged from the workroom exit. They met in the front yard where they stared at the collision on the road before them. Doc gaped at the county sheriff's car parked at an unplanned slant across the dusty, two-lane road at the end of short rubber marks from abruptly applied brakes. Fifty feet or so ahead of the cruiser was one the motorcycles that had been parked behind the house. Another twenty feet beyond that was the blonde man who had tried to kill Doc with the stiletto sprawled across the pavement. One leg was bent at an angle that could never be achieved naturally. He was bleeding from a large, ugly gash on his forehead. He was not moving, although his chest rose and fell regularly.

"Jesus, Doc! Would ya look at that! That scum-sucker got what he deserved," yelled Bear as Doc raced towards the man. Bear followed more slowly. "Serves him right to meet his maker, if ya ask me."

Doc arrived at the man less than a minute after the accident and crouched down so he could listen for breath sounds. The man's eyes were closed, and he did not respond as Doc shouted to him. Doc moved to his head to secure the man's cervical spine, protecting him from further insult. "Get over here, Bear, and hold this guy's head still, so he doesn't move his neck; he's breathing okay and has a good pulse. Don't move him."

"Jesus, Doc; a minute ago, he was tryin' to kill ya and now all of a sudden yer his doctor, savin' his life!" Bear laughed as he stabilized the man's neck. It was not the first time Doc had given him this assignment. He doubted it would be the last. This time, however, Bear would have been more than happy to finish the job started by the sheriff's deputy.

Doc approached the police cruiser as the deputy jumped out, young and scared. "Did you see that? That son of a bitch tore out of that driveway like a bat out of hell! I didn't have time to miss him! I ran right into him! Jesus!" The deputy seemed to have absolved himself of any fault and struggled to take control of the situation. "I've already called for back-up and an ambulance. Is he alive? He must be drunk or something the way he pulled out!" He turned to Doc and asked, "What the hell is going on here? What are you guys up to? Every damn Sturgis Week it gets like this! Have you been drinking, too? Is he still breathing? We should do something!"

Doc listened to the deputy for a few minutes, hoping he would calm down enough to handle affairs. He heard the wail of sirens less than a mile away, and knew he had precious little time to manage the situation the way he wanted. "Well, officer, I'm glad you're here. It sure was lucky the way you came along when you did! This guy, and five of his friends, were robbing the poor woman who runs this art gallery. They hit her, but she's okay; she's lying down inside. The other fellas are inside, tied up by my large friend and me. We already took care of this man's neck. It's sure a good thing you came along, that's for sure. You're doing a fine job," Doc's low voice seemed to soothe the deputy. It was the same voice he'd used to get a woman through a rugged emergency delivery without pain medications. The more Doc told him he was doing a good job; the more he believed it. The more he believed it, the better he actually did. The deputy began to direct the little traffic past the crumpled motorcycle and the man lying with his head, and his life, in Bear's hands. He calmed down enough that some of the squeakiness left his voice, and he lost the adolescent fear that had driven him for the first few minutes after the collision.

Within minutes, two more cruisers arrived with regular deputies and a sergeant. An ambulance arrived and moved their stretcher alongside the stricken man and Bear. The attendants seemed reluctant to bother Bear, but Doc assisted in placing a stiff cervical collar on the man's neck and a backboard beneath him. Together, they moved him onto the stretcher and lifted it. Once its collapsible wheels were locked into place, they moved him to the waiting ambulance. Oxygen was applied, two large bore IVs were inserted, and he was loaded for the trip to Spearfish, where the closest emergency room waited. Doc was worried that he had suffered a significant head injury, such as a skull fracture, bleeding in the brain, or damage to the structure of the brain itself. Doc knew he might never wake up or return to his baseline after a crash like that. He didn't know how his neck was, either. A cervical neck fracture could cause irreparable damage to the soft, flexible spinal cord.

The ambulance raced off, its siren screaming into lower and lower squawks as the vehicle moved away. The police gathered around Doc and Bear, apprehension on their faces. There wasn't a man there that wasn't saying a secret prayer that he'd not have to fight Bear. Doc thought it best to use a little Southern charm to put them at their ease and get them to understand what had happened.

"Well, fellas, we're glad you're here. We've got that guy's five partners hog-tied inside for you. We got here just as they were robbing the place. The lady that owns the place is inside lying down. She got hit a little, but looks to be okay. Come on in, y'all," he sweet-talked the gathering group of police as two more cars arrived.

Doc led the police into the workroom where the other men were securely tied. He explained, very loosely indeed, what had happened over the course of the late morning and afternoon. None of the restrained men cared to disagree and kept their mouths tightly shut. The police at first did not feel comfortable with the two bikers, but then Jeanette made her way out of the bedroom and gave a succinct, but impressive report of what had transpired. Following Doc's lead, she gave little real information about what they had been doing all day, but made it obvious that, in this case, anyway, Doc and Bear were wearing the white hats. As their prisoners awoke, they held their silence to a man, except for the interrogator whose arm had been broken in the first seconds of the fracas. He cursed, cried, and told Doc he would call his lawyer. Doc and Bear were showered with abuse from him, along with a healthy sprinkling of threats and bloody spit from his newly broken teeth. Doc tried to get a little information concerning who they were and what the hell they were doing there in the first place. He got little in return, although he noticed that the threats were always plural: "We'll get you; you'll wish you hadn't fucked with us." Doc realized he'd gotten all he could from the asshole and was glad when the paramedics loaded him onto a gurney and pushed him rather roughly out the door, down the steps, and across the lumpy gravel drive. The man howled like a beaten dog with every bump of the gurney, a sound that made Doc smile.

The police interviewed Doc, Bear, and Jeanette separately, but got the same basic story—break in, robbery, assault, and finally the arrival of the cavalry in the form of the two bikers. Jeanette played the damsel in distress to perfection. The police had little reason to suspect them; the local police had never had any trouble with Jeanette or her friends before, although the police department knew the faded rumors of her remote crime and prison time. Doc smiled as he saw the gangly deputy go from an inane wanderer on Belle Fourche's dusty back roads to a trouble-sniffing law enforcement officer who'd somehow sensed trouble and had come prowling.

Doc was satisfied with the turn of events, although he was very worried about Jeanette. She, in turn, was worried about the angry gash down Doc's flank, although she agreed it didn't look too deep. Doc let her wash it and apply an antibiotic ointment, which stung like fire.

"Damn, that shit burns, Jeanette! Bear, get me another beer, I'll just have to drown the pain with alcohol." His downplay of his injury was pretty much wasted on Jeanette. Bear stood over them like a worried mother hen.

"That looks bad, Doc. I reckon it needs some stitches or somethin'. How about I drive you over to the Urgent Care Center in Jeanette's truck? They'll fix you up." He didn't sound too convinced when he considered that Doc was an experienced ER doctor who'd been doing this kind of care for a long time. Instead, he let Doc instruct him on how to apply adhesive dressing to pull the edges of the angry wound together. Finally, he was satisfied that his two favorite people in the world were bandaged adequately, and he went to grill the steaks that had been sitting in his saddlebags for the last three hours. "Let's eat, and then we can talk this over. Especially this new shit, huh?" He disappeared in the evening air, confident that the late summer light would last long enough for him to prepare supper.

Jeanette and Doc sat at her kitchen table drinking beer and holding the cold cans to their respective wounds. Doc kept the fresh cold beer in his right hand, which was sore from the blow he'd dealt to one of the villain's bellies during the melee.

"Damn, I must be getting old; my fist hurts like hell where I hit that guy in the belly," Doc lamented.

"Bear says they were wearing body armor under their outer clothes, something I find very odd," replied Jeanette. After a brief silence, she said, "I've got to tell you all the awful things they said, Doc. I'll repeat it all for Bear when he's done cooking." She glanced through the open door, hanging loosely on its broken hinges, out to her rusty grill where Bear was cooking steaks and vegetables—Bear-style. She didn't know what concoction of spices and herbs he used, but the food always turned out delicious. He once told her he used an old family recipe, once that he'd just made up the mixture on the spot, and another time that it was something he'd learned in culinary school. She didn't know if she should believe one, two, or all of his stories. It didn't really matter. Like many of Indian blood, she was fully capable of believing multiple contradicting truths simultaneously, something pale eyes were unable to achieve.

"There seemed to be a leader, his lieutenant, and four muscle-bound oafs," started Jeanette. I was in the kitchen, cleaning up, when the door crashed in, less than five minutes after you left. The boss—they called him 'Booster'—kept asking questions while the tall, blonde man held me. I heard Booster refer to him as 'Fist.' What an ugly name, although he didn't hit me, only Booster did. The other guys kind of stood around, as back-up, I guess, until they started knocking over my stuff. I never heard them say any other names, just 'Booster' and 'Fist.' Doc—she paused. "They kept asking where you'd gone and where you'd left 'the papers.' I think they were looking for the memory stick with all the information on it. I was afraid they'd see me looking at it. The damn thing was right in front of me in the computer, and I was afraid they'd realize that they'd found it, and then they wouldn't need me anymore. I was afraid they'd kill me, I really was. Oh, Doc, those guys would have killed us both—"

She hid her face in Doc's shoulder as he moved closer and wrapped his arms tenderly around her. She cried for a few minutes. The only other noise was Bear's voice coming through the doorjamb as he sang some vaguely obscene song, out of tune, at the grill. Doc didn't say anything. He didn't feel he needed to. She was free to continue talking out the recent trauma, as he knew she must before she could move beyond it. He kissed her cheek tenderly, where the swelling and bruising continued to increase.

"They said someone had sent them after you! Booster said that after they finished with me he was going to find you when you weren't with Bear and kill you. That horrible-smelling Fist sneered and said, 'Slit his fucking throat.' Doc, I think they'd do it, too! They seemed intimidated by you, but terrified of confronting Bear. I think Noel sent them after you. I know it's crazy. I don't have any proof, but I know it! He wants you dead!"

Doc sat back a minute and looked into her deep, dark, red-rimmed eyes. He saw the tears and the fear there—fear for him, and Bear, and herself. He was sad because harm had come to Jeanette through him.

Intense regret and dull red anger flooded through him. He had Jeanette to thank for her courage and refusal to give in to the bastards and tell them what they wanted to know. It would have been very easy to give up that tiny, insignificant memory stick, but he knew that the wonderful, beautiful, bruised woman sitting in front of him was fighting for the Lassiters and Jake Epstein as hard as he was.

30

Sunset

Bear easily re-established his reputation as a chef with tonight's offering. Doc was surprised to find Japanese flavor to the vegetables when he knew that they'd only bought mundane, US-of-A spices. The South Dakota beef was succulent, although Jeanette passed on it because of her swollen jaw. Doc provided her with a few choice prescription medications from his tool bag. She seemed a little sleepy from these and her stressful day, but her faculties were fully engaged as they discussed what Bear had dubbed "The Battle of Belle Fourche." Bear placed the steaming food on the kitchen table as he mumbled snatches of verse about the melee like some medieval minstrel composing an epic song for future generations.

Doc's appetite was increased by the violence. He ate heartily, as though he was preparing himself for the next struggle. In a way, he was. He agreed that Noel was probably behind the attack. He prayed to whatever gods would listen, thanking them that Jeanette had not received worse injuries. She seemed to be handling the violence well, but they both knew it wasn't over. The roiling cloud of brutality may pass from Belle Fourche, but Doc knew it would follow Noel like a foul smell following a grave-robbing ghoul.

Bear was almost pensive as he cleared mounds of beef and vegetables from his plate. He smacked his lips as he drained yet another beer fetched from Jeanette's laboring refrigerator. "What's our next move, Doc? Why is this pecker still here in Sturgis? Do you think he's waiting to kill someone else or for some dope deal? If he is, we have to follow him. He won't be stupid, an' I doubt he'll be ignorant enough to pass drugs right in Sturgis; there are too many cops around, ya know?" He was the only person Doc knew that could shovel in such a huge mouthful of food and talk without making a mess. Not many things bothered Doc, but he hated watching people eat with their mouths open, spilling food as they chewed or talked.

"Well, we've got to catch Noel with his hand in the cookie jar, Bear, that's for sure. If we don't, there's no way we can get the police involved. We just don't know Noel's next move. What do you think, Jeanette?"

Jeanette thought for a moment before speaking. "I think you're right, Doc. Either we figure out what he's up to, or we tail him and catch him red-handed. It'll be hard to shadow him out here; there isn't much to hide behind if you're trailing him across the prairie. On the other hand, if we—"

Jeanette stopped mid-sentence and held her head at a slight angle as though listening intently. "Do you hear that? It's the third time I've heard a cell phone ringing. Does it belong to one of you two, or is it out on your bike?"

Doc and Bear looked at each other as they pulled out their phones to confirm it wasn't theirs. Doc stood and wandered over to the entrance to Jeanette's workroom. He paused, listening for a moment and then shot forward, moving aside some of the debris from the earlier altercation. He leaned down in the dark, and when he stood again, he had a cell phone in his hand. He looked at it quizzically, and then answered it.

"Yeah," he said, trying to make his voice non-descript.

"God damn you, Booster! Where the hell have you been? Did you locate that reprobate Lovejoy? Where are the papers I instructed you to acquire? I've been waiting all day for you to report! I don't have time to wait for the likes of you and your motley crew!"

Doc stood motionless. He had recognized Noel's voice instantly, but didn't know what to say in return. "Uh, not yet," he stammered. He tried desperately to remember what Booster's voice sounded like. He had only heard him utter the threat to Jeanette before knocking several teeth down his throat, changing his voice considerably.

"Why in Heaven's name haven't you accomplished a simple task? You said you had located him in Belle Fourche. What is he doing there, and who is he with? Do they have the documents I need? You have my permission to kill them all if you find it necessary. What is the current situation?"

Doc couldn't just answer in one-word sentences, so he tried the old trick of scratching his fingernail across the mouthpiece while talking indistinctly. "Sorry, bad connection." He crossed his fingers internally, hoping Noel would fall it for at least a little while.

"What do you mean? If you can't find the papers, at least do some major damage to Lovejoy. I need you back here by morning if we are to keep that appointment tomorrow afternoon. I don't feel comfortable making that long a trip with that much money and merchandise on my own. You are being paid to provide specific services, and I expect you to fulfill your end of the bargain! Now, what is going on?" Noel was shouting on his end of the connection, partly to improve reception at Doc's end of the "poor signal," and partly because he was furious. How in the world could he run a business when the quality of the help was so bad? His drug-dealing acquaintance had sworn that this group of biker trash could at least take orders. Noel didn't think he could rely on these lowlifes. Unfortunately, he was forced to do just that. "Booster, report now!"

Doc didn't think the silent approach had much more to offer. He took a deep breath and used his usual voice. "Hello, Noel. This is Lovejoy." Pause. "I know what you are up to, and I'm going to see to it that you fail." That, thought Doc, is what you call the direct approach.

At the other end of the connection, Noel nearly dropped the phone as if a living, writhing viper had bitten him. His mouth hung open and he tasted the bitterness of his own evil bile. He couldn't believe it. It couldn't be Lovejoy, it just couldn't! He'd almost had him and the documents that fool Lassiter had brought. Almost! He willed himself to be calmer and decided against hanging up the phone at once. He forced his words out through teeth clenched so tight Noel was afraid they'd shatter.

"Lovejoy, you haven't the faintest idea of what is transpiring, but I can promise that you will die. I'll see to it if it's the last thing I do. I swear it."

"Don't make promises you can't keep, Noel," Doc continued in his slow, quiet voice. It seemed to infuriate Noel. "Just because you murdered Jake and Todd and Tracie, don't think I'll be easy. I'm not. I'm a lot different from them, and I'm going to be your worst fucking nightmare. Today you made the worst mistake of you life, you bastard. You hurt a kind, gentle lady, and now I'm out for revenge. And revenge is going to be very, very sweet, my friend. "

Before Noel could respond, Doc hung up. He thought what he just said would inflame Noel so much that he'd overplay his hand, make a mistake and suffer for it.

Doc returned to the kitchen, where Jeanette and Bear were beginning to wonder at his disappearance. He sat back down and tossed Booster's cell phone onto the table, where it rolled a few times before coming to rest between the empty plates and Bear's drained beer cans.

"Whose phone is that, Doc?" Jeanette asked, although she thought she already knew the answer. She'd not heard the muted conversation in the next room, but she suspected Noel had been involved. In her heart, she sensed that Noel was aware of them; he seemed to be ahead of them at every step. Noel now knew they were onto him and had Todd's extortion documents. Noel wanted the documents, and he wanted them dead. Very badly. In her mind, she was reminded of how Sauron, JRR Tolkien's Dark Lord, searched for his ring of power with a never-sleeping eye. It gave her the creeps, and a shaking chill passed over her. She reached out to the phone, but stopped with her hand hovering over it, as though she could feel the bad vibes. She withdrew her hand.

"It's Booster's. It must have fallen from his pocket during the struggle and slid under some of the wreckage. That sound was the phone Noel calling him repeatedly. He had some irritating custom ring programmed into it." He paused for Bear and Jeanette to absorb what he was saying. "At first, Noel thought it was Booster on the line, so he ranted and raved. You were right, Jeanette; he wants those documents, which he still thinks are on paper. He doesn't know about that little memory stick. Noel hired those guys to come after me and get the papers he supposed Todd gave me. He had pretty much given them free rein and suggested they kill me."

Jeanette inhaled sharply. "I knew it; I just knew it. This guy is evil incarnate!"

"He has something planned for tomorrow. Noel wants Booster and his buddies to go with him to some rendezvous. It sounded like he wants them for physical back-up," Doc continued.

"I bet it's a drug deal!" Bear shouted. "That rat is usin' a beautiful place like the Black Hills for his rotten deals! It's probably cocaine, I bet! An' ya know what? I bet me an' Doc'll be there to fuck it up for him! Won't we, Doc?"

Doc looked thoughtful for a moment and spoke slowly "We need to do that, all right, Bear. But I don't think we can count on any help from the law; they don't trust us on the best of days. Noel comes across as Mr. Clean when he talks to the police. Look at how he shifted suspicion to me about Todd's accident, and even Tracie. This one we'll pretty much have to do on our own."

"Yeah, we gotta be creative an' stuff," Bear mumbled. "I can think of at least ten ways I'd like to rearrange that creep's face."

Jeanette wondered, aloud, "What can we do if Noel gets those guys out of jail? I'm sure they'll call him, and he'll make their bail—possibly by morning. What are we going to do, Doc?"

"Well, here's my plan—" Doc began.

31

WATCHING THE RAT HOLE

An exhausted Doc left Belle Fourche on his comfortable old Wide Glide by eight PM, as the sun was only a red-orange memory in the west. He headed back down I-90 to the Buffalo Chip. He stopped long enough in Sturgis to call Erin and fill her in on what had happened during the long, tiring day. He told her briefly about the interview with the highway patrol. He described the "Battle of Belle Fourche" but he skipped his own injury. She thought he and Bear sounded very brave fighting what she called "Noel's Army," but Erin could tell he was very upset by his friend, Jeanette, being injured. Twinges of jealousy gripped Erin's heart for several beats when Doc spoke of Jeanette with such feeling. She didn't know Jeanette, and she reminded herself that she'd just met the man, and certainly didn't own him. She wasn't surprised to hear that Noel was dealing drugs, but she hadn't expected him to go to such extremes. From what Doc had to say, he had developed a deep hatred for Noel, even if he didn't say so.

When Doc asked Erin to meet him, she readily agreed to come up to the Buffalo Chip in Jim's pick-up and stay with Doc while he kept an eye on Noel. He offered to let her get some sleep and meet him in the morning, but she jumped at the chance to meet that evening. Doc couldn't guess that she'd sing in the shower and smile the whole way up I-90. Maybe it was better he didn't know. His habit of paying total attention to a woman when he was with her, listening to what she had to say, and ensuring that she enjoyed their lovemaking as much as he did was having its usual effect.

Doc entered the Chip through the steel gate and cruised discreetly past Noel's trailer. He saw Noel's Big Dog Mastiff parked in front. He didn't actually see Noel, but the lights were on inside, and he assumed Noel was present. He hurried to the line of vendors along the western edge of the amphitheater area where the first band had just ended its set and people were milling around.

Death in Sturgis

It was a hot night, and people were enjoying the cool spray of water coming off the overpass at the entrance to the area. Women took full advantage of the situation by exposing their breasts as they passed through the refreshing spray, to the delight of the crowd. Many of these same women would compete in the Buffalo Chip's renowned weenie bite and pickle-licking contests. Doc always thought that anyone who needed a detailed description of these contests was either woefully undersexed, or didn't understand the things that could be done on a slowly moving motorcycle by properly motivated, consenting adults. He still had a scar on the inside of his right calf from a hot exhaust pipe while attempting an unusual sexual position in his youth. He still enjoyed the unusual, but tried to be a little more careful at it and seldom tried positions he couldn't handle as he looked at his early fifties.

Doc located the vendor he wanted, remembered from his previous walk through the area. From among various biker gear and camping equipment on display, Doc selected a pair of Nikon Sporter 10x36 binoculars. There were a few more expensive models available, but Doc felt these would be sufficient. The power of the binoculars, ten, in this case, described magnification, so that an object would appear ten times larger than it would to the unaided, naked eye. However, the more one magnified an image, the less light actually got through to the eye. The second value, thirty-six, indicated the diameter of the front, or objective, lens in millimeters. Therefore, the larger the front lens, the more light got in and the better visualization at lower light levels. The Sporter, Doc knew, used a roof-prism design that made it smaller and lighter, something of value on a motorcycle or if you just happened to be following someone discreetly. A single focusing knob and twist out eyepieces were useful for the same reasons. It had a field of view of about three hundred feet at a thousand yards, meaning that when looking at something or someone approximately a thousand yards away, objects within three hundred feet of each other could be kept in focus at once. The Sporter also featured anti-reflective coatings that were a good idea in the bright Dakota sun.

Although Doc already had a knife in his pocket, he bought a good, cheap buck knife that he thought might come in handy over the next day or two. It was sharpened and honed to a razor's edge by the vendor's wife, who looked bored with the whole experience. She had the aura of a woman who traveled endlessly from bike show to bike show and was thoroughly tired of life. Sad, he thought. When there are only so many days for each of us, it was a shame not to savor and appreciate each one. Not a sentimental type, Doc still felt that in some mysterious but wonderful way, everyday was Thanksgiving. He thanked her, told her she looked beautiful, and wandered off to the beer stand. Even with the crap of the last few days, he was glad to be alive and thirsty.

Doc sat at a small table, drank cold beer, and tried out the new binoculars, watching the roadies set up for the next show. Doc had worked as a roadie in his teens, and still remembered the sweaty, backbreaking work done in the dark with impatient musicians and fans on either side. He had fit in beautifully with his black clothes and strong work ethic, but he tired quickly of the prima donnas prancing about on the stage while bitching and whining to the sound crew and roadies. He'd learned some good lessons from the job, but he was not at all eager to repeat it.

Erin arrived four beers later, when the headliner band was starting. Another classic band from the seventies and eighties, Doc vaguely remembered. He had no doubt of the band's fame and quality (they were at the Chip, weren't they?), but there were parts of the seventies he just didn't remember that well. Drugs, alcohol, early dementia, or using his remaining brain cells for something more important, he figured. Many things blurred together for Doc, while others retained crystal clarity years and years later. Doc easily recalled their opening song playing on some tinny radio. No doubt, he'd heard it while smoking a joint or fooling around in the back seat of some long-forgotten car. He smiled, although he couldn't have told you the name of the band or song. In fact, probably only one person performing on stage tonight had actually been in the classic group. Doc laughed softly when he remembered a cartoon that proclaimed that only the guitars and drum set were from the original band.

Doc predicted that Noel would not likely be leaving for his appointment anytime soon. He and Erin eventually relaxed somewhat, but they occasionally returned to a small rise from which he could observe Noel's trailer while remaining invisible. The bike was still parked in front of the trailer, as he could plainly see with the binoculars.

Erin found it extremely funny when a large, beefy man with a red face came huffing and puffing from his RV wearing only his boxers. With loud wheezing voice, he accused Doc of using the field glasses to observe him and his wife having sex. Doc denied it and apologized profusely amid some drunken stumbling from side to side. He only found it humorous when the man's wife came to the door wearing a small towel to cover her 300+ pounds of sweet love. He smiled and waved half-heartedly, while Erin convinced the man of their innocence. Finally mollified, he agreed to share some cold beers with them before the rally ended, and they parted as new friends.

At last, he felt sure that Noel was going to stay put for the night. Doc took Erin back to his tent and put a last call in to Bear and Jeanette for a final bit of reassurance. "Hey, Bear; it's me. Noel is holed up for the night. Everything going all right up there? How's Jeanette?"

Bear replied, "Jes fine, Doc. Jes' fine. We had another big meal, or at least I did, and I'm ready to go to bed now. Jeanette's already in her room, asleep. She didn't even have the heart to clean up that workroom o' hers. It's sorta like her art is her kids or somethin'. Anyway, I hope that little ole couch of hers can hold me up. Are you sure you still want to go through with your plan? I think you're askin' fer trouble, but then, you always say to expect the worst an' hope for the best."

"I don't see any problem, Bear. Erin will be there by eight in the morning or so, and then you can come down this way. That way we'll be able to follow Noel while I feel safe about Jeanette. There's not much chance of those creeps bothering her again, but something tells me we should cover all our bases. I figure Noel is laying in his trailer thinking of a thousand different scenarios, and we should try to be prepared for as many of them as we can, that's all."

"Don' you figure it's like mixin' fire an' gasoline to put them two women together? I think yer crazy, myself!"

"Why? They're both good, strong women. Let's just wait and see, okay? Call me in the morning when you're about ready to leave Jeanette's."

"Yeah, okay. I'll light out of here jes' as fast as I can, once those two females get together. I don't even want to be around. I've seen 'em look at you, Doc, an' I bet there's goin' to be an explosion!"

"Good night, Bear. Erin says good night, too," Doc closed as Erin was kissing his neck and beginning to take off his shirt.

"Yeah, I bet she does. I bet goin' to sleep's the last thing on that little girl's mind right now. See ya in the mornin'." Bear chuckled and hung up.

Erin looked into Doc's eyes and smiled a slightly drunken smile that came close to matching Doc's exhausted one. They had both enjoyed a number of tequila shots and cold beer after deciding the rat would stay in his hole for the night. Doc wanted to get up early for the evil day he expected. Erin, however, eagerly anticipated a little exercise with Doc before sleep. He helped remove his shirt, moving very stiffly on his injured right side. As he slipped the shirt to the ground, she stopped abruptly.

"Oh, my God, Doc!" she shouted when she saw the bandages on his right flank. The dried, crusted blood appeared black in the dim light of the little tent. Doc had intentionally kept the lantern a little on the dim side so the bandage and wound would not frighten her. He had, it seemed, failed miserably. "What in the world happened to you? I mean, you said you guys were in a fight, but you never said you got hurt. Oh, my God! My sweet, sweet baby!"

Erin switched speedily from shocked-girl mode into concerned, healing, mother mode. She lost the horny, sultry look in her eyes and changed to a more professional, clinical persona. As she began to take down the dressing, she explained about working in the emergency vet office for several years before moving to grooming full time. Doc said he felt much better knowing she had experience in caring for stricken Chihuahuas. She frowned, knowing that he would use humor to cover up pain as well as the seriousness of his wound. Biting her lip, she used a bit of beer from her half-full can to soak the areas where Doc's clotted blood had converted the cotton bandage into what felt like a piece of iron. Doc moaned softly and told her a bit more detail of the fight. In his version, he had stood there gaping while Bear single-handedly fought western South Dakota to a standstill. Initially, he did not mention the fracture/dislocation he had inflicted on Booster, although he did admit to stopping him from hitting Jeanette. Erin was sure he was playing down the violence of the day as well as his involvement. As she worked, she got most of the details from him. She realized Doc was fully a match for the devil she envisioned when she heard the name Noel.

Doc told Erin of his worry that Noel would make bail for the four ambulatory members of the group and that they would return to Jeanette's looking for documentation of Noels crimes. He thought that Jeanette being in the house alone would be a bad idea. Jeanette was a strong woman, but her strength radiated from within and gave her little protection from physical violence. He did not think she would tolerate another round with these thugs. Erin would be good company for the next day or so, Doc explained.

Once the new bandage was in place, Erin lay him down and began to rub his back. After a pause during which she was afraid he was falling asleep, she burst out, "Oh, Doc, you could've been killed! This guy is a real bastard! What are you going to do with him?"

"Well, we'll follow him tomorrow because I think he has a big dope deal going down. If we can't break that up, then at least we can follow either the dope or the money. I figure one of these will lead us to the bottom of things. Then, if we can't get the police to pick up Noel based on what we have now, at least we can get enough hard evidence to get them to pay attention. But I'll be honest with you, Erin. I don't just want him to go to jail for what he's done. I want him to pay for hurting people. Pay for killing Jake and Todd and Tracie. Pay for hurting Jeanette. Pay for all those whose lives he's ruined with his cocaine. I want him to suffer as they have. And if I can help that happen before the cops take him away, if they take him away, so much the better."

He stopped talking, and she looked into his eyes. Usually they were bright blue. Now she thought they looked as black as a cavern. She saw none of the joy or happiness often dancing in his eyes when he was with her. That had been replaced with wanting justice for those who had been wronged and would never speak for themselves again. She nodded and laid her head on his chest, listening to his quiet, regular breathing. She was sure they'd make love tonight, but right now, all she wanted to do was touch him, hold him, and be near this complicated, intense man.

32

ON THE TRAIL

FRIDAY

Doc groaned as his alarm went off at seven. He was worn out from the day before, his right flank wound burned, he was hung over, he'd made love with Erin for over two hours, and he just wanted to roll over and pass out again. Erin was nestled closely at his side, wrapped in the meager cover provided by his sleeping gear. She felt warm and secure in his arms. She murmured softly when the alarm sounded and moved further under the blanket, away from the cool morning air. A light drizzle had fallen from four until five, dropping the temperature and making the warm sleeping bag and even warmer girl all the more attractive.

Already, bikers were moving about the Chip and starting their rides. Some would ride south into the Badlands, some west into the Black Hills. Others would stay at the Chip all day and just wanted to hear the reassuring rumble of their beloved Harleys. Doc drained his bladder and returned to the tent, where Erin was having no trouble sleeping through the rising noise. He smiled and woke her by gently rubbing her back. She half-opened her eyes and took his hand in hers, guiding it into the depths of the sleeping bag, against her smooth, young skin. He was immediately aroused but able to encourage the big head to win out over the little head by thinking of what Noel had done to Jeanette and the others. A fire began to burn in his heart and behind his eyes. His hand stopped the firm, repetitive movements it had begun on Erin's receptive body, and he withdrew it into the morning chill. She began to complain, but on seeing the look in his eyes, she gave him a quick kiss and began to dress, as well. He brushed his teeth outside the tent, brushed his hair, and pulled it into a ponytail, then turned to find Erin coming out through the tent opening. She came to him and settled into his arms. He held her tightly for a moment and whispered into her ear.

"Morning, darlin'. It's going to be a long, long day. Are you ready? If not, you can go back down to Tilford, no questions asked."

"Oh, Doc. I'll do whatever you want. You know that. We can't let that bastard get away with what he's done. It's up to us to do our best to stop him, right? I mean, it's the right thing to do, you know?" She looked up at him, her lips moist, but set.

"I couldn't put it better myself, Erin. Some things are just bigger than we are. They demand our attention. I'd rather be out drinking, riding, and making love to you, but right now, there's something I have to do. In the old movies, they'd say that the problems of two little people didn't add up to a hill of beans. I guess now those beans are worth a pretty penny, but the sentiment's the same, even after all these years. I'll go take a quick look at our rat while you get yourself ready, okay?" he asked, already knowing the answer. She nodded, and he walked over the low hill beyond the creek to check out Noel's trailer. The Big Dog Mastiff was still there, but the door to the trailer was open, and Noel was moving about. Doc hurried back to Erin.

"Shit, darlin'! He's getting ready to move! We'd better get ready, too. Put your stuff together and drive to that address I gave you. Remember the directions?"

"Sure, Doc. Just head up I-90 to Spearfish, go north on US-85 and follow the side roads to Jeanette's. I'll make it, and we'll be fine, you'll see. But, Doc—"

"Yeah, darlin'? Something the matter?"

"No, well, yeah. I mean, please, please be careful. I know you will, and I know Bear will go with you, but you know, be extra careful, you know, for my sake—" she had trouble completing the sentence and turned so he wouldn't see the tears in her eyes. She had no idea how she could feel so much for a man she'd known for such a short time. She didn't want him to see her this way. Jeanette was strong, she knew. She tried to be strong, too.

Doc smiled gently and kissed her softly on the lips. "I will. I'll be real cautious every step of the way. We'll get together again tonight when it's all over, okay? You and Jeanette take care of each other today. Get to know her; she's a fantastic lady. I'll call to check in with you when I get the chance. Remember what I said, and watch your ass. Don't trust anyone."

"Don't worry about us. Girls can take care of each other, you'll see. And this girl can take care of herself! I'll-I'll see you then," she said, as she climbed into the pick-up and started its engine. She blew Doc a kiss and drove off as he waved. Doc quickly finished getting dressed and rode to the amphitheater area where he bought a number of bottled waters. He didn't know where today would take him, and he didn't want to end up high and dry. Even though it was cool this morning after the rain, it could still be a scorcher by afternoon. He waited off to the side near the Sons of Light Ministry's free pancakes. He grabbed some juice from them and made his usual small donation. After a minute, he tossed in another couple of dollars. Doc figured he needed all the help he could get today!

The wait was a little longer than he'd expected. Around nine, Noel pulled through the area looking neither right nor left. He cut off a couple on a Road King as he cruised back out the steel gate, earning himself two middle fingers, one from each of them. Doc merely shook his head, pulled on his sunglasses and pulled out onto the access road, being careful to keep well behind Noel. With the amount of motorcycle traffic this close to Sturgis, it would easy to tail Noel without being seen. Once he saw which way Noel was headed, he'd give Bear a call and direct him to meet them. If he were heading up I-90 toward Spearfish, he'd tell Bear to sit tight. Bear would have to haul ass to get back down this way if Noel headed south. So far, it was a wait-and-see game.

Noel headed into Sturgis and passed through without a glance at the excitement beginning to build. He entered I-90 and headed north. Bear's phone call would have to wait. Doc followed about a quarter of a mile behind Noel, changing lanes and sometimes riding with others to maintain anonymity. Where could the bastard be headed?

Doc raised his eyebrows even more as Noel exited at Spearfish and headed north toward Belle Fourche. As he continued north, Doc began to suspect that he was going to Jeanette's studio, although he felt relieved when he thought of Noel knocking on the door only to have Bear open it! What a surprise that would be for the miserable prick! Instead, Noel continued on past Snoma Road, which led east to Jeanette. For a moment or two, Doc was puzzled when Noel stopped on Eighth Street and entered the police station. The guy has balls, he admitted. Doc didn't know if he was holding or just had drug money with him, but he was walking into the building as bold as hell.

Doc phoned Bear. "Get over to the police station. I think Noel is bailing out his pals. We'll follow their asses!" He whispered, even though Noel was in the building and couldn't possibly hear him. Shit, he thought, I'm starting to think he's some sort of vampire or something. Doc waited two streets down, trying not to look suspicious.

Fortunately, there were a lot of longhaired bikers in the little town, so he was safe on that account.

Before Bear could arrive, Noel walked out the front door alone. He went to his ride and waited, pacing on the sidewalk. Fifteen minutes later, from around the corner, came four men on their motorcycles, free as birds and irritable as hell from their overnight visit with the authorities. They stopped at the corner long enough to take orders from Noel. Two rode off to the south along Eighth Street, and the other two went west with Noel.

Shit, thought Doc, they've split up! He had a number of alternatives. He could follow Noel and get to the dope deal he anticipated, but he didn't know where it was going to happen, and Noel might spot him. He could wait for Bear, and then try to follow Noel, although his head start might be too big, and then Doc would lose the trail. Alternatively, he could follow the two that were heading south. God, he hoped they weren't heading back to Jeanette's. Since Bear wasn't even here yet, he could try to follow Noel while Bear followed the other two. Crap, too many possibilities, and not one stood out as the best choice! Finally, Doc decided to play his hunch and pulled out, heading west just as Noel stopped at a traffic light two blocks away. He followed Noel and hoped to see Bear as he passed.

Luck was with Doc as Bear passed the two riders heading south. In their eagerness for whatever chore Noel had assigned them, they did not recognize Bear. He would have turned and followed them if he hadn't seen Doc a hundred yards farther north, still near the police station. With a roar of his engine and a burst of speed, Bear caught up with Doc just as he turned west. The light changed two blocks away, and Noel turned south onto US-85.

Together, Doc and Bear followed Noel south for a little over a mile, until Noel and his accomplices turned west on State Road 34. Doc looked at Bear beside him and shrugged his shoulders. He had no idea where they were headed, but he was worried about the other two who'd turned off back in Belle Fourche. He dearly wished he'd had time to call Jeanette and warn her. But he wasn't sure that was where they were headed anyway, and he knew Erin would be there soon, if she wasn't there already. His heart was sick with worry, but he had to devote his concentration on the pursuit if he was to have any chance at success. He shook his head to clear it and squinted into the western sky.

The sun was behind him, and it was a truly beautiful South Dakota morning, just a little after eleven. It was going to be a gorgeous, if sizzling day. Actually, Doc liked it that way. Rain would make their hunt difficult, if not impossible, and make them miserable. A really hot day would keep Noel moving, he hoped, and get this cat-and-mouse game over with as soon as possible. Sometimes the wind picked up so much on these scorchers that it was like riding through a sandstorm. Visibility would be zero, and the sharp grains of dust would strike exposed skin like a million tiny knives, all doing their best to get around your glasses and into your eyes. Doc swore these storms had minds of their own. Sometimes Mother Nature smiled down on you and made being out on a ride a truly wonderful thing; other times, the bitch did everything she could to make each second unpleasant.

There was little traffic on the little two-lane road this time of morning, other than semi's and farm trucks. They followed Noel from about a half-mile back, straining their eyes to keep him in view. After about eight miles, Noel showed no signs of slowing at the state line, where the road changed to Wyoming 24. Like western South Dakota, this area consisted of undulating hills and small rock outcroppings where range-fed cattle roamed, chewed their cud, and looked stupid.

The day was beginning to warm, and Doc loosened his jacket zipper with his left hand while he kept the throttle steady with the right. He looked around at the breath-taking terrain, carved by seasonal creeks that were dry and dusty in the late summer heat. Doc's mind tried to absorb the history and immensity of all he saw. In another time, Lakota boys chased each other on quick ponies over these same rises. Their world was beautiful, yet harsh, innocent, yet soulful. They knew fear, anger, and love just as Doc did. They valued humility, bravery, and perseverance as sacred. Now, Doc feared, today's youth cared more about their video games, rap artists, and baggy pants than any ideals to make them better men, proud to be a part of their world and people.

Doc smiled as he remembered a tirade he'd read once about the failings of youth. The author ranted about the lack of respect, appreciation, and their desire for fun, fun, fun at the expense of becoming responsible adults. In some ways, he agreed with what the writer had said, but was properly chagrined when he learned that the author was the famous Greek philosopher, Aristotle, more than 2000 years ago. Doc's mind tended to ponder such things as he rode, and he forced himself to pay closer attention to keeping Noel in sight, but not crowding him.

The three bikes ahead of them rode on along Hay Creek, crossing it and re-crossing it with the miles. They passed through the small town of Aladdin with its two small side streets and one fine bar, the Stone House. Any other day, Doc would have made it a point to stop in for a few icy cold beers. Unfortunately, Noel continued west, past Route 111, which would have taken them back south to I-90. Bewildered, Doc and Bear rode on. They covered another fifteen or so miles, passing through another scenic small town, Alva. Noel stopped briefly at a small 'Quickie Mart' for gas. Doc and Bear pulled to the side of the rode and watched Noel through the binoculars. They waited before following him again. Still, Noel rode on into the west.

Ahead lay Hulett, Wyoming, infamous for its 'No Panty Day' every year during the Sturgis rally. That awe-inspiring event took place on Wednesday of the rally week. Although the Wyoming state troopers cracked down on speeding or motorcycle horseplay, the long lines and congestion made the whole area a massive traffic jam on Wednesday. With so many people and so many boys in blue, there was very little nudity anymore. Any woman who cared to share a little look at some flesh was immediately surrounded by dozens of horny guys with their cameras, shoving, and jostling to see something racy. Such groups always reminded Doc of a bunch of teenagers who'd never seen boobs or a pussy before and were about to beat each other over the head for a chance to photograph it. Do what you want, he thought, but their behavior sickened him and cheapened nudity by taking a hundred digital photos to drool over with the other immature boys back home. Or to use as ammunition the next time the boy-man was whacking off. Whatever. Today, there would still be plenty of riders around, but nowhere near as many as two days earlier.

Just beyond Hulett, Route 112 led north to Alzada, where Todd had enjoyed his last meal of bull balls and beer. Noel ignored it and continued west on Route 24. Now Doc knew where he was headed. He was somewhat saddened by the thought of the beautiful region ahead being used for drug dealing. It, too, had been sacred to many Indian tribes, and Doc felt Noel was defacing it much as the white man's civilization and its blatant lies had defaced the Black Hills themselves.

Any minute now, they'd start getting glimpses of one of the most awe-inspiring geologic formations Doc had ever seen. In his mind, it ranked with Yellowstone and the Grand Canyon. It played a sacred role in the religions of many of native peoples of the region, as well. Soon, quick peeks between hills and over the intervening ridges would reveal the climax of *Close Encounters of the Third Kind*—the Devil's Tower.

33

The Devil's Tower

Many, many seasons ago, a Kiowa family lived in the north. There were seven sisters and one little boy in this family. The boy was, like all little boys, quite rambunctious. He played tricks on his sisters and often chased them in the woods where they lived. One day, he pretended he was a bear and chased them, growling and roaring and holding his hands up in the air like paws. On this day, he was so convincing that he actually began to turn into a bear. He grew larger, meaner, and very hairy, just like a real bear. His sisters became very afraid and climbed onto a large rock for safety. The bear that was a boy became bigger and bigger. The girls cried and prayed loudly to the Great Spirit to save them. Hearing their prayer, the Great Spirit caused the rock to rise higher and higher. As it grew into a mountain, the bear became very angry and scratched its sides with his claws. Long, ragged lines formed from the claw marks up and down the mountain that formed in front of him. The girls were still afraid and cried even more. Finally, the Great Spirit felt pity for them. He saved them by turning them into seven stars and put them into the night sky as the Pleiades. They can still be seen rising near dawn at the beginning of the planting time and setting near dawn at the time of the harvest.

This was a version of the Kiowa legend that explained Devil's Tower. Doc felt that in its way, it made every bit as much sense as the white man's explanation of plate tectonics, magma, and prismatic crystallization. Like many ancient people who lived close to the earth and its seasons, origin stories were not meant to give the specific details of how something happened or what someone did. They were meant to teach physical, cultural, and psychological lessons as well as answer questions beyond the technology of the group. Doc was reminded of the ancient Celtic legends of the Irish heroes Cu Chulainn and Finn MacCool. No actual person could have done the incredible physical feats attributed to them, but they conveyed important cultural themes from generation to generation.

Even our highly evolved, technological society wasn't completely certain what the Devil's Tower was, or how it was formed. It was reasonably sure that the surrounding area of Wyoming was sedimentary, that is, formed at the bottom of ancient seas. No volcanic rocks, ash, or lava flows are anywhere nearby. Instead, we found soft, gritty sandstone, limestone, and siltstone stained with iron oxides—rust. This gave a deep, rich, red color to many of the nearby rock outcroppings, often alternating with light green and cream layers. One thin layer is stunning, pure white gypsum, laid down around 160 million years ago. At about the same time the Black Hills were formed, magma forced its way under what is now the tower. There was evidence that this colossal mass of magma forced its way up into the surrounding sedimentary rocks. This laccolith, which is what the geologists would call it, formed deep beneath the earth's surface—up to a mile deep, in fact, and took thousands of years to cool.

Over the intervening eons, the softer sedimentary rocks had been eroded, primarily by the drainage system of the nearby Belle Fourche River. Now the harder laccolithic rocks remained, protruding some 1267 feet above the surrounding surface. Even this had eroded around its edges, creating a pile of talus at the base of the tower.

As Doc saw it, this angry, vigorous mass of hot rock raped the softer, yielding minerals above and around it, forcing its way into, and filling every possible crevice. Then, its forward movement exhausted, it stayed in place and slowly cooled. Rather than shrink away and withdraw, it crystallized into huge polygonal columns with long, vertical joint cracks. This remnant of the earth's fury retained its hardness, much more so than the surrounding rock. With the countless cycles of summer heat and winter cold, wet, and dry, the weaker rocks withered away. Slowly the more resistant tower began to emerge from the ponderosa pines and clinging grasslands. With even more years, the tower's outer edges were slowly destroyed, dropping huge columns onto the surrounding area as a memory of its previous ardor.

Indians of over twenty tribes had come to the Devil's Tower over the millennia and regarded it as a holy place. To the Arapahoe, it was the Bear's Tipi. Cheyenne legend tells that Sweet Medicine, the great hero who brought the Four Sacred Arrows of the warrior societies, tribal government, law, and ceremony to the people was buried at the

Bear's Lodge. As he lay dying, Sweet Medicine foretold of a dark and evil time when white men would come with the horse, when the buffalo would die, and the people must learn to eat slick beasts with split hooves. He told of the white man flying above the earth, taking thunder from the sky and killing the earth by digging in it and draining it of life. The Crow called it the Bear's House, or Lair, and believed it was put there by the Great Spirit and was therefore different from all other rocks. The Kiowa called it Great Lifted Rock and provided the legend of the sisters and their brother. Lakota Sioux referred to it as Mato Tipila or Bear Lodge, Ghost Mountain, and (Doc's favorite) Penis Mountain. They often camped at the tower during the winter, where they prayed, fasted, and worshipped the "Great Mystery." This was the very essence of Lakota spiritual and religious life. There was archeological evidence of sweat lodge ceremonies as late as the last century. Often shamen performed the healing ceremony at Bear Lodge. According to the Sioux, the tower is considered the birthplace of wisdom because it was here that the sacred languages and ceremonies of healing were imparted to Lakota shamen by the Great Bear, Hu Nump.

Oral legend relates that Crazy Horse, Sitting Bull, Spotted Tail, Red Cloud, and Gall, the five great Sioux leaders in the 1870s, came together to pray for guidance from the Great Spirit at the tower before the genocidal war to follow.

The Lakota Sun Dance was traditionally held at the tower near the summer solstice, June 21. This was the day with the most sunlight and the shortest night. This ceremony consisted of dancing, fasting, and sacrifice. It was held to cleanse the universe through individual and tribal purification. The Sun Dance continued being celebrated at the tower even today. Many tribes had lobbied to have the Tower declared a holy place, off-limits to climbers. Some felt this was sacrilege, an insult to the Tower. Many climbers answered that, for them, climbing was a religious experience, a spiritual act, and that the Tower should be open to climbing year-round. The National Park Service had compromised and requested a voluntary ban on climbing during the month of June, a request the majority of climbers have observed. Some have objected, claiming the Tower was a church for rock climbers, and it was unfair to 'lock them out of their church.' It's only fair to point out the irony that it was a federal offense to climb Mount Rushmore, a federally sanctified sacred monument to American expansionism. So far, lawsuits instituted by climbing enthusiasts and the Mountain States Legal Foundation have been rejected by federal judges, but that doesn't mean they won't try again. Although not a direct correlation, Doc saw a sad resemblance to the demeaning and defacing of synagogues in the 1930s that helped in the dehumanizing of the Jews before their wholesale execution in Nazi Germany in the 1940s. Didn't we ever learn?

The first report of the tower by "civilized" man occurred in 1875, when a surveying team of the US Geological Survey saw it. Another old Indian name, the Bad God's Tower, seemed most appropriate, and the white man's name of Devil's Tower came into being. July 4, 1893 saw the first official climb to the top, using wooden ladders, although the owners had probably climbed it first to verify it could be done. It became a popular tourist attraction, named the country's first national monument by President Theodore Roosevelt in 1906.

Like all of life, the Devil's Tower and the surrounding area continued to change. The forces of erosion had been modified by rerouting the Belle Fourche River in the late 1930s after it washed out the access road repeatedly. The straightened riverbed no longer meandered around the base of the tower, depositing silt year after year. In 1952, the Bureau of Reclamation authorized construction of the Keyhole Dam as a flood control and water management project, in other words, it made things easier for those who made roads and bridges as well as providing water for cattle, irrigation, and recreation. All good and upstanding ideals for those who desired to bend the earth to their will. Unfortunately, since that time, we have realized that the cottonwood and willows that make the Devil's Tower region so beautiful require yearly flooding to generate new growth. Since the dam was constructed, few new trees have grown naturally along the river. There was a plan to begin planting new trees by hand.

Alien species have been introduced to the area and spread, partially because there were fewer native plants to compete with them. Many types of thistles grew in the area; they were sprayed regularly by the National Park Service. These same folks manually removed the seed heads of another alien, Houndstongue. Beetles have been imported from Eurasia to prevent the spread of Leafy Spurge by gnawing on its roots, opening the plant to fungal attack.

One of Doc's favorite things about the Devil's Tower area was the abundance of birds, although the type of bird seen varied with the season. Being somewhat of a bird watcher, he'd seen many raptors, such as golden eagles, an occasional bald eagle, northern harriers, and

American kestrels. Hawks are frequent. He'd seen red-tail hawks, sharp-shinned hawks, Cooper's, goshawks, and rough-legged species. Water-loving birds, such as mallards, wood ducks, mergansers, Canadian geese, and great blue herons frequented the area, amazing considering how little water was available. Doc had also seen a number of woodpeckers, especially the common ones such as downy and hairy woodpeckers, although there were also redheaded woodpeckers and flickers. He once saw a great horned owl sitting in a pine above a number of Indian prayer bags. Not sure if it was real or a spirit, Doc walked quietly on down the trail. On any afternoon, one could see turkey vultures as they made their slow, faltering way along the uplifts of warmed air from the surface, their tiny heads and rocking motion making them discernible from the many hawks and eagles. A great number of birds at the Tower were common at Doc's feeders: western pewees, redwing black birds, brown-headed cowbirds, juncos, robins, chickadees, nuthatches, phoebes, Eastern kingbirds, swallows, crows, jays, crossbills, siskins, bluebirds, and wrens. A number of vireos and warblers could be found, but it was beyond Doc's meager powers to distinguish between them. Whether he could identify them by sight, song, or flight, he was glad they were there; they seemed to touch his soul. Birds had always been special to him. They lifted him up when he needed it and let him know that life was going on around him, even when he didn't necessarily feel a part of it. In many native legends, birds were messengers from the gods. Doc tried hard to listen to whatever they had to say. Night or day, summer or winter, they spoke to him.

Mammals were not seen as frequently as birds, primarily because of their more secretive habits. The careful eye and quiet foot would find the most. As the saying went, "Keep your eyes open and your mouth shut!" You could frequently find mice, voles, and wood rats. Porcupines were present at twilight and sunset. Weasels, skunks, foxes, and coyotes were also present, but seldom seen, being creatures of stealth and the night. Formerly, black bears and grizzlies could be found, as could wolves, beavers, black-footed ferrets, buffalo, and bighorn sheep. White-tailed deer and their larger cousins, the mule deer, were still commonly seen, even in the daylight.

Snapping turtles lived in the rivers and lakes, feeding on common carp, shiners, suckers, catfish, and sunfish. From time to time, Doc saw snakes, mostly bull snakes, yellow-bellied racers, garter snakes, and the more threatening prairie rattlesnake, the only snake of any danger to humans in Wyoming. Traditionally, the Sioux did not kill rattlesnakes. There was an old Brulé legend about three brothers who disobeyed the Great Spirit. In anger, they were turned into rattlesnakes, but they told their youngest brother to tell all the people that even as snakes, they would remain faithful Sioux. For this reason, they were spared whenever encountered. Doc could never comprehend many people's apparently deep-rooted fear of snakes and had a hard time understanding those who would kill any snake at any time with any means possible.

Sadly, man had also stepped in to modify nature by suppressing wild fires. Traditionally, ranchers saw all fire as "bad" unless they were tightly controlled. This made sense on their farms and ranches. However, nature didn't work that way. Periodic fires were essential to the ecology of the plains and forests. Fires removed pine needles, dead branches, and trees. This allowed new growth and fostered a diverse ecosystem. Some trees required fire—the lodge pole pinecone had such a thick layer of resin over its seeds that only a cone that had been subjected to a forest fire could spread its seeds.

Prairie fires were also needed from time to time. The removal of the buffalo, taming of the water supply, and elimination of wildfires had changed and continued to change the Great Plains. Even the buffalo droppings were essential, as were their hooves, pushing the life-giving materials deep into the soil. Thankfully, enlightened natural resource managers now utilized prescribed burns, planned ones, over the region at fifteen to thirty year intervals. In this way, they hoped to maintain wildlife diversity, and infection and drought-resistant strains. It reminded one of the intentional prairie fires set by Neolithic peoples. They knew a lot more than we gave them credit for. Maybe, Doc thought, it's not too late to keep us from killing the earth.

Normal people could be involved in abnormal events. Sometimes they rose to the occasion and displayed their finer aspects, sometimes they didn't. Likewise, our governments and institutions could also be touched by events much larger than they were or ever could be. And like individual people, governments could rise and soar like eagles, or sink and slither like snakes. Throughout the years, movies have shown this in extraordinary ways.

Doc's favorite movie of all time was *Close Encounters of the Third Time*. He saw it when it was first released in 1977, directed by Steven Spielberg, known then for his thriller movie, *Jaws*. He even went to lectures given by J. Allen Hynek, professor of astronomy at Ohio State University, chairman of the astronomy department at Northwestern University, astronomical consultant to the United States Air Force's Project Blue Book, and technical advisor to the movie.

Overshadowed that year at the box office by the first Star Wars movie, it still made its mark on movie making and on many of the people who saw it. Whether you'd seen it once or dozens of times, it remained a powerful film, going beyond the theme of earth meets the flying saucers. The film explored ordinary people exposed to and involved with a very extraordinary event—close contact with extraterrestrials. It described how duplicitous our government could be when the demigod "national security" was invoked.

The movie brought together elements often thought unrelated, and tied them together—mysterious power outages, Bermuda triangle disappearances, UFOs, and alien abductions. At the movie's climax, the aliens decided to contact humans at a beautiful, yet remote location—one filled with religious overtones as well as a huge phallic symbol, visible from miles away—the Devil's Tower. It's no wonder Doc stayed up to the wee hours to catch the movie again whenever he could.

34

Close Encounter

The morons repairing the road ahead were obviously lazy idiots who stood around with their hands on their hips while someone else did the actual work. It wasn't at all uncommon to see five of six workers standing around watching a sole employee labor. Noel was disgusted by the incompetence and laziness, but what was he to do? He was forced to wait ten minutes in the ridiculous line of traffic while slothful National Park Service embarrassments toiled in their slow, indolent fashion.

The sun was getting hot, but Noel refused to remove his jacket. He wanted to maintain his image of control and superior breeding even in these barbaric environs. The two dirty bikers in his employ waited behind him, slouching lethargically, and smoking cigarettes with their engines idling at low rumbles. They spoke to him as little as possible and, truth be told, he rather preferred it that way. He had bailed all four out from that hick jail this morning. He'd responded to the phone calls from Booster in that backwater Spearfish hospital where he was to have orthopedic surgery for his fractured and dislocated shoulder. He had called Noel with the disappointing update, blaming everything and everyone but himself. Apparently, Lovejoy had employed a giant with kung fu skills as a bodyguard. No matter; he'd pay him off or scare him off. Hired mercenaries had the dependable characteristic of little personal loyalty. Noel counted on these predictably despicable traits in his dealings. The underlings with him told Noel that Lovejoy had broken their leader's arm during the melee at that woman's art gallery. Noel would make him pay for that. They had also informed him of Fist's accident with the police cruiser. Given the severity of his reported injuries, Noel thought him likely to die of internal bleeding or traumatic brain injury. That was acceptable. He had failed at this assignment, was a potential risk to Noel, and he was a drain on society anyway, as far as Noel was concerned.

Noel had decided to split his forces and send two of them back to Jeanette's gallery to obtain any documents Todd had passed on to Lovejoy. They had been instructed to take whatever they could find and kill the woman. They would use the untraceable Sig-Sauer 9mm pistol he'd slipped them before they separated in Belle Fourche. Noel had provided them with a short but intense "pep talk," and made it very clear that their own lives would be forfeit, should they fail as badly as they had the day before.

For at least the last half-hour, Noel had known he was being followed. The traffic had been sufficiently meager for him to detect the riders trailing him from Belle Fourche. When he'd stopped for gas near the little town of Alva, the riders had stopped well behind him, always keeping him just in sight. That was quite unlikely to be pure coincidence in his estimation. From his vantage point, Noel had been able to sneak in a number of furtive looks at his pursuers. One man was much larger than the other; he was probably Lovejoy's bodyguard. He wondered what Lovejoy's face would look like when he bribed the man's allegiance away from him. He'd done it before with bodyguards, and he was sure he could do it again. It was deflating for the adversary's forces to melt away and to find former allies aligned against one in the balance of power. Let that smug fool smirk his way out of that, Noel laughed quietly under his breath.

The shrill piping of the prairie dogs to his left caught his attention with no small amount of irritation. Dirty animals. Prairie rat was a more appropriate nomenclature. They lived in filthy holes in writhing piles of fetid, disease-ridden flesh. Noel had read about them in medical school. The flea-covered carcasses of prairie dogs and their ilk around the world were a squalid breeding ground for diseases such as typhoid, bubonic plague, and Hantavirus. The disgusting creatures reminded Noel of the dirty, malodorous, in-bred biker trash he found everywhere he went in this godforsaken country.

He recognized the moneymaking aspects of the event, and he couldn't deny that the Black Hills had a certain rugged beauty. Still, he preferred the healthy green, manicured greens, fairways, and roughs of a respectable, private country club. He felt at home in such surroundings. He felt in control. He would strut and preen amid groveling waiters, butlers, and servers, anticipating and meeting his every need and want. Here, he felt vaguely out of control. The massive hills and mountains, deep, rich forests, and wide-open sky made him feel impotent and vulnerable. The worst had been the endless heavens spread above him when they rode to Little Bighorn. Nature's indifference to him made him aware of his own insignificance. Nonsense, he railed in his heart. He wasn't insignificant, damn it! He was a respected, successful, world-class cardiologist, and the renowned medical institute in which he ruled was damned lucky to have him. His importance was proved by how much money he made. Of course, he was a good and important doctor. He had a beautiful, impressive home in an excellent neighborhood, didn't he? He was able to send his children to selective private schools. He vacationed at the right ski resorts and Caribbean islands. He owned both a Lexus and a Hummer! He had a lovely wife who acted properly at the country club. This world just didn't recognize his magnificence. After this deal went down, his brilliance would be even more fantastic. He was convinced that he was justifiably one of the most important persons in the civilized world!

Hah, civilized! That didn't necessarily apply to his current surroundings. At last the peons working on the road either had attained some vague goal or decided to take another break to indulge their slothfulness. The traffic began to move. Without a look or a word, Noel pulled forward, sure his minions would follow him. Their thoughts tended more to whether they had to extinguish their smokes or not on the short remaining road to the Devil's Tower visitor center and parking lot. They glanced ahead, barely even seeing the monolith looming in front of them.

Within minutes, they had located an area for parking slightly away from the other bikes. Noel scanned the people milling about around the small, log building that functioned as the visitor center. He cared little about the history of the place. It was suitable for a few photos or a postcard, but the importance of the pending exchange of cash for cocaine outweighed anything else in Noel's mind. He nodded his head toward the building and went around the rear of the structure to relieve his bladder in the well cared for men's room, accompanied by his two sleazy assistants. He entered a stall and checked the money cache under his coat, as well as the second Sig-Sauer, a pistol he had used only in target practice, but had no doubt he would use accurately and without hesitation. Noel had purchased the guns after careful and thoughtful evaluation and secreted them on the motorcycle he had shipped to Rapid City.

The German Sig-Sauer P-226 pistol was the elite of the "wonder-nines." It was a double-action, locked-breach model, accepting a double-column magazine capable of holding fifteen rounds of 9mm Parabellum ammunition. A Colt-style 1911-type magazine catch was more advanced than the older heel-clip style. Only 7.7 inches long and weighing a scant 29 ounces, the pistol had a simple but comfortable handle with wrap-around plastic grips. It was an efficient combat weapon, with Von Stavenhagen white dot-bar insert sights. The double-action pull of the trigger was smooth, and Noel found it very comfortable when he trained with it at twenty-five meters.

Noel admired its finely machined construction much as he did all things featuring German engineering and efficiency. Yes, he thought the mechanistic, almost computerized approaches to "the final solution" of Hitler's regime—concentration camps and extermination camps—were worthy of respect, both for their ideals and their implementation. He remembered photos of Nazi officers standing behind kneeling Jews and "terminally managing" them with a quick, definitive shot from their pistol. Held at arm's length, just inches behind a helpless sub-human's skull, the pistol held a strong sexual attraction for him. He wasn't ashamed to admit it, although he probably wouldn't do so aloud especially among all the liberals, pacifists, and Jews he found himself forced to work with every day at the hospital.

He confirmed that he had a round in the chamber and left the stall. Noel washed his hands thoroughly and methodically, almost as if he was going into the operating room or catheterization lab before exiting the restroom into the bright sun. It was hot and getting hotter with a few clouds beginning to build up in the west. Like as not there would be a good downpour before sunset, and he wanted to be sure his merchandise was well protected from the elements. The two thugs fell in behind Noel as they headed towards the parking lot. Noel slowed just as they came around the edge of the visitor's center and scanned the hot pavement.

Yes, there they were, just getting off their bikes. Next to Lovejoy was a giant of a man with bushy hair and a large beard. The two men behind Noel sucked in air audibly as they sighted him and stopped in their tracks. There was no mistaking him; he was the one who had knocked their heads together so forcefully yesterday that they'd been stunned and dizzy for much of the night. They prayed they would not have to get physical with that behemoth again today. They didn't know

Death in Sturgis

Noel was packing, but they weren't and without a club, knife, or gun, the hoodlums were afraid of Bear.

Noel's attention was on another group of riders, much closer. Five men stood silently by three bikes and a pickup with California plates. He recognized the tallest of the group from their first meeting last month. The man had promised Noel that he would provide as much cocaine as he wanted for the proper price. This was to be the first of many profitable exchanges. The man, a Mister Gunther Popp, was to provide Noel with twenty kilograms of pharmaceutical quality cocaine for $50,000 each. At $170 per gram, Noel anticipated a profit of approximately three million dollars, which would not have to be split with Todd or Jake. He planned on immediately reinvesting the money to achieve an even better return. Distribution channels were already in place and all that remained was to make the exchange and transport the merchandise back to Ohio. He planned to leave in two days, when his bike would be loaded back up on the trailer waiting in Rapid City. His motorcycle would be secured in the back of the vehicle, along with ten to twenty others. His bike, however, would have its saddlebags full of cocaine. If the drugs were discovered by the authorities prior to his retrieving the white treasure, he'd throw a complete fit about the drug addicts hauling his precious motorcycle. Tim, the man in charge of the trailer, had a drug conviction on his record, and he would be an easy mark. The plan was flawless, and it would succeed if Lovejoy kept his nose out of things. Noel was sure he had the documents Todd had threatened him with before he died. Noel would get those back and eliminate Lovejoy at the same time. Noel had laid awake much of last night, plotting and planning the best and most satisfying way to eliminate that obscene embarrassment, that thorn in his side, that fucking pain in the ass! That Lovejoy!

35

THE EXCHANGE

Gunther Popp was angry. He didn't like this place for an exchange. True, he had suggested it first when dealing with Noel. Noel had acted like a pompous ass each time they met, but he seemed to have money and a lot it. Gunther enjoyed the prospect of doing business at the same time he enjoyed the rally. He'd been Sturgis once before and enjoyed getting away from Los Angeles from time to time. Like Noel, though, the natural beauty of the area began to wear on him after a few days. Not that it wasn't breathtaking, it was; but the hills and pinnacles reminded him of going to church with his grandmother, and the big, open skies made him feel small. Gunther Popp really didn't like either sensation. His grandmother continually pulled him by the ear during Mass and admonished him to be quiet and sit still whenever he sniffled or fidgeted in his pew. After several bitter years of this, he began to hate church. He stopped attending as soon as he moved out on his own and joined the military. Even now, the thought of going to church, even for a friend's wedding or family baptism, sent cold chills down his neck, and stepping through the arched doors resulted in a cold sweat and sick, sour nausea. The only use he had for God or Jesus was when he cursed, which was frequently.

Even more than Noel, he hated the sense of feeling small under the big open skies. He felt like his goddamned grandmother and her God were looking down on him disapprovingly. He wanted to hide and squirmed like a worm on a microscope slide under such scrutiny, and he simply loathed that feeling. At home, there were buildings, trees, and hills, and he would be back on his home turf. It was an experience seeing all the bikes here, but he'd much rather be where he belonged. He could hide there, from his grandmother and God. In addition, it was green back in LA, at least some of the time. He'd never known there could be so many depressing variations of gray and brown. The dark green Christmas trees on these hills might look nice, but he missed flowers and palm trees. He missed the noise. The rumbling of the bikes was noise, but he missed the ebb and flow of millions of people living and breathing all around him. This damn place just seemed dead and lonely. Even the people that lived and worked here had a flat, dead look in their eyes, and their crow-footed faces and deep tans looked like a combination of a zombie movie and a western. He'd be damn glad to make the deal and get the hell back to the city. They had hauled their bikes in a trailer while they rode in the truck and van. Most of the ride had been along I-15 from Barstow to Las Vegas and through to Salt Lake City, where they'd spent the first night. Next, they had hauled ass across boring, boring, boring Wyoming to Sundance, where they were staying. Gunther and two of his boys had gone into Sturgis to see the sights, and he had gone with the other two over to Hulett for the No Panty Day party. They'd kept a low profile, but they were bored and ready to head back to civilization tomorrow. Already he'd been here longer than he'd wanted and would be more than happy to get out from under that glowing, knowing sky.

Gunther had watched Noel drive up and wondered where he had gone in such a hurry. Then he remembered that the restrooms were behind the little shack that pretended to be an official government building. He hated the log cabin façade, reminded of episodes of Disney's *Davy Crocket*. It felt like it was out of the fucking 1950s or 1960s and he wanted no part of it. Jesus Christ, did these yokels eat this shit up or what? He waited impatiently for Noel to come out of the john and began to wander across the parking lot and up the trail towards the Devil's Tower itself. Again, it was imposing, but he felt like God or somebody was watching him. Shit, it made him shiver.

Maybe Gunther didn't actually feel Doc's binoculars on him. Doc had glassed him a few minutes earlier and moved on. Gunther was just another biker milling around the noisy parking lot, no one special, so far. Doc picked up Noel as he peered from around the edge of the building for a few minutes and began to move after Gunther. Doc could tell from the way he moved that he'd seen whoever it was he was looking for; he was moving with purpose. Noel walked boldly upright across the hot asphalt, as though expecting the sea to part and people to automatically make way for him. That wasn't something the biker crowd was likely to do, not knowing he was the most important person in the world, and all. Hell, they probably wouldn't have moved then, either.

As they reached the trailhead, just as it split to encircle the Tower, Noel stopped and looked back. He had seen Doc and seemed to be daring him to move. He stared directly at him, and Doc was treated to a 10x image of Noel's superior sneer. He slowly dropped the binoculars to his chest, and it seemed as though an electric current passed between them. Noel slowly patted his chest, either to reassure himself that his automatic pistol was still in place, or to let Doc know he was packing. What a fool, Noel thought. Come along, Lovejoy, I'll kill you just as surely as I killed the others, and I'll love doing it. He hurried on down the path and was immediately out of Doc's sight. Doc couldn't tell if he'd gone north or south.

The Tower Trail wrapped around the base of the edifice in a twisting, climbing, and dropping 1.3 miles. Mostly gravel, there were large stretches of paved path and frequent benches. It was still a bit early, and more of the visitors seemed to be in the parking lot and visitor center than on the trail. The majority of hikers were still near the trailhead watching a group climb the tower. They had been toiling up the steep walls since very early in the day and were now plainly visible in their brightly colored climbing clothes, although they were not much bigger than specks in the distance. A few crows cawed from the trees, and turkey vultures floated nearly motionless in the bright blue sky, not far from the rocky rim of the Tower.

Doc and Bear hurried across the lot and rushed up the short incline to where the path parted. Noel and his colleagues were nowhere to be seen.

"Let's split up here, Bear. We can't just wait for him to waltz around the Tower for us. You go left, and I'll go right. I'll take the binoculars."

"Yeah, that's sounds good. An' be careful, Doc, we don't know who he's meetin', or how many creeps he has up here," Bear answered.

"Watch your ass. I think the asshole has a gun."

"What do we do if we have to hurry outta here? You know there ain't no phone service up here or nothin'. Where should we meet up?"

Doc thought for a minute and answered, "Beat's the hell out of me, Bear. I guess we just play it by ear. Keep your cell phone on, though. If we are separated, and you can't reach me on the phone, plan on meeting up back at Jeanette's. I think that's best. Let's go."

Doc headed to the right, and Bear to the left. Within a minute, they were lost to each other's view. Doc scrambled along the path, breathing a little hard with the exertion of climbing some of the steeper sections of the trail and feeling the cut along his flank begin to reopen. A warm trickle of blood ran down his side and was absorbed by the shirt. What the hell, he thought. It's a black Harley shirt, and no one will even notice. The few people sharing the trail gave him barely a glance as he hurried along. He went slower after a few hundred yards, because he didn't want to walk right into a dope deal going down. That kind of thing led to bullets and all sorts of unpleasantries. He frequently stopped and strained to pick up the sound of voices ahead, but heard little more than his pulse pounding in his ears. By this time, he estimated that he'd gone well over five hundred yards. How much further could they be?

Just before a particularly sharp bend, Doc trusted his senses enough to peek through the branches of a short aspen tree at the trail ahead. Less than twenty yards away, Noel stood with his two bullies behind him and a small, dark green backpack on the ground in front of him. Five men stood facing Noel from less than fifteen feet away. The shortest, obviously the one in charge, was counting money while two of his companions were pulling brick sized packages from their own backpacks. Although Doc had never seen a big drug deal go down, this had to be the buy Noel had planned.

Gunther, the evil-looking man with the money, stood with his feet well apart, as though ready for action. His friends, muscular and scarred, stood menacingly behind him. One kept his eyes on Noel, and another kept his eyes on Noel's thugs. The other two watched the trail in both directions now that they'd emptied their backpacks. All had guns in their hands and seemed used to firing them. Noel loaded the packages into his backpack. He stacked them like bricks, but he handled them as though they were gold or could explode at any second. Everyone was as tense as the high-E string on Doc's guitar when he tightened it up a little too much. It didn't seem like it would take much to invoke a full-fledged firefight. In fact, Doc thought, that might be a very good idea!

With no warning at all, Doc stepped around the bend in the trail and announced loudly, "Good job, Noel. We've got them just where we want them; now shoot the bastards!" He ended the last part with a scream and threw the binoculars as hard as he could at the leader. As he did, Doc flung himself back the way he'd come and pitched to the ground. He heard gunfire immediately behind him and crawled, then ran, to a pile of boulders fifty feet or more off the trail. After five or six shots rang out, there was confused shouting and cursing. One person moaned, indicating he'd been hit.

Noel looked down at the two thugs he'd brought with him. He had wisely refrained from pulling his gun; he'd be dead now if he had. When Doc had burst out like that, the two tough guys with Noel had jumped forward. That had been a very bad move; the Los Angeles crooks had shot them down in a brief, but deadly flurry of gunfire. One of the men sprawled at Noel's feet, a ragged red hole in his chest from which a few last drops of blood were spreading. The other was holding his abdomen and uttering moans interspersed with curses. Noel slowly looked up, his mouth hanging open, and gaped stupidly into five pistol barrels, all pointed directly at him.

Gunther smiled crookedly at Noel and motioned two of his men to go down the trail in Doc's direction. The other two stayed beside their leader. Gunther was beginning to like the situation. He could take the dope back and keep the money, too. He hadn't originally planned on doing this, but when the opportunity arose, he was just the man to seize it. He was smart enough to realize that Noel had not planned this fiasco and that the man who'd bounced the binoculars harmlessly off his wide chest was not the partner he'd met with Noel in the past. He assumed correctly that he had been trying to cause a fracas and get either the drugs or money, or both for himself. It only works that way in movies, my friend, Gunther thought coldly. He waited for his men to return and held his gun pointed directly between Noel's eyes.

"Gunther, you know this wasn't my—" Noel began, but was motioned into silence. It was very quiet, he noticed. The commotion had silenced the dozens of birds he'd heard chirping and singing just a minute before. In the strange quiet, he could only discern moaning behind him, and he thought he could hear the rushing of body fluids as the corpse at his feet began to cool.

"Now, Doctor Herrod, hand the cocaine back to my friend to my right. That's it. Slowly. Slowly."

Noel rigidly extended his right arm, which held the strap of the backpack he'd just filled with cocaine. He stepped back after the nearest crook took it from him. One package was left on the ground near his foot. He slowly exhaled, waiting for his death. Damn that fucking

Death in Sturgis

Lovejoy. He's ruined everything, and now this low-life bastard is going to kill me! He was afraid he was about to lose control of his bladder as the demon in front of him widened his smile. He saw his dirty, crooked teeth. They reminded him of a rat's teeth, yellow and deformed. Only the tiniest bit of his tongue protruded between them, looking vaguely obscene in the intense Wyoming sun. He felt a rivulet of sweat run down his armpit. He hated dying without even pulling his own gun. What the hell had he bought it for, anyway? As far as he could tell, Gunther didn't even know the gun was under his jacket.

"What a fucking waste of money," Noel uttered.

"What? What are you saying?" asked Gunther, afraid he was missing something vital. His quick but evil mind saw no problem with shooting Noel between his narrow, shifting eyes and walking away with both the money and the dope.

"I just said we could still make a deal, maybe more money than we had initially planned," Noel stammered at first, but quickly found his slick, snake-like tongue.

"No, I don't think so, Doctor. I'm afraid you've made your last deal."

36

Off to the Races

Gunther held his gun out at arm's length, its black barrel pointed squarely at Noel's forehead. He grinned as he saw the cold sweat run down Noel's face and drip off the tip of his nose into the dirt.

Two of his henchmen were still covering Noel with their automatics; the other pair was out of sight as they searched for Doc. Suddenly, a loud noise like an oncoming freight train made Gunther turn. A fast-moving blur rapidly became Bear and two short, stout female park rangers running down the trail. Bear was still thirty feet away when he saw the drawn weapons and skidded to a stop, the two women running into him from behind.

"Are these the hoodlums that are starting a fire?" blurted the first ranger, peeking around Bear. The other was still hidden behind his bulk, wondering what in the world was going on. The Los Angeles criminals were unnerved by the sudden arrival of this unlikely cavalry. Gunther wavered, his gun first pointing at Noel, and then at Bear, barely seeing the two rangers cowering behind him. He realized, however, that he was in a public place and that his time was running out. Each passing second brought the possibility of more people on the scene. He couldn't kill them all, and he didn't know what had happened to Doc after he started the commotion. He had also lost the opportunity to kill Noel, although he dearly would have loved to pop a cap in this fucking doctor's ass. Gunther made a decision and called his men to him, planning a quick regroup, followed by an even quicker exit. As they returned, Bear began to bellow for Doc, and the rangers started jabbering into their walkie-talkies, summoning help for what Bear had apparently told them was arson in progress. Squawking noises warned Gunther that reinforcements were not far off and getting closer by the second.

Faster than Gunther could react, Noel bent down and scooped up the remained kilogram of cocaine. He tucked it under his arm like a football and ran straight at Bear. Gunther spun around and squeezed three quick shots at the fleeing doctor. Two shots went wild, ricocheting off the hard granite rocks with high-pitched whines. The rangers hid behind the largest, safest object they could find—Bear. Noel pushed past the three and ran down the twisting path. He was gone from sight in five seconds. Gunther heard shouting from more people coming up from along the trail they'd just come up. Holding the bags of dope and Noel's money, he shouldered his pistol and nodded his head back down the path, indicating to his men that they should retreat. His men put their weapons away and ran after him, giving Bear and the women a brief hateful glance as they, too, disappeared from view.

Doc popped up about forty feet to the southeast and scrambled over the boulders to where Bear stood his ground and the two diminutive women hid. Bear, for once, was speechless and stared at Doc for ten seconds before Doc realized something was wrong.

"Fuck, man!" screamed Doc as Bear coughed and a small trickle of blood ran from his mouth. Then he swayed a little. The two rangers grabbed the giant by his enormous arms and sat him heavily into the dust of the trail. Doc ripped Bear's leather jacket and shirt open and found a red, wet area where a small, pencil-sized hole leaked blood from the enormous man's right chest, about two inches above his nipple. He held his ear up to Bear's chest and heard good, loud breath sounds. Then Doc poured a little of the bottled water from the container he'd stuffed in his pocket earlier that morning over the wound. There was no bubbling or sucking at the wound site, which reassured him. A quick scan of Bear's back showed no exit wound, meaning the bullet was still rattling around somewhere inside the big man.

"Hell, Doc. I feel like a mule kicked me in the chest. Did I get shot?" he questioned.

"Yeah, man, fuck yeah. It missed your heart, and your lung hasn't collapsed, at least not much. But we need to get you to a hospital. Like, now!" Doc stated emphatically and turned to the rangers. He, too, heard voices from both directions of the path. "Activate your EMS as though a climber has fallen; they can get a chopper here faster that way."

One of the stocky little rangers, P. Hoover on her nametag, picked up her walkie-talkie and spoke authoritatively, asking for a medical air transport helicopter. She had never had a man shot at the Tower while she was working, but she'd trained at least twice every year to call in a helicopter when someone was seriously injured scaling the Tower. Same procedure, she thought, as she opened a small first aid kit and began to apply a bandage to Bear's chest. Doc was impressed. The ranger began a very professional job of preparing Bear for the air transport team, who had just received a stat notice over seventy miles away at the Rapid City Regional Hospital, the nearest trauma center.

Doc and the other ranger, W. Hubble, her tag read, checked Noel's associates, which he had callously left behind. One was stone cold dead from a heart shot and lay sprawled on his back. There were already flies buzzing around the still-open eyes. The other thug sat against a small boulder holding his stomach. His breathing was slow, but his eyes were closed, and his clammy skin was ghostly pale. Doc felt his pulse and found it very thready and fast. He moaned incoherently when Doc tried to rouse him. Doc knew he was bleeding badly from his gut wound. The Belle Fourche police had confiscated the body armor he'd been wearing at Jeanette's gallery. He probably had an injury of the aorta, the largest blood vessel of the body. It sent blood coursing from the heart to be distributed to the blood hungry organs of the belly, muscles, and brain. He was already in an advanced state of shock. Such ominous findings in such a short time indicated a massive, exsanguinating wound. Doc had seen this far too many times when he worked in a Level I trauma center that received gunshot wounds at all hours of the day. The man had less than ten minutes to live without emergency surgery and would probably do very poorly even then. Without the facilities for emergency abdominal surgery, the man was as good as dead.

Doc's rapid triage of the three victims was based on a system established by one of Napoleon's military surgeons, Dominique Jean Larrey. The word triage meant "to sort." Like Doc, he was faced with multiple injuries and limited resources. In this system, trauma patients were divided into four categories. The worst were those who were already dead, like Noel's associate with the chest wound. These were termed "the deceased"—beyond any help and deserving only a very short prayer. Alternately, those people who were seriously injured and needed immediate transportation with urgent medical and surgical intervention were termed "the immediate." The gut shot bully and Bear were definitely immediate patients. Bear needed emergent evaluation to determine the extent of his wound, although it was obvious that he had a serious lung injury. The bully, on the other hand, was on the verge of moving into the deceased category very soon if he didn't have an emergent laparotomy, the immediate surgical opening of his abdominal cavity to repair whatever was bleeding so badly. Simple broken bones were judged less urgent and labeled "delayed" injuries. Patients with delayed injuries would be transported and treated when the immediate patients had been evacuated or managed. Finally, those with scratches and bruises or bloody noses constituted the walking wounded, considered minor injuries. These people were usually made into assistants and used to move and manage the more seriously wounded. They were in no serious danger of death or loss of limb and constituted the largest number of victims when a serious disaster occurred. Because they could move about on their own, they frequently arrived at emergency departments first and flooded the facility before the more badly injured people arrived via EMS squads.

Doc determined there was nothing he could do for these people. Ranger Hoover waddled up to him and announced that a Medivac helicopter was twenty minutes out from their location, and could transport either Bear or the gut-shot thug, but not both. Doc told her the bully would be dead by then, and that Bear would be transported upon their arrival. She nodded and smiled a crooked smile.

"Gee, guys, what a day. We trained for injuries, you know," she stated somewhat nervously. She wiped her brow under her Smokey the Bear hat. "He said someone was setting fires, and we needed to follow him. We had to run off from the tour we were leading about a hundred yards back in order to get here. I'm still winded."

"Y'all did a fantastic job. Listen, I have to go. He'll go to Rapid City, won't he?" Doc nodded towards where Bear was sitting with ranger Hubble. She was taking his pulse and talking quietly with Bear, keeping them both calm, Doc thought. Ranger Hoover affirmed that Bear would indeed go to the Rapid City ER.

Doc ran quickly over to the pair. "Bear, I've gotta follow those scumbags. Yer gonna be okay, ya hear?" A strong southern twang had crept into Doc's voice, indicating his stress level. First Jeanette, and now Bear, shit!

"Yeah, ya go ahead. Kick that fucker's ass fer me, Doc. I'll get patched up and follow ya; it shouldn't take too long," Bear grumbled.

Bear's breath sounds and pulse were checked again, and Doc finally felt that he could leave to pursue Noel and those bastards. He didn't know exactly what he'd do when he caught up with them, but he planned on causing some serious pain and suffering, even if they had guns and he did not. It took a lot to get Doc riled up like this, but beating one of his friends and shooting another certainly qualified.

Doc ran back down the path after the Los Angelinos. It was the shorter of the two trails circling the Tower. Doc offered silent prayers to the Indian spirits that he was sure still inhabited the area. His prayers were intermixed with his harsh breathing. His right side burned like fire, but he didn't let up. Damn, he thought, I don't run like this very often. Maybe I should get more exercise than drinking, riding, and fucking. He brushed past the other people on the trail; Gunther and his men had already shoved many aside roughly. Most got quickly out of Doc's way although some felt they would not be pushed twice in one day and tried to stop Doc. The dark look on his face and the blood on his clothes changed their minds rapidly. The blood was a mixture of Bears, the bully's, and his own from the flank wound now bleeding freely from exertion.

When he arrived at the trailhead, he had to stop to catch his breath; he could not run any further. Several people stopped to tell him that the other men had run down to the parking lot and left amidst squealing tires. A handful of rangers were rushing up the trail while the rest prepared for the helicopter that was still a good fifteen minutes from landing. He assumed they'd put down in one of the small, clear fields nearby. They certainly couldn't land very close to where Bear waited on the rocky, heavily forested, rugged path. He was surer than ever that the gut wound would be fatal long before paramedics arrived. He certainly didn't envy the paramedics who had to carry Bear over the rough terrain on a backboard. They would remember this day for a long time!

Doc half-ran, half-walked down to the parking lot. The five men had roared out of the area several minutes earlier. Most of the people in the lot backed up and gave Doc plenty of room once they laid eyes on him. Doc cursed silently and turned back to where he'd left his bike, but found himself looking down the barrel of Noel's 9mm pistol, less than thirty feet away.

"You worthless fool!" Noel screamed. "You are going to die for your blasted interference!" He had lost almost every bit of self-control and held the pistol with a shaking fist. He was soaked with sweat from his race around the backside of the Tower, and his chest was heaving. But Noel was younger and in better shape than Doc, plus he wasn't bleeding from a wound, as Doc was. He waved the gun from side to side, and people scrambled to get away. Women screamed shrilly, and the rough and tough biker crowd backed away from the insane look on Noel's face, as much as from the quivering gun.

Noel pointed the gun at Doc's head and squeezed the trigger as Doc jumped to his right and rolled behind a pair of Honda Gold Wing motorcycles. Noel pulled the trigger three times and punched the same number of 9mm holes into the metric bikes protecting Doc. Doc began to scramble towards the front of the bikes, unsure what he'd do if Noel simply walked over to him for a better shot. He faintly heard the wail of an approaching siren on the hot, dry air. Apparently, Noel heard it better, because he spun on his heel and ran to his Big Dog. He unlocked it, started its powerful engine, and pulled hard on the throttle to race from the nearly abandoned parking lot. Doc leapt to his feet and charged for his own bike. His side howled in protest as he threw his leg over the seat. The engine kicked over, and Doc headed down the road after Noel. A green and white NPS truck rushed past him in the other direction, its siren changing from a shrill pitch as they approached each other to a lower whine as they moved further apart.

Doc raced down the road, weaving in and out around slowly moving cars, trucks, and many, many motorcycles. He barely heard the curses thrown at him as he sped through the KOA campground and approached Route 24. He saw people standing, looking, and pointing to the south, where he assumed the crooks, and then Noel had hurried. You had to have faith, Doc thought. He barreled down the road where it met with the larger US-14 at the tiny town of Carlile Junction; he ran the stop sign. He had no way to know which way to head. Both directions would lead him down to I-90 in ten to twenty miles of curving, twisting highway. He had no way of knowing that the crooks had turned left toward Sundance, where they were staying. Nor could Doc know that Noel, too, had headed east less than a minute and a half ahead of him. Doc could only guess, and he guessed correctly, scraping the foot pegs of his bike as he ran yet another stop sign and leaned fiercely into the turn at over forty miles an hour.

He rolled on the throttle and took the curves of US-14 at speeds much greater than he would normally have done. Doc's fears of another crash were temporarily pacified by the sheer hate that coursed through his veins. He might be a fool chasing Noel like this, considering that Noel and his friends were all armed, but the mere thought of Bear sitting in the middle of the trail with a bullet hole in his chest really, really pissed him off. Not many people ever came close enough to Doc to be considered a true brother, but Bear had earned that position through many years and bond-building experiences. Doc would kill Noel with his bare hands, if he could get them around his scrawny chicken neck!

He came around one of the hair-raising turns and caught sight of Noel racing ahead less than a quarter of a mile further down the road. Alone. Good, he thought. He continued to give chase along the dangerously winding road. Doc was much more familiar with riding in these hills, and his Wide Glide quickly ate up the distance between them, despite the difference in horsepower and torque. Noel had seen him and suddenly slowed as they passed a road sign indicating they had only six more miles to Sundance. As Doc pulled alongside Noel, he again saw the ugly, grim visage of Noel's gun. Doc braked hard and dropped back about fifty feet as brief puffs of smoke were washed away from Noel's gun by the rushing wind. Two angry bullets passed hotly through the empty space where his body would have been had he not hit the brakes so abruptly. Doc pulled up behind Noel; he knew Noel wouldn't be able to control his bike at this speed and still take shots at him with any accuracy. People only bumped each other or tried to hit each other from moving motorcycles in badly done B-movies, but he wasn't sure if Noel knew that. Apparently, Noel didn't because twice he hit the brakes abrupt enough to force Doc to swerve and hit his own brakes. Any collision, no matter how brief or glancing, at these speeds would send them both into an ugly confrontation with the hard, unforgiving rocks and boulders along the road. Doc dropped back another hundred feet.

The pair swiftly approached Sundance, where Doc knew there would be more side roads and traffic before they reached I-90. He didn't like racing down these curvy little roads, but he certainly wasn't looking forward to the high speeds they could attain once they were on the broad, sweeping interstate.

But Doc wouldn't have to worry about the problems on the highway. His plans all changed as an eighty-year-old farmer pulled his dusty pick-up out right in front of him from a side road and blocked both lanes, leaving him nowhere to go.

37

THE GIRLS

Erin sat in the small kitchen, while Jeanette fetched her a cup of coffee. The rich, black coffee was as thick as the tension in the air. There had been little in the way of introduction; she pulled into the driveway at the same time Bear roared out. He'd waved and shouted, "She's in the house." There was only the smell of exhaust and dust in the air to confirm Bear had even been there. Erin had taken her bag from the truck and knocked gently on the door. The petite Indian woman had let her into the kitchen and tried immediately to put her at ease.

Still, it was hard for the women to talk or look at each other until they understood their respective relations with Doc a little better. Jeanette was impressed with how young, healthy, and vibrant Erin appeared so early in the morning. She kept her eyes down as she spoke. "Doc speaks highly of you. He says you work with animals. I think that's wonderful."

Erin chose to pursue the graciously offered opening and elaborated a little about her experiences. Jeanette listened politely and asked a few succinct questions at the proper points. After a half-hour of hearing about animals, sick and otherwise, the conversation came to a jolting halt again.

This time it was Erin's turn, "Did you do all the beautiful art here? How did you learn to do all this?"

Jeanette gave her the down and dirty version. She told her about the nuns, the art gallery, her abusive husband, and going to prison. Erin listened attentively to every word. This petite, quiet woman entranced her. The time spent in Chicago gave her chills, and when Jeanette told her about the all male jury and male judge, she came around the table and hugged her. They held onto each other for several minutes, amid an unexpected burst of tears. When the embrace ended, Erin had acquired a sense of respect for Jeanette, and in the biker world, there was nothing more important than a healthy sense of respect. It didn't matter if you were respecting someone's scoot, woman, or club colors—proper respect is what kept the world turning. The only sure way of getting your butt stomped at any collection of bikers was to blatantly show disrespect for them. In most cases, respect was something that had to be earned. Young prospects and almost all wannabes had no concept of what that meant. Older, seasoned bikers no longer needed to use their fists to command respect; they did it with their words and actions. By the time Erin understood what Jeanette had been through, she looked at her in a new light. They had become closer, and although you couldn't really say they were friends, they knew each other in a way men wouldn't understand. Women were like that, Doc would say.

"Tell me how you and Doc met," Erin asked. She took a deep breath and slowly released it. Jeanette returned to the table with refills of their coffee. It was only mid-morning, and the day was beginning to heat up quickly.

Jeanette sat at the small table and began to tell Erin about the young man who had sat down to enjoy a sunset those many years ago. That was unusual enough in a world where a sunset was something most people only really saw on a postcard and seldom took the time to sit down and appreciate. She talked about how close she had gotten to Doc over the next few years and how they had a special, if not typical, relationship.

"Here, let me show you something," Jeanette said, and led Erin into her workroom, where debris was still scattered across the floor. She went over to a large cabinet where she stored supplies for her kiln and reached beside it to pull out the painting she'd done of Doc as she remembered him when they first met. She placed it on an undamaged easel and turned a small spotlight on it. "That's how I remember him, not so many years ago. There weren't as many wrinkles and no gray hair back then, but he still looks pretty much the same. He still thinks the same, and he still makes love the same."

Neither woman said anything for ten seconds or more as they studied the painting. They really didn't need to. Erin turned to Jeanette and began "Ya know—" with a knot in her throat.

Jeanette went on, "I know, sweetheart, I do. He's a lot of things to a lot of people, and none of us can ever tie him down. To change him to be more like what we want would be to kill him, and I wouldn't want to do that. There's that old saying about letting something go, if you really love it, and if it comes back to you... That's how he is. It took me years to learn that, and I couldn't expect you to feel that way. I couldn't be mad at him, anymore than I could be mad at a puppy that plays with another woman. I couldn't be jealous of you because you have become a part of him in your own way. I understand that. It's not really that simple, but it's hard for me to explain any other way."

Erin found a tear rolling down her face, and they reached for each other. They clasped hands as Erin said, "I think I know what you mean, even though I've known him for such a short time. It's like that song by Neil Young about love being like a rose that you had better not pick because it starts to die if you pick it and claim it as your own... I mean, you just can't do that."

"Exactly. Some things you can share, and some things you can't. Here, I want you to have this." Jeanette walked into the display area of the gallery and brought back a smaller painting of an eagle soaring above the prairie. "This always reminds me of his love and need for freedom." She handed Erin the beautiful watercolor painting and smiled warmly. She wouldn't let Erin refuse, and the exchange cemented a growing friendship between them.

For the next hours, they straightened the workroom. Erin picked up broken shards of pottery and pieces of blown glass. Jeanette worked constantly with a small broom and dustpan. Every time she had to throw away a finished piece of art, she let loose a few sobs. She had put a great deal of love and effort into the collection, and it cut her to the core that they had been destroyed. They felt like children to her. She knew in her heart that such emotion was excessive, but she had established a relationship with just about every piece in the studio. Some pieces she refused to sell if she didn't think the person buying it would appreciate it or take care of it. From time to time, Erin would comment on the beauty or uniqueness of a piece, and Jeanette would describe what it was, how it was designed, and what it meant to her. In that way, piece by broken piece, they forged a bond between them.

Around two o'clock, they decided the area had been cleaned enough that Jeanette could work again. There would surely be some tears, but she could start creating again. Jeanette suggested they fix lunch and have something cold, as the afternoon was rapidly approaching the sizzling heat that she could survive only because the humidity was so very low. Erin excused herself to take her new painting out to her truck and walked from the room.

Erin was gone less than a minute when Jeanette heard her scream. She ran to the kitchen door, only to find Erin backing into the house with two of the ruffians from yesterday in her face. It looked like Bear or Doc had broken the nose of the one in front, as well as providing two black eyes. He held a dark gray pistol in his right hand, and its barrel was pointed directly at Erin.

"Alright, bitch," he addressed Jeanette. "Yesterday, you were lucky. Today we're gonna get what we should've gotten yesterday. And today you don't have that fucking monster to save you. First, give me the papers—whatever Lovejoy left with you yesterday. Do it now!" The dirty man with the battered face forced Erin against the kitchen table, where she found herself leaning her over backwards.

The other lowlife approached Jeanette with his fist balled up and brought his arm back, as though he was going to strike her. Recalling the pain inflicted the day before Jeanette flinched and stumbled backwards. Instead, he put the flat of his palm on her shoulder and pushed. Hard. She fell back towards the refrigerator and protested, "But I don't have anything. I don't know what you're talking about. Leave her alone, and let us go, why don't you?" She knew exactly what he wanted—the memory stick that now rested in Doc's pocket. She couldn't tell him that, but frankly, she didn't know what to say. He put his hand out to push her again when Erin spoke.

"Hold it, you guys. He gave it to me. I'll get it for you. Let me up." She spoke in a quick staccato, her voice high and tense. She started to straighten when the guy put his filthy hand around her delicate neck and squeezed it brutally hard. She gasped and felt as though she was going to pass out.

"Then get it, cunt, before I lose my temper. And then—then we can have some fun." His oily smile matched his slimy laugh and even greasier hair. He ran his hand over her breasts—leaving no doubt as to what he would consider fun. She laughed nervously and moved around the table like a crab sidling along the water's edge at the beach. Greasy Hair followed her into the workroom, where Erin pointed to her bag on the floor. She bent over to pick it up, her back to the threatening hoodlum. He grabbed a handful of her ass and began to run his hand down her butt and between her legs. He let out a disgusting chuckle as he thought about the rape and murder he planned in his dark, evil mind. Erin had no doubt about what he had planned, but was determined to change his malevolent little mind.

She picked up her bag and turned to face him. He was caught a little off balance, and he took two staggering steps backwards, putting him about four feet from Erin. She raised the bag to chest level and pushed it towards him, as though she wanted him to take it from her.

"Take it out of the bag, bitch. Give it to me!"

Death in Sturgis

Erin smiled an odd little smile and said, "Oh, you'll get it, all right," as she fired two shots from the Smith & Wesson 686 Plus revolver through the bottom of her handbag. The well-placed .357 rounds entered his chest just to center of his left nipple as two small, dark holes. They exited his back as one huge gush of blood, bone, and lung, throwing him off his feet and sending him crashing into the wall. He slid to the floor, leaving a bloody trail on the wall, and lay still. The roar echoed in the small workroom, and the smell of cordite filled the air.

Erin initially felt deafened and smothered, but she also experienced exhilaration unlike anything she'd ever felt before. It wasn't that she had enjoyed doing what she had just done, but she had acted to save her life and Jeanette's, too. She had no doubt that the men would have raped them both before killing them. It was just that simple. She was glad she'd taken Jim's registered weapon from its place in the truck and packed it into her bag this morning. At the time, she thought just the weight of it would be enough to fortify her during the wait for Doc and Bear. She had never expected in a million years that she would have to use the damn thing. She'd give Jim a big hug and kiss for insisting she and Tammy take lessons and frequent target practice to become familiar with the weapon. He'd even insisted on a concealed-carry permit. Now she had another slime ball rushing her way to see what had happened.

As the second man crashed into the workroom, he didn't see Erin standing behind the door. He stared at his friend in mute disbelief and began to back up, and then he felt the barrel of Erin's gun touch the back of his neck. He started to turn, but he heard the unmistakable sound of the hammer being drawn and cocked. Erin cooed, "I killed your asshole partner, and I'll be glad to kill you, too, if you keep moving! Drop the fucking gun!" The gun hit the floor with a dull thud.

She called Jeanette into the room and had her tie the man's hands while she kept the gun trained on him. She felt like a heroine from a mystery novel until she started shaking so badly she couldn't hold the gun anymore. She released the hammer and laid the gun on the kitchen table, well away from where they had tied up their captive. Jeanette hugged her tightly as she began to sob, no longer feeling like any type of hero in any book. They made sure the greasy man was dead, and then called the Belle Fourche police department.

The young deputy from yesterday was the first to arrive again today. As the day before, they gave attempted robbery as the motive. He seemed to have grown in experience since the previous day and calmly called in back-up. Once again, Jeanette's driveway looked like a parking lot for a police convention as they swarmed to inhale the excitement of the broiling afternoon.

It was after six by the time the last policeman left. They washed down the wall where the blood had smeared before sitting on Jeanette's front porch in her matching rockers. They opened fresh cans of ice-cold beer and sat rocking. This morning, they had been wary adversaries, ready to fight over Doc like chickens fighting over a bug. After what they had endured this afternoon, they were joined at the soul, sisters who had fought for each other and would never, ever forget.

38

Back to the Earth

Jasper Pendergast may have been approaching eighty, but he still did a full day's work. His small ranch on the outskirts of Sundance, Wyoming held over one hundred cattle, but could have supported more. Early each morning, he saw that there was enough feed and water to round out what they could get off his meager acreage. Late each afternoon, he rode the fences, ensuring the wire was intact, and nothing had become entangled in it. In between, he carried out a hundred other chores familiar to cattlemen around the world. Today, for example, he had used his aging manure spreader to fertilize his fields between US-14 and I-90 where Sundance Creek and Cundy Creek drained the stubborn, rocky terrain. Then he ran the powerful sprinklers there for an hour, to ensure last year's thoroughly decayed and aged manure began to enter the soaked ground. It smelled awful, but that was just part of ranch life here in Northwestern Wyoming. Now he had to head into town for some new saltpans; his old ones had seen better days, and he was down to just two. If he hurried, he could get back in time to lay out some bait traps around the barn. Yes, it was another busy day for Jasper.

Suddenly, he had to slam on his brakes before pulling onto the road. He just missed another damn fool youngster on a motorcycle, flying by like a bat out of Hell. Didn't these people have to work? This one had gone by at over sixty miles an hour, if he was going twenty. Irritated, but still needing his saltpans, Jasper pulled his 1978 Ford F150 out onto the road. This old baby had been through the wringer over the last twenty-plus years, but like Jasper, it worked day in and day out, whether it was a scorcher like today or a sub-zero Wyoming winter. Colder than a witch's tit in an iron bra on the shady side of an iceberg, Jasper thought, slowly moving his wheezing, beloved truck out onto Route 14, right into Doc's path.

Jasper vaguely saw the next motorcyclist come barreling along, way too fast for comfort. There was no way he'd be able to get around him on this little two-lane blacktop. The rider pressed down very hard and fast on the right handgrip. This moved the entire front tire to the left and forced him into a very sharp right turn. Fortunately, he was able to get enough purchase on the pavement to keep upright, although he leaned so far to his right that he scraped his shiny chrome exhaust pipes, and Jasper thought he'd fall over. The old rancher braced for impact but the bike cut to its right and entered the farm lane he'd just exited. Instead of a rending crunch of metal, all Jasper got was a shower of dust and gravel across his hood and against the left quarter panels of his truck. The bike disappeared with a cloud of dust behind him but Jasper figured there was little chance of him staying upright on the rough, worn macadam. He brought the truck to an abrupt halt and backed up to re-enter his property. That boy was going to need his help when he finally got that machine stopped.

Doc saw the pickup crawl onto the road after Noel passed it. It entered the main road from a small farm road to his right. The driver was so busy watching Noel disappear that he never glanced back to his left to see Doc approaching. Doc knew instantly that the truck was moving too slowly to get back into its lane by the time he reached it. The drainage ditches on either side left him no avenue of escape. He was moving too rapidly to brake in time to prevent crashing. The only option left was to try a severe turn to the right, onto the small lane the truck had just exited.

After he made the turn that avoided the truck and impressed the old rancher so much, Doc found himself speeding down a road that was apparently used to store potholes until they were needed elsewhere. He began braking, but instantly began wobbling as the bike bounced over the irregular surface, which looked like it had been imported from the dark side of the moon, craters and all. He did an admirable job of hard braking without locking up the front brake, but the bike just could not stay upright when the rear brake locked up, as he knew it must. He finally high ended at a respectable twenty miles an hour. He felt the bike go out from under him and pitch him over the top of his scoot. At least I'm not under the heavy Harley, he thought in the milliseconds he had to enjoy the flight. Doc pulled his arms and legs in tight to protect himself, should he roll when he finally hit the ground. Lord, he hoped the ground was soft. Maybe someone left a pile of unused mattresses or a mound of chicken feathers for him. He heard the bike go down in the gravel just an instant before his own soaring ended, leaving him face down in the field Jasper had just watered after fertilizing it with tons of aged manure.

Cow shit saved my life! Doc had to laugh when he finally stopped sliding in the foul mixture. He left a slick, slimy trail over thirty feet long through the malodorous muck, which found its way into every fold and pocket of his clothes in less than two seconds. Sure, fresh manure was bad enough, but this stuff had been reaching a state of shit perfection as it stewed in Jasper's compost pile for almost a year.

Slowly, Doc flexed each limb and felt his neck to make sure nothing was seriously injured or broken. He stood shakily as the old truck pulled up along the narrow gravel road. He had lost sufficient velocity in the turn, and the potholes had helped him to dissipate enough of his remaining momentum, that he had survived. Of course, a lot of credit had to be given to the benevolent spirits that had prompted the rancher to prepare his field this way, today, of all days.

"Damn, young fella. Are you okay? I figured you for dead," called the old man from his truck window. He matched his faded truck perfectly. They say couples look more and more like each other as the years go by. Others say you tend to resemble your dog. In this man's case, Doc thought he and his truck had aged along similar lines, molded by the Wyoming sun, wind, and cattle. Jasper would have taken it as a compliment to be compared to his well-worn truck. He alit from the cab and sauntered over to where Doc was walking from his field. "I guess that cow shit provided you a little bit of cushion, huh?"

"Yeah, I think so, Pops. I think so. I wouldn't recommend getting off yer bike that way, though! Let's see how my scoot is doing'."

They walked over to the silent motorcycle lying on its left side on the macadam and gave it a good looking over. With a few grunts, they were able to get it upright and onto its kickstand. The bike had numerous scratches, a golf-ball sized ding in the tank, and the right foot pegs were slightly crooked. Doc bent the mirror back into an acceptable position. The engine rumbled to life on the very first try, and Doc failed to suppress a shout of joy.

He grinned at the rancher, "I reckon the good Lord was watchin' over me today, huh, old timer?" Doc began wiping some of the foul slime with his hands and shaking them off. Bits of sour material fell as he tried to shake like a dog. Jasper wrinkled up his nose when he had to get very close to Doc or stood downwind.

"Yes, sir, he certainly was, young man. If you like, you can come up to the house and wash off there. I don't know what you smelled like before, but you sure do stink now!" the old man cackled.

"Well, that sounds good, sir. That sounds good. I'm in an awful hurry, but I guess I should hose myself off before this stuff sets like concrete!" Noel was far, far down the road by now, and there was little Doc could do to catch him. He planned on a quick rinse with the rancher's hose, and then hauling ass back to Jeanette and Erin. Moreover, he had to check on Bear, although he was sure the lung injury was on the benign side, as far as gunshots to the chest go.

Doc followed the rancher's truck two miles over softly rolling fields, where cattle stood in small groups watching them with little interest. They pulled up outside a few sun-faded buildings where Jasper had a hose. He and Doc exchanged names and a few other pleasantries while Doc stripped nude and washed off with the cold water. It felt good in the hot sun, and it was great to get the crap off his body; it was rapidly hardening into nasty-smelling cement from Hell. Jasper found a pair of worn, but serviceable overalls for him. They were a bit tight around the middle, but fit well enough otherwise. Jasper didn't seem to have a spare ounce of fat on his wizened body, whereas Doc had bellied-up to a few too many bars and did much less physical work.

Doc thanked the old man repeatedly for his help and for preparing the field for him. Jasper laughed and guided him back to the main road. Doc took a long look up and down the lanes before pulling out and riding the short distance to a truck stop Jasper had recommended. The old farmer, who stood next to his beloved pickup truck, returned his wave. Doc's ride was seriously short on gas, and he thought he could wash a little more thoroughly at the station.

The Shovelhead rode and performed with no indication of serious damage on the short trip to the truck stop. After filling the tank, he parked it near the entrance to the men's room and as far as possible from the two State Highway Patrol cruisers sitting silent and empty by the main entrance. Doc couldn't help but notice that a few heads turned as their noses alerted them to his aromatic presence. He bought some shampoo, aftershave, and deodorant in the convenience mart before making his way to the men's room to wash his hair and try to get off the worst of the stench.

He washed in one of the large sinks where truckers often shaved and washed their upper bodies during long trips. Others came and went, a few sniffing at the fetid reek, but none said anything. Perhaps they didn't want to mess with the biker, but he figured they just didn't want to get too close to that awful smell! Most avoided the sink on either side of him, too. Fortunately or not, few men washed their hands after pissing unless their mothers or women were with them on the road, anyway.

Doc was rinsing his long, thick hair one last time when he looked into the mirror and recognized Gunther Popp behind him, standing at the urinals. He was draining his bladder, seemingly unaware of anyone around him. Perhaps the smell or innocent act of shampooing at the sink made Doc appear no threat. There were no others in the john. Doc slowly and silently crossed the room as Gunther shook the last few drops of urine from his pecker and pulled up his zipper. Doc waited for him to turn from about four feet away. Recognition flared in Gunther's eyes as his hand raced to his jacket opening, where Doc was sure a pistol waited. Doc closed with him and gave him three rapid right jabs in the face before Gunther could say a word or pull his weapon.

Gunther collapsed into the urinal, but Doc grabbed him by the collar, removed his gun, and kept him from falling to the floor. He threw the gun into the pile of clothes by the sink and turned his attention back to the groggy Gunther. He vigorously pummeled Gunther's face and abdomen, rendering his eyes into swollen bags of meat, and his nose into a bloated mass of putty. He broke at least one yellow tooth before he stopped and dragged Gunther into the farthest toilet stall from the door. Gunther's hands were tied together using his bootlaces, and he was propped on the toilet like a king on a throne. Doc stuffed the man's mouth with a dirty rag found on the restroom floor. Perfect, he thought. Now what? Doc's mind raced for a few minutes. He had to decide whether to call the troopers outside and alert them to the guns, drugs, and money in the possession of Gunther and his crew. However, the last thing he wanted was to be a snitch. Traditionally, he solved his own problems and seldom, if ever, involved the law. This time, however, was different. For one thing, the possibility of him successfully taking on the other four Los Angeles thugs was very slight. Other than the boss man himself, he had no beef with the hired help. After all, Gunther had fired the shot that hit Bear. Doc detested him for dealing drugs with Noel, but he couldn't kill him for it. No, he finally realized with a sigh, it's probably all right this time to use John Law to get the desired results. He dug around in his wallet, relieved that the contents had remained reasonably dry during his recent swim in Lake Manure, and pulled out Lieutenant Shelton's card. He finished rinsing and redressed. He checked that Gunther was still in nighty-night land, emptied the thug's pistol, and left it in the toilet at Gunther's feet. Then he gathered his clothes, poured a healthy dollop of aftershave over his body, and left the restroom. He used the hall phone to call the lieutenant. When told that Shelton was out on a call, Doc declined being patched through to him and instead told the trooper on the phone where he could find Gunther and what his claim to fame was. He then walked into the restaurant portion of the truck stop, ordered something cold to soothe his parched throat, and sat where he could watch the troopers eating their hamburgers and French fries across the room. He saw the rest of Gunther's gang sitting by the window, looking very sullen, and he tried his best to look invisible, to both the troopers and the hoodlums. After about five minutes, the four men rose from the table and moved towards the restroom, no doubt looking for their leader. How long did he take to piss, anyway? Just then, the small radios perched on the troopers' shoulders began to chirp their little songs. The men leaned their heads over to hear better, reminding Doc of the old RCA-Victor dog. He almost burst into laughter when they jumped up, knocked over their chairs, scattering half-eaten French fries, and made a bee-line for the men's room. He hoped they'd get a big surprise when they found Gunther and company. He imagined the troopers would ask all the right questions.

Doc drained the fresh, tart lemonade he'd ordered, left the restaurant, and returned to his bike. Fortunately, his scoot smelled better than he did. As the storm clouds that had been slowly building to the west made their way over Sundance, he made a call to Jeanette and told her a little of what had happened. She said next to nothing about her day, but said that she and Erin had gotten along quite well. Doc was relieved they had not come to any harm and that Bear's fear of a major explosion seemed unfounded. He arranged to meet them at Jeanette's, and then they could travel down to see Bear in Rapid City.

Doc predicted that the rain would hit just about when he reached Jeanette's. Good timing, he smiled. For the first time, all day, good timing. He pulled onto I-90 as the first cool, fat raindrops hit the pavement behind him and evaporated almost instantly on meeting its simmering heat. Two speeding Highway Patrol cruisers exited the highway at the same time, their lights flashing. It took little guesswork to predict where they were going. He rolled on the throttle in an effort to outrun the storm and put some distance between him and Sundance. Lightning began to flash behind him, followed by a deep bass rumble as thunder announced the storm that had waited all day for its chance to raise a little Hell. He saw and smelled serious rain about ten miles to the west.

He needed a good bath, all right, but Doc preferred it in a nice bathtub full of hot water, with a cold drink in his hand and a warm woman washing his back. With one of those little smiles on his face, he rolled on the throttle just that much more.

39

Rainstorm

Doc barely beat the rain as he pulled into Jeanette's driveway and ran in her backdoor. A cold wind had been chasing him for the past half hour, bringing the kind of storm that follows a scorching South Dakota day. He found the women sitting in the kitchen, where they had relocated from the front porch as the storm blew up. They barraged him with questions until his stench made itself known.

"Oh, my God, Doc, what is that smell? I mean, I've smelled a lot of dog crap, but that's really rank!" Erin announced as Jeanette waited for enlightenment with a small smile. She began running the shower so he would have some hot water and laid out a fresh towel.

"Well, it's a long story, but basically, I just had my life saved by cow shit!" He chuckled as he indicated his small bundle of foul smelling clothes on the back porch stoop and began to strip off Jasper's overalls. Nude, he continued to talk to the two women standing together in the bathroom door and climbed into the tub-shower. The hot water felt good but it tended to dribble out under low pressure like many rural homes with a cistern. He missed the biting needles of a good, steaming shower, but enjoyed the rich lather he was making with Jeanette's lavender soap. He might smell a trifle like a little old lady, but it certainly beat eau d'manure! As he scrubbed, he shouted over the sound of the water and the storm blowing outside. He told them about his close encounter at Devil's Tower and Bear's wound. He tried to make it sound serious, but not too grim, because he truly expected Bear to be observed overnight and sent home in the morning. He'd done that himself with patients suffering certain gunshot wounds. Finally, he described his swan dive into the manure field and meeting Gunther again in the Amoco Travel Center. Doc almost apologized for calling the troopers, but they agreed he was right in not trying to tackle the whole group by himself. The shower finished, he climbed out and toweled off.

He grinned sheepishly at the two women and asked how their day had been.

Jeanette described how they'd spent much of the day cleaning until two thugs arrived and started pushing her around. Doc stopped smiling and stood with his mouth hanging open as Jeanette described Erin's quick thinking and facility with a handgun. He shivered when she described shooting the man and wasn't sure if it was from the cool air blowing the curtains in the bedroom window or his fear over the two thugs and relief about Erin being a modern Annie Oakley. Slipping into a clean pair of jeans from his saddlebags, he crossed the room and reached out to them. For a long moment, they all embraced, until each began to feel a little awkward and separated. He made them tell him the story again, from the moment Erin arrived, until the last policeman departed. He was visibly shaken at how close they had come to being raped and murdered.

"Lord, Lord, you two! I figured y'all could take care of each other, but I never thought you'd be doin' all that!" he exclaimed. He had not been surprised when Erin told him about Jeanette standing up to the creep to protect her, but frankly, he hadn't expected Erin to have a gun, much less know how to use it! He was thoroughly impressed by the both of them and told them so. "Those sons of bitches never figured on fuckin' with y'all! I'm proud of both of you!" he drawled. A noticeable twang was present in his voice, from fatigue, emotional upheaval, and their actions.

The three moved from Jeanette's bedroom, where Doc had finished dressing while talking with them. Erin had felt a little uncomfortable there, knowing Doc and Jeanette had spent many nights in that room and in that bed making love. She wasn't angry, and she didn't think she felt jealous, she just felt like she was looking in the window from the outside, watching two old friends in a private moment.

In the kitchen, Doc took the time to drink three cold Coors beers that were still in the fridge, one after another. He wiped his mouth and smiled at the women. He wasn't planning to drive, anyway. They agreed to take Erin's truck and Jeanette's venerable Wiley Jeep, which had sufficed through many dry, hot summers and bone-freezing prairie winters. Erin was planning to leave in the morning with her family and head back to Indiana. One of them could still spend the night with Bear and fetch his motorcycle from the Devil's Tower in the morning. Erin was hoping for time alone with Doc before she had to leave. She very much wanted to explain to him how much he mattered, and how much Jeanette had come to mean to her, too.

They reached the Rapid City Hospital and located Bear's room easily. He was being kept for overnight observation. As Doc had thought, the leather jacket Bear was wearing, as well as the thick muscle of his chest, had slowed the bullet considerably. It had passed through his lung and was lodged in the muscle layers of his back. No ribs had been fractured, the lung had not collapsed, and there was no reason for surgery. Doc soothed Bear's apprehensions about being in the hospital overnight and reassured him that they'd get his '47 knucklehead from the Devil's Tower by the time he was released tomorrow. There was no way to get it past the locked gates of the parking lot after closing time, anyway, On the ride to Rapid City Doc had arranged for someone he knew from the Black Hills Harley Davison dealership to fetch it in the morning and keep it for Bear until he got out of the hospital.

"Well, Doc, I s'pose ya know best, ya've done alright so far. An' Hell, them ladies done alright, too! I'm proud of 'em. Me, I'm just sittin' here, takin' up space until they let me out tomorra. I'm no good to ya like this, I'm afraid," he pouted for Erin.

"Now, Bear," Erin laughed, "those rangers were very impressed with you, I think they may be in love!"

"Yeah, but not with me, I hope! If I can't have Jeanette or Erin, I don' want nobody," he roared in return. Jeanette turned a little red and smiled softly. She was tired and ready to go to sleep. Erin gave him a hug, and then apologized for bumping his bandages. "Hell, girl, ya don't have to say sorry for rubbin' up against me! I like it! What I didn't like was those FBI bozos."

Two FBI agents had already been to visit Bear's hospital room because the shooting had occurred on federal property. Bear had been circumspect, telling them he thought they were defacing public property and was just doing his part to keep the National Park clean. The agents, in Rapid City on other business from the Minneapolis field office, probably believed little to none of his story. However, they had gotten essentially the same story from the two park rangers that were the new heroes of Devil's Tower, having risked death to protect their charge. Still, they had two dead bodies to work with, and they placed great stock in forensic evidence.

There was no easy way to connect these deaths with the investigation by the Highway Patrol into the deaths of Todd and Tracie, or the arrests of California drug dealers in Sundance in the last hour. Likewise, because of the splintering of law enforcement in this country, with its associated chaos and selfish guarding of information between agencies, neither the FBI nor the state troopers were aware of the disturbances and deaths at Jeanette's art gallery in Belle Fourche over the last two days. A simple digital database shared between the groups would immediately pick up the common threads running through the events, and at least ring a little bell for someone to look deeper into what was going on. Criminals had appreciated this chaos for years, and at least for the minute, so did Doc. The last thing he wanted was to spend the day in an interrogation room answering questions.

Doc saw the fatigue in Jeanette's face and watched her stifle a yawn. As Bear's closest family member (according to Bear, at least), she was going to stay the night on a small pullout bed. Doc and Erin were staying the night in Bear's hotel room. In the morning, she'd take Doc back up to Jeanette's for his Wide Glide and then return to the Tilford campground; Jim and Tammy wanted to leave for Indiana by noon. She was not looking forward to saying goodbye to Doc at all.

When visiting hours ended, they took their leave of Bear and visited the ER. Doc's friend, Dr. Jim Foster, was working the night shift. As he introduced Erin to the ER physician, he looked her up and down and said, "Boy, Doc, you sure can pick them. You must be doing something right to meet beautiful, young girls like this and stay out of my emergency department!"

Doc agreed on both counts and turned the conversation to the toxicology results from Todd's autopsy. Dr. Foster nodded his head vigorously. "Yeah, man, after I called the pathologist about something as bizarre as killing someone with Antabuse and booze, she ran the specific tests right away. Apparently, it takes some fancy gas chromatography, but she was able set it up and run it pretty quickly. His disulfiram levels are still being calculated because they have to dilute the blood repeatedly, but they were sky high. They also checked acetaldehyde levels, and they knocked the top off the test tube. You were right. The pathologist and I want to write up the case; do you want to co-author with us? Man, I never heard of anything like this before. Who did it? Why did they kill him? Can you tell me about it?"

"Well, I really can't say much since the cops will be investigating, but the creep who did it is still on the loose. I plan on calling him in just a few hours to get a rise out of him."

Dr. Foster looked confused. "Still on the loose? Who's running the show here? The pathologist tried to tell the coroner about this, but they want to handle it as another drunken biker who wrecked his ride. And why would you want to agitate this guy? Isn't that dangerous? Aren't you going to let the police handle it?"

Doc shook his head. "I don't think the police have it together enough to figure out what's going on, even if we tried to tell them. It's an old problem; the cops think of bikers as adversaries, as if we're all one-percenters who want to steal their cars, rape their wives, and sell drugs to their daughters. There's a point of honor here, too. Not only has this asshole killed at least three people, he is directly responsible for serious injury to two of my very best friends. And for that he's going to have to answer to me."

Again, Erin saw the intensity Doc felt about his friends getting hurt. On the ride down from Belle Fourche, he had said Noel was the cause of not only Jake, Todd, and Tracie's deaths, but because of him three of his hired guns were dead, and two more were seriously injured. Doc had explained that when bad things like this went down, someone needed to stand up and make the asshole account for what he'd done. Sometimes a big guy did the job, sometime a little one—male or female, young or old—someone had to do dirty work, and often got no thanks at all. Hell, sometimes you suffered for standing up against the evil right in front of you.

"I still think you should help write the case up with us. You could even write a book using that as part of the plot, you know—a medical mystery. We could sell the idea to *CSI: Miami*. Or that guy, Michael Palmer, who wrote that book with the longhaired ER doctor?" Dr. Foster found it all very funny. He didn't see the black gleam in Doc's eyes or hear the chill in his voice.

"Naw, go ahead and write it up if y'all want; I don't mind. Publishing is the furthest thing from my mind right now," Doc continued. He pulled Erin close to him and smiled a bit. "Come on, darlin', let's leave this poor doctor to slave away the rest of his shift. What is it eight or twelve?"

"Oh, we take it easy on ourselves here; it's only an eight-hour shift. Then I can go home and dream about writing this article and beautiful young girls!" He grinned broadly at Erin, who found his attention a little disconcerting. She'd never known any doctors, and this guy came on a little strong. Doc, on the other hand, didn't really seem like a doctor at all. He seemed, well, she wasn't sure what he seemed or how she felt right now. The stress of the day, and knowing she would be leaving him in the morning, made her feel very tired. They left the busy ER holding hands, something simple that felt very, very good. She walked with him, thinking with her singing heart. Doc was thinking with his heart and his brain. Neither was singing...

He knew from his initial conversations with Todd and Noel, almost a week ago, that Noel was scheduled to fly back east at three o'clock the next afternoon. He doubted Noel would feel lonely without Todd. He doubted that the bastard felt much of anything at all. However, Doc planned to make him feel a great deal today. He was sure Noel was furious over the collapse of his drug deal and would do almost anything to get back at him. He was also sure that any encounter with Noel would be dangerous; Noel would kill him, given half a chance.

Doc's plan started with calling Noel in the very early hours and irritating the shit out him. He would offer to trade the information Todd had so painstakingly collected. Noel would probably offer money or some such thing. Without his hoodlums helping him, there was a chance he could outwit Noel without having to fight him. True, Noel still had had his gun, and so far, had shown no reluctance in using it. Doc had no gun, just a buck knife, and his wits. You never take the wrong weapon to a fight, he'd learned. Taking a knife to a fistfight often ended up with the knife-bearer getting the crap knocked out of him. If he set this up right, Noel's gun would give him no advantage at all—similar to the way Gunther couldn't shoot with dozens of bystanders and potential eyewitnesses he'd have to face later in a courtroom. The only problem was constructing a scenario where Doc could come out ahead.

Erin too, was quiet, wrapped in her own thoughts, on the walk back to her truck in the hospital parking lot. They drove back to the Black Hawk Super 8 Motel around eleven o'clock. The room was cool with air conditioning, as well as the rain. It looked like it would rain all night. They had a few drinks from a bottle of Jack Daniels bought before they'd left Rapid City. Doc had been pulling from the bottle on the ride, but she'd waited until they got to the room and she could get a glass and some ice cubes. He opened the window to let in some fresh, cool air. She heard the rain as it beat against the pavement and vehicles in the parking lot. He stared into the night as she came from behind and wrapped her arms around him. He half-turned and put his right arm around her. He moved slowly from the cut on his side, his flight over the lake of cow shit, and his less than perfect landing. He was more than a little stiff, but the warmth of the Tennessee sour mash whiskey and the even warmer young woman at his side was beginning to relax him. He'd thought enough about how to handle Noel tomorrow, and he was ready to relax. It was a skill he'd learned years ago, when he decided he'd spent enough energy on some problem, he would let it go until a better time arose.

Doc put his head down and began to kiss Erin's face slowly. He kissed each closed eye and her cheeks. As he did, he softly stroked her neck with one hand and pulled her closer with the other. Minute by sensual minute, they stood slowly kissing, deeply probing each other's mouth. He sensed her building excitement as she breathed more deeply, occasionally sighing or uttering a low moan.

He began to harden. She felt it through his pants as she moved against him. She kneaded his chest with one hand and began to fondle him with the other. His hand wandered down to her left breast and started to squeeze it rhythmically. As she moaned louder, he unbuttoned her blouse and slowly drew it off, kissing her shoulders. She reached behind and unsnapped her bra.

"Hey, I was getting there!" he said into her open mouth.

"I know, Doc. I can't wait; you're driving me crazy. I mean, I've never felt this way. If only I didn't have to leave in the morning. I hate it! I don't want to go; I—"

"Shh, we're here now," he whispered as his fingers began to twist and pinch her nipples softly. "We're here now, and we don't even know if we'll be alive tomorrow. Hell, we were almost killed today. But here I am, alive and very, very happy to be right where I am, right here, right now. Let's enjoy what we've got while we've got it. There's no place in this whole damn world I'd rather be than where I am. With you. Right now." He leaned over and covered her mouth with his; he lifted her, as though she weighed nothing, and carried her to the bed.

His hands and tongue were everywhere at once. She helped him take off her clothes and slipped under the covers as he pulled his shirt over his head and undid his belt. She reached out to unzip his pants, which slipped over his ass and fell to his feet. Her hand found his already erect cock and used it to pull him into the bed with her. She quickly slid on top of him to rescue him from the cold covers and leaned down to kiss him and rub her taut, eager breasts against his chest, the hairs bringing her nipples to their hardest. He continued kissing her face and neck and the valley between her breasts. His other hand found her clit and began to massage it, softly at first, and then more vigorously.

Finally, she could stand no more and pushed his hand away, grabbed his swollen dick, and slid it fully up into her vagina. The suddenness and stretched fullness brought a sharp gasp from her. She reassured him that she wasn't in pain and proved it as she began to move up and down the length of his dick. Erin used her position on top to control the speed and depth of their lovemaking. She held onto the headboard for stability and rode him quickly. He warned her she was going to make him come, and she smiled happily. She continued her grinding motion until he came with a low growl. She sat there for a long time, looking down at him, before dismounting, and curling in his arms. For the first time that day, she truly felt safe; he did that for her, and she loved him for it.

Outside, the storm's fury intensified and a fine mist blew into the room through the open window. It didn't bother the two lovers as they lay holding each other tightly. They dozed off under the covers as the storm passed and the still of the night deepened. The skies cleared, and overhead, the summer Perseid meteor shower blazed away with dozens of meteors an hour. If they had been awake, Erin would have insisted they make a wish on every single shooting star.

40

PRIMING THE CHUMP

SATURDAY

The night was almost silent, with barely any traffic on I-90 as Doc arose at three o'clock to start his campaign to infuriate Noel. He still had Booster's cell phone from the First Battle of Belle Fourche. He dialed Noel's phone; it rang for several minutes before Noel answered.

"Yes?" Noel spit out with all the venom of a cobra. Doc paused just long enough to irritate him. Before Noel could hang up or start talking, he spoke.

"Time is up, Noel. Your little party is ending. You can try to go back to sleep, but it's only a matter of time before I come for you. And I will come for you. Today. And you're going to pay for what you've done, you pitiful bastard."

Doc spoke very slowly and quietly. He used his most intimidating voice to build fear and tension in Noel. Apparently, it worked because Noel shouted in a loud, but shaky voice, "Lovejoy, you no-good, son of—"

Doc hung up and turned off the ringer on Booster's phone. Noel could call him as many times as he liked and he wouldn't have to listen to the thing's shrill call for attention. By keeping it on with the ringer turned down, the phone would ring much longer than if he just turned it off. Just another way to piss off Noel. And a pissed off Noel would be easier to handle than a rational, logical one.

After another hour of sleep, he rose again and checked the phone. Noel had called over and over again, the last time only fifteen minutes ago. Hopefully, he had gone back to sleep and was just entering REM cycle. That was the optimal time to disrupt rejuvenating sleep. Doc could be cold and calculating when he wanted to be. This time, the phone rang five times before a seething Noel picked it up. "Now listen to me, Lovejoy, if you think—"

"Noel, Noel, Noel," Doc interrupted. "There's really nothing you can do or say. First thing in the morning, I'm taking the extremely incriminating documentation I'm holding in my hand to the Highway Patrol. They know about the disulfiram, too." There was a long silence while he let that sink in. "Yes, I guess you're just not as smart as you thought you were. They also found DNA evidence linking you to poor Tracie's murder. And you know the shootings at Devil's Tower occurred on federal land, so now you're facing a federal rap, too." Doc knew he had him hook, line, and sinker; Noel listened in infuriated frustration. Doc was using educated guesses and lies, but they were fabrications that Noel was more than ready to believe. I must keep him off balance, Doc thought. "Another one of your creeps was killed in Belle Fourche yesterday, too. Yep, sorry about that, but at least the other one is alive and well, singing his heart out to the police at this very minute. You're trapped, jackass, and there's not a thing you can do." Noel remained silent, but Doc could hear the air whistling in and out of Noel's nostrils. Doc chuckled malevolently and hung up.

Noel only called back twice during the next hour. The rain had stopped, and it was starting to get light again to the east, when Doc picked up the phone and dialed again. This time, Noel picked up the phone instantly, and just said, "Yes," in a very flat voice. Doc had a little trouble telling if he was so angry, all emotion had drained from his voice, or if he was starting to wear down.

"Look out your window, Noel, it's just starting to get light outside, but in a few hours, everything you've done will be out for everybody and their brother to see! I'm going to let the Highway Patrol in on what you did to Todd and Tracie; the Belle Fourche cops know you were behind the assault on those women, and the FBI know about the drug deal you had the balls to try to carry out on federal land. Gee, Noel, they're gonna fight over you like hounds over a kitten. It's gonna get real messy. I guess there won't even be enough of you to send home—"

"What do you want, Lovejoy? I don't believe you're calling only to taunt me. You may be a reprobate and an embarrassment to our profession, but you're not stupid. I don't know why you associate with those people as you do... What do you want from me? What do you want?" His voice went from tired and defeated to loud and defiant. He must still have a lot of fight left in him, Doc thought. He needs a little more tenderizing before I meet him and that pistol of his.

"I'm not quite sure what I want. I know you grabbed that dope when you ran off like a scared rabbit; man, I didn't know you could move so fast! I tell you what, Noel—you think about what you have to offer. What you could possibly have to trade that will keep me from wringing your scrawny neck like a chicken for the pot? You'll hear from me in another hour. I know you plan to leave this afternoon, so we only have a few hours and a few chances to barter. And I'm not going to be easy to deal with!"

He hung up before Noel could respond. There, he thought, the seed was planted, and all we have to do is let it grow for a while. He returned to the still dark bedroom and stood at the open window facing east. A glow along the horizon grew minute by minute. The pre-dawn light was difficult to describe; it might have been blue, white, or even green. The sky was clear, without a cloud in sight, and the only real light came from a first quarter moon high in the sky and the brilliant morning star shining with a faint green cast just above the horizon. The cool, sweet morning breeze was beginning to stir, and the smell made Doc inhale deeply—a mixture of earth, sky, and motorcycles. He wondered briefly if Crazy Horse had ever stood breathing the passing night air on such a morning as this. After a few more minutes, he returned to the warm, young woman snoring softly in the bed. She nestled in his arms and dreamed a woman's dreams, something he doubted he would ever be able to fathom.

At six o'clock, he rose and went into the bathroom again to make the next call to Noel. This time we'll put his core values in jeopardy, thought Doc. He sat on the cold toilet seat with Booster's cell phone in one hand, and the cool, square-bottomed bottle of Jack Daniels in the other. He contemplated the bottle for a few minutes.

Old Jack started bottling his whiskey in earthenware jugs with his name stenciled on the side of the jug back in Lynchburg, Tennessee in 1866, just a few years after the bloodletting known as the American Civil War. He followed the demands of the market and switched to those new-fangled glass bottles sometime in the late 1870's. A new model with a fluted neck and a square bottle became the container of choice for Jack by 1895.

The drink got its distinctive mellow taste by filtering the sour mash through ten feet of sugar maple charcoal over a ten-day period. It was then stored for months in huge barrels of American white oak, where the whiskey and the barrels interacted with each other, swelling and shrinking with the weather, trading organic chemicals complex enough to scare the hardiest chemist. It should probably be considered a health food; it has only seventy-two calories per fluid ounce, with no fats, sugars, starches, or cholesterol. Doc used it as one of the major food groups.

After a long, slow drink that burned all the way down and brought aromatic fumes back up through his nose, he had started to dial Noel again when he saw that Booster's phone was being called. With the ringer off, he hadn't heard it, of course. It was Noel.

"You're getting anxious, Noel." Doc said very softly and slowly. He wanted to keep the pace of the conversation slow, to build more anxiety in his counterpart.

"Yes, Lovejoy, I suppose I am," Noel replied in a rapid, clipped voice. "Perhaps we can make a deal."

"A deal? Why, Noel, what kind of deal can we make? I'm notoriously hard to deal with, you know. But it's so sad; you'll lose your big house. Your beautiful wife will be so lonely while you're gone. Gone to prison, that is. I'm not sure which jurisdiction will win out in trying your sorry ass, but you'll go away for a long, long time. What do you have that I could possibly want that'll keep me from seeing you fry?"

"I can get you money, Lovejoy, lots of money. I can make you a very wealthy man."

"What do I want with money, Noel? You said it yourself, I'm a reprobate, and I'd probably just piss it away. What else have you got?" He didn't want to push it too hard, because when you really got down to it there wasn't anything in the world Noel could offer him that would matter. Nothing could prevent the swift justice hurtling down the highway like an out-of-control Mack truck. "Think about that for the next hour, Noel." Instead of hanging up, Doc paused to listen to the silence on the line. There was no doubt that Noel was listening. Doc let out a little more slack and sat back to watch his fishing line spread out across the ether.

Nothing except heavy breathing came across the connection. Noel was following the path to doom Doc portrayed. When Doc had him convinced there was no way out, that no way to save himself existed, he would finally offer Noel a carrot. Not yet; now was the time to hang up and wait another hour. He did so without another word.

Death in Sturgis

During the next sixty minutes, Doc planned what he would do if Noel took the bait, and how he'd handle Noel's inevitable attempt to double-cross him. As Doc was sure would happen, Noel lay awake in the dark of his rental trailer and played possible scenarios in his head. He even began to count the minutes until Doc made his next call. It was a curious battle, this struggle between two men in the dark, miles apart, communicating via invisible digital signals on their respective pathways from cell to cell.

Noel answered on the first ring. He had not tried to call Booster's phone for the last hour. "What will it be, Noel? The sun is up now. What can you offer to save your sorry ass? I'm still awfully pissed about my friends being hurt, but I'm listening, so go ahead."

"I propose we meet face to face. We can thrash out our differences and attain some fashion of compromise. I sincerely hope we can reach an accord. That may or may not comprise of monies or other, shall we say, commodities." Noel sounded regrouped and ready, smug and confident. That could only mean he had contrived a sneaky trick that would get him what he wanted and most likely leave Doc dead.

"I think a meeting can be arranged, Noel; I have a place picked out. You must bring the cocaine you ran off with, your money, and your gun. Is that agreeable?"

"Certainly, I am at your disposal. Where and when? I am, as you know, on somewhat of a schedule." Damn, he has something up his sleeve, Doc thought.

Doc inhaled deeply and started, "All right, let me give you directions. Write this down."

41

Shake Hands With the Devil

Once, the Sioux people lived underground and called themselves Pte Oyate, the Buffalo Nation. They came to live aboveground, where life was very, very hard. To help them, Tatanka, a magical holy man, came to them in the shape of a buffalo and gave the people everything they needed. The people used his tanned hide to make moccasins, winter clothes, pipe bags, quivers, and tipi covers. His rawhide produced shields, buckets, ropes, saddles, moccasins, headdresses, and drums. Cups, spoons, and ladles came from his horns. Decorations were formed from his tail and beard. The rendered fat of his body was used for soap and cooking oil, while his bones made knives, scrapers, and war clubs. His manure burned hotly without much smell or smoke. The people used his stomach and bladder as buckets, cooking pots, and cups. Rattles and glue were made from the hooves, and his hair created headdresses, halters, ropes, and pillows. The tongue was considered the tastiest part of his meat, although the people used the muscles for meat, jerky, and the sinews were needed for lashing and making bowstrings. Buckskin was tanned using his brain. A special bond existed between Tatanka and the Sioux.

When the white man arrived, there were over sixty million buffalo versus a few dozen horses. By the early 1800's over two hundred thousand buffalo were slaughtered annually on the plains, in addition to a tremendous loss of habitat incurred through farming and the fencing of huge amounts of rangeland. Buffalo robes were very popular items back east and in Europe. Their bones were burned and sent back east for their phosphorous content, a valuable fertilizer component. By 1886, zoologists were hard-pressed to find a herd of more than twenty to thirty animals, and by 1893, less than three hundred animals were left on the entire continent.

Death in Sturgis

In the twenty-first century, there were over five thousand buffalo in South Dakota alone. Most lived on the Triple U ranch, northwest of Fort Pierre. Like Lonny's horse from Interior, they were used in the Kevin Costner movie *Dances with Wolves*. Many others lived on Indian reservations. Over two thousand resided on the Cheyenne River Reservation, and one to six hundred on some of the others. Custer State Park had a herd of over fifteen hundred and hosted an auction of several hundred each year to keep the herd size stable.

The buffalo was more closely related to the bison of Europe and Canada, than to the buffalo of Asia and Africa. Scientifically speaking, the American Buffalo was a bison, and as such was a member of the Bovidae family, the same family to which cows belong. Call it what you will, the buffalo played a tremendous role in the history and culture of this continent for both white and dark-skinned peoples.

Noel fussed and fumed as he rode his Big Dog down I-90 and headed south on Route 16, traveling many of the same miles crossed when he took Tracie to Mount Rushmore to meet her fate. He stayed on Route 16 through Hill City and continued past the Crazy Horse Memorial. In Custer, he found a parking spot at the end of a long line of bikes on the main road. He shook with fury at having to meet Lovejoy's demands. He fervently hoped he could get the documents from him before he killed him. He planned to kill him slowly and painfully if possible, but would choose a quick kill if he had to. The thought of pain spreading across Lovejoy's face as blood spilled from his body brought a good feeling to Noel's heart. God knew why Lovejoy had insisted on meeting him in Custer; other than a few bars and smelly biker-types, there was little here. He was immensely glad to leave the Buffalo Chip, the loud degenerates, and their foul, disgusting women. The noise, the raucous music, and the constant sound of motorcycles had driven him almost to the end of his rope.

As instructed, he found a place to park along Mount Rushmore Road. He winced at the sophomoric street name. Typical, he thought. It was typical of the western jejune mindset. He missed his home with his wine collection and paintings. Lovejoy's insinuations that he would lose all that had made him angry and brought his killing instinct to the searing, burning surface of his soul. He locked his bike once and left the fork lock undone; he might want to leave this mud-hole of a town quickly. He couldn't leave it unlocked altogether; one of the slimy thieves around him would steal his magnificent motorcycle in a heartbeat.

He walked east and found the drinking establishment Lovejoy had identified as their point of assembly—the Frontier Bar and Lounge—how utterly romantic. Leave it to that embarrassment of a doctor to select such a disreputable locale. He approached the paired swinging doors that looked like something out of an old 'B' movie, looked both ways, and walked in. He was at an immediate disadvantage because of the poor lighting. It took a moment for his eyes to adjust, and then he saw Lovejoy sitting alone at a table toward the rear. Damn! The saloon was crowded with unbathed, drunken, good-for-nothings laughing and carousing. It was the kind of place where he couldn't deal with Lovejoy as he wanted. There were too many people like him there that would leap to his defense should anything happen. He couldn't use his gun openly due to the tight confines. He suspected that many of the degenerates around the bar were comrades of Lovejoy, ready to jump on him and beat him to a pulp using their numbers against him.

Doc sat at the table with a bottle of Jack Daniels and no glass. He pushed a chair out a few feet across the sawdust-covered floor towards Noel with a kick. Noel paused, but finally took the seat offered in so gentlemanly a manner. He felt a wave of nausea as he inhaled the sour smell of beer and sweat that wafted over the unwashed crowd. He waited a moment for a waiter, but none appeared. Doc sat across from him like an enigmatic criminal, dressed in a black leather jacket and an American flag doo-rag. His dark sunglasses hid his eyes, making Noel guess where he was looking and what he was thinking. Damn him and his malefactor's ways!

Finally, Noel started, "Doctor Lovejoy, I think we, as two intelligent men, can come to an agreement in this matter."

For a long minute, Doc said nothing and watched Noel begin to squirm. He noted that Noel kept his hands in his pockets and had his jacket open enough to pull a pistol from it if need be. His short, dark hair was slicked back, and he was already sweating in the hot, dim bar. No waiter approached, of course, and that seemed to make Noel suffer as well. Doc drank from the open bottle and wiped his lips with his open hand.

"Before we talk trade, Noel, I suggest you pull out that pistol very carefully and lay it gently on the table. Put it in this bag. Then maybe we can talk," suggested Doc. He barely moved, other than to toss a small leather tool bag across the table in front of Noel. His eyes never left Noel's face.

Death in Sturgis

For a full minute, neither of the two men made a move or said a word. Finally, Noel blinked. He snorted and took the Sig-Sauer pistol from under his jacket, slid it from its holster, and placed it in the saddlebag. Doc reached forward and snatched it from the table before dropping it to the floor behind him.

"Now maybe we can talk, you slippery bastard. What do you have that I could possibly want? All I want is to kick your fucking ass from here to hell and back for what you did to some very decent people. They never messed with you, and you felt you were enough of a god to snuff them out or hurt them badly. You're a miserable piece of shit. Do you know that? What could you possibly trade me?"

Noel looked from side to side like he expected some creature to crawl up and bite him hard. When he seemed satisfied there was nothing there, he said, "Money, my friend. I can see that you get more money than you ever thought existed. I can promise you one hundred thousand dollars a month for the next sixty months. That's six million dollars—all of it tax-free. Even you can't imagine that much!" He waited, snake-like, for Doc to respond.

"Well, for one thing, you fuck, I can imagine a lot, an awful lot. For another thing, I don't want your drug money—shit money made from the suffering of others! That's just plain no good, Noel, no good at all." Doc leaned back and took another drink, without ever taking his eyes off the man across the table. He looked at ease but was so wound up on adrenaline it was hard to keeping from leaping to his feet and beating the crap out of this scumbag.

"Very well, you may not be interested in a share of the product I move. You needn't do a thing—simply sit back while the profits roll in. Visualize yourself enjoying the fruit of my effort. While I slave away, you skim the cream from the top. You say how long and how much!"

Doc spat back, "I guess the little ride you just took bothered your ears a lot more than your candy ass! I don't want your money. Is that all you think is important? Money, houses, possessions, belongings, cash, dope? All that stuff? None of that means a thing in my life! All it does is show me how sick and decrepit your soul is, you fuck! You ain't got shit!"

Noel was sweating freely, and as he talked, he shifted in his seat, as if his ass was crawling with biting insects. "Well, maybe you'd like to let your little lady friend die? At this very moment, she's tied up, hand and foot, back at that shit-hole gallery of hers. If my men don't hear from me in the next half-hour, they're going to take turns raping every hole in her filthy body, and when they're done, they'll let the dogs have what's left. I already bought off your giant—that oversized idiot that can't even find his way in the dark. He's left town by now, a little smarter and a lot richer after throwing in with me. When he saw that you had little to offer, he took my money and hit the road. You've got nothing now, and when my associates are through, you won't even have your little slut up in Belle Fourche!" Noel's voice had risen as he spoke, and although he laughed from time to time as he ranted, not a word of it rang true. Doc hadn't needed the call from Bear and Jeanette twenty minutes earlier that they were waiting for the inevitably delayed discharge paperwork from the Rapid City Hospital to know Noel was lying through his teeth. He read lies in Noel's every move, glance, word, and inch of his black soul.

In one smooth move, Doc reached forward and slapped Noel hard across the face, knocking him to the floor. The loud, sharp sound echoed throughout the small bar and rose above the talking, the laughing, and the rock music pouring from the stereo. Suddenly, every eye in the place was on Noel where he sat on the floor with a small trickle of blood at the edge of his mouth. His face was crimson, his eyes bulged, and a small vein pulsed in his temple as he glared up at Doc.

"Noel, you're a fucking liar! You don't rate the respect I'd give a pile of dog crap. You've played your last card, and now it's time to get what's coming to you!" Doc shouted as he turned the table over with one hand and stood, taking his jacket off to free his arms. Even with the wound down his side and the aches and pains from his wreck the day before, he moved like a well-oiled machine. He towered over Noel and spat, "Get up, you fucking murderer; I'm gonna kick your sorry ass."

People in the bar moved back and left an open area in anticipation of a good old-fashioned bare-knuckle fight. No one had called the police, yet, although the bartender would, once the fight actually began. Usually, when Doc was forced into violence in a bar, he tried to end it with a few well-placed punches or kicks designed to incapacitate his opponent before a real fight broke out. That way, the fight was over before anyone had time to call the law. This had worked well enough that he had never lost a fair fight and never been arrested, although he'd had to talk to the cops more than once to explain that some smart ass had needed a quick lesson in respect. In most instances, the police knew the offender was a jerk or quickly came around to Doc's way of thinking. This time, Doc didn't care. When he thought of all the pain Noel had caused, and the deaths for which he was responsible, he grew angrier and angrier. With the empty threat of violence against Jeanette, he'd lost it altogether, and he was ready to pound the shit out of Noel. He envisioned hitting him repeatedly. He imagined the sound of connecting with the cartilage in Noel's nose, crushing it, and sending blood spraying in all directions. He could almost hear the dull thump when he pummeled him so hard it lifted his body off the floor.

Noel stood slowly and took out the knife he'd been fingering in his pocket as he sat at the table. He held it in front of him and leaped at Doc with a snarl. His move was so quick that Doc barely had time to deflect the blade from his face, but he still took a long cut down his forearm. An irate cry of anger came from the crowd, unhappy that Noel had resorted to a knife. Off balance after the failed lunge, he fell on the ground near the upturned table and sighted the tool bag containing his gun. He was unable to reach it, however. If he had, the fight would have ended much more quickly. As he turned to jump at Doc, he felt a burning impact on his wrist as Doc kicked the knife away. A brief cheer rose from the crowd; they thought they'd get to see a good fist fight after all. Noel, however, scrambled away from Doc and around the table and chair. He grabbed the bag and began to remove the gun. Doc came upon him before he saw what he was doing. He reached down and took Noel's jacket in his grip, lifting him up, and forcing him around to face him. As he drew back to strike Noel again, he caught a glimpse of the cold, gray barrel rise towards his face. Doc never heard the screams as people in the crowd caught sight of the gun in the coward's right hand, nor did he hear the explosion as the gun went off. A blinding blast of yellow and white fire exploded from the barrel in front of him, and he pitched backwards onto the floor. Noel wiped his bleeding face with his left hand as he stood over Doc's body and breathed great, heaving breaths.

The gun came up again, aimed directly at Doc's chest, before anyone in the crowd could move either towards or away from the battling pair. He smiled an evil smile through swollen, bleeding lips, and squeezed the trigger.

42

SOME SLIPPERY SHIT

Sheila was pissed, in a major way. First, her beer gets spilled when some guys start a ruckus. Then, one of the guys in the fight, a real pussy, resorts to pulling a knife. As if that wasn't enough, the son-of-a-bitch didn't have the balls to fight with his fists or knife and pulled a goddamned gun! Sheila had spent a large part of the last forty-five years in biker clubs and bars with her old man, Elvis—God rest his soul. Since he'd died seven years ago, she still went out with the club and traveled to biker events, but found she had been elevated to some sort of elderly wise-woman. Young men came to her for advice on how to get laid, others on how to rise in the club. Hell, she was just a woman, and as such had no official role in the club, anyway. Elvis had never told her about the inner workings of the club, the intricate by-laws or secret goings-on when the club flirted with outlaw activities back in the eighties. But she'd learned about respect and standing up for what you believed. She was always proud of doing right by her old man, and she'd done all she could to be the best damn biker bitch around. The word bitch wasn't an insult in biker circles, it just described who and what she was. Now that he was gone, she still heard him talk to her from time to time, just as if he was at her ear. She didn't mention it much, because people gave her a real funny look and walked away muttering when she did. But Sheila was happy. She had always made her man proud. Her tall, thin Elvis had liked it just that much more when she lost her teeth. Even though she couldn't fuck as well since her back surgery, she could still do him right in the mouth department!

Yes, she was proud of who she was and what she stood for. One thing she and Elvis didn't stand for was fighting dirty or kicking somebody when they were down. She was pissed at how this one son-of-a-bitch was fighting. When she saw him draw down on that guy on the ground, she heard Elvis whisper in her ear, "Knock this fucker down." Without a moment's hesitation, she launched her three hundreds pounds across the twelve feet or so that stood between them. She didn't use her fists or head-butt him, she just hit him broadsides with her hefty bosom, and although she only stood an even five feet tall, she carried a lot of momentum. Noel was thrown about ten feet to his left, and the bullet he was firing disappeared into the wooden floor no more than three inches from Doc's right ear.

A cheer rose from the crowd around them as Sheila turned around for another pass at Noel, like a bull at the corrida de toros. He staggered to his feet and waved his gun from side to side, not at all sure where the little truck came from that had plowed into him. People shouted as the gun pointed in their direction and ducked, almost as if they were doing the wave at a sporting event. Noel tried to refocus his eyes, but Sheila hit him again. She moved like a little freight train driven by that old engineer, Elvis. She could almost see him, as well as hear him, standing beside her in his faded jeans, leather vest, and his bolo tie. He would have smiled real big under his white handlebar mustache and patted her ample buttocks.

Noel bounced from her like a pool ball caroming off the cushion with a good amount of English spin. He turned like a top, and just when it seemed a dozen hands would catch him, he fell hard against the wall. His gun flew from his hand, and he cursed a blue streak. He began crawling crab-like towards the door amid showers of laughter and derision. His face red, Noel made it through the door with the help of a good, swift kick in the ass from Sheila. She thought that one up on her own, without any help at all from Elvis, but she was sure he would have approved. The crowd certainly did. A chorus of cheers and laughter followed Noel onto the sidewalk.

People applauded Sheila and began helping Doc to his feet. He kept blinking his eyes and rubbing his ears. The bottom of his goatee was gone, burned to the chin by the blast from the pistol. A few burning grains had gone up his nose, and he sniffed and snorted like a bull in front of a matador. At first, his eyes were blurred, but this rapidly cleared the longer he stood. Doc was amazed to be breathing. He was sure the bullet had hit him somewhere, but he was not disappointed to be alive and seemingly without gaping holes in his anatomy. He did a quick trauma assessment and was pleasantly surprised that the damage appeared limited to burns to the lower face and maybe a bit of injury to his eardrums—much too close to the pistol when it went off.

Once he was more stable, he looked around for Noel. Bystanders told him Noel had crawled out the door on his hands and knees, and although it was a picture they'd never forget, Doc wasn't done with him. He still had a major beating in store for Noel. Doc took a long, deep drink of the cold draft beer pressed into his hand by one the bystanders, and picked up his jacket. He swung it on as he left the bar, still staggering a bit from the ordeal he'd survived. Sirens were crawling down the mountain road as he passed through the swinging doors. A few passers-by eagerly pointed the direction in which Noel had fled. Fortunately, Doc's bike was in that direction and when he reached it, he hopped on and started it up. He backed out and cruised down the long row of bikes, looking for the characteristic Big Dog Mastiff on the road or Noel's malevolent face in the crowd. He didn't want to be blindsided by that fucker. He felt bad that he hadn't anticipated the knife. Doc had felt smug about getting the gun out of the way so early, but he'd not put the pistol completely beyond Noel's reach, and that was a mistake. He was not going to make a mistake with Noel again.

Doc rolled along evenly on his Wide Glide, dripping blood as his slashed right forearm soaked through the leather jacket. Doc didn't give it a second glance and proceeded on down the road, headed west. He'd take care of the wound once he was done with Noel. And he did plan on finishing with Noel—today. People turned to watch once they noticed the dripping blood, but he paid them no heed.

About two hundred feet farther down the street, Noel revved his engine loudly and sprang into the narrow gap between the rows of bikes. He headed directly for Doc, accelerating as he proceeded. People cursed at him and scrambled out of the way of the heavy, powerful machine. Doc saw him almost immediately and rolled on the throttle as if they were playing a bizarre game of motorcycle chicken. At fifty feet, he realized Noel had no intention of stopping, and Doc hit the brakes and edged as far to the side of the four to five-foot-wide path as possible. He bumped the back of a few bikes doing so but none were unbalanced enough to fall. At twenty feet, Doc heard the roar of Noel's 117-cubic inch engine and saw the murder in his eyes. He stopped and ducked at the last minute as Noel passed him on his left and lashed out at him with his left arm. Doc toyed with the idea of trying to knock Noel from his bike, but decided not to, in order to keep folk from being injured in the crash that was sure to follow. Moreover, Doc didn't like the idea of damaging so many bikes, especially his own Wide Glide—it had taken enough of a beating for one Sturgis week!

Noel screamed Doc's name in frustration as he passed, like a knight whose jousting quarry had dodged his lance at the last moment. Doc didn't have enough room to turn around in the narrow space and gunned his engine to reach the end of the row a little over two hundred feet to the west. Noel tore east and continued on US-16A toward Custer State Park. By the time Doc reached the end of the row of scoots, Noel had a quarter-mile head start. This time, Doc was determined that Noel would not escape. People shouted and jumped to safety as the two raced out of town before the police got anywhere near them. Doc heard the scream of a Highway Patrol cruiser far behind him as he, too, headed for the ruggedly beautiful state park.

Within two miles, they'd reached the entrance to the park and crashed through the entrance, making the young, bored ranger leap back into his small booth. He crept out like a small mammal emerging from its den in the spring. He stood in their wake, a pair of park passes held forlornly in his outstretched hand. Hearing the wail of police cars, he wisely stepped back into his protective booth and waited for the authorities to pursue the bikers into the park. His mouth was still hanging open with the standard warning speech about grazing animals on the road on the tip of his tongue. Oh well, he'd give the memorized discourse to the next vehicle that passed through his station at something less than the speed of sound.

Neither Doc nor Noel had the time to appreciate the beautiful lake to their right as they weaved in and out of stopped, slowed, and moving vehicles. It was a mad game of catch-me-if-you-can, with Noel in the lead, and Doc quickly closing the gap. The anger and hatred on Noel's face was matched by the determination on Doc's as he prepared to stomp Noel's ass. Fortunately, there was little gravel on the road and most riders and drivers were able to slow a bit or pull to the edge of the lane as the two careening motorcycles approached at high speed.

As Route 87 merged with the US-16A, more traffic appeared, and the chase became much more hectic for a little over a mile, until some of the traffic headed north to Mount Rushmore or the Sylvan Lake Lodge. As they passed the split in the road and the traffic thinned, Noel hit the throttle hard and passed a line of four or five cars coming to a stop in front of him. He saw nothing in the on-coming lane and accelerated. He looked over his shoulder and laughed as he passed the front car and went crazily into the approaching series of sharp S-turns. Doc backed off his throttle just a bit, until he could determine what was stopping the short line of vehicles ahead of him.

Noel glanced briefly over his shoulder. When he looked back, he was horrified to see a large portion of the Custer State Park buffalo herd spread across the road, less than twenty yards ahead of him, passing from right to left. Panicked, he hit the front brakes like a ton of bricks and started to lock them up. He never even hit the rear brakes, but as the rear end of the bike had started to leave the ground already, it didn't really matter. The front wheel finally locked up completely, and the rear of the bike flew up and over the front end, a mere three feet before he hit the broadside of a huge bull buffalo. Noel was launched head first over the handlebars in a low, flat trajectory at over eighty miles per hour.

Noel's thighs hit the not-quite-stationary handlebars and mangled his femurs with shattered, open fractures. Pieces of thighbone poked through the muscle at multiple places and twisted his legs into obscene angles. He hit the 2200-pound bull with his head and upper body. Although the animal's side seemed soft and furry to the hand, at this speed, it was like hitting a concrete wall. The bull exhaled noisily and twisted to the left quickly enough to impale Noel's left shoulder with its amazingly sharp fourteen-inch horn. It pushed through his leather jacket and into the soft tissue running from his acromion, the tip of the shoulder, and burying itself in the tissue at the base of his neck. With a savage jerk, it threw his body up and out, so that his shattered legs whipped around the front of the huge beast as though he were performing a macabre ballet, pirouetting his way around the creature's shanks.

The motorcycle landed with a crash that terrified the dumb brute; it rapidly backpedaled from the screaming metal and sparks. Several cows bashed against the massive old male as it retreated with Noel still alive on its sweeping horns. By this time, Noel had recovered his first inhalation. He used it in a loud, pained scream. As the herd scattered from the steel and chrome, the male shook his head twice more. Each time, Noel's fragile frame was shaken like the last person in line at crack the whip. His boots flew from his feet from the incredible force brought into play by the thick muscles of the bull.

As the bull stopped backing up, Noel slid from its horns and lay moaning in front of the furious beast. Instinct took over as the broken

Death in Sturgis

body was treated like any wolf or puma that had attacked the herd, which is surely how the old male saw it. He put his head down and speared Noel again, lifting him quickly by the abdominal wall and flinging him twelve feet into the air. Apparently, Noel was still conscious enough to scream, although much more faintly than before. The maddened animal pawed him repeatedly with his front hooves, breaking bones loudly enough to be heard from twenty yards away. The sound became muddy as the huge beast brought its mass down, time after time, into the pulverized flesh. After three or four minutes of such punishment, Noel was a nearly unrecognizable mass of bloody meat and gristle, mixed with the cocaine he'd carried under his jacket. The herd seemed satisfied and began to move on, its dignity preserved by the huge old male. In a timeless ritual, some small measure of respect had been regained. A few of the younger animals dropped large fragrant lumps of dung onto what was left of Noel as they moved on.

Doc watched the entire encounter after stopping his bike well back from the herd. Although he would have preferred to deal Noel's punishment himself, he found it strangely fitting for nature, the buffalo themselves, to have brought final justice to him. As the lumbering animals moved to the left of the road, he became vaguely aware of the commotion behind him and the arrival of the Highway Patrol cruisers. He smiled; things had been evened out. An infinitely satisfied Doc had absolutely nothing else to add.

43

ONE LAST SUNSET

The last drops of yet another beer raced down Doc's throat, headed for his stomach, soon to cause havoc with his brain cells after a short trip through the vascular system. He and Bear had been drinking beer and Jack Daniels since seven o'clock, and now that midnight was approaching, they both had every reason to feel real good. Real good and drunk, that is. They were nursing the wounds of the past few days, and they wholeheartedly agreed with the biblical axiom that a little liquor was good for you. And if a little bit was good, a whole lot must be...

Down in Custer State Park, Doc had successfully avoided the Highway Patrol when they arrived at the scene of Noel's death. No one had attempted to scatter or disperse the buffalo herd and instead let them wander off at their own pace. The big bull that had turned Noel into a bloody stain on the roadway returned to chewing his cud and ambled off to the admiration of all the buffalo bitches. No doubt, they liked the look in his eye, that small piece of Noel's shirt still on his left horn, and the specks of blood and gore spattered on his thick, brown fur and hard, black hooves. It wasn't clear if any of the cocaine spread across Noel's mangled corpse made it up the animal's nostrils, but he didn't show it if it had.

Horrified bystanders had rushed to the spot where the broken body was smeared across the pavement, curious and repelled at the same time. One well-prepared soul had captured it on video and was already counting the money he would make when he sold it to the TV station, America's Most Disgusting Videos, or something of that ilk. Mothers hid the scene from their children's eyes while craning their own necks for the best view. One enthusiastic person burst through the crowd, announcing she was a paramedic, and kneeled down in an attempt to find a pulse. First, she had to find an identifiable wrist. After a few confused moments, she cleared her throat, rose to her feet, and solemnly announced that the mass of bloody jelly was dead. It was oddly reminiscent of the Munchkin coroner pronouncing the Wicked Witch of the East dead after an entire house crushed her. The proud paramedic, having done her duty, walked in a very official manner over to the approaching troopers to present a formal evaluation. Surely, someone, somewhere, could rest securely with that paramedic on the job at night.

An entire photo album of snapshots were taken by the tourists that formed a ring around what was left of Noel; they were enjoying their time in the Black Hills wilderness, far from the death and pain and crime of their hometowns. Cars began edging around the spot, careful to keep their tires out of the bloodstained areas. No one seemed to know what to think of the chunks of white powder mixed in with the muscle and torn skin. The Highway Patrol would take care of it, whatever it was.

As the troopers began to guide the traffic more smoothly and look for eyewitnesses, Doc started his Wide Glide, backed it around, and rode slowly and discreetly back through the park entrance and into Custer. He thought of stopping back at the Frontier Bar and Lounge but decided it would be better to head back to Rapid City and join up with Bear and Jeanette. He rolled up US-16, past Crazy Horse, and through Hill City toward the hospital in the southeast part of the city.

As he rode along, he shook his head from side to side to clear his mind of the image of Noel being torn apart by the bull. In its mind, Noel had attacked the herd, and the beast was merely doing what needed to be done to protect the cows and calves. There had been no malice in its heart, unlike the vicious coward that had perished beneath its hard hooves. Doc made a conscious effort to think of other things.

Not surprisingly, Erin's face and sweet young body came to his mind. She was a definite improvement over Noel's last stand, although his last memory of her was bittersweet. She'd cried and cried those few hours ago when he was leaving for his fatal rendezvous with Noel, and she was heading for Tilford Campground. She had gotten very attached in a very short time, and he had been as gentle as he knew how in parting. He promised to call her when he got back to Ohio, and reassured her that her Indiana town was only a matter of hours away. He'd done his best to let her know that she was something special, not just a one-week Sturgis fling. Erin had sobbed on his shoulder and apologized for being a baby and acting foolish. Doc had dried her tears and held her gently, only to have the fat, wet drops spring forth again. Finally, he'd told her he needed to leave in order to get to Custer before Noel. She had been a little snotty then, but when he assured her that he was going not just for himself, but for Jake, Todd, Tracie, Bear, Jeanette, and even her, she seemed to understand. He'd held her and kissed her tears long enough that she calmed and could smile a little as he left. He'd hauled ass down to Custer in time to set up the table where he wanted it and wait for Noel. He truly did plan to call Erin and might even ride over to Indiana for a visit. At least, he'd meant it when he said he would.

When Doc arrived at the hospital, Bear and Jeanette had left just ten minutes before him. He called Bear on the cell phone and agreed to meet them in a few hours in Belle Fourche. He told them little about the strange end of Noel at the hands (hooves?) of Tatanka, but promised to fill them in more completely over some cold beers and whiskey, a promise he was sure he'd keep. Bear and Jeanette were on their way to the Black Hills Harley-Davidson dealer to pick up Bear's Knucklehead, which had been retrieved from the Devil's Tower in pristine condition while they'd waited for the endless hospital paperwork to be completed for Bear's discharge. Bear swore he felt no pain, and in fact, had never been better in his life. Apparently being shot agreed with him, although he was a little disappointed when Doc told him the sole bullet probably wouldn't set off metal detectors in airports or courthouses.

A few questions in the emergency department revealed that Jim Foster was off that shift and not expected until the morning. Damn, he thought, he really wanted the gash on his arm cleaned and dressed. Doc didn't think it would take stitches, just soap and water, followed by well-placed steri-strips. He didn't want to sign in officially and be seen by a doctor he didn't know; that would just lead to a whole lot of questions that he had no intention answering, especially once the police were called, as the law required when a knife or gun wound was treated in the ED.

Once again, Lady Luck was with him. Doc was able to locate a cute, friendly nurse from his previous visit that remembered him. She was quite curious because Foster had told several people about Doc's NO-CPR tattoo, and she was anxious to see it. She broadly hinted on seeing more than just the tattoo, and made it clear that he could see as much of her as he wished, but unfortunately, she was on duty for the next eight hours. This is one damn friendly hospital, Doc admitted cheerfully.

Death in Sturgis

It was a mercifully slow day in the ED, and she was persuaded to take him into an empty procedure room to clean and dress his newest wound and the burn under his chin. In exchange, she wanted a private showing of his tattoo-work. The wound management required about twenty-five minutes (it seemed longer) and the viewing another thirty-five (it seemed shorter). Fortunately, the room had a stout lock on the door and soundproof walls. When they were done, they left the procedure room with satisfied, shit-eating grins on their faces. Doc left with many thanks and a new phone number.

He rode back up I-90 to Sturgis and stopped at the Buffalo Chip for his belongings. He really loved the Chip and wished he'd been able to spend more time there over the past week. This dying, fighting, fucking, and drinking took up so much time. The Chip being its usual trustworthy place, he found his belongs exactly where he'd left them yesterday morning. He quickly rolled up his sleeping bag and packed his few belongings into his saddlebags. Of course, he couldn't leave without a cold beer or two. Once again, the main concert area was rapidly becoming crowded as the warm-up band struck up one of their well-known classic tunes. Doc clapped and cheered as he washed some of the dust from his throat before slowly riding through the beautiful iron gate. It still brought a little lump to his throat each time he passed under it. See you next year, Woody and Carol, he thought, and rode back into Sturgis to the west.

Route 34 was quiet after the eternal commotion of the Buffalo Chip and party-crazed Sturgis. Doc enjoyed the quiet and felt like he was finally home when he turned into Jeanette's dusty back lot. There sat Bear's '47 Knucklehead and Jeanette's Jeep, looking calm and happy in the growing South Dakota dusk. They were waiting for him on the front porch with two cases of cold beer and two bottles of Jack Daniels Old No. 7. Three chairs were laid out with small stools to rest their weary feet. Bear was already working on the first quart of Tennessee whiskey, and Jeanette was nursing a cold wine cooler, one of the few indulgences of her old age, she argued.

Doc was happy to find the porch littered with over a dozen small white boxes along with the beer and whiskey, the product of Belle Fourche's China Garden restaurant, a sparkling pearl of the Orient nestled within gritty South Dakota. His friends had slaved long, hard hours over the take-out counter at the China Garden to provide him with this exquisite cuisine after a day of fighting crime and protecting the dignity and honor of women and children throughout the free world, or so Bear proclaimed, as he offered him a beer and some chopsticks. Doc dug in with a gusto belying his fatigue after the events of the day. He ate his fill while relating the final ride and last stand of the infamous Dr. Noel Herrod. Jeanette closed her eyes tightly when he gave the Reader's Digest version of the buffalo literally stomping the shit out of Noel.

Doc had also found out from his new nurse friend that Booster had been released from the hospital into police custody that day for the break-in at Jeanette's two days before. Four hours of surgery had been needed to reassemble the pieces of his arm bone and fit the humeral head back into the shoulder socket. He'd carry the metal plate and pins in his arm to the grave, which at this rate, wouldn't be terribly far into the future. The police were terribly interested in him, especially since his two cronies had been shot down like dogs at Devil's Tower. Maybe someone in law enforcement was beginning to detect a pattern in the deaths and shootings. Maybe.

Fist remained in a coma, and it was doubtful he'd ever fully awaken. This news brought tears to Jeanette's eyes, even though she had no fond memories of the man. Bear merely grunted at the news. It was hard to think of any rider being turned into a vegetable after a collision with a car, even one of Noel's rent-a-thugs.

They talked for a while about what they should do with the memory stick that had somehow survived the wild ride in Doc's pocket for the last few days. If he wasn't trying to drown it in a downpour, he was subjecting it to hazardous wastes, like pureed cow shit. Then he took it into battle with him, where it was almost stabbed and shot. It was more excitement than most poor little memory sticks had in a lifetime! After much discussion, it was decided to leave it with Jeanette. She had already planned a sculpture that would encapsulate it deep in a chunk of clay, within a ball of steel, within a globe of glass. She dreamed of a beautiful design to hide the ugly, dark secrets contained in the silicon depths of the stick that would form a memorial to Jake, Todd, and Tracie. It was a dream only someone like Jeanette could envision and create.

As the sun set, a hush fell over the three of them. Doc and Jeanette moved to the edge of the wooden porch and let their legs hang down, barefoot in the gathering dusk. She rested her head on his shoulder, and the only sound was the occasional car off to the south and the squeaking of the rocking chair as Bear slowly moved back and forth.

Death in Sturgis

Just after the sun went down, a coyote called from less than a hundred yards down the road, a lonesome sound that seemed to sum up all that had happened over the last week. Lives had been lost and others had been changed. People had died, and somewhere, babies had been born. In the gathering coolness of the evening, it all made sense on a crazy, cosmic level. Even though they were separated by over a hundred years from the Sioux who had once roamed this land, for just a while they all seemed connected. Some link existed, strong enough to sense, even if you couldn't touch it, see it, or smell it. They were glad to be alive in the way that only those who had faced death could understand. And they keenly sensed the loss of those who had died because of Noel's greed and avarice. Even though they'd never met, Jeanette felt Jake, Todd, and Tracie near them. Maybe it was her Apache blood. Hell, maybe it was because she was a woman. Or maybe it had to do with the danger and nearness of death over the last few days.

One by one, the stars came out, and the day's heat began to lift from the hot, baked earth. Jeanette wandered among her few shrubs in the front yard, and Bear warned her about scorpions and her bare feet. She laughed as though nothing like that had ever hurt her or ever would. When she returned to the porch, they opened another quart of the fine, amber liquid that had come all the way from Tennessee to burn their throats and lighten their hearts here in the dark of a South Dakota night. They drank and laughed for another hour as the sky darkened and a few meteors shot by overhead. When that quart was gone, Bear grabbed a blanket and crawled off to sleep on Jeanette's couch. Soon his snores could be heard mixing with the sound of night insects and the occasional owl.

Doc stood stiffly and helped Jeanette up by the hand. They went to her room and closed the door. Doc slowly undressed her in the dim light, sighing happily, as each piece of clothing came off, as if he'd never seen a woman's body before. She reveled in his attentions over the hours as they made love slowly, slowly. The night slept on as a thousand prairie creatures lived and died outside her window.

44

The Taste of Iowa Bugs

EPILOGUE

Six o'clock came much too soon in the morning, and both men groaned and rolled over to return to sleep—Doc in Jeanette's bed and Bear on the couch. Without complaint, Jeanette arose and busied herself in the kitchen making a huge breakfast for her two men. By eight o'clock, breakfast was ready, even if Doc and Bear weren't. The inviting smell of bacon and fresh coffee helped them open eyes that the previous night's whiskey had closed so tightly. Amidst good-natured cursing and fussing, the two men found their way to the breakfast table. Bear put away a whole plateful of food before his eyes were fully open. Fortunately, the second course included the maximum dose of ibuprofen, to be washed down with cold beer. Doc wasn't sure, but he suspected the beer brought him back to feeling human again.

The two men cleaned the table and washed the dishes after they had devoured every bit of breakfast put before them. The sight of the two men crowded at the little sink made Jeanette shake with laughter. She tried to push them away, but they insisted.

"Please, guys, I'll do that later. Just let it be for now," she pleaded.

"Now, ma'am, just let us be. We're proud to be able to help an' all. Look at all you've done fer us this past week," Bear protested.

"Yeah! We're what you call domesticated boys. Why, at home, I even take the dishes out of the sink before I piss in it," Doc joined in.

Bear howled at such highbrow humor and continued to block Jeanette's approach to the dishes. At last, they had all been washed, dried, and put away without a single plate, cup, or saucer being broken. With a final cup of coffee, they retired to the front porch, where there was shade from the early morning sun.

Death in Sturgis

Then, as she sat and silently watched, the two bikes were packed with their owners' meager traveling goods and readied for the road. Oil tanks were topped off before the ride. Older Harley's are oil-hungry brutes, and the wise rider always had an extra quart hidden away somewhere. Doc checked the controls, fuel lines, and brakes extra carefully, because of the trauma his bike had gone through over the past week. Bear's scoot got a similar going-over, not because of its abuse, but because it was about a quarter of a century older than Doc's ride. They'd check tire pressure and top off their gas tanks at the Cenex station before hitting the highway.

By eleven o'clock, they were ready, although not eager, to leave. As always, Jeanette stood quietly and spoke little. Bear gave her one of his famous hugs and swung her around. She pecked him on the cheek as he held her almost three feet off the ground. If he hadn't lifted her, she never could have reached him without the help of a step stool. Then he spent a few extra minutes fooling around with his bike and checking things he had already checked twice while Doc and Jeanette said their goodbyes. She seldom made eye contact with Doc at times like this, partly because she didn't want to cry, and if she did, she certainly didn't want him to see it. After a long hug, a longer kiss, and whispered words of farewell, he mounted his bike and started it with a roar. Bear started his Knucklehead and after allowing a good five minutes for warming up the oil that circulated through their scoots, they gave Jeanette a final wave and pulled away. She waved back and stood on her porch for a long time after they had disappeared before returning to her now silent house. Each of them was teary, but Bear blamed it on the wind, which only seemed to blow that certain irritating way whenever he left someone he genuinely cared about. Neither man said a word at the service station, nor did they have to.

They drove south on US-85 to I-90, and then took the interstate to Wall, where they refueled. From there, they went south through the Badlands on SR-240, and stopped in Interior, where Doc had met Todd and Noel only a week before. They stood in the bright early afternoon sun drinking frosty beers and looking south into the Pine Ridge Indian Reservation.

Only thirty miles away lay Wounded Knee, where the last massacre of Indians at the hand of the US Army had occurred in 1890. Two years earlier, the Ghost Dance had swept the western reservations after Paiute shaman Wovoka taught that the old ways would be restored and the buffalo would return. This would only happen if the Indians turned from the ways of the white man and purified themselves. He taught that non-violence and forsaking alcohol would enable the earth to be reborn in a pure, aboriginal state, and that Indians, even dead ones, would inherit its riches. They must fast, he said, and pray, and most importantly, they must dance. During the Ghost Dance, they would briefly die and see the reborn earth.

Not all on the reservations liked the non-violent ideas of Wovoka, especially two Miniconjou mystics, Short Bull and Kicking Bear. They preached that the Ghost Dance shirts would protect the dancers from the white man's bullets in a violent uprising. Troops entered the reservations to suppress the dance, but only agitated the residents. The rebuilt Seventh Calvary, still smarting over the defeat of Custer fourteen years earlier, rounded up three hundred fifty Indians in the southeast corner of the Pine Ridge Reservation. Only one hundred and twenty of these were men, the rest were women and children. After a scuffle, some five hundred soldiers opened fire on the Indians with repeating rifles and rapid-fire artillery, called Hotchkiss guns, firing grape shot, similar to giant shotguns firing handfuls of lead ball bearings. In less than an hour, three hundred Indians had been slaughtered. A sad and infuriating fact is that almost twenty Medals of Honor were handed out for killing unarmed women and children. Doc had made several trips to the Wounded Knee site and mass grave, but he couldn't do it without crying. After the week he'd just had, he found he lacked the emotional strength he would need for another visit.

Usually, Doc took only state roads and avoided interstates whenever he could. This trip was to be no different. Bear was headed for Birmingham, Alabama; he would travel with Doc at least across South Dakota and down part of the western edge of Iowa. By staying out of Nebraska, they could avoid wearing helmets. Doc could go helmet-free all the way to Ohio by driving through South Dakota, Iowa, Illinois, and Indiana.

Staying on the back roads cost them a few hours, but the scenery along the way and the people they met were worth it. They stayed overnight in Parkston, where Doc tried to stay at least once each trip. There, they checked into a little motel across the street from a bar and restaurant. Some good South Dakota steaks disappeared, along with a number of beers, and they turned in early.

Death in Sturgis

In the morning, they continued east on SR-44 along the southern part of the state before hitting I-29 near Lennox. From there, they could travel southward together down the eastern edge of the state until they hit the junction of the Big Sioux River and the Missouri River at Sioux City and crossed into Iowa. Together, they traveled south another twenty miles until Doc headed east for Dension and US-30, while Bear continued south on I-29.

The two men stopped at Doc's exit and stood looking out at the lush hills of western Iowa. To the immediate west was the Winnebago Indian Reservation. They spoke little, saying the most with a simple handshake before returning to their respective bikes. No long goodbye was required, and neither man felt like talking anyway. The engines fired into life, and the two friends parted, one headed east, and one south.

As Doc rode up and down the curvy, two lane roads of backwoods Iowa, he breathed in deeply. It was early afternoon as he thoroughly immersed himself in the ride. He enjoyed talking with the clerks in the gas stations and the waitresses in the little cafes along the way. It was good, he reflected with a smile, good to be alive.

Almost four hours later, as Doc neared Cedar Rapids, he came over a hill and hit a cloud of busy, buzzing insects. He wiped a few off his sunglasses and spat out more than a dozen. Funny, he thought, wood. Tastes like wood. These Iowa bugs tasted just like wood...